the
yadayada
Prayer Group
GETS TOUGH

the yadayada *Prayer Group* GETS TOUGH

a Novel

neta jackson

INTEGRITY®
PUBLISHERS
Nashville

THE YADA YADA PRAYER GROUP GETS TOUGH

Published by Integrity Publishers, a Division of Integrity Media, Inc.,
5250 Virginia Way, Suite 110, Brentwood, TN 37027.

HELPING PEOPLE WORLDWIDE EXPERIENCE *the* MANIFEST PRESENCE *of* GOD.

Published in association with the literary agency of Alive Communications, Inc.,
7680 Goddard Street, Suite 200, Colorado Springs, CO 80920.

Scripture quotations are taken from the following: The Holy Bible, New
International Version. Copyright © 1973, 1978, 1984, International Bible Society.
Used by permission of Zondervan Bible Publishers. The King James Version of the
Bible. Public domain. The Holy Bible, New Living Translation®, copyright ©
1996. Used by permission of Tyndale House Publishers, Inc., Wheaton, Illinois
60819. All rights reserved.

This novel is a work of fiction. Any references to real events, businesses, organizations,
and locales are intended only to give the fiction a sense of reality and authenticity.
Any resemblance to actual persons, living or dead, is entirely coincidental. However,
some of the events in this novel were inspired by a rash of "hate incidents" on the
campus of Northwestern University from 2000 to 2003.

Cover design: Brand Navigation | www.brandnavigation.com
Interior design: Inside Out Design & Typesetting

Library of Congress Cataloging-in-Publication Data

Jackson, Neta.
The yada yada prayer group gets tough / by Neta Jackson.
    p. cm.

Summary: "The Yada Yada Prayer Group has been together for a whole year and so
many good things are happening. However that's just when the Enemy knows to
attack. The Yada Yada sisters realize they need to get tough"—Provided by
publisher.

ISBN 1-59145-358-5 (tradepaper)

1. Women—Illinois—Fiction. 2. Christian women—Fiction.   3. Female friendship—Fiction.   4. Prayer groups—Fiction.   5. Chicago (Ill.)—Fiction.
5. Prayer groups—Fiction. I. Title.
PS3560.A2415Y334   2005
813'.54—dc22   2005022353

Printed in the United States of America
05 06 07 08 09 DPS 8 7 6 5 4 3 2 1

In memory of

Ricky Byrdsong,

Former head basketball coach at Northwestern University,

Our friend and brother—

Murdered by a white supremacist

While walking with his children near his home,

July Fourth weekend, 1999

Prologue

*T*he four-door sedan swung into a Permit Only parking spot, coughed, and died as if it knew it was trespassing. "What's wrong?" The young woman in the front passenger seat turned to her companion. "Will it start again?" When they finished what they had come to do, she wanted to be able to *leave*.

The dark-haired youth—twenty or twenty-one—rolled up the windows and reached into the back for his backpack. "Don't worry, Sara. It just got overheated. It'll cool off by the time we get back. Come on."

Reluctantly, the girl opened the car door and stepped out onto the concrete of the bi-level parking lot at Northwestern University. A breeze off Lake Michigan a hundred yards away made her shiver in spite of the mid-May sunshine. That's the way it always was in Chicago—cooler by the lake.

She grabbed her sweater and pulled it around her shoulders before locking the car door. She shivered again, wishing she could've worn jeans and a sweatshirt. Would've been perfect for a cool, sunny day. But no, Kent said if he was going to wear a suit and tie, she needed to wear a dress. After all, they were representing their Cause and wanted to be taken seriously.

Huh. When it came to supporting the Cause, she'd rather be back at the office stuffing envelopes. She wasn't good at this activist stuff.

"Here." Kent pulled a bundle of pamphlets out of his backpack and handed them to her. "You start with this row; I'll go down the other side." He moved off, sticking pamphlets under one windshield wiper, then another. She thought he looked a little silly in his black suit and tie with a ratty backpack slung over his shoulder, but she had to admit he was good-looking in a thin-faced, gangly sort of way. His straight, dark-brown hair, so carefully combed back, had a cute way of falling over his forehead, giving him a boyish look. Not that she would ever tell him. He was quite determined to be a serious grownup.

"Sara! Get busy!" His shout from several cars away made her jump, and she hustled to catch up. She worked fast, sticking pamphlets under windshield wipers, eager to show she *was* committed to the Cause . . . or maybe eager to get the pamphlets on the cars and get out of there before they got caught. At least the top level of the parking lot was only half full. Sunday afternoon wasn't a high-traffic day at the university; they'd be done in ten minutes and could get out of here.

A middle-aged man carrying a briefcase topped the short flight of stairs to the open second level and headed for his car, keys jangling. She pretended not to notice and kept moving from car to car. But a quick side-glance told her he'd stopped, reached for the pamphlet on his car window, and scanned its front page.

"Hey!" he yelled. "You can't leave your garbage here! This is private property!"

Sara glanced anxiously at Kent, one row over. "Keep moving," he hissed. "For all that guy knows, we're students here and have every right."

The man waved the pamphlet angrily over his head. "At least have the guts to present your wacko ideas personally," he shouted, "instead of blitzing cars anonymously!"

The invitation was too much for the young man. "Good idea! We'll do that!" He waved back, a smile plastered on his face.

Muttering, the man started to drop the pamphlet on the ground, hesitated, and then tossed it into his car.

"He took it!" Kent said gleefully.

Sara frowned. "Did not. He just didn't want to drop it. Those professor types never litter."

"Doesn't matter. He took it." The young man fished a campus map out of his backpack. "C'mon. Let's go to the student center." He looked up, scanning the buildings. "I think it's right over there."

"No, Kent. Let's just do the cars." But he was already heading in long strides for the exit stairs.

She sighed and followed. Under other circumstances, she'd enjoy a stroll around the Big Ten university campus, which had been practically in her backyard all her life. The grounds were beautiful this time of year. Soaring spires mixed with modern architecture. Graceful willow trees coming into bud, swaying in the breeze. Lake Michigan lapping along the boulder-studded shoreline. Flowering bushes and winding walks everywhere. Why hadn't she applied here? Her grades and SAT scores had been topnotch. She'd graduated from a prestigious high school here on the North Shore two years ago. But what was it Kent had said? *You gotta decide what's most important—dedication to the Cause or getting a so-called education watered down by all this politically correct mumbo-jumbo.*

Right. She admired Kent's dedication to the Cause. He'd taken her under his wing when the "popular" girls at New Trier acted as if she didn't exist. He explained things to her. Told her people had a right to stick up for what they believed.

She just didn't like conflict and confrontation, that's all.

They found the Norris University Center along the narrow campus drive and pulled open the big glass doors. "It's Sunday," she murmured. "Won't be many students."

"That's OK," he said. "More opportunity to leave the truth unhindered." He headed for the nearest bulletin board—crowded with fliers announcing everything from roommates needed to frat parties to the next theater production. "Heathens," Kent muttered, punching a pushpin into the bulletin board, leaving their pamphlet front and center.

They scurried down the wide stairs to the ground level, where Willie's Food Court, a cafeteria-style eatery, and Willie's Too—dispensing gourmet coffee, sub sandwiches, smoothies, and pizza—opened out into a large room with square wooden tables and booths along the far windows looking out over the Northwestern Lagoon. Several students sat at the scattered tables with drinks or sandwiches, talking or studying.

Kent straightened his tie and approached the first populated table. "I think you'll be interested in these facts." He thrust a pamphlet at a young woman bent over a large textbook.

The student glanced at the paper he held out to her. Her eyes narrowed. "Get that out of my face, or I'll call the campus cops!"

He barely flinched. "Not open to the free exchange of ideas? I thought—"

"I mean it! Get away from me!" The student grabbed her book and flounced to a table on the far side of the room.

Sara tugged on her companion's sleeve. "We should've worn casual clothes," she murmured anxiously. "They know we're not students, dressed up like this."

Kent ignored her and headed for two male students in T-shirts slouched in one of the booths, watching the hanging TV. One ignored them, eyes glued to the ball game; the other took the pamphlet, shrugged, and tossed it on the table.

Sara was relieved when they finally left the student center. At least it was Sunday. No classes. The campus proper was practically deserted. But as they pushed open the double-glass doors, Kent studied a bright flier taped to the glass. "See that? There's a Jazz Fest going on. It's gotta be over soon." He studied his map. "Come on!" Grabbing her hand, they followed the sidewalk signs pointing toward the Pick-Steiger Concert Hall.

The wait wasn't long. Soon a rowdy, laughing mix of students in shorts and bare midriffs, dreads, and buzz cuts pushed through the glass doors of the concert hall, rubbing shoulders with jazz fans from the local community. Once again, Kent dug into his backpack, pushed a stack of pamphlets into Sara's hands, and hustled to catch up with any moving target.

Sucking up some courage, the girl held out her pamphlets—mostly to females—steeling herself for the typical reactions: "Keep your stupid trash." . . . "You believe this stuff?" . . . "Guess it's a free country, even for weirdos." . . . "Stuff it up your—!"

The words she'd practiced rose to her defense. "Thought we had free speech in this country! So much for tolerance."

Her defenses soon crumbled, and she finally fled to a grassy knoll with the rest of her pamphlets, sinking onto a bench beneath a graceful weeping willow, its long tendrils bursting with the bright green buds of May. Kent found her there ten minutes later, her wedgies off, rubbing her arches. "My feet hurt," she moaned. "Let's go."

"Your feet hurt!" He snorted but sank down onto the bench beside her. "Passed out all my pamphlets?" He made a face when he saw the remainders. "Want me to pass those out?"

She shook her head. "No! Let's just *go.*"

AFTER A FEW TURNOVERS, the old sedan started, and they headed up Sheridan Road, back toward the posh bedroom communities along Lake Michigan's North Shore. But a few blocks north of the university, Kent took a left at the traffic light at Sheridan and Lincoln Avenue.

Sara frowned. "What are you doing?"

Kent shrugged, pulling over to the curb along the tree-shaded street of large brick homes, with ivy climbing up the wraparound verandas and neatly manicured lawns. "Might as well finish the job. We can stuff a few mailboxes, and we're done."

It was useless to argue. He was already out of the car. Reluctantly, she took several of the remaining pamphlets and scurried up the sidewalk, leaving a pamphlet tucked in the iron railing on one set of steps, in the mailbox at the next house. When her supply was gone, she hung back as her companion, still holding a few pamphlets, walked up the steps to a neat brick two-story with ivy hugging the walls. Boldly lifting the mail slot in the door, he started to push the pamphlet through . . . when the door suddenly opened.

It was hard to tell who was more taken aback—the pale young man on the stoop, hand outstretched, frozen in time . . . or the tall, goateed African-American in the gray velour sweatsuit coming out of the house, car keys in his hand.

The man spoke. "What do you want?" The tone was mildly hostile.

"Uh, don't think you'd be interested." Kent started to back away.

"What's this?" The man snatched the pamphlet out of the young man's hand, scanning the first page. He flipped to the second. Even from where Sara stood, she could see the muscles in the man's face tighten like the face of a clock being overwound. Her heart clutched. She saw the man stab his finger into Kent's chest, right in the middle of his tie, forcing Kent to back down a step. "If I *ever* catch you . . . in this neighborhood . . . *ever* again . . . with this . . . this—"

"Mark?" A woman's voice floated out from inside the house. "Is someone at the door?" The accent was foreign—British or African or something.

"*Git!*" the man hissed. Kent nearly tripped backing down the steps, but he recovered his dignity and sauntered back to where Sara waited anxiously on the sidewalk. His withering look still focused on Sara and Kent, the man called into the house, "Uh, nobody. Just some environmental types wanting signatures for Greenpeace or something." Then, glancing at the pamphlet he still held in his hand, the man shoved it into the ivy flanking the doorway till it was hidden, stepped back into the house, and shut the door with an angry *thud*.

When he and Sara were about two houses away, with the tension released, Kent dissolved into laughter.

1

*T*he wedding cake—a modest three-tiered creation from the Bagel Bakery—sat resplendent and untouched on the pass-through counter of Uptown Community Church's kitchen. Ruth Garfield, a navy "church hat" parked on her frowzy brown hair, stood in front of it, hands on hips, muttering something about ". . . marriage can't be consummated if the newlyweds don't cut the *cake*."

Yo-Yo Spencer, back in a pair of dry overalls after her baptism in Lake Michigan less than an hour ago, jerked her blonde, spiky hair in Ruth's direction as we folded the friendship quilt the Yada Yada Prayer Group had made for Avis's wedding. "What's got *her* tail in a knot, Jodi? We can still eat the cake. Heck, my brothers could demolish the whole thing in a couple of hours—oh." The spiky-haired twenty-something looked at me, stricken. "Guess I ain't supposed to say 'heck' now that I been dunked, huh?"

I stifled a laugh just as a crack of thunder outside covered for me. The threatening storm that had cut short Yo-Yo's baptism—and

Bandana Woman's, which had shocked the socks off everybody—finally unloaded over the north end of Chicago, washing the high, narrow windows of Uptown Community's second-floor meeting room. Ben Garfield and my husband, Denny, were taking down the Jewish *huppah* Ben had built for Avis and Peter Douglass's wedding. My son, Josh—Mr. Clean himself with that shaved head of his—was bossing around the cleanup crew of teenagers, all of them still half wet from the "hallelujah water fight" the double baptisms had inspired down at the lake. José Enriques and his father were packing up their guitars. And Pastor Clark sat knee to knee with a shivering Becky Wallace swathed in several layers of damp towels, his Bible open as he showed her the verses about "all have sinned" and "God so loved the world" and "by grace we are saved."

A huge bubble of happiness rose up in my spirit and oozed out all my pores as I hugged the folded quilt with its individual squares embroidered by each of the Yada Yada sisters. What an incredible day! I wished I could capture it in freeze-frame photography and replay it again, moment by moment:

All the Yada Yadas blowing our noses and smudging our mascara as dignified Avis Johnson "jumped the broom" with Peter Douglass right in Uptown's Sunday morning worship service . . .

Yo-Yo in her brand-new lavender overalls "gettin' off the fence and gettin' dunked," as she called it, in Lake Michigan . . .

The spontaneous plunge into the waters of salvation by Becky Wallace—a.k.a. "Bandana Woman," the heroin junkie who'd robbed Yada Yada at knifepoint last fall and ended up as Leslie "Stu" Stewart's housemate last week on house arrest, complete with electronic ankle monitor . . .

Could any of us have imagined such a day a year ago when we'd all met at that Chicago women's conference? A perfect "anniversary" for the Yada Yada Prayer Group!

Except for the cake, that is. I wasn't sure our resident *yenta*, Ruth Garfield, would ever forgive Peter and Avis—soaking wet from the silly dunking he'd given her after the baptisms—for deciding to forgo their wedding cake in lieu of getting into dry clothes and setting off on their honeymoon.

"Earth to Jodi!" Florida Hickman's hand waved in front of my face, breaking my thoughts. "You gonna hug that quilt all day or help me convince Ruth we should eat that cake? Avis would want us to!" She grabbed my arm. "C'mon . . . hey! Look who's back!"

Nonyameko Sisulu-Smith and her husband, Mark, appeared at the top of the stairs that opened into the second-floor meeting room, looking comfy and dry in sweats and gym shoes. "Uh-huh," Florida challenged. "Thought you guys had ducked out on us."

Mark shrugged. "We wanted to leave you guys with all the dirty work, but we need to talk to Pastor Clark about something." He grinned, and probably every female heart in the room skipped a beat. Our African "princess" had definitely snagged herself an American "prince," even if he was a Georgia-boy-makes-good. Dr. Mark Smith was not only a professor of history at Northwestern University and the father of their two polite boys, but—as Florida would say—"that brother is *fine.*"

Nony rolled her eyes. "That's not the whole of it. You should've heard him complaining because he hadn't gotten any wedding cake!"

"Cake, nothing!" growled Denny, still struggling to dismantle the *huppah* with Ben. "Give us a hand with this thing, man, so we can get it out the door."

"Better get your hands dirty, Mark," Florida smirked. "I *know* your grandma taught you: 'Them that don't work, don't eat.'"

Laughter rippled through the motley crew—some damp, some dry—who'd assembled back at the church after the lakeside ceremonies. The original plan had been for Avis and Peter's wedding ceremony to take place during the morning service, followed by a brief reception with cake and punch; then everyone would walk or drive to the lake for Yo-Yo's baptism. But Chicago weather being what it was—the forecast called for scattered showers throughout the day—when the sun came out shortly after the "I do's," Pastor Clark had suggested we all head for the lake for Yo-Yo's baptism and *then* come back for the reception.

Humph. "Best-laid plans" and all that. Hadn't counted on ex-con Becky Wallace getting zapped by Jesus like Paul on the road to Damascus and wanting to get baptized right then and there too, and everybody ending up in the water in an exuberant celebration of God's ongoing redemption. Well . . . maybe the teenagers just saw their chance to dunk their parents or give Pastor Clark a good soaking. Whatever. It had been glorious.

Until the lightning drove us out of the water, that is. Then it'd been a toss-up whether we all ought to split for home and get out of wet clothes or if some of us should go back to the church long enough to do some cleanup first. Most of Uptown's small congregation and about half of the Yada Yada sisters—most of whom attended other churches—decided to go home. (Stu, who lived on the second floor of our two-flat, drove a carload of Yada Yadas so they wouldn't have to ride the elevated train wringing wet.)

Couldn't blame them—that's precisely what I wanted to do too. Walking around in soggy underwear under my damp dress slacks wasn't my idea of a good time. But Pastor Clark hiked up the heat so we wouldn't "catch our death," as Ruth kept muttering, and there wasn't that much left to do. Still, it was nice of Nony and Mark to come back after changing out of their wet African dress and dashiki; they must've left the boys at home with Hoshi, the Japanese university student Mark and Nony had befriended. Nony had told Hoshi about Jesus and then brought her to the Chicago women's conference last year, where twelve of us ended up in prayer group twenty-six . . . and the rest, as they say, is history.

"Don't worry, Ruth," Nony was saying gently. "We can lift off the top two tiers—see?—and refrigerate them till Avis and Peter get back later this week."

"Yeah." Florida bopped into the kitchen and reappeared on the other side of the pass-through. "Ain't much in this here fridge once we take out this stuff." The small-boned woman with beaded braids all over her head and a scar down one cheek pulled open the door of the industrial refrigerator and pulled out two plastic jugs of red punch and a liter of ginger ale. Then Florida gingerly took the top two layers of the wedding cake from Nony and slid them carefully onto the nearly empty shelf. "There! That thang'll be safe here till them lovebirds pick it up next Sunday." As the refrigerator door closed with a soft wheeze, Florida grabbed a large knife from the block. "OK, everybody!" she yelled out into the big room. "Cake cuttin' time!"

"*Oy vey!* Don't be such a nudnik." Ruth grabbed Florida's wrist and took the knife as it hovered over the bottom layer of the wedding cake. "The punch *you* make, Florida Hickman; the cake *I* will cut—with the dignity it deserves after being heartlessly abandoned by the guests of honor." She waved the knife at the rest of us. "Nony, set out those paper plates and napkins. Jodi, tell Ben and the other men to get themselves up here. Yo-Yo, wash those hands! You should be so lucky not to end up with a fatal disease after bathing in Lake Michigan—and tell the other *shiksa* and *shegetz* they better wash their hands, too, or no cake!"

We obeyed. The men had disappeared with the dismantled *huppah,* so I assumed they were wrestling it into the trunk of Ben Garfield's big Buick LeSabre outside. I hobbled down the stairs to the front door as fast as my rodded left leg would let me—that and a missing spleen were the only physical scars left over from my car accident last summer. Sure enough, halfway down the block, Ben was tying down his half-opened trunk, which had slats of white-painted wood sticking out the back like vampire fangs, and Mark and Denny were walking slowly back in my direction, talking intently.

They made an odd couple—and not just because of the black and white. Denny was two inches shorter than the urbane Dr. Mark Smith, attractive in his own way—though "cute" came to mind when Denny grinned, sporting a deep dimple on each cheek. An assistant coach at West Rogers Park High School, Denny didn't exactly hang with the same crowd as the professorial Dr. Smith . . . and yet God had brought us and the Smiths together through Yada Yada. *How cool is that, God?*

"Wedding cake!" I called. "Ruth says hurry, and she's in no mood for laggards!"

Denny gave me a wave and bent his ear toward Mark once more. *Huh. What's that about?* But I hustled back up the stairs, where Ruth was now ceremoniously cutting the cake, and Florida was passing out clear plastic cups of red punch spiked with ginger ale to the cleanup crew. Pastor Clark and the newly baptized Becky, a tinge of pink tipping her usually pale cheekbones, joined us, and we all sat around demolishing our neat squares of chocolate cake with sugary roses in pink and green icing. I noticed our fifteen-year-old, Amanda, had cornered José and his father, Ricardo, and was showing off her not-quite-fluent Spanish, making them laugh at her innocent stumbles.

"Hey," Yo-Yo said through a mouthful of chocolate cake, "aren't we supposed to meet at Avis's apartment next week for Yada Yada?"

"What is she, a hotel? Give the lady a break. She just got married!" Ruth waved her plastic fork. "In the Bible, a whole year they gave to the new couple without any outside responsibilities. Maybe it's even one of the commandments."

I laughed. "Don't think so, Ruth. But we can meet somewhere else." I was just about to offer my house—though we'd just met there last week—when Yo-Yo cleared her throat.

"Uh, you guys wanna come to my crib? Now that I'm 'washed in the blood' and all that, I mean." She hunched shyly inside her baggy overalls. "I could send Pete and Jerry over to Garfield's or somethin'—but don't tell Ben yet, Ruth. Gotta spring it on him last-minute like, or he'll have time to think of a reason to say no."

Meet at Yo-Yo's? We'd never been there. I had no idea what kind of home she'd been able to create for her two half brothers. But . . . why not? Especially since it was her idea. "OK," I agreed. "I'll get the word around."

Denny, Mark, and Ben came tromping up the stairs at last, and Ruth handed them the plates she'd set aside, along with a few grunts of disapproval for being late. "Now eat, eat, so we can send these damp dishrags home before they all end up with the croup."

Fine by me! I was anxious to get out of my soggy clothes. Early May temperatures in Chicago weren't really warm enough to walk around damp—and I was supposed to be careful of getting colds now that I was without my infection-fighting spleen after the accident . . .

I shook off the dark memory. I wasn't going to let anything spoil this wonderful day.

Nony sat down beside me, cake in hand. "Jodi, I haven't had a chance to tell you. Mark's former pastor from Georgia recently relocated to Chicago, and he and his wife are starting a new ministry—New Morning Christian Church. They've been meeting in rented facilities for several months, and already the congregation is growing."

I looked at her with interest. "So that's where you and Mark are attending now?"

She nodded, eyes alight. "Pastor Cobbs has a heart for getting kids off the street. Mark's excited about the possibilities. But . . ."

"What?"

"New Morning is trying to lease a more permanent place to meet, but in the meantime, their current lease ran out. So we're looking for a place to meet for a few months. Do you think . . . ?" She paused, almost as if embarrassed.

"So that's what you guys want to talk to Pastor Clark about!" I grinned. "Sure, why not? He won't bite you." I leaned close to Nony in mock conspiracy. "He's a Mister Rogers clone, all warm fuzzies." We laughed. A few minutes later, I saw Nony and Mark standing off to the side talking with Pastor Clark.

Well. This might be interesting—sharing the same church building with a black church. I wondered when they'd meet. Saturday evening? Sunday afternoon?

ONCE WE GOT HOME, I claimed the bathroom for a long, hot, steamy shower. Josh—still basking in the glow of having his own set of car keys to our minivan—had offered to take José and Mr. Enriques home, along with Josh's two "pierced" friends from Jesus People USA. "I'm going too," Amanda had announced, beaming at José. Denny and I and Becky Wallace had hitched a ride with the Sisulu-Smiths for the few blocks to our house. *Our house,* I thought as I let the hot water run over my head, trying to warm up my bones. I still wasn't used to the idea that "our house" was now Becky Wallace's house, too, since she was living over our heads in Stu's second-floor apartment.

By the time I came out of the bathroom toweling my hair, Denny was in the recliner flicking the TV remote between ball games, with Willie Wonka, our rather deaf chocolate Lab, sprawled happily under his feet. I sat down on the arm of the recliner, which put me half into Denny's lap, slyly wiggled the remote away from him, and hit Mute.

"Hey!" He grabbed and missed.

"Hey yourself." I held the remote high over my head. "You can have it back when you tell me what you and Mark were talking about so intensely on the sidewalk back there."

He smirked. "Wouldn't you like to know?"

"My point exactly." I wiggled the remote temptingly.

"OK, OK." Denny rolled his eyes. "Remember what I said to Mark at our Guys' Day Out a month ago?"

I frowned. "Yeah. Something about he should take a sabbatical from the university and go to South Africa with his family for a year or two." It had been a brave thing for Denny to say, since that issue was a hot button between Mark and Nony. I also remember thinking it wasn't likely Mark would budge on Denny's say-so, when he'd stubbornly resisted Nony's pleas to move to her homeland. My eyebrows lifted. "You don't mean . . ."

Denny's grin got wider and his side dimples deepened. "Yep. Said he couldn't stop thinking about what I said about Nony 'dying by inches here'—or something to that effect. The thing that really got to him, he said, was my comment that 'God put that fire in her for a reason.' Told me he's actually applied for a sabbatical next year. But"—he wagged a warning finger at me—"you can't say anything, Jodi Marie Baxter! not to Nony, not to any of your Yada Yadas who tend to yakety-yak a bit too much, not even to Willie Wonka. Now"—he grabbed it—"give me that remote!"

2

*N*ot say anything? *Huh.* Good thing Avis was on her honeymoon for the next five days, or I'd be sorely tempted to bop into her office at school, spill the beans, and tell *her* not to say anything. But sure enough, although the door to the principal's office of Mary McLeod Bethune Elementary stood ajar behind the main desk as I passed the school office the next morning, the lights were off and the office empty.

Ack! How could Bethune Elementary function a whole week without Avis's magnetic rule? In fact, how did she manage to convince the school board to let her take a whole week off when there were only six weeks of school left? *Sheesh! Wish I had that kind of clout.*

Still twenty minutes before the first bell. I breezed past the school office heading for my third-grade classroom when I heard my name. "Ms. Baxter! Ms. Baxter, wait."

I turned. The school secretary came running out the door of the main office—a thirtyish woman with ash-blonde hair and reading glasses perched on her nose. "Ms. Baxter, did Ms. Johnson *really* get married yesterday?" When I nodded, she smacked herself on the forehead. "I can't believe it! She didn't say anything to the office staff; we just found a list of instructions when we came in this morning. Did she elope or something?"

I chuckled. Indeed. Avis wasn't exactly the blabbermouth type, even when it seemed obvious to the rest of us that she ought to be jumping up and down and shouting for joy. So what if she had passed the big Five-O? Getting married to a man as fine as Peter Douglass was worth crowing about.

Well, it was out now. "No, she didn't elope, but it wasn't exactly a wedding either. She got married during the morning service at our church—just the congregation plus her daughters' families." *And* Avis's Yada Yada sisters, but that was too complicated to explain. "But you know what, Ms. Ivy?" I gave her a conspiratorial grin. "I think we ought to get her good—give her a big shower or something from the school staff when she gets back. Streamers, signs, tell all the kids, make a big fuss, the whole shebang."

Ms. Ivy's eyes widened over her reading glasses. "That's a *great* idea! And we have a whole week with her out of the way to plan it. Perfect . . . perfect . . ." I could practically see mental wheels whirring as she headed back into the office. "And if she gets huffy about the fuss, I'll tell her it was your idea." She laughed and disappeared behind the desk.

Oh, great. Avis would be discombobulated. But who cared? It would be fun shaking her up a little.

I was glad for the few minutes alone before my classroom filled with squirrelly third graders. Dumping my tote bag containing a sack lunch, water bottle, and notebook stuffed with lesson plans on my desk, I began the Monday-morning routine I'd been trying to implement this school year—praying for each child in my room by name. I went up and down the rows, touching each desk, imagining the child who sat there . . .

"Jesus, thank You for Kaya. Thank You for the progress she's made in her reading this year. Bring her up to grade level, Lord . . . Open Chanté's ears, Lord, to remember instructions . . . Bless funny, feisty Ramón, our 'mighty protector,' who takes the meaning of his name a little too seriously . . . and give Cornell patience!—or maybe I'm the one who needs more patience with Mr. Know-It-All . . ."

Through the long bank of windows along one side of the classroom, I could see backpacks tossed helter-skelter on ground still damp from yesterday's rain, as the girls ran in and out of the spinning Double Dutch jump ropes, and the boys got out their kinks with the usual pushing and tagging and running. Only five more minutes until the bell; I needed to speed up my prayers. "Thank You for Ebony, Lord, for her sweet spirit . . . help me to channel D'Angelo's bossy ways into positive leadership skills . . ."

I touched the next desk and paused. "And Hakim . . ." I took a deep breath, trying to override the ache his name still engendered in my spirit. Would this wound never heal? "And Hakim. Lord, help me to love him enough to let go, to let someone else help him unlock the genius inside . . ." My tumbling emotions rested for a moment on the painful but liberating parent-teacher conference a few weeks ago when Geraldine Wilkins-Porter—Hakim's mother, and the mother of Jamal, the teenager who'd run in front of my car that awful day last June—had sat across from me in this very room, and for one brief moment our spirits had touched . . .

"Oh, Geraldine. Can you forgive me?" I had reached my hand across the desk.

To my surprise, she had touched my fingers briefly, then pulled her hand back and looked down at her lap. *"Maybe . . . maybe someday,"* she had whispered.

A loud, brassy ringing jerked me out of my thoughts. The first bell! And I wasn't out on the playground to bring in my students. I scurried down the hall toward the playground door. Outside, my students looked at me reproachfully for making them be the last line to file inside.

Sheesh. Not the best way to start a Monday morning!

But—I smiled at each childish face as it passed—the time spent in prayer was.

SUNDAY'S STORMS HAD HEADED SOUTH, sending a spate of killer tornadoes through the Central Plains. Becky Wallace, red bandana knotted around her hair, was on her knees in our backyard spreading mulch over the flowerbeds from the pile of leaves that'd been left to rot beside the garage—a skill she'd brought from Lincoln Correctional Center, where she'd worked on the garden-and-grounds crew and discovered she had a green thumb. As I shrugged out of my spring jacket and put the teakettle on, I watched her from the window in the kitchen door. She'd already planted the flat of Johnny-jump-ups, petunias, and zinnias that the kids had bought me for Mother's Day—a week early. Now she was turning her attention to the unplanted areas, long neglected. Once she'd spread the rotting leaves in a thick mat, she grabbed the long-handled spade and began to dig and turn, mixing the mulch with the rich brown dirt—dirt that was now weed and root free, thanks to the muscle she'd applied all last week.

A whine near my knees begged for attention. "Wonka! Ohmigosh, you haven't been out yet." I unlocked the back door and called out, "Uh, Becky! Do you mind if Willie Wonka comes out? He's been in the house all day."

"No problem." Becky kept digging, her words coming out in grunts. "He's good company. Doesn't boss me around"—she snorted a laugh—"not like the grounds super at Lincoln." She plunged the spade in once more.

Willie Wonka scrambled down the porch steps as best as his arthritic joints would allow and lifted his hind leg, watering the rusty charcoal grill that had stood out all winter. Why in the world hadn't we moved it into the garage last fall? Oh, yeah. There wasn't any room now that Leslie "Stu" Stewart parked her silver Celica in the garage. Our apartment's two-car garage—kind of like a double bed—was more like one and a half.

Tough luck, Mr. Grill.

The teakettle whistled, and I poured the steaming water over a tea bag in the biggest mug I could find. Then, on an impulse, I grabbed another mug and tea bag, sweetened both cups with honey, and headed out the back door.

"Hey, Becky! How about a tea break?" I held the second mug aloft and sat down on the back steps.

The red bandana turned, hesitated, then Becky laid down the spade and sauntered my way. *How did she get into those tight jeans?* The twenty-something young woman didn't have one spare inch on her lithe frame, and she showed it off to good advantage.

Becky stopped a good two yards away. "Are ya sure ya want me to sit?" She held out her hands, dirt creating brown moons under her fingernails. "These paws are kinda grubby."

I shrugged. "Sure. What's a little dirt?"

Still standing, Becky gingerly took the hot mug, sniffed, and wrinkled her nose. "Tea, huh? Ain't much of a tea drinker. Like a good shot of coffee, though."

"Oh. Sorry . . . I could go make a pot." I started to get up.

Becky waved me down. "Nah. This is OK." She took a tentative sip, then sat down on the bottom step.

I suddenly felt awkward. I'd never been alone with Becky Wallace for more than two minutes in our entire acquaintance. Good grief. How would I just chat with an ex-con, a street woman whose life had no possible relation to my own?

Whaddya mean, Jodi Baxter? No relation to your own life? The Voice inside my head seemed to be shouting in whispers. *Didn't this woman get baptized yesterday in front of dozens of witnesses? Declare she wanted to follow Jesus? Doesn't that make her your sister in Christ?*

Well, yes, but . . .

And isn't she a mother—just like you? Doesn't she live upstairs, your "neighbor" now? And didn't Jesus say to "love your neighbor as much as you love yourself"?

I darted a glance at Becky over the rim of my mug, wondering if she suspected the inner tussle I was feeling. But she just held the mug in both hands, sipping now and then, looking back and forth between the flowerbeds on either side of our postage-stamp backyard.

"Say, Becky. Tell me a little more about Andy, your little boy. I mean, if you don't mind." That'd be a safe topic.

A small smile creased her sober face, and she glanced up at me. "Don't mind. I like to talk about Andy—helps me remember him. 'Cause some days . . ." Her voice faltered and she looked away. "Some days I can't remember what my baby looks like."

"You don't even have a picture of him?"

"Nah. Went to prison with jus' what I had on that day—came out with the same. Don't know what happened to my stuff. Didn't have that much anyway." She shrugged. "Little Andy—he's one cute kid. Whatever else go wrong with his daddy and me, we sure did make a pretty baby. Big Andy's black—think I tol' ya—good-lookin' guy. Lotta muscles. Thought I'd made quite a catch. But . . ." She sighed. "Guess I screwed up. The drugs an' all."

I tried to steer the conversation back. "Tell me about Andy."

She perked up. "Andy got pearly skin and black hair. Not kinky, not straight. Lotsa loose curls. People used ta say he look like hot chocolate an' whipped cream—I'm the whipped cream, ya know." She grimaced. "Not so sweet though. Been messin' up most of my life." A long pause followed while she stared at her tea.

"Andy," I prompted.

"Oh, yeah. That boy, he's bright. Picks up ever' little thing anybody say, say it right back. Trouble is, he picks up the bad words too. He don' know what they mean; still, I don' want him talkin' trash. He's only two years old!" She frowned. "Or was, las' time I saw him. He had a birthday while I was in prison." She stared into her mug of tea. "Must be gettin' big now. Hope his grandmama helpin' him with his letters and numbers. I never did that, really. Didn't have many books. Not a reader myself." She looked up at me again. "You got books for kids? I mean, you a teacher, right? I'd like to have some books to read with Andy when DCFS lets me have a visit—"

We both heard the garage door on the alley side go up and turned expectantly. The sound of a car engine dying—two cars?— and voices. Then the back door to the garage opened, and Amanda spilled out . . . and stopped.

"Hey!" She called back into the garage. "Hold it, you guys. They're both out here in the yard."

Josh's shaved head showed up behind his sister; then Stu's black beret and long blonde hair appeared too. The three looked at each other with mutual shrugs and disappeared back into the garage.

Josh, Amanda . . . and Stu? No telling what they were up to. Though how they hooked up to arrive home at the same time was anybody's guess. Denny sometimes picked up the kids at Lane Tech, but Stu's schedule visiting her DCFS clients was erratic at best.

"They up to somethin'," Becky muttered. She stood up and set down her mug, only half-empty. "Maybe I better get back ta—"

The Three Musketeers came tromping out the door at that precise moment, followed by Denny, and all four of them had a flat of flower sets in their hands. "Happy early Mother's Day, Mom!" Amanda crowed.

"And happy early Mother's Day for you too, Becky," Stu added. They set the flats on the sidewalk in front of Becky and me.

I wanted to laugh. "But you already got me a flat of flowers a couple of days ago. Thought that was my early Mother's Day gift."

"Yeah, yeah," Denny said. "That was just for starters. We all decided that since we now have a gardener *in residence* . . ." He grinned at Becky, whose eyes looked about to pop at the array of marigolds, snapdragons, alyssum, purple lobelia, and dianthuses tucked in their little plastic six-packs, nine to a tray.

"Uh, only one catch." Josh wagged a finger at me. "Let Becky plant 'em, Mom. Face it. Whatever your fantasies about actually getting these babies into the ground, you *don't* have a green thumb!"

OK, let them laugh at me. I laughed too—until I looked at Becky. Tears puddled in her gray eyes, tears she rapidly brushed away with her hands, leaving dirty tracks. She pulled off the red bandana and wiped her eyes and nose. "Sorry. Jus' that . . . nobody never gave me a Mother's Day gift before."

Stu, looking spiffy in her belted leather jacket and black beret, tossed her hair. "Hey, this is just the appetizer. Wait'll you get the *real* Mother's Day gift!"

3

*B*ecky looked confused. I was too. Who was Stu talking to—Becky or me? But Stu just headed up the back stairs that led to the second-floor apartment. "Hey," she called over her shoulder. "You guys want to grill something tonight? I have a couple of chicken quarters we could throw on for Becky and me. Got some crusty bread we could grill too." Stu disappeared into her back door without waiting for a reply.

I looked at Denny. He shrugged. "OK by me. We might have a bag of charcoal left over from last summer . . . somewhere." He moseyed back out to the garage to begin the hunt.

Becky went back to spading the mulch. I picked up her mug and squinted at the sky. Clouds hung heavy overhead, even though the temperature was in the high fifties; we might be in for more rain. *Guess we can always eat in.* I let the screen door bang behind me as I went inside to hunt for chicken body parts in our freezer.

Denny found the charcoal, though it was damp and old, and he had to use half a container of lighter fluid to get it to burn. By the time the coals were hot enough, I'd managed to thaw enough chicken pieces in the microwave to feed the Baxter Four and grated some carrots for a carrot-and-raisin salad—my substitute for a tossed salad once I'd seen how limp and pathetic the lettuce looked that'd been hiding in our crisper. I didn't really mind firing up the grill this early in the month; I'd even wanted to invite Stu and Becky down for supper one of these nights. We'd pretty much left the new housemates alone last week to get settled and sort things out after Becky's release from prison. But Stu had done it again—preempted my good intentions and caught me off guard, unprepared for company for dinner.

I sighed. Probably just as well. Becky might feel more comfortable with something spontaneous anyway.

Sure enough, by the time Denny yelled that the chicken was done, it was starting to sprinkle, so I shanghaied Amanda to set our dining room table for six. I was filling glasses with water and ice when Stu came in bearing the platter of golden-brown chicken, followed by Becky with a basket of grilled bread. "Better switch the silverware, Amanda," Stu chided. "The knife and fork shouldn't be on the same side."

I snorted. *Good for you, Stu. Maybe Amanda will remember if somebody besides me nags her about how to set the table.* Then it hit me. *Oh great. Stu probably thinks* I'm *the one who taught her to do it wrong.* I bit my tongue, waved everybody into seats at the table, and held out my hands to Becky on one side of me and Denny on the other. Becky's eyes darted from person to person as we joined hands for our table grace, then she ducked her head and squinted her eyes shut as Denny "blessed the food" in twenty-five words or less. My husband didn't believe in long prayers while the food was hot.

Becky didn't say much as we all tackled the chicken, letting the rest of us do the talking. Stu asked about prom and graduation coming up for Josh, and what was he going to do next year, and was the Uptown youth group going to do a mission trip again this summer? That got Josh wound up about taking a year off before going to college and volunteering with Jesus People USA here in the city. I eyed Denny. That wasn't a *decision* yet, was it? But every time Josh talked about *not* going to school next fall, the idea edged another inch toward reality.

"And the youth group is going to volunteer at the Cornerstone Festival this summer," Amanda added with her mouth full. "Cheaper than going to Mexico or someplace. You wanna come, Stu? It's *so* cool. *All* the hot CCM bands play at Cornerstone."

"Contemporary Christian Music," Denny explained, noticing Becky's bewildered look. "And Cornerstone is the big music festival sponsored by Jesus People every summer here in Illinois."

"Oh. Never heard of it. For kids like them?" Becky waved her fork at Josh and Amanda.

"No, it's for everybody! Even you, Becky—oh." Color crept up on Amanda's face. "Sorry. Forgot about the . . . the ankle thing."

Becky shrugged. "It's OK. Don' worry 'bout it."

"The ankle thing" was the electronic monitor Becky Wallace had to wear, restricting her to "house arrest" for at least six months as a condition of her early parole. The fact that she was out at all only eight months after a felony conviction—ten years for robbery and assault—was mind-boggling. A case of God at work, mixing together the overcrowded conditions at the women's prison, Yada Yada testifying on Becky's behalf at a special hearing with the parole board, and Stu offering to let Becky stay with her since she needed an address to qualify for "house arrest." A miracle, really.

Funny thing about miracles, though—they're uncomfortable; they upset the natural order. One hardly knows what to do with them; they don't come with instructions. Right now, the only thing I knew to do was hang on to God's promises and hope He knew what He was doing.

"—supposed to meet this Sunday?" Stu was asking. "Jodi?"

"Uh, Yada Yada? We were supposed to meet at Avis's before she up and got married." I grinned. "Yo-Yo said we could meet at her apartment this time. Kinda neat, huh?" My grin turned to a grimace. "Oh, shoot. I was supposed to send an e-mail and let everybody know. Thanks for the reminder."

Denny frowned. "Sunday is Mother's Day, though."

"So? You guys already gave Becky and me our Mother's Day gift. The flats of flowers."

My husband pulled a puppy-dog face. "But we still like to hang out with our favorite mom. Right, kids?"

"Right!" they chorused dutifully.

I snorted in jest. "*Right.* By five o'clock, Mother's Day or not, you'll all be off doing your own thing. Yada Yada might as well pray." I started to clear the table.

"Uh, you guys hang out and do special stuff on Mother's Day?" Becky's question halted the table clearing.

Sheesh. Nothing like sticking my foot in my mouth. She said she'd never had a Mother's Day gift before—maybe never celebrated Mother's Day, even as a kid. "Well, sure," I said. "I was just teasing them. Doesn't have to be a big deal, but it's kinda nice to do something as a family."

Becky's jaw muscles tightened. "Yeah. That'd be nice. That's what I'd like to do for Mother's Day, hang out with my kid." She shrugged. "Someday, anyway." She pushed back her chair and started piling plates and silverware.

Stu caught my eye over Becky's head . . . and winked.

WITH "DON'T TELL" HANGING OVER MY HEAD, I'd almost forgotten what Denny had said about Mark Smith applying for a sabbatical until I got an e-mail from Nony in reply to the one I finally sent out about meeting at Yo-Yo's apartment this Sunday.

To: Jodi Baxter
From: BlessedRU@online.net
Re: Ride on Sunday

Dear Sister Jodi,
I am blessed that Yo-Yo invited Yada Yada to meet at her apartment on Sunday! Mark said he can drop us off—we'll bring Hoshi—but he needs the car to attend a faculty function at NU that evening. Could you bring us home? If so, we'll be there!

(Wasn't Sunday's baptism a glimpse of glory? We need glimpses like that to help us bear the pain and sorrow all around the world.)

Love, Nony

P.S. Has anyone heard from Avis and Peter?

I was still thinking about Nony's e-mail as I walked to school on Wednesday. *Hm. No mention of Mark taking a sabbatical. He must not have said anything to her yet.* But her mention of the "pain and sorrow all around the world" was characteristic of Nonyameko Sisulu-Smith, raised in South Africa, educated at the University of Chicago—where she'd met Mark—but longing to return to her homeland, now that apartheid had ended, to help her people.

"Especially children orphaned by AIDS," I murmured as I tossed my tote bag on my classroom desk and changed out of my walking shoes and sweat socks. I admired Nony's heart for suffering people—though it seemed we had plenty of suffering children right here in Chicago who could keep her busy. *Right here in my classroom,* I thought as the first bell rang, and I headed out to the playground to bring in my class. But still. If Mark could get a sabbatical and give Nony a chance to go where her heart resided, that would be wonderful.

If. What if he didn't?

No wonder Mark hadn't told her yet. Wouldn't want to get her hopes up only to—

I felt a tug on my sleeve as the line of children jostled past me into the third-grade classroom. "Ms. B?"

I looked at the upturned face. Hakim's deep brown eyes seemed to be searching my own. "Yes, Hakim?"

He hesitated, waiting until the last child had gone through the door. I let it close, leaving us alone in the hall. "This gonna be my last week. Mama found a teacher to help me, one of them special schools. S'posed to start next week. Goin' to summer school, too, so I can be ready for fourth grade."

My heart felt like it dropped down into my stomach. "Oh, Hakim." Anything else I wanted to say came up a big blank. How could his mother *do* this, so close to the end of school! Couldn't she

26

wait till next fall, start him in a new school then? *But didn't you tell her you couldn't help him, Jodi? That he needed professional help to deal with his post-traumatic stress, that you realized you needed to let him go?*

I bent down and gave him a hug. "I will miss you very much, Hakim. So much."

He seemed embarrassed. "Um, sorry I scratched my desk." He pulled away and looked up at me quizzically. "Why didn't you ever get it fixed?"

I smiled. The three-inch jagged lightning bolt, scratched with a paper clip, still decorated Hakim's desk. "Because it reminds me of you." I playfully boxed his shoulder. "Only kidding. They're supposed to fix it. Guess the janitor can't do everything at once."

Except I wasn't kidding. I kind of hoped that desk never got fixed, not if Hakim was going to leave. It would remind me of the boy who wore a scar on his heart—a scar I helped create when his big brother ran in front of my car—and loved me anyway.

4

*H*akim's news on Wednesday morning left me with only two days to figure out some kind of send-off. I didn't want Hakim to just disappear with no good-bye. What would be appropriate? I stewed about it all the rest of that day and into the next. *Keep it light. Keep it fun. But let him know he's been an important part of our class . . .*

For some reason my mind didn't churn out the usual string of ideas, and the more anxious I got about it, the more I came up blank. Then I realized this was Old Jodi behavior: stew about it first; pray later, when all else fails.

"Didn't Jesus say God cares about a sparrow who falls out of the sky?" I muttered as I let myself into the house after school on Thursday and put Willie Wonka out. "He's gotta care about Hakim leaving our class." So I prayed aloud as I put a saucepan of water on the stove to heat and started peeling potatoes for supper. "Sorry, God. Didn't mean to be slow talking to You about this. You know the situation; You know how awkward it is that Hakim is even *in* my class! Yet I do want to thank You. Yes, *thank You* for putting Hakim in my class. He doesn't know it, but he's brought so much healing to me just by his presence . . ."

Healing. Didn't Hakim's name mean something about "healing"? I dropped the potatoes I was peeling and hunted up my lesson plan notebook. At the beginning of the school year, I'd made a welcome bulletin board with each child's name and its meaning in colorful bubble letters. I had the list somewhere . . . *there it is.*

"Hakim. *Wise healer.*"

Hm. What could I do with that? He'd been pretty scornful last September when I told him what his name meant. I studied the list, trying to think.

The back door banged. "Mo-om! Wonka's digging up the flowers Becky Wallace just planted!" A split-second lull. "Why is there a pan heating on the stove with nothing in it?"

"Ack!" I made a mad dash for the kitchen and pulled the empty saucepan off the burner. "Boiled dry," I said lamely to my fifteen-year-old, who was holding Willie Wonka by the collar and wearing that *I-can't-believe-how-dumb-parents-are* look. I glanced out the back door window; sure enough, a freshly dug hole decorated with topsy-turvy marigolds had materialized in the newly planted flowerbeds along the fence.

Grabbing a rag from the bucket under the sink, I got it wet and threw it at Amanda. "Make yourself useful. Clean off Wonka's paws," I said, heading out the door to repair the damage. The dog, oblivious to his crime, licked Amanda's face as she bent over his muddy paws.

By the time I'd rescued the marigolds, Amanda had her head in the refrigerator looking for a snack. Refilling the saucepan with water, I put it back on the stove and tackled the potatoes again. "Tomorrow is Hakim Porter's last day in my class," I said, trying to make normal conversation. "Got any ideas how I could make it special?"

Amanda gave up on the refrigerator and raided the cookie jar. "Cupcakes. And play some kind of game. It's third grade, Mom."

I stared at my daughter as she grabbed the phone on her way out of the kitchen. Cupcakes! Of course! And a game . . .

Suddenly I had an idea. I grinned as I plopped the last skinned potato into the now-boiling water. Thanks to God and Amanda.

MS. IVY WAVED ME INTO THE SCHOOL OFFICE the next morning, grinning slyly as if she was guarding a national secret. Ignoring the fact that my hands were full with a tray of chocolate cupcakes, she dragged me behind the main desk, threw open Avis Johnson's office door, and flipped the light switch. "Ta-da!"

Somebody had been busy. A long paper banner on the wall behind her desk said CONGRATULATIONS, AVIS AND PETER! Twisted yellow and green crepe-paper streamers crisscrossed the room like a spider web, and on the desk sat a pile of wedding gifts wrapped in colorful paper and gold ribbon. "Better come in early on Monday if you want to see the look on her face." Ms. Ivy giggled. "Haven't had this much fun since we had a sit-in for two days in the president's office in college—oh! Don't forget to tell your students to say, 'Congratulations, Ms. Johnson' whenever they see her on Monday."

"Except it's Mrs. *Douglass* now—but don't worry. She'll love it. Just ignore anything she says like, 'What's all this nonsense?' and, 'Did you get any work done last week?'"

31

I left Ms. Ivy still chuckling, made it to my classroom without dropping the cupcakes, and hid them in the supply closet. Once the bell had rung and the students were more or less in their seats, I announced that today was Hakim's last day in our class, so I was declaring Friday "Hakim Porter Day" and everyone should try to think of something special he or she could do for Hakim. Embarrassed, Hakim slid down in his seat and put his hands over his ears—but I saw a tiny smile flicker at the edges of his mouth.

A few of the students really got into it. Chanté offered to sharpen his pencil. Ramón said Hakim should be first in line to go to lunch. Cornell broke his candy bar in two and gave Hakim half. During creative arts, several students labored over good-bye cards.

With an hour left in the school day, I told the students to put away their papers and books—to loud cheers—and it was time for Hakim's good-bye party. We pushed back the desks, and on the floor I laid down a number of flashcards with a large capital letter written on each one. "Who can make a word out of these letters?" Jade picked out SEE. D'Angelo put together RAT and OWL. We kept mixing up the letters, and others began to get the idea, finding OR and REAL and HAT. The word game took a detour when Terrell discovered POW and proceeded to act out a few karate kicks: *"Pow! Pow!"*

After marching Terrell to his seat for a five-minute time-out, I noticed Hakim studying the letters intently. Suddenly, he said, "Let me." In thirty seconds, he had spelled out HAKIM PORTER and sat back on his heels grinning.

"But what are the other letters for, Ms. Baxter?" Kaya asked.

"Just to fool us, I bet," scoffed Ramón. "It was Hakim's name all the time, 'cause it's Hakim Porter Day."

"You're right, Ramón. It *is* Hakim's name, but the rest of the letters spell out the meaning of Hakim's name. Remember our bulletin board at the beginning of the school year?"

Several heads nodded. "But I only remember *my* name," said Britny. She stuck her nose in the air. "It means 'England,' and I'm going to go there someday."

A hubbub ensued as several students shouted out the meaning of *their* names. But I finally managed to corral everyone's attention again. "Whoever can put together the two words that are the meaning of Hakim's name can bring out the treat I've got locked in the supply closet."

Again there was a flurry of waving hands. Hakim said gruffly, "Let me. It's *my* name." And in short order, he had spelled out WISE HEALER with the remaining cards on the floor.

I smiled. "You remembered."

He shrugged. "It's still stupid. Can I get the treat now?"

The cupcakes, which also had capital letters spelling out Hakim's name in green frosting, one letter per cupcake, were a big hit; so was the game of pin the tail on Shrek's donkey friend. We played and laughed until the bell rang. "Don't forget!" I called out as the kids scrambled for their backpacks and jackets. "When Ms. Johnson comes back from her honeymoon on Monday, you can say, 'Congratulations, Mrs. Douglass!'"

Hakim lingered, cleaning out his desk and stuffing papers, pencils, colored markers, and other stuff that he had collected throughout the year into his backpack. Finally, he came up to my desk. "Thanks for the party, Ms. B." A frown collected on his creamy brown face. "I—I won't get to say good-bye to Ms. Johnson. Will you"—he fished in his back pocket and pulled out a crumpled, handmade card—"give this card to her?"

I took the card. "Of course, Hakim. She will really appreciate it."

He fished in his other back pocket. "An' this one's for you." He handed me another crumpled, construction-paper card. The front was decorated with curlicues and flowers and stick figures holding hands. Inside were just four words: *I LOVE YOU. HAKIM.*

OK, SO MAYBE TEACHERS AREN'T SUPPOSED TO CRY and give their students big hugs, but I couldn't help it. I was still sniffling as I started home with my tote bag and the empty cupcake tray. Even if Hakim's mother didn't know if she could forgive me, Hakim's "I love you" went a long way to healing the pain in my heart.

No wonder Jesus said we should "become like little children" and "a little child shall lead them."

Besides, I told myself, *wasn't it a* good *thing Hakim would be getting the help he needed?* In fact, so many good things had been happening lately that I should be dancing in the street! Avis getting married . . . Yo-Yo getting baptized . . . Becky getting an early parole . . . not to mention that spring was busting out all over, draping the rough edges of our Chicago neighborhood with a canopy of green leaves overhead, while tiny lilies of the valley embroidered the grass along the rough concrete sidewalks.

Wow, God. Given how this school year started—MaDear throwing a hissy fit at Adele's beauty shop, sending a mirror flying at my husband's head; Bandana Woman busting into a Yada Yada prayer meeting waving that wicked knife; getting screamed at by Hakim's mother at our first parent-teacher conference when she realized who I was—*given all that upset and trauma, it seems like "all things are working together for good," just like that verse in Romans promises.*

As gladness swallowed up my sadness, I even tried skipping down the sidewalk of Lunt Street as I approached our two-flat . . . until I tripped over a crack. OK, forget skipping. I could be happy, but I needed to watch my feet.

That's right, Jodi. Don't let down your guard. I could almost hear Avis's voice speaking firmly in my ear. *Satan likes nothing better than to lull us to sleep spiritually when things are going well. Keep up the prayers. Pray for Yo-Yo. Pray for Becky—you better believe Satan isn't happy about "the ones who got away." Pray for your kids, pray for Hakim and his mother, pray for—*

The phone was ringing as I came in the house. Shedding my jacket and dumping my tote bag on the way to the kitchen, I grabbed the receiver just as the answering machine kicked in. "Hi, it's Jodi! I'm here."

"Oh. So glad you are home, Jodi!" Nony's rich voice seemed curiously breathless. "I have such good news. I can't wait till Yada Yada meets—two whole days. I will burst wide open before then."

I laughed. "What?" I had an inkling. "I'm a glutton for good news."

"It's Mark! He came home from work today and told me . . . oh, bless the name of the Lord! Let the whole world know what He has done! For the Lord is good. His unfailing love endures forever!" Nony burst into one of her Scripture prayers, and I had to wait several moments before she came back on the phone.

"Nony! What did Mark say?"

"Oh, Jodi. He applied for a sabbatical from Northwestern, and it was approved. We are going to South Africa when the boys finish their school year!"

Ha! Take that, Satan, I thought as I hung up the phone a few minutes later. *God's on a roll, doing good things for all the Yada Yada sisters!*

But as I let Willie Wonka out into the backyard—supervised this time, till we put some little fences up around the flowerbeds— the Voice in my head said again, *Be on your guard, Jodi. Pray.*

5

Saturday started out with the usual chores—me nagging Josh and Amanda about cleaning their rooms and doing their laundry—but I added a trip to Home Depot to get some fencing to keep Willie Wonka out of the flowerbeds. I even remembered to measure how many feet I'd need. But as I stood in front of the display of decorative edging and realized how much this was going to cost me, I wished I'd talked to Stu about sharing the expense, since we both used the backyard.

On the other hand, it was *our* dog that had dug the hole and made it necessary.

I sighed, loaded a whole stack of foot-high, white plastic pickets into my cart, and headed for the checkout. Once I got home, I snapped together several lengths, stuck them into the ground, and stood back for a look. *Hm.* Wouldn't keep out a determined dog, that's for sure. I bent down and scratched Wonka's head. I was counting on the fact that our chocolate Lab was old and arthritic.

Denny left to coach a baseball game at West Rogers High at two o'clock, backing the minivan out of the garage just as Stu drove in. "Not bad," she said, stopping to admire the fencing, her arms full of packages. "Gotta do what we gotta do, I guess."

I grimaced. "Yeah. Sorry about this. Willie Wonka apologizes—don't you, Wonka." The dog panted happily. "Did you have to work today?" It wasn't unusual for Stu to visit some of her DCFS cases on the weekend.

"You could say that." Stu hesitated, shifting her packages. "Look, Jodi. Don't say anything yet, but this thing with Becky Wallace has gotten a bit complicated. I have to drop Andy from my caseload. It's a conflict of interest, since his mother now lives in my house." She rolled her eyes.

"Oh no. Becky's counting on you going to bat for her to get visitation rights."

"I know. It'll work out. Another caseworker is willing to work with the situation. I went to talk with her today, to fill her in. Oh!" A grin spread over Stu's face. "On the way home, I stopped at Adele's Hair and Nails to take MaDear out for a bit." Stu chuckled. "She's a handful, all right. Kept telling people on the sidewalk that she was being kidnapped."

My mouth dropped. "She didn't!" So far, Yada Yada's decision to take turns getting Adele Skuggs's elderly mother out of the shop had been working pretty well. Usually MaDear had to spend hours on end tied in her wheelchair where Adele could keep an eye on her, since MaDear suffered from dementia. But one never knew what to expect from the feisty old woman. Being "kidnapped" was a new one.

"Yep." Stu seemed to think it was funny. "And Adele's bugging me to bring Becky into the shop so she can 'do somethin' with that hair.' I tried to explain she's on house arrest, but Adele just said, 'You'll figure out somethin'.'"

"Huh. How does that work? I mean, what about church? Can Becky go to church tomorrow? She got permission for last Sunday—the wedding and baptism and all."

Stu shifted the packages she had in her arms. "Yeah, well, we got a special dispensation for last Sunday. But for regular stuff like church every week, the pastor has to fax a letter on church letterhead to the department, stuff like that. Haven't even had time to ask Pastor Clark to do it."

"What about Yada Yada? She came two weeks ago when it was here at the house. But tomorrow we're going to Yo-Yo's."

"Might be a problem, since we move from place to place each time." Stu shrugged. "Don't even know if she wants to come to Yada Yada." She glanced at her watch. "Oh, hey, I got tons of stuff to do. See you tomorrow, OK?"

I went back to sticking plastic pickets along the flowerbeds, but a moment later Stu yelled down from the second-floor landing outside her back door. "Hey, Jodi! You guys going to be around tomorrow afternoon?"

"Think so," I called back. "Denny's the last-minute type, you know. But I'm *not* cooking my own Mother's Day dinner, that's for sure."

THE SECOND SUNDAY POTLUCK, a tradition normally carved in stone at Uptown Community Church, got bumped to the third Sunday this month in deference to Mother's Day. Too many complaints last year—though it did have the advantage of providing a Mother's Day meal for single moms and others without mothers to celebrate with. I had to admit I was glad I didn't have to throw together a Baxter casserole or salad to take to church—especially since Denny made cheese omelets and splurged on gourmet coffee for breakfast, which he'd served up by candlelight. "Freeloaders," he groused at the kids, who'd long ago given up making me breakfast in bed for Mother's Day. Not that I missed the Cheerios and peanut butter sandwich combos they came up with.

"Hey, Jodi! Where's Avis and that Mr. Peter?" Florida hissed at me as she came up the stairs to Uptown's second-floor meeting room, trailed by nine-year-old Carla and twelve-year-old Cedric. "I thought they was gettin' back yesterday."

I smirked. "Maybe they did. Honeymoon probably didn't wear off yet."

Florida must've caught me glancing behind her to see if her husband, Carl, and her oldest boy, Chris, had come, because she shook her head. "Carl's still in the bed. Don't know if I'm gonna get him to church regular after putting in a full workweek." She rolled her eyes. "'Course, he didn't make it regular when he *wasn't* working. Go figure. But I'm not complaining; thank ya, *Je*sus! A man with a job ain't nothin' ta sneeze at." She sent Cedric and Carla off to find seats, then murmured quietly, "But ya gotta pray for Chris, Jodi. He's the one I'm worried about right now. Why didn't nobody tell me fourteen could be so nasty?"

I didn't know what to say; I just hugged her and nodded, promising to pray. I didn't remember Josh being "nasty" when he was fourteen. At the same time, he hadn't been in the foster-care system for five years like Florida's kids, while she was getting herself sober from years of drug addiction. Frankly, the fact that their family was back together again was nothing short of a miracle.

It was one of those miracles that resisted getting pinned down in a happy ending, though. According to Florida, her oldest was hanging out on the street far too much these days.

Carla had happily joined the ten-year-old Reilly twins passing out carnations to everybody as they came up the stairs—red if your mother was still living, white if she'd passed. I noticed Stu took a red carnation, though I wasn't sure if her parents still lived in the Chicago area or had moved to some other state.

Did Becky Wallace have a mother? A father? She'd basically said she didn't have any family except Andy—and he was currently living with his paternal grandmother. For a moment my insides ached. *Oh God! So many hurting families . . .*

Worship was never quite as spirited when Avis was absent. Rick Reilly, who played guitar for the praise team, was a decent worship leader, but Avis . . . I missed the way she helped us focus on worshiping God for who God is, not just for what He's done. Still, the worship was lively enough, and Pastor Clark gave a good sermon on "Who is my mother and my brothers and my sisters?" from the passage in Matthew 12—reminding us that no matter what our natural family situation is like, we all have a *new* family when we become God's sons and daughters.

"Wish Becky could've heard Pastor Clark's sermon," I murmured to Stu after the service. "She's going to need a new family."

"You guys going to be home this afternoon?" Stu asked me again.

I eyed Denny, who was talking to some visitors. "Probably. My guess is that we'll go out somewhere for lunch. Low-key stuff. Why? . . . Oh, hey. You want to ride with me to Yada Yada tonight? Only hitch: Nony asked if I'd give her and Hoshi a ride back to

Evanston after Yada Yada. Mark can bring them, but he needs the car for something or other."

"I'll think about it." Stu waved as her black beret disappeared down the stairs.

SURE ENOUGH, Denny took us out to eat at Baker's Square—definitely a "family" restaurant. "Hope you don't mind," he murmured in my hair as we followed the hostess to a table out in the solarium. "I'm saving the fancy eats and fancy price for when it's just you and me." He had a point. Teenagers only want burgers or pizza anyway.

We came home with a triple-berry pie to heat up and a half-gallon of french vanilla ice cream. "Mind if I invite Stu and Becky down to share it?" I asked, popping the pie into the oven to warm. Obviously, my family didn't mind—Denny and Josh were already cruising through TV channels to catch the NBA scores, and Amanda had disappeared with the phone.

Going out our front door, I rang Stu's doorbell and waited on the porch until I heard feet tromping down the carpeted stairs. "Hey, you wanna . . ." we both said at once.

Stu grinned. "You first."

"Just wondered if you and Becky want to come down in a few minutes for pie and ice cream. Mother's Day treat."

Stu's grin got wider. "Sure. If you can cut the pie in sevenths. We've got a guest."

"Oh." I was disappointed. That kind of changed things. "Well, sure. About ten minutes?"

"We'll be there!"

Back in the house, I brought out seven dessert plates, forks, and spoons and put on a pot of coffee. Who was visiting Stu? Her mother? That didn't make sense; Stu would go visit *her*, wouldn't she? *Huh. Just goes to show how long you can know a person and still not really know her.*

A few minutes later, I heard voices come in the front, then Denny exclaim, "Hey! Who's this?" his voice high with delight.

Curious, I quickly snatched the pie from the oven before it got too hot, then I hustled down the hallway to the living room. Stu stood off to the side, wearing a grin so wide it threatened to put another pierced hole in her ears. Denny had squatted down on his haunches in front of Becky, who was standing almost trancelike in the middle of our living room with her hands on the head of a little boy—a little boy with loose black curls and skin the color of hot chocolate with whipped cream.

My heart nearly skipped a beat. It *had* to be . . . Andy.

6

*T*he best Mother's Day surprise I'd ever seen sat on a pile of encyclopedias stacked on one of our dining room chairs and tackled his piece of triple-berry pie and ice cream with lip-smacking gusto, complete with a dishtowel "bib." This certainly had to be the best Mother's Day gift Becky Wallace ever had! The thin young woman never took her eyes off her son's face, as though he might disappear if her eyes strayed for even an instant.

The joy of seeing a mother and her child reunited was contagious. Amanda immediately fell in love, even dragging out her much-loved Snoopy dog that she still slept with and using it as a puppet to "talk" to Andy. The TV was abandoned and left talking to itself in the living room, and Josh, working his fingers like a pretend pair of scissors, teased, "Hey, buddy! Wanna trade my bald head for all that hair?" . . . which sent Andy into squeals of laughter, holding his arms protectively over his head.

Stu busied herself chatting lightly, jumping up for more coffee, laughing a tad too easily. I sat back, suddenly realizing the emotional price Stu had to pay for this reunion. Seeing little Andy in the flesh, so alive and downright huggable, so *three years old*, couldn't be easy for her. For it was digging into Andy's DCFS files that had brought Stu face to face with her own heavy secret: Andy's birth date was the same due date of Stu's own baby, the day he should have been born, the baby she'd aborted . . .

I blew out a breath, pushed back my chair, and began clearing the table. *Don't want to go there right now.* Stu was right behind me with a stack of empty dessert plates.

"Well, you sure worked a miracle," I murmured to Stu, sticking the berry-stained plates into the kitchen sink and turning on the faucet full force. "Had no idea you could arrange a visit so quickly— Becky's only been out of prison a week!"

Stu shrugged, taking the rinsed plates from me and sticking them into the dishwasher. "Have to admit I played the Mother's Day card pretty heavy, both with his new caseworker and the grand-mother. In fact, my whole deck was nothing but Mother's Day schmaltz." She grinned. "I was shameless!"

"No, you were brave."

Stu's hand paused in midreach for another plate, as if my words had turned an Off switch. Then our eyes met.

"It can't be easy," I added softly. "It's a great gift to Becky. She doesn't know what it costs you—but I do."

Stu's eyes squeezed shut, and she gripped the edge of the kitchen counter for a long moment. Then she took a deep breath. "No, it's not easy. It helps that you know and understand. Really, really helps, Jodi—I mean it." Her face softened beneath the fall of long blonde hair that fell over her shoulder. "Actually, it's a gift to me too . . . to see Andy. I like to think of David like this—giggling, being silly, fat cheeks, laughing eyes."

David . . . "Beloved." The name Florida and I had given to Stu's aborted baby that weekend the story had all come out.

"OK. Dishes loaded." Stu shrugged off the moment, dried her hands on a paper towel, and glanced at the kitchen clock. "Yikes. Almost four. We better get going. Andy's new caseworker is coming to meet Becky, then I have to take him back to his grandmother. Might be late to Yada Yada; tell the girls I'm coming, though. Oh." Stu cocked her head. "Has anybody heard from Avis yet? Is she going to be there tonight?"

"Who knows? I left a message on her voice mail, telling her we'll be at Yo-Yo's place just in case." I made a face. "But my guess is Peter wouldn't be too happy if Avis skipped out their first evening home."

"Huh." Stu fished for her keys. "They've had a whole week together. Nonstop romance. She probably *needs* some sister sympathy about now."

IT TORE MY HEART APART to see Becky cling to Andy in the back-yard, not wanting to let him go, not knowing when she'd see him again. Stu gently pried him loose and disappeared into the garage with a wailing Andy in tow. Becky stood stock-still in the yard until the silver Celica disappeared down the alley, then she turned and took the outside back stairs to Stu's apartment two at a time.

She did not look like she wanted company. *Or* sympathy.

As Stu's back door slammed behind Becky, I had my doubts whether this had been a good idea after all. Was the pain of another separation worth the few hours of being together again? Then I saw

Amanda head back into the house with her threadbare Snoopy dog under one arm, and I remembered the birthday we'd given it to her. She'd been three—about the same age as Andy. And I knew that if I was in Becky's jeans and that wailing three-year-old had been Amanda—or Josh, for that matter . . . *yes*. Absolutely. I'd have given my right arm to spend two hours with my child. Even if it hurt like fire to say good-bye.

A half-hour later, I was hollering at my teenagers that if they wanted a ride to youth group to come *now*, when the phone rang. My ears tingled when I heard the voice on the other end. "*Avis!* You're back!"

"Alive and kicking," she said. Was that a giggle I heard in her voice? "Can't say the same for my plants. Should've given you a key and asked you to water them; *bedraggled* would be a kind description. Hopefully they'll resurrect by tomorrow—"

"Avis! I don't want to hear about your plants! How was Cancun? What'd you guys do? Did you have a honeymoon cottage on the beach? No, wait; don't tell me. I'm just heading out the door to Yada Yada, and I'm sure all the sisters would love to—"

"Jodi, slow down. That's why I'm calling. Don't think I'm ready for Yada Yada yet after a week on the beach with my man—"

My man. I wanted to snicker. Watching Avis fall in love at fifty-something was like discovering the fountain of youth wasn't a myth after all. At the same time, a smidgeon of jealousy dampened my joy for her. Things were going to be different now that Avis was remarried and had a husband to think about, and I wasn't sure I liked it.

"—so just wanted to let you know we got back safe and sound, and please give my love to all the sisters. See you tomorrow at school, all right?"

An impatient *honk honk* sent me flying out the back door. Josh had already backed the minivan out of the garage and was leaning on the horn. "I know, I know," I apologized as I waved him out of the driver's seat. Why did teenagers immediately obey only when it was inconvenient?

Twenty minutes later, I pulled up in front of an apartment complex in Lincolnwood, not far from the neighborhood of compact brick bungalows where Ruth Garfield lived. The complex was fairly new and only two stories high—part of Chicago's scattered-site low-income housing. I waved at Adele Skuggs and Chanda George, who pulled up the same time I did, and we walked up the outside stairs to the second landing and pushed the doorbell for apartment 2G. Somewhere inside we heard an obnoxious *blaaat.*

"Now why dey can't put a nice ding-dong on de bell?" Chanda sniffed, her Jamaican accent notched up. "When I get me 'ouse, de doorbell gon play a whole tune!"

The door flew open, and Pete and Jerry, Yo-Yo's half brothers, shuffled out, high school sophomore and seventh-grader respectively. "Yo-Yo says go on in," Pete grunted, thumbing over his shoulder. "Say, Mrs. Baxter, next time you Yabba Dabbas meet here, bring Josh so we can go shoot some pool! C'mon Jerry. The ol' man said don't keep him waitin'." Pete grabbed his younger brother by the shirt, and they clattered down the metal stairs in their big shoes, laces flying. I peeked over the railing to see Ruth climbing from the Garfields' massive Buick. The two boys dove into the backseat, and Ben took off for parts unknown.

Adele arched an eyebrow, said nothing, and marched into the apartment. Chanda and I trailed in her wake. A few minutes later, Delores Enriques, Edesa Reyes, and Florida straggled in the door behind Ruth. I arched an eyebrow at Florida. How'd they get here? The el didn't come this direction; would've meant a couple of bus transfers at least.

As if reading my mind, Florida said, "Humph. We shared a cab. But no way we goin' home by cab! Could've fed my kids two, three days for a fare like that." She smirked. "Stu goin' to be our taxi, though she don't know it yet."

I opened my mouth to offer, then I remembered I'd promised to give Nony and Hoshi a ride home. So I joined the rest of the Yada Yadas who'd just arrived and were getting a tour of the small, two-bedroom apartment. Yo-Yo's pale face was flushed, and she seemed nervous having visitors; at the same time, she kept saying, "Know it ain't much, but I'm glad you guys willin' to hang out at my crib."

She was right about that. Her "crib" wasn't much—two tiny bedrooms, a narrow bathroom, a decent-size main room that ran from the front to the back of the apartment and served as both living room and eating area, and a three-sided shoebox of a kitchen just off the dining area. All the walls wore nondescript beige. The living room furniture was sparse—a frayed brown couch, a couple of discount-store padded chairs, a TV and VCR sitting on a scratched coffee table in the corner. No rugs, no curtains, just miniblinds pulled up to let in the evening light of early spring.

You'd think we hadn't seen each other for months, the way everyone was yakking at once, but it was the first time we'd been together since the special events of Yada Yada's "anniversary weekend." The banter was interrupted a couple of times by that awful door buzzer, admitting Hoshi and a flustered Nony, and finally Stu. Ruth kept grousing about the two tiers of wedding cake still sitting in Uptown Community's refrigerator, while the rest of us helped ourselves to Yo-Yo's leftover pastries from the Bagel Bakery.

The lack of rugs and curtains didn't help the noise—or keep Chanda's voice from carrying over the rest.

"Dey don' tell you about dem big taxes!" she pouted to no one in particular. "Me tink I'm supportin' de whole U.S. government wit' me winnin's!" Most of us were a little tired of hearing about Chanda's "winnin's." She could hardly talk about anything else since she'd won the Illinois lottery a few months ago. *Chanda George*, of all people! Single mom, three kids. So much for trying to tell her that playing the lottery wasn't a wise use of her hard-earned money cleaning houses on the North Shore.

I tried to sidle away, but Chanda dogged my heels. "But me startin' to look for a real 'ouse now. No more two-bit apartment! No more paint peelin' from de ceiling. An' a car—oh Jesus! Hallelujah! One of dem fancy cars wit' power dis and power dat." She shut her eyes happily and waggled a hand in the air.

"You got a driver's license yet?" I asked pointedly. The champagne Lexus she'd driven to a Yada Yada meeting a couple of months ago had gone back to the dealer when they discovered she was using a state ID instead of a driver's license.

Chanda was unfazed. "Dat too. Soon as me get some driving lessons."

Delores rescued me by coming by with two big mugs of coffee and tipping her chin toward an empty corner. "I am so disappointed Avis didn't come tonight, Jodi. I know she hasn't had time to look at the friendship quilt we made. Do you have it at your house?" She handed me one of the mugs.

Only then did I notice the bandage on her right forearm. "Delores!" I hissed. "What happened?"

She must have seen the alarm in my eyes and guessed what I was thinking: her husband sometimes went on drinking binges, especially after losing his trucking job. He'd seemed happier since he'd picked up a regular gig with his mariachi band, but . . . She shook her head. "Not what you think. Dog bite." She kept her voice low.

"Dog bite! How?"

She sighed. "Ricardo got one of those ugly dogs last week. A pit bull."

I gaped at her. "A pit bull? But . . ." I hated to say it. But with their family of five kids trying to live on Delores's salary as a pediatric nurse at the county hospital, taking on the expense of a dog seemed ludicrous.

"You know it. I know it. But Ricardo . . ." She grimaced. "He's got some crazy scheme up his sleeve. I can smell it."

I wanted to ask what kind of scheme, but just then Yo-Yo raised her voice. "Uh, guys. I mean, ladies . . . whatever. Somebody want to start this meeting? I'm just providing the four walls. Avis ain't here, so . . . Nony?"

7

ony had seemed a bit flustered when she first came in—ready to burst with her news about Mark's sabbatical, I suspected—but she waited calmly while we all found a seat, some on the couch, some on Yo-Yo's mismatched table chairs, some on the floor. Then, looking like a queen beneath her crown of braids, she smiled. "Sisters, God is so good to us. Let us give Him some praise! Think back upon this week, and let us pour out our gratitude for His mercies . . . His abundance . . . His lovingkindness."

So our chatter turned to praise, not one at a time, but several at once, for all the good things God had been doing among us. "An' that includes Becky Wallace, our new sister in God's family," Florida tossed in.

"And that Becky got to spend time with her little boy on Mother's Day," Stu added. That news sparked several shouts of "Hallelujah!" and "You're a *good* God! Oh, yes!"

I wanted to praise God, too, but the biggest thing on my mind was that Hakim wouldn't be in my classroom on Monday, and I didn't feel thankful about that. Finally I raised my own voice: "Thank You, God, for Hakim, for giving me the privilege of being his teacher this year, for all the gifts and potential You've created within him. And thank You, God, for going with him wherever he is, even though he's no longer in my classroom." My voice caught, and I felt a hand squeeze mine. Hoshi's long, smooth fingers. I squeezed back.

Nony wrapped up our praise time with one of her favorite Scriptures from the Old Testament: "Father God, *thank* You that the plans You have for us are to prosper us, not to harm us, plans that give us hope and a future!"

"That's right," Florida chimed in. "You sayin' it now."

Nony's voice got emotional as her prayer followed the familiar verses from Jeremiah 29: "Even though we sometimes find ourselves in a strange land, just like the Israelites of old, You never forsake us. You have promised that if we call upon You and seek You with all our heart, that we will find You and You will bring us out of captivity, back to the place from which we were exiled. Yes! Thank You! Thank You!" Nony suddenly laughed aloud and clapped her hands. "*Thank* You!"

Startled, I opened my eyes; others did too. Nony wore a smile so wide and joyful it lit up her whole face, even as tears wet her cheeks. Knowing what was behind her joy, I couldn't help it; I started to laugh.

Ruth looked back and forth between us. "So what is this laughing? A secret you two know? Not so nice to laugh in our face." She sniffed.

"Better tell 'em, Nony." Frankly, I was eager to hear more than she'd given me over the phone.

Nony took the wad of tissues someone passed to her and wiped her eyes. "You all know that Mark and I have quarreled many times about my desire to go home to South Africa. God has put such a burden on my heart for my people, wounded by the many years of apartheid, suffering from the ravages of HIV and AIDS—especially the children."

"Dat we know!" Chanda broke in. "We wanna be hearin' de good part!"

Nony laughed again. "All right. The good part! Two days ago, Mark told me the university has granted him a one-year sabbatical from the history department! He said he applied several weeks ago but didn't want to tell me in case it was denied."

"Sabbatical? What's that?" Yo-Yo's forehead wrinkled into tire treads. "Somethin' like the Sabbath?" Yo-Yo, who was anything but Jewish, nonetheless got half her religious education behind the counter at the Bagel Bakery.

Nony's eyes danced. "I had not thought of that. But I suppose it has the same root meaning—a time of rest, a time to set aside your work. For Mark, it means taking a year off without pay, but he can have his job back when he returns."

"So de mon jus' wan' to loaf aroun'? Not work?" Chanda rolled her eyes. "Me had me fill of dem loafers sittin' on dey behinds, eatin' me food and sayin' dey broke."

I stifled a giggle. That would be DeShawn, otherwise known to the prayer group as "Dia's daddy," who suddenly showed up after Chanda won the lottery. Chanda finally got wise to him and gave him the boot . . . though I wondered how long that would last.

"No, no, nothing like that! Mark's taking a sabbatical for *me*, so that we can go to South Africa for a year—together, as a family!"

Adele, sitting on one of Yo-Yo's hard chairs with her arms folded across her ample bosom, *tsked* through her teeth. "Nony, if Mark is doing this for you, there may yet be hope for the male species." Yo-Yo snickered. "Though my guess is," Adele went on, "none of us wants to think about you being gone from Yada Yada for a whole year."

Adele's comment pulled a plug out of the dike. Suddenly everyone was talking at once: "Oh, Nony! We will miss you so much!" and "Are you really going to go?" mixed with "When will you come back?"

Ruth held up her hand like a traffic cop. "What is she—gone already? Let the lady tell us what the plans are."

Nony flashed a grateful smile. "Mark has to finish this semester, of course. And we will have to find a renter for our house—so many things to do! So we haven't set a date yet—maybe August? Oh! One thing I ask for your prayers. Mark has applied to teach at the new University of KwaZulu-Natal in Durban, a merger of several small universities that opens next January. He is quite excited about it; I am too." Her voice softened, almost shyly. "Because then going to South Africa would not be just for me, but for him too."

It didn't take a math genius to realize that if the Sisulu-Smiths left for Africa this summer, but the school year did not start until January, Mark's one-year sabbatical might be more like one and a half. I suddenly felt bereft. That was a long time—too long to be without Nony in my life. And what about Hoshi? Nony and Mark were practically family to her! Her *only* family . . .

"But we need to move on," Nony said graciously. "There are many other prayer concerns, I know. Hoshi? Why don't you begin?"

In her careful English, Hoshi Takahashi asked us to pray for what she should do this coming summer when classes ended in June. "I only have one more year at NU. Then"—she smiled, a bit sad—"even bigger question of what I should do." She left unsaid the painful reality that she might not be welcome if she went home to Japan.

Ruth waived her turn, saying Ben was behaving himself, if she didn't count him being crotchety, and everything else was fine. Delores didn't mention anything about being bitten by the pit bull—just "Keep praying for Ricardo." Her lip quivered slightly, and I wanted to launch myself across the room and wrap my arms around her. *Oh God, how easily I take Delores's strength and upbeat attitude for granted! But it's been almost a year since Ricardo got laid off. She's really hurting.* I glanced at the bandage peeking out from her sleeve. *And maybe scared.*

Edesa Reyes—the young African-Honduran student who often baby-sat for the Enriques family—gave the older woman a quick hug. "I went on rounds at the hospital with Delores recently, and realized many of those sick children might not be there if they had good nutrition, regular shots, and checkups. I have completed almost two years at Chicago Community College in social work, but . . ." She looked around shyly, her bouncing corkscrew curls held back from her warm, mahogany face with a colorful orange head-band. "I've been thinking I could be more help to the Latino community if I switched to public health. Will you pray God will show me what to do?"

I put Hakim into the prayer hopper next. "And pray for me, because . . . I feel like I failed him. I wanted so badly to make it right after discovering he was, you know, Jamal Wilkins's little brother."

"Jodi." The way Adele said my name felt like she'd just told me to sit up straight. "Don't keep beating yourself up over that boy. You can't fix everything—haven't you learned that yet? Give him over to

God, and concentrate on *your* job: praying for Hakim. You can do that."

I wasn't sure if Adele was chastising me or encouraging me—probably both—but I gave her a weak smile. "I know. You're right."

Nony gently nudged us to keep going so we could hear from everyone, and finally it was time to pray. Nony began simply, "El Shaddai, You are the All-Sufficient One, and Your sufficiency is all we need. You already know each of the needs we have shared here tonight, and we *thank* You—yes, thank You!—that Your plans are to prosper us and not to harm us, as Your Word says. But keep us alert, Father, for the Evil One schemes and plots to shake our trust in You . . ."

IT FELT GOOD TO TURN ALL OUR NEEDS, all our tangled feelings into prayers for one another. Before we left, we helped set Yo-Yo's apartment back in order, called for Ben Garfield to bring the boys back and pick up Ruth, and made sure everyone had rides. Stu didn't even blink when Florida announced that she'd been elected for taxi duty into the city.

As promised, I gave Nony and Hoshi a ride home. We dropped off Hoshi at her dorm, then drove another half-mile past the NU campus, turned onto a lovely tree-shaded side street, and pulled up in front of the Sisulu-Smiths' neat brick home with ivy climbing all around the door and window shutters. Nony hesitated before getting out. "Don't think Mark's home yet. I . . . hope everything's all right."

"Why wouldn't it be?"

She gave a half smile. "I'm sure it is. It's just that . . . for some reason he seemed upset just before we left to pick up Hoshi.

Somebody came to the door—getting signatures for something or other, he said—but after that, he seemed all uptight and snappy. We barely spoke on the way to Yo-Yo's house; I'm sure Hoshi noticed." She shrugged. "Oh well. Maybe he was cross about having to go to that department meeting tonight. It's probably nothing." She opened the door. "Better go rescue the baby-sitter. Marcus and Michael tend to pull a few tricks when Mom and Dad aren't home."

"Can I use your bathroom?" I asked, opening my door. "All that coffee I drank at Yo-Yo's is suddenly yelling, 'Emergency!'"

Nony laughed, and we walked up the brick walk together. As she fumbled with her house key, she suddenly peered into the ivy that clung to the brick masonry. "Look at that. Someone stuck trash in there. I hate that!"

She reached toward the ivy, but I danced urgently on my toes. "Uh, can you hurry with that key? I really gotta go."

"Sorry. Forgot." She unlocked the door, and I pushed it open, dashing toward their half bath, which was just off the front hall.

A few minutes later I came out, but the front door was still standing open and no Nony to be seen. Puzzled, I came back outside and found her sitting on their front stoop, her shoulders shaking with silent tears.

"Nony!" I sat down beside her. "What's wrong?"

She turned to me, her eyes frightened, and handed me a crumpled pamphlet—the litter she'd pulled out of the ivy.

"Oh, Jodi," she whispered. "I didn't know . . . I didn't realize . . . such hate existed here in my adopted country too."

8

I took the pamphlet and stared at the bold-faced print: IF YOU LOVE AMERICA, WAKE UP! And then in slightly smaller type: "Don't stand idly by while the worldwide Jewish conspiracy takes over our government, our universities, our financial institutions . . . while the purity of the White Race is polluted by the mud races . . . while our rights as White People for self-preservation and self-protection are being eroded, one law at a time. The time to fight back is now!"

The pamphlet was several pages long, presumably elaborating on these "points," but I couldn't stomach any more. "Who in the world?" I muttered, turning the pamphlet over. There, at the bottom of the last page, it said, "For further information, contact the Coalition for White Pride and Preservation (CWPP)." The phone number had a Chicago area code.

I snorted. "What garbage! Don't give it another thought, Nony. This is the ranting of a few kooks." But I had to admit it rattled me too. *Mud races?* Talk about inflammatory! And what was with this "worldwide Jewish conspiracy"?

Nony turned her head away from me and stared into the branches of the large, majestic elms lining the street, their out-stretched limbs hidden by a profusion of newly minted green leaves. She was silent for several long moments, the only sounds a faint hum of traffic on Sheridan Road a couple of blocks away and a whisper of wind in the trees. Then she sighed. "It isn't just kooks, Jodi. I've seen it before—intelligent white people, people in government and law enforcement and teaching in universities, sincere white Christians who go to church and are good mothers and fathers—saying the same things. Thinking the same things. Except it was, 'If you love South Africa . . .'"

I squirmed, acutely aware that I fell into the "white people" category. Surely Nony didn't think all white people, or even most white people, would agree with this kind of warped thinking—did she? I felt myself growing defensive. Just because Nony had grown up with apartheid didn't mean—

A Voice in my head—or maybe it was my heart—said, *This isn't about you, Jodi. It's about Nony. Put yourself in her shoes.*

I couldn't. I wanted to, but I had no idea what it meant to grow up under apartheid. In fact, to be honest, I didn't know what it meant to grow up in the Jim Crow South, or even on the South Side of Chicago. I wanted to say, "But that's over now! That's in the past!"

Except . . . the pamphlet in my hand would make me a liar.

I reached out and took her hand. "Nony, I'm so sorry. I can't believe this is anything but the drivel of a few die-hard racists. We have civil rights laws now, and most people appreciate that we are a multicultural society. Don't take it too seriously."

She left her hand in mine but continued to stare somewhere beyond the trees. "Unfortunately, Jodi, white Americans are comfortable with a multicultural society—as long as they are still the majority. But that is changing. Tolerance wears thin when you think your own rights and privileges are at risk."

She gave my hand a squeeze, took the pamphlet, and stood up. "Better let the baby-sitter go before I have to pay for another hour!" She grimaced. "Teenagers! They're getting expensive."

Relieved at changing the subject, I gave a short laugh. "Yeah. Their toys are expensive too—CD players, hundred-dollar gym shoes, picture cell phones. Sheesh!" Not that I'd ever bought my kids a pair of hundred-dollar shoes. The Baxter budget coughed up enough for a decent pair from Sears, and if my teenagers wanted a brand name, they had to waste their own money—though their attitude usually made me feel like Ebenezer Scrooge. "Yikes, I better go. Denny will wonder if I cleaned out the bank account and headed for the border." I gave Nony a hug. "Talk to you later, OK?"

As I climbed into the minivan, Nony waved at me from the front door and then turned to go in . . . the pamphlet still in her hand.

I WANTED TO TELL DENNY about the stupid pamphlet Nony had found, but the kids beat me home from youth group, and Denny was helping Amanda study her Spanish II vocabulary. "Da-ad! You don't pronounce it right—not like Edesa!" Amanda wailed as I passed through the dining room on my way to let Willie Wonka out for his final pee.

"I'm all you've got right now, toots. So come on. Give it to me: *jefe, dueño, caudillo.* All meaning . . . what?"

By the time Denny the dad finished butchering Amanda's Spanish vocabulary, Denny the husband had that "bedroom look" in his eyes, and I knew he wouldn't want me to throw cold water on his ardor with a depressing report about some Chicago-area hate group. So I let it go. *After all,* I told myself, *that's what I told Nony to do, wasn't it?*

"Shh!" I giggled as he locked our bedroom door in Willie Wonka's face, then picked me up and dumped me on the bed. "The kids are still awake!"

Denny rolled his eyes as he shed his jeans and shirt. "Number one reason why we should've sent our kids to boarding school when they turned thirteen."

On the other side of the door, the dog scratched and whined.

"Denny!" I hissed. "Let Wonka in. The kids know what we're doing when we lock the dog out." I was having a hard time keeping my giggles quiet.

"Arrgh!" he muttered, but he did let the dog in before shedding the rest of his clothes and slipping between the sheets beside me.

"A roll in the hay on Mother's Day?" I teased as he pulled me close against his bare chest. I caught a whiff of Polo men's cologne. "You're not trying to make a mother out of me again, are you?"

"Jodi!" He sat up with a jerk and looked at me, alarmed. "That's not funny! You're not late or anything, are you?"

"No, silly." I pulled him back down beside me and shut him up with a lingering kiss on the mouth, enjoying the scratchiness of his chin, the warmth of his breath. But I was surprised at his reaction to my little joke. A baby . . . would it be so bad?

You're forty-three years old, Jodi Baxter! What are you thinking?

Denny was right. We were just a few years shy of being empty nesters, except for our nosy dog—if he lived that long.

Suddenly I felt incredibly sad and wasn't sure why. Empty nesters . . . *empty* . . .

The kids had grown up with Willie Wonka; I couldn't imagine the Baxter household without him—or without Josh and Amanda, for that matter, obnoxious as they could be sometimes. At least I'd always have Denny—wouldn't I? We'd celebrated our twentieth anniversary last fall; things were good . . .

For some reason, I saw Nony in my mind's eye, sitting on her steps, her happiness at Mark's sabbatical punctured by that dreadful pamphlet.

I TRIED TO GET TO SCHOOL EARLY, I really did, hoping to yell, "Surprise!" with the other staff when Avis opened the door to her office. But she must've come in an hour earlier, because there she was when the rest of us arrived, already sitting at her desk beneath the canopy of yellow and green crepe paper draped from the ceiling, opening mail, reading reports. The amazing pile of wedding gifts had been neatly stacked on the floor to give her working room.

Ms. Ivy rolled her eyes at me, and I could read disappointment on her face. Several other teachers clustered in the hall, realizing their principal was already there, unsure what to do with the "celebration" plans.

I think I forgot it was a school day and I was a third-grade teacher and Avis was the school administrator. Because I marched into the office and said, "Oh, no, you don't, Avis Johnson Douglass," grabbed her by the hand, and hauled her out into the main office, pulling her office door shut behind me. "OK, we're going to run this like we planned it—right, Ms. Ivy? Places, everybody!"

I dragged Avis, who by this time was starting to laugh—*Oh, thank You, Jesus!*—out into the hallway and out the double doors of the school. "Avis!" I squealed and gave her a big hug. "It's so good to see you!" Then we turned around, and I marched her back in again. The main office was dark; the door was closed. "Go on," I hissed. Avis rolled her eyes, but she obediently opened the main office door and flipped on the light.

Nothing.

Shaking her head, Avis headed for her inner office, opened the door—

"Surprise!" All the office staff and a healthy contingent of teachers had scrunched themselves into her office and launched into, "For she's a jolly good fellow . . ."

By now, Avis was laughing for real and accepted a round of hugs and congratulations. "Thank you, everybody. It's wonderful. I *was* surprised when I got here this morning, but, you know . . ."

"We know. You're shy." My comment got a few snickers from the staff. As Bethune Elementary's principal, Avis Johnson-now-Douglass was anything but shy. More like Condoleezza Rice, the president's no-nonsense chief of staff.

Avis clapped her hands together twice. "All right. Ten minutes until the bell rings. We all have work to do, right? But tell you what: I'll call Peter and see if he can come by after school, and we'll open these gifts and you can all see what a lucky—no, what a *blessed* woman I am."

"Order some pizzas, and it's a deal!" cracked Tom Davis, one of the few male teachers at Bethune Elementary.

"You got it! Pizzas! Now . . . everybody out of my office!" Avis smiled widely and firmly shut her door.

I GOT HOME A BIT LATER THAN USUAL because of the off-the-cuff pizza-catered wedding shower after school. Peter Douglass charmed all the staff, then he charmed *me* by giving me a ride home along with a box of leftover Gino's pizza, which I planned to warm up and serve my family for supper.

I even gave in and let Denny and the kids fill their plates with pizza and hot garlic bread and take it into the living room to watch the news. Make that Denny, Josh, and me. Amanda opted to munch in the kitchen with the phone to her ear.

The news wasn't pretty. Iraqi insurgents chose to ignore the U.S. declaration that the Iraq war was over and were creating havoc. "In other world news . . ." Videocameras zeroed in on a devastated government building in Chechnya, Russia, while a voice-over intoned: "—at least fifty dead and climbing. The truck bombing today offers grim evidence that the separatist struggle has entered a new phase, with Chechen fighters increasingly resorting to suicide missions . . ."

"The world's going crazy," I muttered, remembering why I didn't like eating supper in front of the TV. In front of the evening news, anyway. Hard on the appetite.

"In local news," the news anchor intoned, "Northwestern University officials are disturbed by—"

I stood up. "Anybody want more pizza? Garlic bread?"

"Hey! Hey!" Josh hushed.

"—a swastika painted in the stairwell of one of the residence halls. This follows on the heels of complaints from patrons attending the Jazz Fest on campus yesterday that members of the Coalition for White Pride and Protection were passing out hate literature after the concert, attacking Jews and other minorities. University officials were quick to—"

My mouth hung open. "Ohmigosh, Denny. Those are the same people who were passing out hate literature in Mark and Nony's neighborhood yesterday."

Denny and Josh both turned to stare at me. "What?"

9

I tried to tell Denny about the pamphlet Nony had found stuck in her ivy, but since I'd only read the first few phrases accusing Jews of a "worldwide conspiracy" and calling minorities "mud races," I couldn't tell him a whole lot. "I'm pretty sure it was written by the same group that was mentioned on the TV—Coalition for White Pride or something."

Denny shook his head. "Extremist jerks. Too bad the press got hold of it. Kooks like these should be ignored, not given media attention. Getting on the evening news only encourages those types."

"That's what I tried to tell Nony—she should just ignore it, not take it seriously."

"Not take it *seriously*?" Josh glared at us, a flush creeping up his face. "You don't think painting a *swastika* in one of NU's dorms is serious? Think about it!"

"Josh" Denny's tone was sharp, "there's always going to be some creep trying to make waves by spraying graffiti. I didn't mean the university shouldn't deal with it; I just meant these extremists thrive on media attention. Blows it up bigger than it is."

"No, you said 'ignore.' Both of you." Josh started for the hallway in a huff.

"Just a minute, Joshua James Baxter." If my bigheaded son wanted an argument, he was going to get one. "Your dad and I don't condone this kind of bigotry! I just don't want Nony to take it too seriously, to let it upset her. Like your dad said, ignoring this garbage may be the best—"

"Yeah," Josh tossed over his shoulder. "That's probably what a lot of Europeans said when swastikas first started appearing on the walls of *their* universities." He disappeared, punctuating the air with the loud slam of his bedroom door.

I gaped at Denny. "What was *that* all about?"

Denny seemed about to go after his firstborn, then he hesitated, rubbing the back of his head as if calming his thoughts. "Let him cool down. We can talk later." He leaned back against the couch cushions and hit the TV volume.

"Sheesh," I muttered, collecting the plates with leftover pizza crusts and heading back to the kitchen. Enough drama. I had lesson plans to do—namely, rustling up household items so my third graders could measure rectangles. Should I let them bring items from home to measure? That might be risking irate parents, like the time my first class at Bethune Elementary brought in such no-nos as a treasured jewelry box and a box of tampons. "A list," I told myself on the way to the kitchen. "I'll send home a list of appropriate items to—"

I nearly tripped over Amanda and Willie Wonka, who were sprawled in the doorway between the dining room and kitchen, the phone still attached to Amanda's ear. "Oh, here's my mom. I'll ask her." She beamed up at me. "Can I go to the sophomore dance at José's school? It's not for a couple of weeks—and I already have a dress! From my *quinceañera*." She flitted her eyelashes, as if that settled the matter.

"*With* José, I presume." I stepped over my daughter's body and began loading the dishwasher. *Hey, didn't I cook supper? Someone else oughta be doing this.* On second thought, no, I didn't cook supper. Better to save dish duty for my family when there were lots of pots and pans.

"Mo-om!"

OK, I was stalling. A dance at José's school? What school was that? What kind of kids would be there? What kind of dancing did they do? Was I ready to let Amanda actually *date*? Were Amanda and José getting too—

"Mom!"

I blew out a breath and whirled on my daughter, hand on one hip. "I *heard* you. I'm thinking. I don't know yet. I'll talk it over with your dad. Go do your homework."

"Oh." She put the phone back to her ear. "Yeah, probably. I'll let you know for sure."

Daughter and dog disappeared in the direction of her bedroom. I turned on the dishwasher, plopped down at the dining room table with my lesson plan book, and started to make a list of appropriate household items to teach measurements . . . but I found my mind drifting. Back to Nony finding that pamphlet. The pain in her eyes. The news report on the TV. Josh's fierce reaction.

I sat thinking for a long time.

Finally, I got up and padded back toward the living room in my sock feet. The TV was off, and Denny had team rosters and scoring sheets spread out on the coffee table. I stood there a moment and then announced, "I know why Josh was upset."

Denny looked up. "What?"

"I know why Josh was upset."

"Oh." He patted the couch cushion beside him. "Tell me."

I sat down, leaning my elbows on the knees of my jeans. "Because hearing about stuff like this on TV is one thing. But when I told you that Nony had found one of those pamphlets, that those people had actually come to her house, Josh realized it wasn't just a news story anymore. It was about Nony and Mark now. Somebody we know. Somebody we care about."

Denny sighed. "Yeah. I've been thinking about that too. Easy for us to say 'ignore it'—we're not Jewish or getting called a 'mud race.' But for Nony and Mark, it probably feels personal."

I looked at Denny. "Not just them. What about Avis and Florida? Or Delores and Edesa?"

"Yeah. Ruth and Ben too."

Oh God. What about Ruth? Has she heard about this Nazi graffiti showing up at Northwestern? Did any of her family die during the Holocaust? She must be somewhere around fifty, born after World War II like the rest of us in Yada Yada. What stories had been passed down to her about fellow Jews and family being rounded up by soldiers with that swastika on their armbands?

I need to pray!

I CALLED NONY THE NEXT EVENING but got the answering machine. Wednesday evening, Denny and I got off our duffs and made it to the midweek Bible study at Uptown. Have to admit I wasn't very keen on making it a regular thing on a school night. But the current series was called "Lord, Teach Us to Pray." Funny. Before Yada Yada came into my life, I probably would've thought, *Yeah, yeah, prayer. Just talk to God; that's prayer. What else do we need to know?* But the more I prayed with Yada Yada, the less I seemed to know about prayer—or maybe, the more I wanted to know. Like a pregnant woman who has a craving for pickles or ice cream or Fannie May chocolates.

To my surprise, Avis and Peter were both there. Peter was attentive but quiet during the discussion time, but Avis had a lot of good input about the different parts of the Lord's Prayer—especially the first part: "Our Father which art in heaven, hallowed be thy name." She said we so quickly skip over that part and get to the "Give us this day our daily bread" list of requests, but there's a *reason* we need to focus our prayer with praise and worship first, to get our priorities straight.

Good stuff.

Stu came, too, and afterward I saw her talking to Pastor Clark. Probably asking him about writing a letter on Becky's behalf to send to the parole board. *Hoo boy.* Becky Wallace at Uptown Community. How many more places in my life was my own personal thief going to show up? *Sheesh. Give You an inch, God, and You take a mile.*

I overheard Denny inviting Peter Douglass to the men's breakfast on Saturday—a gig that happened every third weekend of the month. Not sure he got a commitment. In fact, I got the feeling that Peter wasn't all that excited about attending a mostly white church. Before he and Avis got married, he'd been visiting other churches like Salem Baptist, where Rev. James Meeks, one of our state senators, was pastor. I knew this was something Avis and Peter were going to have to work out now that they were married. But I felt a pang. What if . . .

OK, God, I'm not going to go there. But can I put in a request? I really want Avis and Peter to stay at Uptown Community. We need them! It's too easy for us to be a church of "people like us," but the Bible says the different parts of Your body need each other.

And then there was Amanda, still badgering me about going with José to the sophomore dance at Benito Juarez High School. I finally told her to quit bugging me about it, and that she'd get an answer by the weekend.

So it was Thursday night by the time I got hold of Nony. She'd barely said hello before I plunged right in, apologizing for saying she should "just ignore it" when she'd found the pamphlet. "That was insensitive of me, Nony. Easy for *me* to ignore it, to brush it off as the extremist views of a few ignorant white people. Guess I wanted you to ignore it because I don't want you to think that white people in general, or . . . or me in particular, think like that. I was wrong to brush it under the rug, and I'm sorry."

I finally paused for breath, but there was only silence on the other end . . . and then what sounded like stifled crying. "Nony?" *Oh God. I should have called her right away, not let so much time go by. Now she was really upset.* "Nony? I'm so sorry."

On the other end of the line, I heard Nony blow her nose then come back on. Her voice was shaky. "I know you are, Jodi. Thank you. But just today, Mark came home very angry. Some of those young men from that White Pride group were on campus, passing out fliers inviting students to a 'free speech' rally on—wait a minute. He brought home one of the fliers." She was back in a moment. "On 'White Purity and the Mud Races.' They're not students and don't have access to any of the university meeting rooms, but they want to meet at the Rock—it's kind of like a public square at Northwestern."

"Oh, Nony." I was stunned. "Can they do that? I mean . . ."

Denny looked at me funny as he passed me on his way to the kitchen to get a snack. *What's going on?* he mouthed at me.

I held up a finger, trying to listen to Nony. But he hung around until I finally got off the phone. I told him what Nony had said. "Mark's really angry. He's trying to get the university administration to call a meeting of staff and faculty to deal with this stuff."

Denny leaned against the kitchen counter for several minutes, staring at the floor, his forehead knotted, rubbing the back of his head. Then he held out a hand. "Give me the phone."

He was so abrupt and impolite, I almost refused. *Give it up, Jodi. This isn't the time for niceties.* I handed him the phone.

Now I was the one who hung around eavesdropping. "Hi, Nony. It's Denny. Can I speak to Mark? . . . Mark. Denny Baxter. Jodi just told me what's happening at Northwestern. I know you've probably got your hands full dealing with this on campus, but I'm wondering . . . If you can spare the time, would you be willing to come to our men's breakfast at Uptown Saturday morning and fill us in? You've been there before; the guys know you. I might even be able to pull in some of the guys we had at our Guys' Day Out. The rest of us in the community need to know what's going on and talk about what we can do in our churches. And personally, I'd like to know how I can support you, my brother. At the very least, how I can pray for you." He listened for a moment and then gave a laugh. "Yeah, if we'd listen to our wives now and then, these Yada Yadas, we'd finally get it that we should pray first, *then* knock the blocks off these kooks."

10

*D*enny was all over the phone that night and the next, checking with Pastor Clark about inviting Dr. Smith to speak to the Uptown men on Saturday, then calling some of the guys who didn't attend regularly, like Carl Hickman and Peter Douglass.

"Jodi? Do you have the Garfields' number?" he yelled through the bathroom door as I was trying to have my Friday night soak-the-school-week-away bubble bath. I sat up with a jerk, sending water cascading over the side of the tub and soaking the rug.

"Denny, wait! Why are you calling Ben Garfield?" I yelled back.

There was a momentary pause. "To invite him to come to the breakfast tomorrow." Denny's tone said, *Put two and two together, Jodi. What have I been doing all evening?*

I climbed out of the tub and grabbed a towel. "I mean, why Ben?" I opened the door a crack. Denny stood in the hallway, phone in hand. "Why upset Ben and Ruth by all this anti-Semitism stuff? Maybe they haven't even heard about it."

To his credit, Denny actually seemed to be considering what I said. Then he shook his head. "I don't want to upset them, but it's on the news. Three incidents in one week at Northwestern. This White Pride group is obviously stepping up its activities. Ben and Ruth will have heard about it." He snorted. "Huh. Didn't even know they existed a week ago! Frankly, I'd like to get Ben's perspective."

Arrgh. I was back to hoping the whole thing would just go away. But I told Denny where to find the Garfields' number and locked the door again. I sank back into my bubble bath, studying the scars on my body—the almost invisible short scars at the top and bottom of my left thigh, where a rod had been inserted to repair my broken femur, and the vertical scar on my abdomen to remove my mangled spleen. Scarred but not broken. Most days I felt pretty good, though damp weather and too many hours on my feet sometimes left me with an aching leg. For months, I felt awkward about my scarred body in front of Denny, not wanting him to look at me like damaged goods—not that *he* ever made me feel that way. I hated those scars, hated those reminders of that awful day, reminders of my anger and my sin.

I pushed aside the bubbles and traced the scar on my abdomen. That was before I heard God's still, small Voice in my spirit, telling me that those scars were my reminder to *pray*—for Jamal's mother, Geraldine, and for his brother, Hakim. What a revelation! Even scars can have a redemptive purpose.

So pray, Jodi. Soaking in the tub is as good as anyplace else. So I prayed for Hakim, whose seat in my classroom had been empty all week. And I prayed for his mother while my fingers got wrinkled and pink. Prayed that God would continue the healing that had begun when our fingers had touched that brief moment across my desk at the last parent-teacher conference.

Keep praying, Jodi, said the Voice in my spirit. *Others have scars too—scars invisible to you, but scars nonetheless. Wounds that seem healed but still bleed, cut open once again by a careless remark or the lies of the enemy or even by events in the news.*

I slid under the bubbles to wet my hair, squirted some shampoo in my hand, and lathered up my head—and prayed for Stu and the wounds she carried in her heart for her aborted baby . . . for Nony and the pain of race hatred stirred up in her memory . . . for Ben and Ruth, whose ethnic history included genocide—and almost felt like I was drowning under the heaviness. *Oh God! How can You carry the weight of these wounds? They're too big! Too big . . .*

I stayed in the tub so long, I could've qualified for pickling.

JOSH GOT HIMSELF OUT OF BED and went to the men's breakfast with his dad Saturday morning. Well, not exactly "with." Denny left early for a run along the lakefront, ending up back at Uptown Community. I dropped off Josh at the church by eight o'clock, taking advantage of being out and about to get my grocery shopping done early in the day. I knew Denny was pleased. He'd invited Josh a couple of times before, but Josh had never been interested . . . till now.

"Hi, Nick!" I called out to the Greek owner of the Rogers Park Fruit Market, who was helping to unload boxes of Mexican mangoes from a truck. "Got a price on those yet? They look yummy."

Nick grinned. "For you, one dollar each. Tell the girl I said so." Nick held out a box. I picked out two golden-green mangoes then headed into the market with my list: fresh ginger, romaine lettuce, green onions, a bunch of cilantro, fresh parsley, bananas, two beef shanks for soup, chicken quarters . . .

Next stop: the new Dominick's megastore on Howard Street. For some reason, the immensity of the grocery store still intimidated me. Why couldn't I figure out where to find stuff? I finally made it home with my bags of groceries, hoping Amanda was up so she could help carry stuff in. No such luck. Her door was still closed, with no sign of emergent life oozing from her bedroom.

When I went back out to the garage, Becky Wallace was leaning into the back of the minivan. "Thought you could use some help," she grunted, hauling out two or three bulging plastic bags in each hand. Only then did I realize she must have been in the back yard weeding the flowerbeds or something, and I'd totally zoned out that she was there.

"Uh . . . sure. Thanks!"

With Becky's help, we got all the groceries into our house in one trip. "Thanks again," I said as she dumped her load on the counter and headed back outside. I watched as she pulled on some tattered garden gloves and resumed weeding along the fence—the outer borders of her narrow world. For a nanosecond I felt sorry for her. *Sheesh. It's like grounding a full-grown adult.* On the other hand, I told myself as I started stashing canned goods, it's gotta be better than prison. And actions *did* have consequences.

By the time I put away groceries, stripped beds, and started laundry, it was eleven o'clock and still no sign of Denny and Josh. Or Amanda. Impatient, I entered the inner sanctum of teendom and turned on the light. "Up! You've got chores. I've got more errands, and I want to know you're on track."

"Mo-om!" came the muffled complaint from the bedclothes, but I heard the bathroom door slam a few minutes later.

I left a note on the kitchen counter for Denny, another for

Amanda with a list of her Saturday chores to be done *before* she got on the phone or left the house, and backed the minivan out of the garage again. The weekend weather report was for mixed sunshine and showers, and I hoped the sunshine would hold long enough for me to take MaDear for a walk this morning. But by the time I parked on Clark Street near Adele's Hair and Nails, it was starting to sprinkle.

Rats, I thought as I pulled open the door, setting off the familiar bell. The beauty shop was full of customers. All three chairs were occupied by women in various stages of "relaxing" or "curling." Two more sat under hair dryers, with Adele and Takeisha, the other hairstylist, running back and forth between all of them. Three more customers flipped pages of *O* and *Essence* magazines in the waiting area.

Adele looked up from her customer, a jar of white goo in one hand, a brush in the other. "Jodi Baxter! Don't have room for walk-ins today, but you could use an appointment."

Adele was anything but subtle.

"Yeah, yeah, I know." I made a face. "I'm still not used to the beauty-shop routine. Maybe for Josh's graduation. Came by to see if MaDear wants to play"—that got a smile from Adele—"but it's starting to rain."

The jar of goo and brush paused again in midair. "Well, if you're up for it, I've got something you could do with MaDear here in the shop. Come on." I followed Adele past the hair dryers, past the nail station where the not-much-more-than-a-teenager Corey was doing exquisite designs on the toes of another teenager. I curled my bald fingernails into the palms of my hands and followed Adele into the back room, where her elderly mother sat strapped in a wheelchair, dozing.

Adele picked up a shoebox and handed it to me. "Pictures. I've been meaning to get them into a photo album, but *mm–hm.* Another good intention gone straight to hell." I blinked at her language then remembered the old cliché, *"The road to hell is paved with good intentions."* "Thought MaDear might enjoy looking at some of the pictures, might waken some of her memories."

I took the shoebox. "Well . . . sure. But if she doesn't remember who's who, I won't be able to tell her."

Adele shrugged. "Still, maybe it'll be a start." She shook the old woman, shrunken inside a faded, flowered dress. "MaDear. MaDear! Someone to visit you." Then she was gone.

MaDear blinked, her eyes bleary, as she came awake. The brown leathery face, sprinkled freely with freckles and age spots, crinkled in a smile. "I know you. Sissy's little friend, ain't ya?"

Sissy was Adele's younger sister, a grown woman with a family of her own. But I let it pass. There was no use arguing with MaDear; you were who she thought you were.

I opened the shoebox. There on the top lay a sepia-toned photo of a smooth-skinned young woman with large, dark eyes and a full head of hair curled up on the sides forties-style, the rest gathered into a bun at the nape of her neck. But there was no doubt who it was: MaDear. Sixty years younger. "Oh, MaDear!" I showed her the picture. "You were beautiful!"

MaDear took the picture and studied it for a long minute. Then she stabbed at it with a bony finger. "Sally." She nodded. "Sally Skuggs."

"That's right!" Adele had said her mother's name was Sally, though even the customers called her MaDear. I pulled out another picture. No recognition. I decided to fish through the pictures . . .

there. A man, a woman, and two little girls. The woman was obviously Sally; could that be Adele and her sister, Sissy? Oh! This was too much fun!

We looked through all sorts of pictures—snapshots and portraits, all of African-Americans with varied skin tones, some darker, some lighter. Most of the older pictures were brown tint, gradually shifting to black-and-white prints, then color snapshots, all mixed together. If Adele wanted to do a photo album, she sure had her work cut out for her.

Suddenly MaDear's hand snatched a small picture from the box. A family group, obviously from the rural thirties—father, mother holding a toddler, a barefooted youngster about six or seven, a middle girl about ten or eleven, a teenage boy. MaDear held it close to her face. Then her finger traced the outline of the teenage boy in trousers, shirt, and suspenders. "Larry." That's all she said.

I thought my heart would stop beating. *Larry?* MaDear's brother who'd been lynched by white neighbors because they decided he'd gotten too "uppity." I felt torn between wanting to memorize the face of the brother who'd only been a name until this minute . . . and wanting to flee. What was Adele *thinking*, letting me look at photos with MaDear? Did she want to stir up all that pain again? MaDear's painful memories, hidden beneath her dementia and forgetfulness. And Denny's pain, when MaDear mistook him for one of the men who'd killed her brother two-thirds of a century ago.

I tried to gently take the picture from MaDear, wanting to bury it back in the box, but she held on tight. "Larry," she said again. Then she smiled a sweet, sad smile. "Young man who killed 'im tol' me he was sorry—"

Now I could hardly breathe. *That was Denny! She remembered*

Denny coming to ask forgiveness for what happened to Larry. "Because she needed to hear someone say 'I'm sorry,'" he'd told me.

"—an' I forgave him. Yes, I did." Her head bobbed up and down. "Sure do miss Larry, though." With a shaky hand, she brought the faded photograph to her lips, kissed it, and let it flutter to the floor. I put it in the box and replaced the lid.

"Bye, MaDear," I whispered, softly kissing her leathery cheek. The lump in my throat was so big, I made sure Adele was busy with a customer before I walked out, giving her a wave from the door before it tinkled shut behind me.

11

osh was hunched over the computer in the dining room when I got home. Loud music pumped from behind Amanda's bedroom door, and Willie Wonka looked at me expectantly, hoping for—what? A walk? A treat? A scratch on the noggin?

A scratch took the least energy. I tossed my shoulder bag on the dining room table and gave Wonka a good knuckle-rub on his head. "Where's Dad? Did you guys have any lunch yet? How did the breakfast go? Did Ben Garfield show up?"

"Uh . . ." Josh clicked the mouse a few times, peering closely at the screen with the intensity of an air-traffic controller. "Which question do you want me to answer, Mom?"

I stifled a smart retort. "Your dad."

"He, uh"—the mouse clicked again—"had to coach a baseball game at West Rogers High. One o'clock, I think."

I glanced at the clock in the kitchen. Half past noon. *Ack!* Did Denny tell me he needed the car? But as if reading my mind, Josh added, "Don't worry. One of the other coaches picked him up around noon. He said he'd call if he needed a ride home."

"Oh." Didn't sound like I was in trouble. But I felt frustrated. I wanted to tell Denny about the picture of Larry Skuggs—or was "Skuggs" MaDear's married name?—and that MaDear remembered she had forgiven "the man who killed Larry." For an old woman who barely remembered who Adele was some days, that was huge.

And I wanted to hear about the men's breakfast, though Josh didn't look like he was in a chatty mood. "Whatcha doing?" I peered over his shoulder—and recoiled. "Lord, have mercy. Josh! What is that?"

A red background filled the computer screen; across the top ran a black banner bearing the words KIDS FOR WHITE PRIDE in big white letters. On the rest of the screen, cartoon "white guys" threatened violence against cartoon stereotypes of blacks, Asians, and Jews, like a comic strip. "Watch," Josh said, clicking one of the cartoons. The figures immediately came to life, bashing and kicking and laughing until the victim lay in a heap. The animation stopped, returning the cartoon figures to their starting position, ready to do it all over again at the click of a mouse.

I couldn't believe my eyes. "Joshua James Baxter. Why are you looking at that garbage? It's . . . it's worse than garbage! What if Amanda walked through here?" I made a grab for the mouse. "Turn it off—*now!*"

Josh gave me a look and minimized the Web site. He swung around in the desk chair. "Mom. Calm down. I was listening for Amanda and would've cut it off if she came out of her bedroom—though she's got the phone in there talking to you-know-who, so I don't think it's likely."

I glared at him. "Still. Why are *you* looking at that garbage?"

"Because it's all over the Web, and we don't even know about it! Mark—Dr. Smith—told us these hate groups are targeting some of their Web sites to *kids*, like that stuff I just showed you. All this 'fun,' interactive stuff—jokes and cartoons and games, all putting down Jews and blacks and other minorities. And if people like us don't know about it, if we just ignore it, then these hate groups have free rein to do whatever they want!"

I knew I was in trouble, trying to argue with an eighteen-year-old who was on the debate team at school. I wanted to rip the computer plug right out of the wall and throw the whole thing out the window. The computer screen suddenly seemed like a cunning portal through which evil could creep into our house.

I pulled out one of the dining room chairs to give my hands something to do, and sat. "Josh," I said finally, "you're right. We shouldn't be ignorant that this stuff is out there. But I don't want this filth in our house or on our computer. It makes me feel like we've just opened a door and invited all these . . . these *demons* into our house. And I especially don't want my kid feeding his mind with all this hate propaganda—even for 'educational' purposes."

Josh arched an eyebrow. "*Demons*, Mom?"

Well, maybe I didn't know what I was talking about. My religious background certainly acknowledged the reality of Satan. But we didn't get into all that other stuff, like demon possession or "the devil made me do it." Sin and salvation, heaven and hell. That was about it. I just looked at my son—good-looking in spite of his shaved head, taller than his dad, filled out and muscular since his beanpole days at sixteen. Legally a man. Definitely not a child any longer. Definitely with a mind of his own.

I opened my mouth to say something but was distracted by angry yelling in the apartment upstairs, then a slammed door. Stu and Becky? Josh eyed the ceiling with a knowing smirk. "Was wondering when Ying and Yang would stop being polite up there."

Again I opened my mouth, this time to say it was none of our business, when I heard footsteps stamping down the outside back stairs, then rapping on our back door. Sounded like someone was about to make it our business. Had to be Stu. No way would Becky Wallace complain to us if she and Stu had a falling out. I stood up, irritated. I didn't need this right now. But as I started for the kitchen, I said, "Josh, please get rid of that Web site—at least until we can talk more, OK?"

Stu didn't wait for me to open the door; she just charged in. "Ye gads, Jodi. I can't stand it!" She paced my kitchen in a pair of faded jeans and a sweatshirt. "Becky doesn't know the meaning of 'put it back where it belongs.' She takes something out of the pantry and leaves it sitting on the counter for two days. Leaves her wet towel in a heap on the bathroom floor. Dirty dishes in the living room." She grabbed fistfuls of hair on both sides of her head. "Arrgh! I'm going nuts!" Then she looked at me accusingly. "It's not funny!"

I didn't even try to stifle the grin on my face. "I know. It's just that it sounds like my house—except *your* teenager is twenty-five." I shook my head. "Might be too late for reform."

"No, no, it can't be!" Stu sank down on our kitchen stool, head in her hands. "OK, help me think this out. Obviously, living on the street, no real family, Becky's never been taught how to keep a house tidy. Maybe I could, you know, offer to teach her some house-keeping tips, how to organize her stuff—"

"Uh-uh."

"What?"

"Uh-uh. Too paternalistic—or maternalistic, as the case may be. You aren't her mother. She's your housemate. You guys gotta sit down and agree on a contract, an agreement of expectations—what you're going to do, what she's going to do. Who does what chores. Stuff like that."

Stu just blinked at me. Frankly, I felt like blinking at myself. Where did *that* come from? And why hadn't I ever tried that out on my kids? Might work a whole lot better than the nagging I'd perfected.

"A contract." Stu's voice held wonder in it—probably because the idea came from me instead of herself. But she said, "Thanks, Jodi. That just might work." She got off the stool and looked over my shoulder. "Oh, hi, Amanda. How's José?"

Amanda had come into the kitchen to replace the phone. "He's *fine*—or would be if my parents ever got around to deciding if I can go to the sophomore dance at his school." She glared at me.

Stu grinned. "My cue to exit. Thanks, Jodi." She pecked me on the cheek and closed the back door behind her.

Ah, yes. The sophomore dance. "OK, I promise. When Dad gets home, we'll talk about it and give you our answer. OK?"

"Don't know what the big deal is," she grumbled, pouring cereal into a bowl and getting out the milk. "You'll probably let Josh go to the prom—you let Josh do everything—and you won't even know his date, not like you know José."

Prom? I watched Amanda disappear, cereal bowl in hand, dripping milk on the wood floor like Hansel and Gretel dropping crumbs. Willie Wonka followed in her wake, licking up the spilled milk. Of course I knew Josh's graduation was coming up, but so far he hadn't said anything about the prom.

Josh was still at the computer, but to his credit, he was typing something instead of surfing the Net. "Josh, honey?" I pulled up a chair beside him. "Do you want to go to your senior prom? Haven't heard you say anything about it—and it's OK if you don't. I was just wondering." And wanting to peel the lid off any last-minute surprises. Who would he take, for goodness' sake? Josh was a very sociable kid, but he didn't seem that interested in dating so far. Just made friends, like those two girls with green hair and pierced body parts from Jesus People . . .

My thoughts stuck like flies to flypaper. *Ohmigosh. Would he ask one of* those *girls?*

Josh finished typing the sentence he was working on, hit Save, and turned to look at me. "I don't know. I've been thinking about it, but . . ."

"Prom is pretty special." I smiled. "Who would you invite?" OK, I was shamelessly fishing. But he seemed willing to talk about it.

He shrugged. "That's just it. The girls at school . . . they're OK, I guess. But most of them are so immature, always blabbing about some stupid reality TV show and who said what to whom and which guys are hot. I hate that stuff. And there are *no* girls my age at Uptown—not like our church back in Downers Grove. Wish I knew a girl I could *talk* to about important stuff, like Edesa."

I blinked. "Like . . . Edesa? Edesa Reyes?"

Josh rubbed the back of his head sheepishly—the same gesture Denny did so often without thinking. "Well, yeah, like Edesa. Actually, not *like* Edesa . . ." A faint flush crept up his neck. "I'd like to . . . What do you think, Mom? Do you think Edesa would go to the prom with me?" His words began to rush. "I know she's twenty-one and I'm only eighteen, but when you think about it, if it was the other way around, nobody would think a thing about a three-year age difference. And—"

I was so shocked, my mind didn't even compute the rest of what he said. *Josh* had a crush on Edesa Reyes? But Edesa was a . . . a *woman*, and Josh was just a . . . a kid. Wasn't he? And Edesa came to Yada Yada, the world of grownups, and Josh was only in high school. For a few more weeks anyway.

But if he goes to college next year, he'll be a freshman and she'll be a junior . . . not unheard of for college romances.

"Uh . . ." I licked my lips. "It might be better to ask someone your own age, Josh." That was lame, and I knew it. Shouldn't I be ecstatic he was attracted to someone like Edesa, a young woman with a strong faith, who wasn't running around with every Tom, Dick, and Harry—a woman with strong family ties, even if they were in Honduras?

Josh rolled his eyes. "You're not listening, Mom. I don't *like* any girls my age. Most of them are such *airheads*." He swung back to the computer. "Forget it. Maybe I won't go."

I got up and put my arms around him from the back, resting my cheek on the back of his bald head. "I'm sorry, Josh. You just took me by surprise. Honestly, I don't know what to think. Guess the only person who could give you a real answer is . . . Edesa."

12

I snagged Denny when he got home from coaching his baseball game. "You up for an impromptu date? Like *now*? Let's go have coffee at the Heartland."

"Sure." Denny looked at me funny. "Something up?" I rolled my eyes in the direction of the kids' bedrooms. "OK," he said, peeling off his muddy sweats. "Give me ten minutes to shower."

Half an hour later, we were sitting inside the Heartland Café, a few short blocks from our two-flat on Lunt Avenue. Several die-hards in shorts and T-shirts sat outside at the sidewalk tables in spite of the on-again, off-again drizzle that afternoon, but I figured, why risk getting dumped on?

Denny slouched in his chair, one arm over the back, and sipped his black coffee. "What's up?"

"Well, I'd like to hear about the men's breakfast, but . . ." I briskly shook cinnamon on the pile of whipped cream crowning my mocha decaf. "I mean, nothing bad actually happened. Just . . . I don't know what to think!"

Denny looked at me under lowered eyebrows. "Jodi . . ." He had that *I-have-no-idea-what-you're-talking-about* tone of voice.

"OK." I matched him stare for stare. "Josh has a crush on Edesa."

Denny blinked.

Ha. That got him.

"And you know this because . . . ?"

"Because he wants to ask her to the senior prom at Lane Tech! *Edesa*, of all people! She's practically an older woman!"

Denny rubbed the back of his head, the edges of his mouth twitching.

"He did that too!" I accused.

"Did what?"

"Rubbed his head! Like when you're mulling over something."

Denny threw back his head and laughed. "Yeah, well. This one's a corker, all right." He leaned forward, resting his forearms on the wooden table. "Gotta say, our kids have interesting taste in the opposite sex. Got an eye for quality, at least."

"Denny! Edesa's a wonderful person, and if Josh was twenty, I'd say hallelujah." I scrunched up my forehead. "At least, I think I would. Aside from the whopping cultural differences, that is. I mean, she's only been in the U.S. a couple of years, and even in Honduras she was a minority. 'African-Honduran,' or whatever they call black people there. What if he asks her, and she's embarrassed to be asked to a high school prom? How awkward is that going to be?"

My husband grinned. "What if she accepts? How awkward is *that* going to be?"

I opened my mouth and closed it like a goldfish in a bowl. Finally I gasped, "You don't think . . . no! She wouldn't accept. He's just a baby!"

Now Denny did laugh. "Look again, Jodi. He's a good-looking young man, even with that shaved head of his. Takes after me, of course." Another smirk.

"Denny. This isn't funny. And not only that, Amanda is nagging me to death about going to the sophomore dance with José at Juarez High School. The last weekend of this month, I think."

"What's the question? Neither one of them can drive, so one of us will have to take them, hang around as chaperones—though I can think of a lot of things I'd rather do on a weekend night. Take *you* out, for instance." He waggled his eyebrows.

"Denny! Be serious."

"I am serious. Didn't we agree once upon a time that—"

"Yeah, yeah, I know. Say yes unless we have a good reason to say no." I made a face. "Whatever happened to 'No, because I said so'? Worked for *my* parents." But by this time I was starting to giggle.

Denny reached for my hand. "Look, Jodi. Amanda made a vow at her *quinceañera* to save sex for marriage. She's even wearing a purity ring. That's huge for a kid her age. We have to show her we trust her."

I stared into the bottom of my mug. Empty. Why didn't they give free refills on their specialty coffees? I sighed. "I know. I do trust Amanda—at least, I trust her intentions. But some of these high school dances are downright raunchy. Have you looked at MTV lately?" I grabbed my throat and made a gagging noise. "I just don't want to expose my daughter to all that."

"I know." Denny nodded. "We'll talk to them—to both Amanda and José. Share our concerns but say yes. That's how they grow up." Denny leaned back in his chair. "OK. You want to hear about the men's breakfast?"

"Sure." Would rather hear about it with another cup of mocha decaf in my hands, but I couldn't justify another three dollars—*or* all those calories. "Who all came? Did Ben come? Was it good?"

"Real good. Not exactly 'cozy good,' but an important conversation, I think—especially if Mark and Nony's church ends up sharing space with Uptown for a couple of months. And yeah, Ben came. Have to admit I was surprised, but was glad he did. Also Carl Hickman and Peter Douglass, besides the regular Uptown guys. A good turnout."

According to Denny, Mark brought the men up to date about what had been happening on Northwestern's campus in the past week: members of White Pride handing out hate literature, a crude swastika appearing overnight in a stairwell, and young men in suits inviting students to a "free speech" rally on "White Pride and the Mud Races."

Denny shook his head. "I tell you, Jodi. It's one thing to hear this hate group diatribe on the news or talk about it between you and me. But to sit in a room with several black guys and a Jewish guy and imagine how *they* feel hearing that stuff . . . that was tough."

I winced. I couldn't imagine sitting with Avis or Florida or Adele or any of my Yada Yada sisters while somebody—even Mark—repeated such insults.

"Mark admitted it's tempting to dismiss these incidents as the antics of a few extremists. Even *he* said, 'I'm not that eager to rock *my* boat.'" Denny grinned. I grinned too. Big of Mark to admit he had it pretty good—small-town Georgia boy gets PhD and tenure at a Big Ten university, beautiful wife and kids, upper-middle-class home, nice pension.

But I also squirmed. That had been my gut feeling exactly: *Don't want to be bothered . . . Ignore it . . . Maybe it'll just go away . . .*

"But," Denny went on, "Mark said the events of the past week should be a wake-up call for all of us. Even though there've been great strides in civil rights and massive shifts in attitudes, it doesn't take much to bring latent racism bubbling to the surface. Some little spark ignites an explosion, and you end up with something like the beating of Rodney King and the L.A. riots. Peter Douglass didn't say a whole lot, but he quoted that famous line: 'The only thing necessary for evil to triumph is for good men to do nothing'—something like that."

"What about Ben? Did he have any response to all this?"

"Yeah. In fact, Mark asked Ben how it felt, as a Jew, to hear that anti-Semitism is not dead in Chicago. It was . . ." Denny blew out a sharp breath. "I've only read about this stuff in history books, Jodi. It's really different hearing someone you know talk about his own grandparents who ended up in Hitler's gas ovens"—he swallowed— "while a lot of good Christian folks ignored what was happening, or didn't want to believe it, until it was too late. Ben kinda stuck it to us when he asked: 'Will we let it happen again?'"

The supper crowd was coming in, so we finally gave up our table and walked home in the damp coolness of the May evening. Denny took my hand, though I knew his mind was somewhere else. After a full block in silence, I finally prompted, "Any discussion?"

"Well, yeah. Some of the questions and comments got kind of hot. Carl Hickman unloaded at one point—a lot of resentment about 'bigoted cops' and 'a system that keeps you down.' A few of the white guys argued that it's not all one-sided. But mostly we listened." He snorted. "Huh. Josh probably asked more questions than anybody. But it was good. All good."

The two-flat we rented loomed into view. "What now?" I asked.

He shrugged. "Not sure. Pastor Clark closed out the discussion with those verses about the different parts of the body needing each other, and when one part suffers, the whole body suffers. Paul's letter to the Corinthians, I think. Mark seemed moved by that, said it was a good reminder for him not to go off like the Lone Ranger, even though he was very angry and felt a need to respond somehow. So then we prayed—prayed for Mark, prayed for Ben, prayed that we'd all listen to God's voice speaking to our hearts. Even prayed for the people mixed up in this White Pride group that's kicking up so much dust. It was . . ." Denny's voice got a little husky. "We all took hands while we prayed. Peter Douglass was on one side of me, and Ben on the other. And I thought, *The gates of hell can't prevail if we can just hold on like this—together.*"

THE GATES OF HELL CAN'T PREVAIL *if we can just hold on like this—together.*

I would've liked to think about Denny's comment some more, but as we walked through the front door, Amanda accosted us about our answer to José's sophomore dance—and then Saturday night at the Baxter household kicked in. Willie Wonka was everywhere under our feet, whining for his walk; Amanda tore apart her bedroom—the one she supposedly cleaned that morning—hunting for her shoes so she could go baby-sit; Josh wanted to borrow the car after supper. Denny snapped a leash on Wonka, mumbling something about the video store and getting a movie, while I tried to conjure up something edible for supper.

Tacos. That would do it. I was grating the cheddar cheese when the phone rang.

"Jodi." Ruth's voice swept along without waiting for me to respond. "They should carve Denny's likeness on Mount Rushmore, they should." I grinned. I could see his dimples, twenty yards long, chiseled out of stone. "Ben came home charged up like a football player on steroids. Never before has he been asked his opinion about anti-Semitism outside the Jewish community. And they listened. A roomful of *goyim* listened. Mark and Denny made him feel like a man, Jodi." Ruth's voice got wobbly. "Like a man."

I wished Denny were home to hear this. I started to respond, but Ruth got her voice back. "So. To dinner he is taking me. And dancing. Suddenly he is Romeo. Bye. Gotta go."

Couldn't help chuckling as I tackled the cheese grater again. *Romeo? More like Danny DeVito.* But dinner and dancing—that sounded like fun. Why didn't Denny and I ever do that? But I knew what Denny would say, "Me? Dance? Not if you value your feet."

The phone rang again. This time it was Florida. "Jodi! Where ya been? Third time I've tried to get you."

Guiltily, I glanced at the answering machine. The message light was blinking. "Sorry, Flo. What's up?" I cradled the phone between my shoulder and ear and dumped a packet of taco seasoning on the hamburger sizzling on the stove.

"Nothin'. Jus' that Carl came home from that men's breakfast thang an' says he wants ta move. Up on the north side. Be closer to work. Get Chris outta the Edgewater neighborhood an' away from the gangbangers he been hangin' with. Says we need more room for the kids. Huh. 'Course I been sayin' the same thang for months; suddenly it's his idea." She snorted into my ear. "Men."

"But that's good, Flo."

"I know. I'll take it. Anyway, that's why I'm callin'. If you see anything up there with three bedrooms that don't break the bank, let me know. Not one o' them condos. We ain't buyin' . . . yet."

I managed to get the tacos on the table and something into my kids' stomachs before they both took off—Amanda out the front door when her baby-sitting ride showed up, and Josh out the back door offering vague promises to be home by one o'clock—before the phone rang again. I eyed the caller ID: *Mark Smith.*

But it was Nony. "Hello, Jodi. Am I interrupting your dinner?"

"No, no. Just finished." Well, Denny was making his fourth taco and tossing bits of hamburger into Wonka's eager mouth, but that didn't count. "Denny really appreciated Mark coming to talk to the guys at Uptown this morning. Sounded significant."

"Yes." Her voice was low, almost hesitant. "Mark feels positive about it."

I walked the phone farther into the kitchen. "You don't sound too sure."

"No, no . . . I am sure it was a good thing. It's just that . . . Mark came home determined to not let this so-called free speech rally go unchallenged."

"What do you mean? Can he keep those thugs off the campus?"

"No." I had to strain to hear her voice. "He wants to meet them head-on, debate them right there at the Rock."

Goose bumps crawled up my arms. Did I miss something? Hadn't Denny said Mark didn't want to do some Lone Ranger thing? Nony's voice was so low, I almost missed what she said next.

"Jodi. I am frightened."

13

I rolled over in the bed and peered at the glowing numbers on my digital alarm. 1:10 . . . and I still hadn't heard Josh come in. He hadn't called either. *Arrgh.* Why didn't somebody tell me that teenagers ruined your sleep every bit as much as a colicky infant? Denny, on the other hand, was out cold, oblivious to the fact that our son hadn't come in. Probably because he thought a curfew was a bit unnecessary for an eighteen-year-old, even though we were pretty generous with exceptions if Josh called and asked for extra time. But that was beside the point. We'd agreed to the curfew on weekends, then we planned to remove it as a graduation present.

That was when we thought Josh was going off to college. What if he stayed home next year—with no curfew! I'd *never* get any sleep!

I punched my pillow and curled up on my side, facing away from Denny, feeling resentful. One of us had to know when the kids came in—otherwise they could stay out until all hours if they had a mind to. Or something could happen, like an accident, and we might not know until morning.

Calm down, Jodi. He's only a few minutes late. Well, true. And if I was honest with myself, that wasn't the only reason I was still awake. After supper, I'd put together a seven-layer salad for the potluck at church tomorrow, then Denny and I relaxed with a video and a big bowl of popcorn. But even after Amanda got home from baby-sitting and we'd gone to bed, I kept thinking about Nony's phone call.

"Jodi. I am frightened."

That wasn't like Nony. Was she frightened for Mark's safety? I had rushed to reassure her. *"What could happen? It's just going to be a 'free speech' rally—we had tons of those at college in the seventies. I'm sure the campus police will make their presence known; they won't let anything happen. Maybe a few jeers and catcalls—but Mark's got thick skin."* I hoped. *"Besides,"* I'd rushed on, *"Mark's smart. He'll demolish their dumb arguments in two minutes, the NU students will clap and cheer, and it'll all be over."*

Nony had not responded right away. I'd tried to think of some comforting Scripture—the kind of thing she'd do if I was scared about something—but the only thing I could think of was "Be anxious for nothing," and I needed my Bible to quote it correctly. I'd started for the living room to look for it, phone still to my ear, when she had spoken up again.

"I know. But . . . it's suddenly consuming all his time and attention. He threw out the syllabus for his history classes, says he's going to use this opportunity to focus on ethnic hatred in the world today—not just Islamic jihad or ethnic cleansing in eastern Europe, but hate groups right here in the Midwest."

I'd tried to keep it light. *"I should send Josh to Mark's classes. He's all hot to research these hate groups and turn it into his senior debate topic."* But I had to admit I was confused. *"Seriously, Nony, I know it's not a fun topic, but it does seem like Mark's taking a proactive approach, taking advantage of a teachable moment for his students. Maybe something good will—"*

"*That's just the problem, Jodi!*" The force of Nony's words startled me. "*Mark is supposed to be just . . . just finishing up his classes and disengaging his responsibilities at Northwestern—not getting involved in a huge campus issue. I know it's important . . . but why Mark? Why now? We're going to South Africa when school is out. He promised me!*"

Only then had I realized why Nony was frightened. She was afraid Mark would get so involved in fighting this hate group stuff that he wouldn't have time to make his sabbatical happen. Renting the house. Pursuing the position at the university in Durban. Making plane reservations.

She was afraid her dream was about to come crashing down.

But the crashing I'd heard just then sounded more like someone sideswiping a metal garbage can out in the alley. I strained my ears . . . and heard the garage door opening. I eyed the red digits on the bedside clock. 1:30.

I DEPOSITED MY SEVEN-LAYER SALAD on the pass-through counter to Uptown's kitchen the next morning and found a seat. I was getting smart. Made it the night before; nothing to cook on Sunday morning; nothing to *forget* to cook either, like that fiasco with the raw chicken-and-rice casserole the first Sunday Stu had visited Uptown. Who said you can't teach an old dog new tricks?

I put my coat and Bible on the chair beside me, saving a seat for Denny. Fact was, I was proud of myself. When Josh had knocked on our bedroom door last night to signal he was home, I just called, "OK." I figured we could deal with why he was late in the morning.

Denny, of course, snored on, unperturbed. Now if it'd been Amanda who was out—ha! Different story.

"Hi, Jodi. Can we sit here?" Stu broke into my thoughts.

I glanced up. "We" were Stu and Becky. "Sure!" I turned my knees so they could scoot into the empty chairs in the middle of the row. "Hey, Becky. Neat you could come." I didn't state the obvious. Her parole agent must've gotten Pastor Clark's letter.

Becky just nodded, her eyes darting here and there, taking it all in—Josh at the soundboard at the back, Amanda sitting with some of the teens. Her face perked up when she caught sight of Avis talking with Pastor Clark off to the side. "That the lady what got married a couple of weeks ago, right?"

"Well, thank ya, Jesus!" Florida's voice sailed over my shoulder. "Look who's here! Becky Wallace." She appeared at the end of the row, beaming a smile. "Now I know God's got this day in His hands." She jerked her head slightly toward the back of the room.

I twisted around. Carl Hickman was shaking hands with Denny. My eyes widened. "How . . . ?"

She shrugged. "He just got up and came. Didn't explain himself. And *I* ain't gonna question God." With a little wave, she found a row with several empty seats, pulling Carla onto her lap. In a few moments, Carl shoveled twelve-year-old Cedric into the row and sat down with his family.

No Chris, though.

I glanced around the room. No Peter Douglass either. That was strange. You'd think now that he and Avis were married—

"Good morning, church!" Avis stood at the front, her Bible opened. Denny slipped into the chair beside me.

"Mornin', Sister Avis!" Carla piped up in a loud voice. Chuckles rippled over the rows, still filling with latecomers.

"Carla Hickman's got the right idea!" Avis smiled. "Out of the mouth of babes . . . Let's try that again. Good morning, church!"

"Good morning!" everyone chorused. I grinned. Avis was going to make us a talk-back-to-the-preacher church if it killed her.

"If you listened to the news last night or looked at the headlines this morning," she went on, "you might wonder why God puts up with such hate and violence. Does God care? Where *is* God?"

Nods and murmurs all over the room.

"We need to remember that the prince of this world is still working overtime, trying to defeat God's purpose and plans. We shouldn't be surprised. Jesus told us to expect wars and rumors of wars, trials, and persecution. I'm not just talking about yesterday's suicide bombing in Morocco or the years of hostility between Palestine and Israel. I'm talking about the opposition we face in our own lives, too, right here in Chicago. In our neighborhoods. In our families. Within ourselves. But we know something the devil doesn't know! What is it, church?"

Florida leaped to her feet. "The devil's already defeated! Thank ya, *J*esus!"

"That's right!" Avis turned to her open Bible. "The book of Revelation says, 'The great dragon was hurled down—that ancient serpent called the devil, or Satan, who leads the whole world astray. He was hurled to the earth, and his angels with him. . . . They overcame him by the blood of the Lamb and by the word of their testimony.'" Avis looked up. "Did you get that? 'The blood of the Lamb'—that's the price Jesus paid, His own life. 'And by the word of their testimony'—that's us. That's because the battle isn't over yet. There's a war going on in the spirit world—"

105

Becky seemed mesmerized. "That Avis can preach," she murmured.

It was true. This was Avis's first Sunday back after her honeymoon, and she was on fire. We hadn't even had the opening song yet.

"—but God has given us the weapons to block Satan's offenses. And one of those weapons is praise! The devil can't operate in an atmosphere of praise to God. So let's fill this room with praise! Let's fill our hearts with praise! Let's not give the devil any room to work!"

Rick Reilly, the praise team leader, hit the first chord on his guitar, and the rest of the musicians plunged into a new gospel song by Kurt Carr we'd been learning: "We lift our hands in the sanc-tu-ary! We lift our hands to give You the glo-ry . . ."

It was impossible to sit and sing such a song. The Uptown congregation of about a hundred and fifty folks joined Florida on our feet, raising our hands, some clapping. Becky was grinning, not singing the words, but clapping right along. "Hallelujah in the Sanctuary" was followed by "I'm taking back what the devil stole from me . . . I'm takin' it back, takin' it back . . ."

As we filled the room with praise, Nony and Mark crowded into my mind. I hadn't had any time to talk with Avis, to catch her up on what had happened since she and Peter left town. But the Scripture . . . the songs . . . what Avis was saying about the weapons of spiritual warfare—all seemed on target for what they were facing.

Or maybe it was for me, to help me remember how to pray in times like these . . .

"CHURCH ALWAYS LIKE THIS?" Becky sat down across from me at the long table, her paper plate full of pasta and chicken and salads from the array of dishes crowded on the pass-through counter. "I mean, lots of get-down singin' an' clapping?" She shoveled in a big bite of macaroni and cheese. "Avis, she was up there practically dancin' outta her shoes."

I grinned. "Well, that's Avis. She just gets . . . full, she says. Full of God's Spirit."

Becky shrugged. "Well, I like it. Wasn't so sure about comin' to church—ain't never been much. But Pastor Clark tol' me a new Christian gotta learn how to grow." She chewed and swallowed. "Guess I shoulda figgered church was part of the deal when I did that baptism thing. But I wasn't thinkin' much that day. Just knew I wanted to be, you know, washed clean. Start over. Get God's help."

I could hardly stifle my amazement. Becky was being downright talkative. "That's right. We all need God's help—oh, hi, Avis! Yeah, sit." I patted the chair beside me. "No, I'm not saving it for Denny. He's . . . who knows where."

Avis sank into the metal folding chair. "Someday," she murmured, "God's going to figure we've suffered enough with these awful chairs and send padded ones from heaven."

"Amen to that!" Stu sat down next to Becky, delivering coffee. "Maybe we should start a chair fund. I'd be willing to head up . . . What?" She looked at us, puzzled, as Avis and I burst out laughing.

"Nothing! Nothing, Stu." Avis was still chuckling. "We do love you, just as you are. Here." She dug in her purse, pulled out a five-dollar bill, and tossed it on the table. "The beginning of the chair fund."

I dug in my own purse. "Me too." Only three ones, but they'd have to do. "Get a basket, Stu; pass it around. Who knows?"

Stu snatched the money and stood up. "OK, I will. You'll see."

Becky looked bewildered. "What's she talkin' 'bout?" Obviously padded chairs weren't high on her agenda. She glanced around. "Where's your new husband?"

Avis shook her head. "Sick. We went out to eat last night. A couple of hours later he had the runs. Probably the fish."

I felt relieved. At least he wasn't off at some other church. "Poor guy," I murmured dutifully. I poked Avis. Stu had reappeared from the kitchen with a basket labeled Chair Fund in big black letters on a scrap of paper and was passing it around to the tables. "See what you started?"

Avis buttered a roll and started in on my seven-layer salad. "Well, Jesus took the little boy's five loaves and two fish and fed five thousand. What's a couple hundred chairs?"

Again Becky frowned. "What fish? Is that in the Bible some-where?"

Avis and I passed a look. Then Avis said, "Becky, do you have a Bible?" Becky shook her head. "Would you like one?"

She shrugged. "Well, yeah. If it's not too hard to read. I'd kinda like to read that bit about the armor Pastor Clark preached about today—you know, to protect you from the devil. 'Cause . . ." She shifted in her chair and her eyes went down. "'Cause I know the devil's still after me."

Avis reached across the table and touched Becky's hand. "We'll see that you get one."

Stu returned with the basket and set it down in front of us triumphantly. "There!" The basket indeed had a lot of bills—mostly ones, a few fives. "Gotta start somewhere." She picked up her plastic fork. "Josh OK, Jodi? I heard him hit the trash can when he came in last night."

"You heard him?" I groaned. "I thought I was the only one who lost sleep waiting for my kid to get home." I eyed Avis sympathetically. "You have three girls, Avis. Did you and Conrad get *any* sleep when they were teenagers?"

The moment I said it, I wanted to bite my tongue. How thoughtless to mention Avis's first husband a mere two weeks after she'd remarried.

Avis just shrugged. "Didn't lose any sleep. We used an alarm clock."

"What do you mean?"

"Conrad's idea. We set an alarm clock for their curfew—a loud one. We put it outside our bedroom door and went to sleep. If they got in by curfew, they shut off the alarm, and we slept blissfully until morning. But if that alarm went off and woke us up . . . those girls were in trouble."

An alarm clock! How simple. How brilliant.

I was so delighted with Avis's solution to the curfew/sleep dilemma that it was only later, when we drove into the garage and I saw the dented trash can, that I wondered if Stu had been insinuating something else when she asked if Josh was "OK."

Did she think he'd been drinking?

14

ad Josh been drinking? The thought so unnerved me that I forgot to put a filter in the plastic basket before I scooped in the coffee, and I brewed up a whole pot of gritty mud—what my dad used to call "field coffee" from his stint in the army. I started a new pot and went looking for Denny, but he'd changed into a T-shirt and sweatshorts and was heading out the door for a run by the lake.

Not a good time to say we needed to talk.

Willie Wonka stood in the kitchen doorway, looking up at me, eyebrows wrinkled, tail wagging, as if to say, *You can talk to me—if you take me for a walk.* Not a bad idea. The afternoon sun had pushed the temperature into the midsixties. What was I doing in the house anyway? I poured some half-brewed coffee into a travel mug, got Wonka's leash, and headed for Touhy Park—about as far as I thought Wonka's legs would hold out.

The big, old elms along Lunt Avenue were almost in full dress, and the offspring of last year's daffodils, tulips, and crocuses sprouted in strange places. Should have sent my spirit leaping. But I felt like kicking myself instead. If I'd been my typical nosy self last night, I would've gotten out of bed when Josh came home, and then I'd *know* if he'd been drinking or not. But what could I do now? Wait until next time? Be at the back door when he comes in? Ask him outright?

"Were you drinking last night?"

"Sure, Mom. Had a few beers with my buds, hit the trash can when I came home."

Yeah, right.

We finally ambled to the park at old-dog speed, and I flopped on a bench while Wonka diligently sniffed each tree, checking out which neighborhood dogs had last come this way. "Wish your ears worked as good as your sniffer," I grumbled at the dog's rear end. Used to be we could count on Wonka barking his head off if *anyone* came in the door, day or night. Now it was a toss-up who could sleep through the most racket: Willie Wonka or Denny. *Arrgh.* Just a few hours ago, I thought I'd finally found a solution to my weekend sleep deprivation. And to think we were actually going to lift Josh's curfew when he graduated. Ha! No way was I going to—

Jodi Baxter, just listen to yourself. I sat up straight. The Voice in my spirit cut straight through my grumbling. *You're fussing and fuming—about what? You don't even know if there's a problem. You haven't asked Me for wisdom. You're leaning on yourself, when you could lean on Me.*

I shook my head and started to laugh. Old habits die hard. "OK, God," I said aloud. A boy shooting baskets nearby stopped and looked at me funny. Laughing even harder, I made a grab for Willie Wonka's leash and started on the slow walk home. "You're right,

God! I don't even know if there's a problem. I don't want to accuse Josh—but if there is a problem, I don't want to ignore it either. So I need some wisdom. Your wisdom."

Just ask him, Jodi. Don't accuse. Just ask.

Well, yeah. Why not? Josh didn't always tell us everything—like that protest march he went to a few months ago. But if asked outright, he was usually honest.

Was this the wisdom I just asked God for? Maybe that's what Jesus meant when He said, "Be wise as serpents, harmless as doves." Be alert, be aware, be watchful, be prayerful; but don't get all messed up without knowing the facts, and trust God with the outcome.

Wonka finally did his business a block from our house, so I did the pooper-scoop, good-citizen thing and then cut through the alley to dump it in the closest trash can. Hauling the dog and his arthritic behind up onto our back porch, I almost missed Becky Wallace sitting on the stair landing going up to Stu's apartment, smoking a cigarette.

"Hey." She nodded at me and took another drag on the cigarette. "Been on a walk?"

I nodded. A note of envy tinged her simple question.

She sighed and ground out the cigarette stub with her shoe. "I'd do it for ya if I could—walk the dog, I mean."

"Thanks." What do you say to someone who can't even leave the yard? I tipped my chin toward the flowerbeds. "The flowers look great. I've finally discovered the secret of successful gardening: let Becky do it." I grinned.

She nodded but didn't return the smile. "Yeah. Helps pass the time. I'm goin' bonkers, know what I mean?"

I didn't really. But I said, "Yeah. I'm sorry about that. But one of these days you'll get that thing off"—my eyes slid to the EM strapped to her ankle—"and you can start a new life. For real."

She fished another cigarette out of her pocket and a book of paper matches, the kind you pick up at restaurants. Where in the world was she getting this stuff? A moment later, a long trail of smoke drifted down the stairs. "If I make it till then," she muttered.

Huh. What did she mean by that? But by this time, the coffee I'd drunk before walking the dog was prompting an urgent call of nature, so I just said, "See ya" and made a beeline for the bathroom.

While still in the bathroom, I heard Amanda hollering. "Josh! Are you done with the phone yet?" When I came out she collared me. "Mo-om! Tell Josh to get off the phone. He's had it half an hour *at least.*"

A strange complaint coming from a teenager whose own phone-call record hung around the two-hour mark. I opened my mouth to put things in perspective, when Josh's bedroom door swung open, and he thrust the cordless at his sister. "Here, shrimp. Now quit bugging me." And he disappeared once more, slamming the door behind him.

I waited until Amanda flounced into her own lair with the phone, then I knocked on Josh's door. No answer. I knocked again.

"What!"

I turned the knob and peeked in. Josh was sitting on his bed, earphones encasing the dome of his smooth head like quotation marks, pouring some kind of music into his ears. "You OK?"

He shrugged, moving his hands to the beat in his head, as if playing imaginary drumsticks.

I stood in front of him, working up courage to ask about last night. "Josh?"

He sighed and took off the earphones. "Look. I just called Edesa about prom and she said no. It's fine. I'm fine. But I don't feel like talking right now, OK?" He plopped the earphones back on his head.

Oh. Even Jodi Open-Mouth-Stick-in-Foot Baxter knew this wasn't a good time to talk about dented trash cans. I backed out of the room.

MONDAY . . . TUESDAY . . . WEDNESDAY came and went before I realized something spectacular: the week was blessedly dull. Boring even. At least on the home front. I spent the week teaching story summaries and reviewing measurements—inches and centimeters; ounces and kilograms; gallons and liters. Some of my third graders even got it. The weather cooperated with my field trip to the branch library to replace lost library cards. I'd sent home a note asking each parent to send one dollar to cover the fee, but of course a third of my class showed up empty-handed Thursday morning. I didn't care. Best ten bucks I'd spent in a long time.

The top news stories that week covered an earthquake in Algeria and the president's announcement that he was lifting sanctions from Iraq. Definitely big news . . . over there. I almost felt wrapped in a cocoon, the rumblings in the world distant and far away. Nothing in the news about Northwestern; nothing about the so-called Coalition for White Pride, which seemed to have faded into the background like a pimple in a sea of freckles. Maybe this whole hate group thing was just a lot of hot air and would blow over after all.

Even the phone calls and e-mails from Yada Yada that week had mostly to do with where we were going to meet this weekend. Avis's? (Since we'd skipped her last time.) Or Adele's, next on the list? Ruth was adamant. "Newlyweds we should leave alone." So that was that. Adele said fine.

By Thursday afternoon, I was pleasantly tired, looking forward to the long Memorial Day weekend, thinking we should do something special as a family. After all, how many family holidays would we have together once Josh graduated from high school? It was easier when they were younger. "Special" could be a trip to the zoo. The occasional circus tickets. Or, once in a blue moon, maybe an eye-popping evening at Medieval Times to eat dinner with our fingers and watch armored knights on thundering horses knock each other off their steeds with long, buffered lances. But what would be "special" to a fifteen- and an eighteen-year-old—*with* parents?

I was chewing over the possibilities as I unlocked the front door, dumped my tote bag, and brought in the mail. Besides the usual glut of junk and utility bills, there was a letter from Uptown Community and a package sitting on the front porch addressed to Josh Baxter. Plain brown paper, packing tape. No return address. Postmark said "Chicago." Heavy, like books.

Huh. Wonder what that is?

I put the package on the dining room table, let Willie Wonka out the back door, and opened the letter from Uptown. *Ah.* The request from New Morning Christian Church to rent space from Uptown until they found their own facilities. Well, good. Looked like that was moving ahead. I was glad for Nony and Mark.

While I waited for Wonka to finish his doggy business, I put a pound of ground beef into the microwave to thaw. Spaghetti tonight. It just felt like a spaghetti kind of day. The temperature had dropped to the low fifties, a briskness to the air, tempered by a bright sun, a deep blue sky, and the cawing of crows.

Ack. The crows were back. Oh well.

Half an hour later, Amanda waltzed in, let Willie Wonka lick her face, grabbed the phone and a bag of potato chips, and waltzed right back outside again. So much for my fantasy that my daughter would kiss *me* and say, "Anything I can do to help you, Mom?"

I had dinner ready to whisk to the table by the time Denny and Josh got home. "Awesome," Josh said. "I'm starving. Hurry up and pray, Dad."

Hot pasta, Jodi's secret spaghetti sauce, hot garlic bread with dill, and tossed salad with croutons made it around the table in record time as my family filled their plates. "Oh, Josh." I twirled spaghetti noodles around my fork. "You got a package." I tipped my chin toward the computer desk, where I'd had to move it. "Over there."

Josh glanced at it then turned back to his food. "OK."

My fork stopped in midair. "Aren't you going to open it?"

"Sure. After dinner. I'm hungry."

I glanced at Denny, but he was helping himself to more garlic bread.

"Maybe it's a graduation present," I suggested.

Josh shook his head. "Don't think so." And he filled his plate again.

The package sat on the computer table until dinner was over and we'd all cleared the table. Denny and Amanda loaded the dishwasher while I put away the leftovers. When I peeked into the dining room, the package was gone.

No package. No Josh.

What was going on?

OK, enough politeness. I marched to Josh's bedroom door and knocked. He came to the door and opened it a few inches. "Yeah?"

"Josh, what's in the package?"

"Some books I ordered."

"Oh." I blinked. "Why all the secrecy? Feels like you don't want us to see them."

"Don't want Amanda to see them. Like you said."

"What are you talking about? I never said—"

He opened the door wider, pulled me in, and shut it again. "Look for yourself, Mom. You won't like it . . . but if you insist."

Several paperback books of various sizes rested on his bed, the brown wrapping paper tossed aside. Stark white covers with bold black-and-red titles. I walked over and read the words. *The Pro-White Creed . . . The Final Solution: A History of the Coalition for White Pride and Preservation . . . Why White Will Win . . .*

My whole body went numb. I stared at the books. The titles mocked me with horrified fascination, like traffic slowing down to gawk at a mangled car wreck. A sick feeling settled in the pit of my stomach. *Where did Josh—? Why?*

It didn't matter. I whirled on my son. "Get those books out of this house this instant, Joshua Baxter," I hissed. *"Now!"*

15

I started to snatch up one of the books and then recoiled. "You do it. Get rid of them!" My voice came out a harsh whisper, though inside my head I was yelling.

"Hey, Mom, hold on a minute. Dad said I could—"

"He *what?*" Now heat flooded my face.

"Mom." Josh said it patiently. "Slow down a minute and listen to me, OK?"

I folded my arms, pulled them tight against my body, and pressed my lips into a thin line. I'd listen, but I wasn't going to like it.

"OK." Josh sat down in his desk chair. I stayed on my feet. "Already told you I want to do something about hate groups for my senior debate team project. But if I'm going to debate it, I need to know what I'm talking about! I've gotta do research, and Dad said I could—"

"Why didn't you just go the library? Or read the stuff online? At least you can turn it off. But this!" I grabbed the brown paper wrapping—and stopped, staring at the address. *Josh Baxter . . . Lunt*

Avenue . . . "Ohmigosh, Josh. You ordered these books directly from this group! Now they have your name and address! They'll put you on a mailing list and send you all sorts of . . . of evil literature." The heat drained from my face, and I could hardly push the words out. "They know where you *live*."

My debate team superstar looked at me for a moment, speechless. Then he squirmed. "Didn't think about that. I went over to the Reillys' last Saturday to use their computer, 'cause, you know, you didn't want me calling up that stuff when Amanda was around, and—"

"Amanda was baby-sitting Saturday night." I tapped my foot.

"Yeah, I know. But, face it, Mom, *you're* the one who's all upset. So I asked Mr. Reilly if I could do my research over there—*after* the twins were in bed, natch. Dad said it was OK if the Reillys didn't mind."

Rick Reilly and his wife not only were raising ten-year-old twins and provided the backbone of Uptown's praise team, but they somehow had energy left over to ride herd on Uptown's youth. I unfolded my arms. "You were there all evening? Like, until you came home?"

Josh nodded.

"So you weren't drinking Saturday night?"

"What? Mom! What made you think—"

"I heard you come in." I made a face. "Heard you hit the trash can."

Josh rolled his eyes. "I *know* I hit the trash can. Wind or something had tipped it over. Couldn't see it in the dark. Really, Mom! Why didn't you just ask me?"

I nodded sheepishly. "I know. So I'm asking now. *Have* you—"

Josh threw his hands up in front of his face. "Uh-uh. No fair digging, Mom."

I hesitated. "OK. But you do know it's illegal under twenty-one, and—"

"Yes, Mom, I *know*. And I'm not going to drink and drive. Never, Mom. That's a promise."

The promise hung in the air for a moment. "Good," I said. "I'm glad." I still didn't budge. "About the books . . ." I didn't know what to say next. I did *not* want them in the house. What if one of my Yada Yada sisters saw one of those lying around? Did we really have to immerse our minds in muck in order to fight it? And they'd been mailed to this address. *Our* address.

Oh God, help me here. I don't know what to do!

I wanted an Elijah-style answer, God's voice like a thunder crack. Maybe a bolt of lightning, too, consuming those books—and nothing else, of course—like Elijah's wet sacrifice on the altar. But . . . nothing. I turned on my heel and left the room.

I JUMPED ALL OVER DENNY for saying, "*Sure, Josh, go ahead, order those white supremacist books, put 'em on my credit card, send 'em to the house, tell 'em where we live.*" Well, whatever he said, same thing. We ended up sleeping two feet apart in the bed, backs turned like a Hatfield married to a McCoy.

The next morning I was so upset I didn't even take time for prayer on the fly, much less reading my Bible. Denny drove both kids to Lane Tech before heading for Rogers Park High; I dumped the breakfast dishes in the sink and left early for school, hoping to catch Avis in her office before the bell rang. Not that I wanted to tell her the titles of those books—*ack!* That would feel like slapping her in the face! But I did need some prayer, some way to focus so I could get through the day.

The day was gorgeous—if I'd bothered to pay attention. The TV weather guy was predicting a beautiful Memorial Day weekend. Might even make it to seventy degrees. But all I could think about as I navigated the uneven sidewalks to Bethune Elementary was my conversation with Josh last evening. Sure, I was relieved he'd been at his youth leader's house last Saturday and not out drinking with a bunch of buddies. He even made a promise never to drink and drive. So. Did that mean I could breathe a sigh of relief? Relax?

Probably not. There was always the problem of *other* drunk drivers, other teens who drank irresponsibly . . .

Don't go there, Jodi. At some point you have to trust God!

Right. But then why did Stu assume the worst and get me all worked up?

Bethune Elementary loomed up ahead. The playground was still empty. Good. I was early. Good thing my feet were on automatic, because my mind was definitely not paying attention to where I was going. I kept seeing those paperback books spread out on Josh's bed. And every time my mind alighted on the books, a flicker of fear licked at my spirit, like a tiny campfire flame feeding on kindling, searching for a good, solid log of fuel to make a roaring fire.

Why? What was I afraid of? Was the group violent? I didn't know that for sure. There were tons of violent video games out there—some just as nauseating as what Josh had found on that White Pride Web site. We just avoided them. Didn't buy them for our kids; didn't let our kids play them. And we ordered other stuff on the Web and didn't worry about people having our address . . .

I pulled open the door of Bethune Elementary and headed straight to the office. Ms. Ivy and the other secretaries weren't in yet. But the light was on in Avis's office, and her door was open a crack. I marched in.

"Jodi!" Avis looked up, slightly surprised.

"Can I talk to you for a minute?" I blurted. "I need some prayer." I didn't wait for confirmation, just flopped into the chair on my side of the desk and rambled on for five minutes. She had to back me up a few times—she didn't know about Nony finding the pamphlet stuck in her ivy—but I finally got it out, about Josh actually ordering books from this hate group that were now sitting in my house. I stopped short of mentioning the titles.

Avis was silent for several moments after I stopped. Then she stood up and came around to the front of her desk, leaning back against it. "I agree with you," she said finally. "I don't think it was wise of Josh to order those books directly from that White Pride group, using your address. Maybe nothing will come of it. But I do understand your concern." She reached out and took both of my hands. "It's also true that fear is one of Satan's greatest weapons. The spirit of fear can be contagious, Jodi. It feeds on itself, until we feel paralyzed and powerless—or we go overboard protecting ourselves from whatever we're afraid of."

Well, she hit the nail on the head there. I gripped her hands.

"Lord, again and again You told Your disciples, 'Do not be afraid.' And Your Word tells us that fear is not of God . . ."

It took a moment for me to realize that Avis had started to pray. I did not close my eyes—just stared at our two hands, fingers entwined, brown and beige, manicured nails and nails badly in need of an emery board, her new wedding ring set and my old one, as she continued praying against fear. Finally, she squeezed my hands and returned to her seat behind the desk.

"Do you have a Bible here at school?" she asked. I nodded. "Read Psalm Fifty-Six." She glanced at the clock on the wall and smiled. "You have ten minutes before the bell."

I MANAGED TO READ THE PSALM before my third graders, giddy with spring fever and a long holiday weekend ahead, pushed and shoved their way into the classroom. But I knew right away why Avis had suggested I read it. King David, who seemed to attract enemies and slander like flypaper attracts flies, kept repeating himself: "When I am afraid, I put my trust in You. . . . I trust in God, so why should I be afraid?"

By the time I got home from school that Friday, that refrain was going around and around in my head like a mantra.

The message light was flashing on the answering machine. "Jodi? It's Avis. After we talked this morning, I had one more thought. This stuff is spiritual warfare. So do battle, sister. Pray over those books. Ask God to send His angels of protection on your family and on your house. Rebuke Satan and all his lies contained in those books. Then fill your house with praise. Satan can't do his dirty work in an atmosphere of praise to God."

Whoa. That sounded like heavy-duty stuff. I was supposed to do this by myself? I listened to her message again. *Hm.* Maybe Denny would pray with me when the kids weren't around.

I checked the kitchen calendar. Denny had a game after school today, followed by a sports awards banquet. *Rats.* He probably wouldn't be home until nine or so. With the sophomore dance still a week away, Amanda had invited José to come up and "hang out" Friday evening—though when José actually arrived, they talked Josh into going with them to see a movie at the local discount theater.

Which left me alone with Willie Wonka. And those books.

I was sorely tempted to gather them all up and take them to the trash can—maybe even dump them in somebody else's trash can. "Sorely tempted," I told Wonka as I loaded the dishwasher. But footsteps moving back and forth overhead gave me an idea. Stu. Maybe she'd come down and pray over those books with me. She wasn't exactly a prayer warrior like Avis or Nony or Florida, but hey, the Bible said, "Where two or three are gathered in My name . . ."

I gave a last swipe to the kitchen counters, headed up the back stairs in the soft twilight, and rapped loudly on the window in Stu's back door. I could hear the TV and voices inside. I rapped again. "Stu!" I yelled.

But it was Becky who came to the door. "Oh, hey, Jodi." She just stood in the doorway.

Somebody yelled from the living room, "Beck! Where's the f— remote?" A male voice.

I found my own voice. "Is Stu here?"

Becky shook her head. "Nah. She pulled a hard case today— runaway foster kid or somethin'."

"Oh." My mind was racing. Did Stu know Becky had company while she was gone? Had she anticipated this? And who was it? Should I ask? Was it any of my business? "Sorry to bother you," I said. "Didn't know you had company."

"Yeah." She jerked a thumb over her shoulder. "Old friend of mine dropped by."

I definitely wasn't being invited in to meet Mr. Old Friend. "Oh.

125

Well, if Stu comes home soon, tell her to give me a ring, OK?"

"Sure. No problem." The door closed once more. The bolt moved in the lock, and the kitchen went dark.

"*Old* friend?" I muttered to myself as I scurried back down the outside stairs and in our back door. I made sure it was locked. "As in, from her *old* life?" A life that had involved drugs, alcohol, and armed robbery—a fact I knew all too well.

I flipped on all the lights in the house—even the lights in the kids' bedrooms—and put on the loudest praise music I could find. If Satan couldn't do his dirty work in an atmosphere of praise, well, Willie Wonka and I were going to raise the roof!

16

J was on my third run-through of an Israel Houghton CD—after cranking up the volume so I could hear it while enjoying a long soak in the tub—when the music suddenly went dead. In the silence I heard, "Jodi?" Denny's voice. Loud. "Where are you?"

"Tub!" I shouted back. "Be out in a sec." I toweled off, pulled on a big T-shirt and a pair of sweatpants, and came out to find Denny rummaging in the refrigerator. "How was the awards banquet? Didn't they feed you?"

"Sure. Hours ago." He gave up on the refrigerator and threw a packet of microwave popcorn into the microwave. He lifted an eyebrow at me. "What's with the earsplitting music? Could hear it a block away."

"Driving out demons." I said it lightly.

"And husbands," he muttered under his breath.

"Sorry." I got out a bowl for the popcorn and then touched his arm. "Actually, I *am* sorry for jumping all over you last night. Forgive me?"

He looked at me sideways. "Only if you jump all over me tonight."

"Denny!" I swatted his shoulder. "I'm making a serious apology here! And I need to talk to you about something."

The microwave beeped. Denny pulled out the puffed-up bag, opened it gingerly, and dumped the hot popcorn into the bowl. "Apology accepted. Want some of this? Where are the kids?"

I trailed Denny to the living room and flopped beside him on the couch. "Movie. They took the el, but Josh went with them, so they should be OK. Amanda and José, I mean. But I wanted to talk to you before they got back . . ."

Dipping into the popcorn bowl, I told Denny about my talk with Avis, what she'd said about spiritual warfare, and about the message she'd left on the answering machine. "You weren't here to pray about those books, so I went upstairs to see if Stu was home. She wasn't, but Becky had a friend over. An *old* friend. Male. Made me nervous. I mean, what sort of people did she hang out with before she went to prison? So, OK, she's been clean for eight or nine months now, and she got baptized spur of the moment, John the Baptist–style. But I don't know how long her new life will last if all her old buddies suddenly show up."

Denny crunched popcorn and nodded thoughtfully. "Don't think Stu is home yet—at least her car wasn't in the garage when I came in. Should I go upstairs and meet this 'old friend'? You know, let him know another guy is in the house?" He snorted. "If you didn't drive him out already with that deafening music."

"Ha. Maybe I did." But I shook my head. "No, don't go up. Maybe this sounds weird, but I *would* like to pray, you know, like Avis suggested. Pray against any evil that could come into this house through those books, pray for protection on this house, protection for our family. Protection for Stu and Becky too."

He sat silently for a moment, as if wrapping his mind around the idea. Then he nodded. "Sure. Why not? Guess it's up to us to pray, and up to God to sort it out."

THE KIDS GOT HOME ABOUT ELEVEN—José had already headed home on the el—but by then Denny and I had walked hand in hand around our house, praying in each room, praying for protection from the Evil One. We lingered in Josh's room, praying especially that God would protect his mind and his heart as he grappled with the ugly things written in those books. We ended by praying for Nony and Mark Sisulu-Smith and their children, for the students on Northwestern's campus, that the upcoming "free speech" rally would be peaceful, and that the hateful ideas of this White Pride group would fizzle out.

Both kids home. House saturated with prayer. I slept like a baby.

Guess Stu didn't, though. The next morning, she stormed into our kitchen about eight o'clock and started venting. "I am *so* mad, Jodi! Do you know what happened last night?" She plopped down on our kitchen stool, no makeup, wisps of hair falling from a hasty twist. "I got home late, maybe ten-thirty, after a *killer* day. Had to follow up on a runaway foster kid—turns out he had a good reason to run away. Ended up having to call the police and file a complaint against the foster mother's boyfriend, who'd been . . . never mind." She rubbed her temples. "Anyway, got home, *dying* for a hot bath, some hot milk and honey, and some peace and quiet so I could curl up with a good book—and there was Becky with some . . . some strange guy in my house, a man I didn't even know. Laughing, watching a dumb car-chase video he'd brought, eating my food. Dirty dishes everywhere. Worse, they drank all the milk. Every drop!"

She left the stool and started pacing from one end of the kitchen to the other, but I knew she wasn't done, so I poured another cup of coffee and waited. She stopped abruptly and wagged a finger in my direction. "But you know what makes me *really* angry? I don't know if I have any right to be angry! I mean, Becky *lives* here—I invited her myself, didn't I? And she's stuck in this house, day after day, can't go out as long as she's wearing that electronic monitor. So of *course* she wants to have friends come over." Rolling her eyes, she plopped down on the stool again. "I just . . . I don't know, Jodi."

I sure didn't know either. Seemed like we were stuck with Becky—or she was stuck with us. But did any of us know what we were getting ourselves into? An "old friend" comes over to watch TV one day—but what next? I didn't want to mention my own fears. A parade of "old friends"? Druggies? Street people? A lover?

Oh God. Help.

"We've got to get Becky some new friends," I blurted. "And get her that Bible we promised her."

I WAS SO GLAD YADA YADA WAS GOING TO MEET this weekend that I made chocolate-chip cookies from scratch to take to Adele's. Had to slap a few greedy hands or the cookies would've disappeared by the time Sunday evening rolled around. I almost called the sisters to ask if we could meet at my house and do some of that "praying for protection over the house" as a group. But it wouldn't have worked. Uptown's youth group had been cancelled because of the holiday weekend, so Josh was holed up in his room reading up on White Pride, and Amanda and her dad were cranking out some serious homemade ice cream in the backyard.

"Maybe we should invite Becky down to help crank the ice cream, give her something to do while you women 'yada yada,'" Denny said. There was no humor in his eyes. "Did you Yadas think about meeting *here* so Becky could attend?"

"Yeah," I said defensively. "But you forget we don't have a family room or a basement rec room anymore. You and the kids would end up stuck in your bedrooms all evening. Or out in the yard with Willie Wonka." It wasn't the first time I'd let Denny know I missed our spacious house out in Downers Grove.

His comment stuck in my brain as I bundled up Avis and Peter's friendship quilt in a garbage bag to keep it clean, grabbed my plastic container of chocolate-chip cookies, and made a beeline for the garage before Becky showed up to crank ice cream. It *was* awkward, taking off for Yada Yada and leaving Becky behind—though what could we do about it? Just because *she* was on parole didn't mean the rest of us had to be on house arrest.

I fumbled for the minivan keys as a figure showed up in the door to the yard. I looked up, expecting to see Stu.

"Mom!" Josh's six feet filled the doorway. "You're going to Yada Yada, right? Can you give this note to Edesa? Uh"—he looked at my loaded arms—"where should I put it?"

I just stared at him, mouth open. A note for Edesa? Grinning, he stuck the envelope in my mouth and said, "Bite easy!" Then he squeezed out the door just as Stu showed up. "Hi, Stu. Bye, Stu."

Stu looked after my son, then back to me as I stood between the cars, my arms full, Josh's note in my teeth. "I'd better drive," she smirked, opening the passenger door of her Celica and squeezing me, bulky garbage bag, and container of cookies into the front seat.

"What's that?" Stu spun out of the alley and headed for Clark Street.

That's what I'd like to know. I took Josh's note out of my mouth and stuffed it into a pocket of my jeans as I patted the garbage bag. "Avis's quilt."

"What have you still got that for? Don't you see Avis every day at school?"

"Yeah." I shrugged. "But some of the Yada Yadas asked me to bring it to the next meeting and give it to her there. Most of the sisters didn't get a chance to see the quilt squares the others made." Understatement. The quilt had barely gotten stitched together in time for Avis's wedding, where it showed up draped over the Jewish *huppah*. And the reception, where we were supposed to have time to gawk at the quilt, had fizzled out because of the free-for-all baptism at the lake.

"Oh. Good point." She merged into the two-lane traffic on Clark Street, thick with pedestrians as well as cars enjoying the Memorial Day weekend. Handcarts and sidewalk vendors sold everything from corn dogs to enchiladas and burritos. "Humph," Stu grumbled. "Would've been faster to take the side streets."

Denny's comment still niggled in my head. "Stu, should we invite Becky to come to Yada Yada?"

Stu swung her gaze from the traffic and looked at me. "How could we do that? She can't leave the premises. I mean, sure, she can come when Yada Yada meets at your apartment or mine, but other than that—hey!" Stu slammed on her brakes just in time to miss hitting a pedestrian who insisted on crossing the street in the middle of the block, dodging cars. "Stupid jerk!"

I waited until the car started to move again. "Yeah, I know. We'd have to make adjustments, like meet at our house most of the time. Or"—I glanced at her sideways—"get permission from her parole officer to leave the house every other week. Couldn't we do that?"

Stu was quiet for several moments, threading the car through holiday-happy youths, most of whom were yelling at each other in Spanish. Then she shrugged. "I don't know. Guess we could try. But usually those requests have to come on letterhead from some organization. Last I checked, Yada Yada doesn't have letterhead."

I giggled. "Yeah. Even if we did, not sure what the state of Illinois would think of letterhead that said 'The Yada Yada Prayer Group.'"

Stu laughed. But her smile quickly sobered, almost to glum level. "Gotta be honest with you, Jodi. I'm not all that excited about inviting Becky to Yada Yada. I mean, I *live* with her. She's in my living room, my kitchen, and my bathroom whenever I come home. She's coming to church at Uptown now. I'm not eager to have her in my face *every*where I go." She grimaced. "That sounds really selfish. But there it is."

I looked at Stu; her face was flushed. The calm, cool, and collected Stu I'd known for just over a year had let down her guard with me twice in one weekend. She was being honest with me. I felt . . . honored. My up-and-down relationship with Stu had definitely turned a corner.

But it put me in a bind. How did I respect her feelings—I certainly understood them!—and still deal with the growing certainty in my gut that Becky *needed* to be part of Yada Yada? We didn't like her "old" friends, but how else would she make new ones? And Becky was a new Christian, like Yo-Yo. Brand-spanking new.

Didn't she need the kind of sister support and prayer and Scripture challenges the rest of us needed? That *I* needed, even though I'd been a "good girl Christian" most of my life?

Yada Yada had turned *my* life upside down. Maybe "rightside up" would be more accurate.

How could I keep that for myself and shut Becky out?

17

A loud buzzer released the door in the foyer, and we
climbed the short flight to the first landing, where Adele
stood in her open doorway. I handed her the cookies.
"Sweet," she said. "Go on in. I'm bringing drinks in a minute." Our
hostess shuffled off in a pair of worn slippers.

As usual, all the shades were pulled, and the front room was dim.
MaDear sat in a corner by the front window, wedged into her wheelchair by a foam cushion shaped like a large highchair tray. She didn't
seem to notice us coming into the room, even though Florida, Hoshi,
and Edesa showed up right on our heels, chattering like a high school
reunion. Delores came in, too, though she looked a bit preoccupied.
They must have met up at the el station and walked to Adele's
together.

I spread out Avis's friendship quilt over a couple of chairs and
moved out of the way as the others crowded around to "ooh" and
"ahh." "Adele! Do you mind if I open the shades? So we can see the

quilt better!" That was my excuse, anyway. All those drawn shades on a bright, spring evening made me feel claustrophobic.

I thought I heard Adele grunt from somewhere in the direction of her tiny kitchen, so I squeezed behind a big overstuffed chair and pulled on the bottom of the shade. It rolled up with a loud snap. Adele's window now framed a brick wall not five feet away with a facing window, shade pulled. *Oh. Oh well. Still lets in some light.* I sidled over to the front windows—three in a row—and raised the shades, gently this time. The late afternoon sun had already slid behind the buildings across the street, but the bright daylight seemed to startle MaDear. She looked around, bewildered. "Eh? Mornin' already?" She squinted up at me. "Yo' not Adele. Where Adele at?"

I leaned over and gave MaDear a kiss on her leathery, freckled cheek. "She's coming. No, it's not morning. Just a sunny evening."

Adele brought in a tray with lemonade and the chocolate-chip cookies, eyeing the bald windows dubiously. I noticed she handed MaDear a sippy cup, like the ones I used to give my kids when they were little. I felt a pang. How humiliating to get so old one had to be treated like a toddler again! On the other hand, the sippy cup was brilliant. MaDear could drink on her own with no spills. "Good idea," I said to Adele.

"Don't know about that," she grumbled. "I keep those shades down so people can't look in here. This is a first-floor apartment, you know."

It took me two seconds to realize Adele thought I was talking about putting the window shades up, not the cup. "Oh! I'm sorry, Adele. I can put them down again."

She waved me off. "Leave 'em. We'll pull 'em when we have to turn on the lights."

The door buzzer interrupted, and she shuffled off to let in the next batch of Yada Yadas. Turned out to be Avis and Chanda. "Sorry to be late," Avis said. She was dressed down—well, "down" for Avis—in slim jeans and a short-sleeve sweater top. "We've been circling the block for ten minutes looking for a parking space."

"An' when she find one," Chanda pouted, "we have to walk t'ree blocks!"

"Now see?" Florida crowed, helping Adele pass out glasses of lemonade. "Bunch of us who came by el was the first ones here." She simpered at Chanda. "You sure you wanna get that fancy new car? Bein' poor has its 'vantages. No parking hassles."

Chanda sniffed. "Maybe me get a chauffeur, too, drive me aroun' like a movie star, drop me off at de front door."

But her braggadocio was lost as Avis caught sight of the quilt and actually squealed. "It *is* a quilt! Mine, right? Mine?" Her eyes were wide as she reverently touched the tiny stitches and then gave us a sheepish smile. "I was beginning to think the quilt I'd seen draped over the *huppah* was a mirage." For several minutes we all gathered around, pointing out all the different embroidered designs each one of us had done on the muslin quilt squares. Avis kept shaking her head in delight, tracing the names "Avis and Peter" on the center square. "How did you ever . . ."

"Delores's idea." Edesa dimpled. "She got us started *way* before you got that ring."

Avis's mouth dropped, even as her smile widened. "A bit *rash*, don't you—"

The buzzer rang again, and Yo-Yo bopped into the room—alone. She guzzled a glass of lemonade as if she'd just crawled off the Sahara and then wiped her mouth. "Ruth ain't comin'. Said she don't feel too good. Mr. Ben drove me over anyway. Told me to get one o' you Yada Yadas ta drive me home, though."

"Nony will not be here as well," Hoshi offered. "She and Mark flew to . . . to . . ." Her smooth forehead puckered into a frown. "To visit elderly grandmother."

"Really?" half a dozen voices chorused. Obviously none of the rest of us knew that Nony and Mark had gone out of town. Out of state, to be more exact. Mark's grandmother still lived in Georgia. *Probably a good thing*, I thought. Maybe the Sisulu-Smiths could put all this hate group stuff aside for a while and just enjoy the holiday weekend away.

On the other hand, I'd been counting on Nony to fill us in on when this "free speech" rally was supposed to take place. I didn't really want to be the one to bring it up. But I knew we needed to be praying—big-time!

"—so guess we can get started," Avis was saying. "Let's worship the Lord for a few moments, focus our minds on Jesus, put aside other distractions—even those to-die-for chocolate-chip cookies."

Yo-Yo had just bit into one of my cookies, and she stopped, mouth full, and looked around guiltily. Edesa Reyes giggled and gave her a hug. "Go ahead, *pequeña hermana*," she stage-whispered. "I won't tell."

"What'd she call me?" Yo-Yo swallowed the bite of cookie.

Edesa just flashed a teasing grin, and I was suddenly mesmerized by the Honduran student's effervescent beauty, spilling over like champagne bubbles when the cork is removed. Her wide smile and dancing eyes beckoned like a playful elf, but I couldn't help noticing her skin, glowing like dark polished oak, surrounded by bouncing corkscrew curls and jangling earrings. No wonder Josh had a crush on Edesa.

I suddenly remembered the note. Should I give it to her now? Murmured prayers were already traveling around the group. "We love You, Lord" . . . "Thank You for the privilege of talking to You with my sisters" . . . "You are an *awesome* God! Jehovah-Jireh, my Provider! Thank ya!" . . .

I kept my head bowed, but for some reason I felt awash, like I'd just been cut loose from the dock and was being swept out to sea. My son, my firstborn, stood on the cusp of manhood, about to graduate from high school, but he continued to resist our expectations about attending college next year, and the "girl" he pined for was a woman. Someone I considered *my* friend, even if she was twenty years younger.

Even more unsettling, I'd left him sitting at home plowing through those awful books—books I didn't even want to mention by name, not here. What would my Yada Yada sisters think of Josh—or our family—if they knew what he was doing? Even if it was for a good cause—or was it? Was a senior debate topic worth dabbling in the rhetoric of hate?

Oh God, I groaned silently. *I feel so helpless.*

Just then, I heard Delores speak into the prayers. "*Gracias, Padre*, for letting us come to You when we don't know what else to do. When we don't understand what's happening to our families. When the world seems to be sweeping them away from us." Her voice trembled a moment, then strengthened. "*Gracias, gracias*, that You hold onto us when it seems we can't hold on any longer."

Good grief. Had the woman read my thoughts? "Ditto, God," I murmured. But I heard pain in Delores's voice. What was going on with the Enriques family? José hadn't mentioned anything amiss when he showed up Friday night. I peeked through my eyelashes at

Delores's arm. No bandage. The dog bite must have healed. But what was going on?

Florida started singing a song I hadn't heard before, but it was easy to pick up.

> *Hold to His hand . . . God's unchanging hand . . .*
> *Hold to His hand . . . God's unchanging hand . . .*
> *Build your hopes on things eternal*
> *Hold to God's unchanging hand.*

Florida filled in the verses—at least three—and by the time she sang, "If your earthly friends for-sa-ake you, still more closely to Him cling," we all jumped in on the vamp: "Hold to His hand! God's unchanging hand!"

As the last notes and claps died away, we all jumped as MaDear suddenly screeched from her corner: "Help me, Jesus! Help me!" And she started to wail.

"It's all right," Adele murmured, rising heavily and heading toward her mother. "Old songs like that bring up a lot of old stuff. She'll be all right."

We all sat in silence for several moments as Adele ministered comfort at the far end of the room. The words of the song—an old song, Adele said—still hung in the air. Then Yo-Yo heaved a big sigh. "Well. Gotta tell ya, Delores, your prayer said it for me. I don't unnerstand teenagers anymore."

Our laughter broke the tension. Yo-Yo wasn't that far from being a teenager herself. But I knew raising her half brothers on her own wasn't a laughing matter.

"Pete—that boy's got me comin' an' goin'," she went on. "Wasn't so bad when he and Jerry were shorties. Thought I could be the mama they never had. But, man! I'm about ready to throw that wannabe 'hood rat out on his butt. Comin' in late, stinkin' like weed." She cussed under her breath.

"Yeah," Florida jumped in. "Throw the Hickman teenager into that pot. No sooner does Carl get a job and things be lookin' up for us, than Chris start hangin' out on the street. Lord, *help* me. He's not listenin' to either one of us. Wish Carl would knock some sense into him, make him toe the line. But Carl workin' a lot of hours now—an' I'm grateful for that, thank ya, Jesus. But he ain't around that much, and when he *is*, all he does is yell at Chris. Fat lot of good that's doin'."

"Sisters." Avis said it like a call to order. "We need to understand what's going on here. God has been answering many of our prayers. Yo-Yo chose to be baptized, Carla has been returned to her family, Carl Hickman got a job. Didn't we pray on our face before God for these things?"

"Yeah," Stu added, "and we prayed that Mark and Nony would quit fighting over which continent to live on, and now Mark is taking his family to South Africa."

"I prayed I could forgive Becky Wallace. And I did." Hoshi's voice was quiet but firm.

"An' Becky gettin' an early release. God sure messed with the system big-time in her case." Yo-Yo laughed.

"You an' Mr. Douglass gettin' married," Chanda giggled. "Now dat's *good*."

Avis smiled. "That too. All these and more are blessings from God, answers to our cries. But we need to keep alert, because Satan doesn't like to see our prayers answered. He doesn't want our trust in God to grow. The apostle Paul told the Ephesian church . . ." She paged through her Bible. "Here it is. Chapter six, verse twelve: 'Our struggle is not against flesh and blood, but against the rulers, against the authorities, against the powers of this dark world and against the spiritual forces of evil in the heavenly realms.'"

Was she talking to me? *"Spiritual warfare,"* Avis had called it when she left that message on our answering machine—after I'd told her about the books Josh had ordered.

But that was confidential! I hadn't planned to tell anyone else.

"Guess you could say that's what's happening at my house too," Stu said. My heart stuttered . . . then steadied. Stu didn't know about the books. Not from *me* anyway. And she said at *her* house, not mine. "God did answer our prayer about Becky Wallace," she went on. "Could say I even pushed God on that one."

Both Florida and Yo-Yo snickered. "Could say that."

Stu made a wry face. "But I have to admit it's kind of tough right now. Becky's going nuts being confined to the apartment and yard, and she's driving *me* nuts. We no sooner get something worked out—like cleaning out the tub or hanging up wet towels—than something else happens. Now it's her 'old friends' dropping by! When I'm not home, to boot." Stu shook her head, her face gloomy beneath her blonde tresses. "Didn't think about that being 'spiritual warfare'—but I'm about ready to surrender and call it quits!"

18

For a moment no one spoke. What did Stu mean? What would happen to Becky if she actually called it quits?

Adele raised her eyebrows. "*Humph.* Sounds to me like Becky Wallace needs a new posse. Needs a couple of hours in my shop, too, but that's another story."

Florida snickered. "You speakin' the truth, girl—on both counts. I'm thinkin' we left Stu in this soup all by her own bad self. Maybe some of us could drop by her place from time to time, give Becky a little company. Like we do for MaDear." She jabbed a finger in my direction. "After all, the devil was workin' overtime when B. W. came bustin' into Jodi's house last September. Then God worked overtime gettin' that mess untangled. Maybe it's time for the rest of us to put in a little overtime, before the devil turn ever'thing inside out again."

Heads nodded. But I squirmed. Was Flo thinking *I* should "put in a little overtime" relating to Becky, since I lived in the apartment below? Decided it was just a stray "guilt germ" and squashed it.

"Thanks, Flo," Stu said. "Would appreciate that. Still . . ." She shook her head.

143

"We need to put in some overtime on our knees too," Avis said. She flipped her Bible again and ran her finger down a page. "Listen to this. 'If the owner of the house had known at what hour the thief was coming, he would not have let his house be broken into.'"

"What?" Yo-Yo yelped. "Jodi didn't 'let' Becky bust in. That don't seem—"

Avis held up her hand, putting Yo-Yo on Pause. "Jesus liked to use examples from everyday life to help people understand spiritual principles. Here He's talking about being alert and ready for His return from heaven. But it applies equally to being alert and ready for attacks from the enemy. It's not enough to wait till something happens and *then* pray about it. We need to sharpen our spiritual weapons, fill the house with praise so Satan can't get a toehold, and pray for the battle that's already going on between God and His angels and Satan and his demons."

"Then I want us to pray for Mark Smith." A worried frown creased Hoshi's forehead. "That White Pride group is staging a 'free speech' rally on the university campus next Friday, and Dr. Smith plans to speak up against their ideas. Nony is upset about it, but Dr. Smith seems quite determined."

There. It was out. The room began to buzz. "White Pride *what?*" "What kind of free speech rally?" "Thought all that Ku Klux Klan stuff went out with the civil rights movement." "Nah, they're different. They've been in the papers—swastikas and stuff." "I don't get it." "You don't even wanna know!" "Lord, have *mercy*."

Adele's mouth tightened, and I saw her eyes retreat behind a mask.

I kept my eyes on my shoes. *Please, God, don't let Avis ask me to fill in the blanks.*

"Those hatemongers—ain't no different than street gangs," Yo-Yo piped up. "Got their own rules, can't reason with 'em. I met a few white supremo chicks in prison. Best to just ignore 'em, in my opinion. Let 'em have their ol' rally, talk to themselves, nobody show up."

Made sense to *me*.

"Girl, you think that'll make 'em go away?" Florida wagged her head. "Them White Pride types need attention, an' they goin' to get it, one way or another."

"I think," Delores said slowly, "Hoshi and Avis are right. We need to pray. We need to prepare for the battle. Jesus, have mercy. It's already upon us."

Little bumps stood up on my arms. All this talk about spiritual warfare made me feel creepy. Were we making too big a deal out of this? And what in the world did Delores mean, *"It's already upon us"*?

Avis nodded. "Absolutely. We must pray. That is our strongest spiritual weapon. Each of you, just speak out what God puts on your heart. We have mentioned several things already." Avis began, "Lord God, Your Word tells us to take up the shield of faith and the sword of the Spirit, Your Word . . ."

The coil of tension in my gut unwound a few notches. At least Yada Yada was praying about this hate group stuff without me having to say anything about Josh and those books. After all, I hadn't actually opened them; I didn't really know what they said.

Maybe I wouldn't have to.

WE WERE GIVING NOISY GOOD-BYE HUGS when Chanda called out, "An where we meetin' next time? Soon as me gets my 'ouse, we can be meetin' dere. What you t'ink?"

We laughed. "That'll be great," said Stu. "But for now, you'll have to put up with my apartment. I'm next on the list."

Edesa was helping Delores into her jacket. "I vote for Stu's. Then Becky Wallace can meet with us. I think . . ." She glanced around at the rest of us. "I think it would be good for her to come to Yada Yada all the time. We should pray about that, *sí*?"

And pray about whatever's bugging Delores too. Maybe I'd give her a call later. Or should I ask Edesa if she knows what's going on?

Edesa. My fingers went to the pocket of my jeans. I almost forgot to give her Josh's note! I hesitated. I didn't want Edesa to think I was some kind of go-between or that it was *my* idea for Josh to ask her to his prom.

Florida poked her head back inside the door. "The Hickmans are fixin' to move soon as we find a place in Rogers Park. Keep your eyes open, ya hear? Pray about it. Movin' the Hickmans ain't gonna be no picnic. Edesa? Delores? You comin'? Best to walk to the el together this time o' night."

It was now or never. I caught Edesa's arm. "Edesa, Josh said to give this to you." I pulled out the envelope—rather crunched from its ride in my jeans pocket.

"Oh! Good." Edesa took the note and smiled. "Josh said he'd send it with you. Bye." She gave me a kiss on the cheek. "That's for Amanda."

I stared at her back as the el crowd evaporated through Adele's front door. *Josh said he'd send it with me?* Were those two talking by phone? Surely they were both mortified by Josh's rash invitation to the prom. So what—

"Come on, Jodi!" Stu waved a hand at me impatiently. "Yo-Yo needs a ride home."

Stu and I didn't say much after we dropped Yo-Yo off at her apartment. I wondered what Stu was thinking about inviting Becky to Yada Yada on a regular basis. One thing for sure, she wouldn't have been able to blurt out the "housemate problems" they'd been having like she did tonight. Not if Becky was sitting right there.

As for Josh and Edesa, guess I should be glad Edesa was still on speaking terms with Josh. But—passing notes?

SO MUCH FOR A BAXTER FAMILY OUTING on Memorial Day. When I got home from Yada Yada, Josh was on the phone organizing a couple of vanloads of Uptown kids and friends to go to Six Flags Great America. Denny interrupted the Dagwood sandwich he was making to peck me on the cheek. "If they get twenty warm bodies to go," he murmured in my ear, "they get a group discount— fifteen bucks off each ticket. Wanna go?"

I snorted. "Yeah, right." His mouth kind of sagged. "Wait a minute. You're serious?"

"Why not?" He grinned. "Could be fun, don't you think?"

Losing my stomach on the Raging Bull or knowing for sure I was going to die on the Vertical Drop wasn't exactly my idea of fun anymore. "Tell you what. If they hit nineteen and still need another warm body, I'll consider it. *If* you go—what, Josh?"

Josh had leaned into the kitchen, holding the phone against his chest. "I've got Chris Hickman on the phone. He doesn't come regular to youth group, but he and Cedric *are* Uptown kids. He says he doesn't have any bread. Can we, uh, help out a little?"

I grimaced sideways at Denny. God knew our bank account was skinny enough. But if Florida was worried about Chris hanging out on the street, a trip to Great America with Uptown kids might be a good alternative—at least for one day.

Denny nodded. "Tell him he's gotta pay something, but we'll help with the rest."

"And call Yo-Yo's brothers too!" I called after the back of Josh's shaved head. "That'd be two more!"

Josh no sooner hung up the kitchen phone than Amanda snatched the receiver. "I'll see if José and Emerald can go!" she said, disappearing in the direction of her bedroom.

I smiled smugly and headed for the bathroom. The body count was rising. I wasn't too worried. Still had a lot of escape hatches. But I'd get brownie points for being *willing*—

"Why not?" Amanda's voice rose behind her half-opened bedroom door. "The more kids we get the cheaper it is . . . José! It's not your job to support your family. You're only a kid! . . . Well, if we get twenty people, they give one free ticket. How about that?"

I paused in the hall. Financial problems. That had to be what was bothering Delores. Ricardo still hadn't gotten regular work since the trucking company downsized last summer. And her paycheck as a pediatric nurse had to be stretched thinner than plastic wrap these days—and they had five kids. I *really* needed to give her a call.

"It can't take *that* long to exercise the dog. Wish you didn't have to do it, anyway. That dog is mean . . . Look. I'll pay for your ticket. Or Emerald's." Amanda obviously wasn't taking no for an answer. "Why not? I've got lots of baby-sitting money . . . Nah, I don't need any summer clothes . . . It'll be fun! *Please*, José?"

NONE OF MY ESCAPE HATCHES FUNCTIONED. After burning up the phone all evening, Josh and Amanda indeed rounded up eighteen victims who enjoyed scaring themselves to death, two warm bodies shy of the necessary twenty. Denny was practically rubbing his hands with glee. "We don't have to tag along with the kids. They're big enough to take care of themselves. We can even do the kiddie rides if you want—Roaring Rapids or whatever."

Yeah, right.

Between the fifteen-passenger church van (Pastor Clark was a pushover when it came to using the van for youth activities) and our minivan, we had enough seats for the assortment of Uptown kids, siblings, and friends who showed up at the church—but my mouth dropped open when José and his sister Emerald showed up with Edesa, looking cute as a Gap model in her white capris, bright orange T-shirt, and an orange wrap holding back her curly hair, bringing out the mahogany shine of her skin.

She just grinned at me. "Josh's idea. Said he needed a few more adults to supervise the rabble." Her dark eyes rounded in nervous anticipation. "I've never been to a—how do you say?—*parque de diversion*. Josh says my experience in the United States is not complete unless I ride the American Bird."

I giggled. "American Eagle. It's a roller coaster." Well, it would be fun to have Edesa along. But was she with Denny and me—or Josh?

Turned out to be neither. Edesa mostly took special pains to look after Emerald Enriques, who wanted to do everything the older kids did—though at one point I saw Emerald grab both Edesa's and Josh's hands as she walked between them, laughing up into their faces. Chris Hickman managed to show off his shoulder-rolling "gangsta walk" for about one hour—then he started running from ride to ride and horsing around like all the other kids. Pete and Jerry Spencer too.

This was good. Very good. *Thank You, Jesus.*

Denny finally talked me into getting on the Demon, a roller coaster that looped upside down a few times. *What was I thinking?* I didn't know which was worse: watching Amanda and José, a few cars in front of us, hold their arms high in the air as we flew over the heartstopping crests, or feeling like I was going to get launched into outer space at every turn. Had to admit it was crazy fun screaming at the top of my lungs and holding on to Denny for dear life. But I was still glad to be in the first carload to poop out and go home.

"WHOO-EE," Denny said, kicking off his gym shoes and propping his feet up on the coffee table. One toe peeked through a hole in his sock. "What a gas. Glad you called time-out, though. I'm beat."

"What?" I deadpanned. "Aren't you planning your annual Memorial Day Grill Fest in the backyard? I invited all those kids to come back here for burgers tonight!"

The tan on his face faded at least two shades. I burst out laughing. "Gotcha! Oh, Denny. The look on your face was worth the price of admission."

"Oh," he groaned. "Don't *do* that to me. Just give me the phone, and I'll order a pizza. For two."

Still laughing, I headed for the kitchen to get the phone, where the answering machine message light was blinking. Three messages. I punched Play.

"Jodi!" Stu's voice. "Thought you guys would be home today. Andy's caseworker brought him over here for a couple of hours to

visit with his mom. Sorry you missed him. Hope you don't mind—
I let Willie Wonka out in the yard, so Andy would have somebody
to play with. The dog was a trooper. OK, bye."

Hm. Too bad. I would've liked to see little Andy again. I hit
Erase.

"Jodi?" For a moment I wasn't sure who had left the second
message. I could barely hear the caller; the voice sounded low,
despondent. "I . . . please call me, *mi amiga.*" Delores! She sounded
terrible. I reached for the phone to call her right back, but the third
message started up.

"Denny, this is Mark Smith." *Oh yeah, Mark and Nony are home;
thank You, God.* "Listen, brother, give me a call, tonight if you can.
I'd like to talk to you about getting some of the brothers together
Thursday night to pray—before this White Pride rally on Friday.
And . . . I know you've got to work, man, but . . ." Mark's voice
sounded strained. "It would mean a lot to me if you could come to
the rally, be there for some support. I appreciate what you did giving
me a chance to talk with the guys at your men's breakfast a couple of
Saturdays ago. The flier these nuts have been handing out says four
o'clock. Any chance you could get away?"

I raised my finger, almost willing it to "accidentally" hit Erase.
No way did I want Denny to go to that rally! But I just stood there,
my finger raised. What was it Denny had said after that men's
breakfast?

*The gates of hell can't prevail if we can just hold on like this—
together.*

19

The nightmare stalked me again just before the alarm rang the next morning. *I'm in the street, dodging cars, trying to get to the other side, rain plastering my hair to my head, sticking my eyelashes together. And then, headlights bearing down on me—*

I sat up in bed, clammy with sweat. I hoped it was sweat anyway. I was too young for hot flashes, wasn't I? I sank back against my pillow—then sat up again. Wait a minute. The dream was wrong, flipped around, as if my memory had turned inside out. I shouldn't be the one in the street; I was supposed to be in the car. I . . .

Denny sighed in his sleep and heaved his body onto his left side, facing away from me. And then I knew. This dream wasn't about the accident that happened nearly a year ago. It wasn't a memory at all.

It was fear.

I gave up on sleep, slid out of bed, grabbed Denny's robe off the door hook, and followed Willie Wonka to the back door for his morning ablution. I started the coffee while keeping an eye on the dog as he waddled in the early morning's half-light to the corner back by the garage to do his business. The patchwork of Johnny-jump-ups, petunias, and marigolds nodded happily along the fences, enjoying an early morning breeze. Looked like a nice day. Should be a nice day. But apprehension stitched my insides into a knot.

I dreaded the coming week.

It wasn't just because my classroom tended to run amuck after Memorial Day, even though the long holiday weekend signaled "summer" to the third-grade collective brain, and they all came back to school acting like Mexican jumping beans. (My MO for the last few weeks of school? "Just get through them—somehow!")

It wasn't just because the sophomore dance at José's school was next Saturday, although Amanda had been acting as if all the sands of time, all cells and molecules, all the stars and the moon and the sun, all significant historical events, scientific discoveries, and great literature had been created for this one weekend.

The coffee maker gurgled its final burp. I poured myself a mug, stepped out onto the back porch in Denny's oversize robe, and sat on the aging porch swing. No, the main reason I dreaded the upcoming week was because Denny hadn't even blinked when Mark asked him to come to the rally next Friday. "I'll be there," he'd said when he returned Mark's phone call. "Just tell me where."

And because Josh, when he heard what was going down, leaped on it. "Me too, Dad."

Oh God, I groaned. *I don't even know what I'm afraid of.* The unknown. I mean, what in the world were we getting ourselves into? It was bad enough that Nony's husband wanted to take on these white supremacists toe to toe. But why drag Denny and Josh into it? *What if . . . what if . . .*

My mind zeroed in on its target like a heat-seeking missile.

What if the rally got ugly? What if some of the minority students got offended at this "white is right" harangue and reacted violently? Were they going to distinguish *my* "white guys" from the White Pride nuts? I rolled my eyes. Wouldn't they just *love* to know Josh had a stack of that White Pride filth under his bed!

Wonka finished his morning business and wandered back toward the house, pausing to sniff the new day. Grabbing the pooper-scooper, I hustled down the porch steps in my bare feet. It suddenly seemed very important to get rid of Wonka's poop *now*.

HALFWAY INTO THE WEEK, I realized I still hadn't called Delores to find out what was troubling her—*or* Ruth, to see if she was feeling better.

Hadn't been upstairs to see Becky Wallace either.

Some friend you are, Jodi Baxter, I scolded myself as I came in the house after school on Wednesday. I'd been so busy keeping myself busy so I didn't have to think about this rally business, I'd been neglecting—well, a lot of stuff. Prayer. Friends. Promises.

Dumping my tote bag and kicking off my shoes, I headed for the kitchen in my sock feet, let the dog out, grabbed the phone, put on the teakettle, and pulled open the freezer door to see if, by some miracle, a magic elf had left an already-prepared supper there.

"Hello?"

Good grief, whose number had I dialed? "Uh . . . is Delores there?"

"No, Mama's at work. Do you want her to call you?"

Which Enriques cutie was this? Wasn't José. Didn't sound like Emerald. "Yes, please. Tell her Jodi Baxter called, OK?"

"*Si.* Bye, Miz Baxter."

Admit it, Jodi. You're not very good at multitasking. I took a big breath, put some pork chops into the microwave to thaw, poured hot water over a tea bag, and sat down before I made my next call. The phone on the other end picked up.

"Garfield." The voice was gruff. Curt. Male.

"Ben? It's Jodi Baxter. I'm calling to see if Ruth is feeling better. We missed her at Yada Yada on Sunday."

The briefest of pauses, like a skipped heartbeat. "Yeah, sure, she's OK. Some low-grade bug she's been fighting, nothing serious. Or maybe it's, ah, you know, a female thing. But she's at work today. Be home in an hour or so."

"Oh." I swallowed my disappointment. So would my family, and once supper, the evening news, kids on the phone, and homework kicked into gear—and oh, yes, tonight was midweek Bible study at Uptown—it'd be bedtime, or tomorrow, before I'd get a chance to call again. "Just tell her I called, OK? Thanks, Ben." I started to hang up.

"Hey! Miss In-a-Hurry. You called me. So talk." The gravelly voice at the other end chuckled. "Actually, I've got a question. Is Denny there?"

"No. Baseball practice after school, you know."

"OK, that's not my question. What I want to know is, is your good-looking husband going to that sicko rally at Northwestern on Friday?"

Now it was my turn to skip a heartbeat. "Yes," I admitted. "Josh wants to go too."

"Good for the boy. Good for Denny. Tell both of 'em to keep me in line just in case I'm tempted to wipe the mouth off a White Pride kisser or two."

I think I made a strangled noise. Couldn't be sure if it was me or static on the line.

"Jodi, sweetheart. Just kidding. I'm going to behave myself. Mark Smith asked me to be there, so I'm going to be there. Glad I'll have some company. OK. Now you can hang up."

"Wait! Ben?" Ben Garfield had to be older than Ruth by at least ten years—she was close to fifty, which probably made him fifteen or twenty years older than I was. For some reason, his teasing and gentle gruffness made me feel like a little girl being hugged by my daddy. And I found myself blurting out the whole business of Josh ordering books from the White Pride people, and there they were, sitting in my house, making me feel like a party to all this mess.

Ben listened. At least he was quiet while I bumbled along. Then he said, "The kid's got guts. What's he finding out from these books?"

"Uh, I don't know. He hasn't said anything."

"*Said* anything! Of course he's not going to say anything. This kind of venom isn't exactly dinner-table talk. I meant, have you looked at these books? Didn't you tell Yo-Yo once upon a time—one of you Yada Yadas did—that parents or guardians better watch what their kids watch, read what their kids read, listen to what their kids listen to? Of course, this is different, because Josh is educating himself about this mess. Still, I'd go look at those books if I were you, Jodi."

How long had Wonka been scratching at the back screen door? "Um, thanks, Ben. You're probably right. Don't forget to tell Ruth I called." I hung up quickly, getting rid of the phone like a hot potato. Absently, I let the dog in.

Did I want Ben Garfield telling me I should look at those books?

No.

Maybe because it *was* Ben. Maybe because Denny had told me

some of Ben's family history during the Holocaust. If Ben Garfield thought I should look at those books, maybe . . .

I glanced at the kitchen clock. Amanda might be home any minute; I wasn't sure about Josh. Denny wouldn't hit the door until six thirty. But for the moment, I had the house all to myself.

Slowly, I walked to Josh's bedroom. The door was ajar. Usually I pulled it shut when I passed by, not wanting to see the puree inside, as if bedclothes, dirty socks, ratty jeans, gym shoes, underwear, books and papers, soccer equipment, and a hundred CDs had been dumped into a giant blender. Out of sight, out of mind, I figured— until the next cleaning orgy at least. But today I pushed it open and entered. *Don't go snooping into anything else, Jodi Baxter,* I told myself. *Just the books.*

Took me several minutes to find them, stuffed under his bed. What else was under there, only God knew. Probably Josh himself had no idea. I shuddered. As long as it wasn't crawling, growing mold, or multiplying, I'd let it go. For now.

I pulled out the books. Most were thick, four hundred pages at least. But I picked up a small booklet. *The Pro-White Creed—A Summary of What We Believe.*

A summary. That would do it for me.

I glanced at the table of contents. It read almost like a religious handbook, designed to instruct the novice believer. *"The Ten Commandments of White Pride"* . . . *"We Believe—A Daily Affirmation of Faith"* . . . *"Fifteen Principles of Healthy Living."* I steeled myself for a twisted form of Christianity, like the Crusades or the Ku Klux Klan. But the more I read, the weaker I got in the knees until I ended up on the floor.

"We believe our race is our religion. . . . The inferior races are our

avowed enemy, and the Jewish race is the most dangerous of all." The enemy? Dangerous? I didn't get it. I mean, by definition racists thought other races were "inferior"—but why the "enemy"? And why the Jews? I always thought of Jewish people as "white." They looked that way to me.

"Christianity was invented by the Jews to destroy the White Race. . . . Christianity rapes the minds of otherwise intelligent White Men." My eyes practically bugged out of my head. *What?* What in the world did they mean, "invented . . . to destroy the White Race"? Seemed to me most Jewish people got rather offended by Christians claiming Jesus was the Messiah. But hey, if these White Pride types didn't believe in God or Jesus, that was fine with me. Gave me less to apologize for.

"What is good for the White Race is the highest virtue. . . . There is nothing more despicable than a traitor to his or her own race." I read that one over at least three times. What were they talking about? Mixed marriages? Disagreeing with them?

"Eat only raw vegetables . . . drink no poisons like coffee or alcohol . . . exercise regularly. Build up the White Race!" OK, so they were health nuts. I flipped more pages.

"It's a law of nature to protect one's own. . . . Do nothing illegal. But be ready to defend yourself. Racial war is only a matter of time—"

A door slammed. The phone started ringing. "Mo-om! Where's the car? Can we go shopping? I need new underwear for the dance!" The ringing phone cut short. "Hello? Baxter's Beauty Barn . . . Oh, hi, Mrs. Garfield. . . . Mo-om! It's for you!"

I quickly shoved the books back under Josh's bed, scrambled to my feet, and met Amanda in the kitchen with a smile plastered on my face.

20

S o. It's Baxter's Beauty Barn now, is it?" I could practically hear the smirk on Ruth's face. "Sorry about that, Ruth. I *did* teach my kids phone manners once upon a time." I aimed that last salvo at Amanda, who ducked and scuttled out of the kitchen.

"So. You called?"

"Yes! Yo-Yo said you weren't feeling too good Sunday night. How *are* you?"

"How should I be? This body's got nearly half a century hanging on it. A tune-up I need. Still, I could be dying and Ben wouldn't take it seriously. 'Ben,' I say, 'can you bring me some Pepto-Bismol?' 'What?' he says. 'Can't you get it yourself?'" Ruth snorted in my ear. "*Husbands.* God help us—'cause *they're* sure not going to."

I giggled. "Oh, come on, Ruth. Ben sounded kinda worried about you when I talked to him a while ago."

"*Humph.* Maybe, maybe not. Would it break his face to *show* me he's worried?"

"Are you still sick?

"I should be so lucky. A little attention I might get. A queasy stomach is all . . . So how was Yada Yada? What's the latest melodrama?"

Movement in the kitchen doorway caught my eye. Amanda was bouncing on the balls of her feet and pointing at the clock. I turned my back on her. "Ruth, I'm sorry. Amanda thinks the end of civilization will be upon us if she doesn't get new underwear *right now* for the dance at José's school this weekend. Let me call you back, OK?"

"New underwear! Jodi, Jodi. Go put your feet up. My grandmother Zelda, God rest her soul, had one thing to say when the boys began to call: 'Always wear your ragged undergarments, young lady. More likely to keep your clothes on.'"

My turn to snort. Knew *that* would go over like spinach at a birthday party. But maybe I could put off Amanda until Saturday, at least, since Denny and I'd been trying to make it to the Uptown Bible study on Wednesday nights.

As it turned out, we didn't go. The phone rang during supper, and Denny answered. "Uh-huh . . . uh-huh . . . I can do that . . . What? Sure, I'll hold . . . Yeah, still here . . . OK. No problem. I'll ask her."

I raised my eyebrows into question marks as he sat back down at the table.

"Uh, that was Mark. He hasn't been able to get hold of Peter Douglass or Carl Hickman about getting together tomorrow night to pray, and he has to attend some meeting tonight at the university. He asked if I'd call them. Then Nony told him to ask you to come— maybe Avis and Florida too."

"Not just the guys?"

Denny shrugged and tackled his now-growing-cold mashed potatoes. "Guess not. Nony wants to be there."

"Can I come?" Josh asked. "I want to see Dr. Smith about something."

Denny's mouth was full, but he managed, "Guess so."

I sat up inside. The cobwebs that'd been clouding the corners of my spirit all week vanished, as if they'd been dusted out. *Praying together.* That's what I needed. Hadn't been able to pray by myself all week—why was that? If Denny, Josh, and some of the other guys were going to this rally, too, it'd be great if we could all pray together first. *Avis could probably come with Peter. Would Florida need a babysitter?*

I got up to get my Yada Yada phone list then glanced at the clock. "Oh! Denny. What about Bible study tonight?"

"Not me. Not if we're going out tomorrow night." He didn't even look guilty.

Amanda pounced. "You're not going to church tonight? Does that mean we can go shopping?"

Grandmother Zelda's "recipe for virtue" almost popped out of my mouth. Instead, I said, "It can wait till Saturday morning—if we go at all. I'm not sure it's necessary, Amanda. Nobody's gonna *see*—"

Amanda's mouth dropped. "Mom!" She grabbed my arm and dragged me into the kitchen, out of hearing of her father and brother. "That's not the point," she whispered. "I just want to feel, you know, *special* from the inside out on Saturday night. It's, like, my first real date."

I studied my daughter. Her first real date. With José. Yes, I was aware of that. For a moment, I put aside mother bear mode and tried to remember what it was like to be fifteen and going on a "real" date. Well, sixteen in my case. My parents had a solid spot in the Strict Parents Top Ten, just under the ones who advocated arranged marriage. But I could remember that awesome feeling of knowing that somebody—a boy, a *nice* boy—liked me. Liked me enough to ask me out and be seen in public with me. Remembered all the nerve endings that felt naked and exposed for days leading up to the date. *Will I do something dumb and humiliate him? Humiliate myself? How am I supposed to act? Is my dress dorky? Should I dip into my college savings, just this once, and—*

"All right," I said. "Saturday morning."

"OK." She shrugged. "Can I have the phone?"

I snatched it first. "No! Your dad and I have to make some calls about this prayer meeting tomorrow."

Amanda's mood-o-meter swung from mild compliance to mutiny. "Mo-om! You won't take me shopping, and now you won't let me use the phone. Nobody *ever* lets me do *anything!*" She flounced out of the room and disappeared. A door slammed.

I came back into the dining room, hoping to send Denny after his melodramatic daughter. I found him in the living room, already engrossed in a TV special on the fiftieth anniversary of the first ascent of Mount Everest.

Which was *nothing*, in my opinion, compared to raising teenagers.

WHEN WE GOT READY TO GO Thursday evening, Josh showed up lugging his old school backpack, the one with the broken zipper. I started to ask what happened to the new one we got him this year, but Amanda interrupted. "If everybody's going to be gone, can I go upstairs and do my homework with Stu and Becky?"

That's nice, I thought. Except when we went out to the garage, we realized Stu's car wasn't there. *Uh, God? I'm leaving my daughter alone with an ex-con. Does this make any sense?*

"They'll be OK," Denny said. "Let's go." But at the last minute, he ran up the back stairs and asked Becky not to have any "friends" over while Amanda was there.

"What'd she say?" I hissed when he climbed into the minivan.

"She said, 'I'm cool with that.'" He flicked the garage opener and backed into the alley.

Josh gave a snort from the middle seat. "Maybe we could just let Amanda live upstairs all the time."

Hm. Tempting.

Nony met us at the door of their ivy-covered brick home in north Evanston. "Denny! And Josh too! Go on through the kitchen. Mark's in the family room with Avis and Peter." She gave me a warm hug, wrapping me in the folds of the yellow-and-black caftan she was wearing. "Thank you for coming, Jodi. Would you help me carry in the tea?"

In the kitchen, Nony picked up a tray with a teapot wrapped in a cozy, cups, a honey pot, and a small pitcher of cream. *The real deal*, I grinned. "Bring that lemonade, too, will you, Jodi?" she said. "And glasses—up there in that cupboard."

The TV was on in the family room as we came in with the drinks and munchies. I threw a smile at Avis, who was sitting patiently at one end of the comfy couch while the guys were all glued to the TV. A couple of news anchors were bouncing all over the president's announcement that U.S. troops would remain in Iraq "indefinitely," even though the war was supposed to be officially "over."

"It's not over," Mark muttered. "Not by a long shot."

The doorbell rang, and a moment later Nony ushered Florida and Carl Hickman into the room. And Stu. Stu? *Oops.* Should I have called everybody in Yada Yada about this prayer meeting?

"Don't think I'm not grateful for the taxi service, Leslie Stuart," Florida was saying, drowning out the TV. "But, girl, you need to get a bigger car if you gonna haul around the likes of Carl and his long legs."

"Flo!" Carl's color deepened.

Stu grinned. "Why do you think I drive a small car? You really have to *need* a ride to call me up."

Nony shut off the TV and sat down next to her husband. They looked like a photo shoot straight out of *Ebony* magazine. "Guess we're all here. Stu, can you stay? We're going to pray about the rally tomorrow."

"Well, OK. Haven't been home yet, but I could stay a little while." Stu sank into an overstuffed chair.

Josh slung the backpack off his shoulder and handed it to Mark. "These might help give you a heads-up for tomorrow, Dr. Smith."

"What's this?" Mark reached into Josh's backpack and pulled out a book, then another. I stared. *Those books.* I glared at Josh. Was my son out of his *mind?* I could guarantee Nony would be upset seeing that venom in her house.

All the books were dumped on the coffee table, tea and lemonade forgotten. Peter and Carl each picked up a book, turned it over, and read the back, frowning. Stu grabbed one, too, and began paging through it. "Good grief," she muttered. "Glad Ruth and Ben aren't here. These people really hate Jews, don't they?"

"Jews *and* blacks *and* Asians *and* Christians," Josh said. "And whites who 'mingle' with, um, non-whites." He grinned at his father and me. "We're all traitors."

I could tell Mark was fascinated. "Where'd you get these?"

Josh told about finding the White Pride Web site and ordering the books as research for his debate team. "Pretty nasty stuff," he admitted. "But they might give you a clue what these jerks are going to say at their 'free speech' rally tomorrow."

"Yeah. Yeah. Thanks, Josh. I appreciate it."

Nony did not pick up any of the books. She sat on the couch, arms folded against her chest, hidden within the roomy caftan. I caught her eye. *Where are the boys?* I mouthed at her.

She pointed toward the floor and mouthed back, *Play room. Downstairs. Video games.* Then she pressed her lips together. Nony was not a happy camper.

"Listen to this," Peter said, and began to read the "Ten Commandments of White Pride." Avis got up from her end of the couch, threaded her way through the bodies and knees populating the Sisulu-Smiths' family room, and disappeared into the kitchen. Didn't blame her. Maybe I'd go use the bathroom next. Stick my finger down my throat and throw up.

"Whassup with this, Mark?" Carl was shaking his head. "These guys talk about preparing for 'racial holy war.' Man! I thought all that was in the Middle East."

Denny spoke up. "It's not too late to reconsider, Mark. No one in this room would blame you if you decided to just ignore these guys tomorrow. That might be the wisest thing anyway."

Everyone had an opinion. Comments flew back and forth. Short snippets from the books got read. Josh was engaged with men he respected; *that* part I could be grateful for. But I felt unsettled. The tension in the room—spoken and unspoken—was high.

Stu whispered something to Florida. "Hey, everybody." Florida raised her voice over the hubbub. "Hate to break up the party, but didn't we get together tonight to pray? Stu's gotta go in a few minutes, maybe some of the rest of us too. Kids, you know."

"Yeah, yeah, of course." Mark started stuffing the books back into the backpack; then he looked at Josh. "Could I keep these till tomorrow? I'd like to look at them a little more carefully." At Josh's nod, Mark glanced around the room, as if searching for a place to put them.

"Not in here!" Nony snapped. "Take them up to your office. I don't want the boys to see them."

"Right. Be back in a minute." Mark disappeared with Josh's backpack.

"Where's Avis at?" Florida frowned. "She's been gone a long time. But if we're gonna pray now, she's gonna want to be here."

"I'll get her," I said, getting up. Avis had been gone a long time. Too long for a trip to the bathroom.

I found Avis in the music room—a little alcove off the front foyer with an upright piano, a floor-to-ceiling bookcase, a violin case lying on the floor, and a music stand. The room was dim, lit only by the light from the foyer, but I could see Avis was walking back and forth, her lips moving, murmuring. Sounded like she was praying in tongues.

I cleared my throat. "Avis? Um, they're ready to pray now."

She turned. A slight smile—it seemed sad—gentled her face. "All right."

Everyone was standing in a circle holding hands when we came back into the room. "Lord," Mark was saying, "You know I'm the type of person who tends to act first, then asks You to bless it. But thank You for these brothers and sisters willing to pray with me. And we're asking Your blessing on what happens tomorrow."

Denny prayed that the rally would not get out of hand, that students would not react in negative and harmful ways, that reason and calm would prevail . . .

"And, Lord, give wisdom to Dr. Smith, that he will know how to speak the truth, and that people will listen." That was Josh. I peeked. My son's shaved head shone in the lamplight, his eyes tightly closed.

Peter Douglass spoke. "Father God, it's a good thing for me to pray with a mixed group like this. And I don't mean gents and ladies." He cleared his throat. "I mean, black and white together. A good reminder to me that this isn't about race or color—not in Your eyes. It's about hearts stunted by hate."

"And about One heart full of love, thank ya, Jesus!" Florida added. "The Son of God died for the haters too."

Whoa. That wouldn't be my first thought. Still, she was right.

A few more prayers, and the room quieted. We stood hand in hand in silence for a few moments. Maybe we were done. But then Avis spoke for the first time. "Brothers and sisters, I feel strongly in my spirit that we need to pray against fear. Fear. That's our biggest enemy. God isn't the author of fear; fear is a weapon of the Evil One. Again and again Jesus said to His followers, 'Don't be afraid! It is I.'"

I heard movement and opened my eyes. Avis walked over to Mark and Nony, a tiny bottle in her hand. Anointing oil, probably. I knew she carried it with her. I saw her tip the bottle between her fingers and then touch Mark's forehead. "Mark," she said, "do not be afraid of those who kill the body but cannot kill the soul."

The hairs on the back of my neck prickled.

Avis turned to Nony, tipped the bottle, and gently rubbed the oil on Nony's forehead. "Nonyameko, my sister, when Jesus left His disciples to return to His Father, He said, 'Peace I leave with you; do not let your heart be troubled and do not be afraid.'"

The room hushed, as if everyone had stopped breathing. *Whew.* Powerful words about not being afraid. Enough to *make* me afraid if I wasn't already.

Frankly, what Avis said was kind of creepy.

21

I awoke in the night. Something felt wrong. I sat up. The nightmare again? No. Didn't even remember dreaming. The red numerals of my digital alarm glowed 2:17. I listened. Nothing. Just the muffled drone of nighttime traffic on Sheridan Road a half-mile away, and Denny's not-quite-a-snore nasal breathing.

Sheesh, it's hot. And it's not even June yet. I got out of bed in my oversized Bulls T-shirt—my "nightgown" of choice—and opened the bedroom window a couple of inches. A gentle breeze blew in off Lake Michigan, freshening the room. Huh. It was high time we put the screens in so we could keep the windows open. Maybe Denny would do it on Saturday—

Saturday. Saturday was the sophomore dance at Benito Juarez High School. Amanda and José were going. Probably should talk to Delores and agree on expecta—

Delores. *Delores never returned my phone call. And I'd called her two days ago!* Was she avoiding me? Nah. Probably didn't mean anything. Fact is, I'd left the message with one of her younger kids. Likely she never got it.

Still, I should try calling her again. She didn't seem herself at the last Yada Yada meeting. Maybe her name came to mind in the middle of the night because God wanted me to pray for her. Well, why not? I was wide-awake now. Pulling on Denny's robe, I shuffled down the dark hallway toward the living room.

Could probably use the extra prayer time. Hadn't exactly used up my prayer minutes this week. Even last night—

The back of my neck prickled. Last night. The prayer meeting at the Sisulu-Smiths.

That's what was bothering me.

I sank down in the recliner near the front windows. A cold nose pushed against my hand, and I stroked Willie Wonka's soft forehead. Faithful old dog. "Sorry for waking you up, Wonka," I murmured. Yeah, I felt unsettled about last night's prayer meeting. But why, exactly? Avis's words to Mark and Nony? She'd taken them right from Scripture. But still. Kinda creepy. And anointing them with oil. Why did she do that? Made it seem so . . . so serious.

The whole thing was disconcerting. Not to mention having all those White Pride books on display! *What was Josh thinking?* The anger I'd stuffed down last night in polite company had been simmering all night. I was sorely tempted to march into Josh's room right now and hold my own free speech rally.

Nope. Shouldn't go there. I reined in my thoughts and backed up a step. What *was* Josh thinking? I pondered that one, trying to be honest. Guess I couldn't really blame him—he thought the books would be helpful to Mark. And Mark did seem to appreciate that he brought them.

OK. Maybe I was just anxious about the rally, which was only—I counted on my fingers—less than fourteen hours from now. It was natural to be concerned. Even Mark had asked for prayer support last night. Only thing was, we'd gotten all those people together and didn't really pray. Not for long, anyway. Almost like a P.S. But this wasn't a P.S. kind of situation! The rally was obviously designed to provoke anger and harsh words. To stir up division. And my husband and son were going to be there. And Nony's husband . . . and Ruth's husband . . . and maybe Peter and Carl.

And a lot of unpredictable university students.

Anything could happen.

Oh God! I groaned. *If fear is the main enemy, then I'm licked already.* I wanted last night back so we could do some serious praying. Like what Avis called it when the whole hate group thing came up: *spiritual warfare.* Wasn't exactly sure what that meant or how you did it. We prayed last night. Sincere prayers. But looking back on it, it didn't feel like "warfare" to me. More like, "Now I lay me down to sleep, I pray the Lord my soul to keep . . ."

Now it was too late. What could we do?

Pray, Jodi. A Voice within overrode my whining. *Cover the rally with prayer.*

Well, sure. I reached for the old afghan on the back of the recliner and pulled it around me. Of course I was going to pray during the rally. School would be over; I'd be home by then. I'd make it a point—

At the rally. Cover the rally with prayer. Pray for the people you see there.

Whoa. I didn't like the direction this inner dialogue was going. "I don't even know what to pray!" I fussed aloud. "And, OK, God, I admit it. I don't want to be there. Those people are scary. I just want it to be over. I just want them to go away."

When you don't know how to pray, pray the Word.

Pray the Word. OK, that was a good idea. Nony was usually good at that. Not last night, though. In fact, I couldn't remember Nony praying at all. Wished she had. She'd probably know some good Scriptures to—

Pray the Word that's in your own heart, Jodi.

A pair of headlights came down our one-way street and lit up our living room for one brief sweep. As the car's red taillights winked between the cars parked bumper to bumper along the curb, the psalm I'd half-memorized filled my thoughts.

"When I am afraid, I will trust in God. I trust in God; why should I be afraid? . . . When I am afraid, I will trust in God . . ."

"JODI? JODI!" A hand shook my shoulder roughly. "What are you doing sleeping out here in the chair?"

I blinked my eyes open. Daylight streamed through our bay windows. Sunlight tipped the tops of the trees outside. Denny stood over me, unshaved, hair on end, wearing only his sleep shorts, looking like a modern caveman.

"When I am afraid, I will trust in God. I trust in God; why should I be afraid?"

I sat up, tossing the afghan aside. "Denny? This afternoon—could you pick me up? I'm going to the rally with you and Josh."

OF COURSE, *this* had to be the morning I tipped over my mug of coffee and sloshed it all over the breakfast table, sending a tidal wave onto Denny's clean slacks. By the time we mopped up the mess, threw the slacks in the washer (after dumping a load of Becky Wallace's left-behind clothes in a wet heap on top of the dryer), and found Denny a clean pair in the still-unfolded pile from last week, we were all late getting out of the house.

Which meant I arrived at school late. Another teacher had to bring my class in when the bell rang, earning me a look that said loud and clear, *If we had to vote on teacher of the year, it wouldn't be you.*

The day was warm for the end of May, the kids hot and restless. Somehow we made it through our final unit entitled "City Bugs and Insects" and picked up litter from the playground as part of the school's "Leave the World a Better Place" contest. I finished the last activity in our "Understanding Illinois History" unit, broke up three fights, and reminded students who failed to bring back their Thursday take-home folders that Monday was the absolute, final, drop-dead day to bring signed permission slips for our Garfield Park Conservatory field trip next week.

After the end-of-the-week stampede that cleared the room at three o'clock, I collected a pink sweater, a windbreaker, a Mickey Mouse watch, and a torn backpack, threw them all into the Darn Lucky Box—already overflowing with unredeemed lost-and-found items—and staggered out the front doors of Bethune Elementary.

No Denny.

Well, OK. A momentary surge of relief overrode my frustration. Maybe Denny forgot and went to the rally without me. Or maybe it had been cancelled altogether, and I just hadn't gotten the word yet. I could just walk home as usual . . .

Not likely.

I went inside, hoping to get a word with Avis, maybe even a chance to pray together about the rally, but Ms. Ivy said she hadn't been in all day. A consortium of Chicago school principals or something.

A knot tightened in my stomach. *I don't know if I can do this, God!*

Denny and Josh finally pulled into the parking lot at three forty-five. "Sorry, babe." Denny got out and loaded me and my school bags into the middle seat of the minivan. "Had a flat tire. But I didn't have time to go home and change." A five-inch smear of black grease decorated one of Denny's pant legs.

Flat tire. Figured.

I was quiet during the fifteen-minute drive north on Sheridan Road to Northwestern University, but Josh kept tossing questions at his father. "Isn't Northwestern a private university? I mean, like, private property? How can an outside group come on campus without permission and hold a rally?"

"I asked Mark the same thing. He thinks there are a few students on campus who are members of this group. So, technically, they can call this a 'student-sponsored' rally. Besides, they're gathering at the Rock, which traditionally is kind of a free-for-all place. Students paint it, plaster signs on it, whatever."

"What if there's trouble? Can the campus police arrest the off-campus people?"

My husband snorted. "Don't forget, we're off-campus people too."

I was beginning to regret my leap of faith in coming along. Even shopping for underwear with Amanda would be better than this.

Denny parked on a side street, and we dodged cars as we crossed Sheridan Road to the main campus entrance. Finding the Rock was easy enough; a group of about fifty people were milling around a small plaza, like a tiny brick lake fed by three or four separate sidewalk streams. Some construction blocked one of the sidewalks. Two imposing buildings faced each other on opposite sides of the plaza; a budding maple tree rose in the middle. A third side boasted a low stone wall, populated by a dozen or more students. Well, presumably students. Twentyish. Assorted Wildcats T-shirts. Mostly African-American; mostly male. They stood on the wall like a Secret Service detail circling the president. Behind the bodies on the wall, I could see a huge boulder about my height, painted a garish red.

Mark Smith noticed us and muscled his way through the small crowd. He looked every inch the casual university professor—goatee neatly trimmed, open-necked burgundy dress shirt, wrinkle-free slacks. I nonchalantly stepped in front of Denny's grease-stained pant leg, hoping Mark wouldn't notice. "Hey, Josh, thanks." He handed Josh the bulging backpack with its broken zipper. "Hope you didn't need this today."

Josh slung the backpack over his shoulder. "Nah, it's my old one." He looked around. "So what's goin' on?"

Mark's smile was sardonic. "We'll find out, won't we?"

"Is Nony here?" I asked, though I suspected I knew the answer. Mark shook his head. "Home with the boys. It's best."

Where I should be. I felt as out of place as a *Leave It to Beaver* rerun on MTV.

The crowd was starting to swell. My eyes traveled, looking for a bunch of skinheads with tattoos, wearing leather and chains or something, trying to figure out who the White Pride members were. A contingent of about twenty people arrived together, all white, but they seemed an odd assortment. Several wore suits and ties; five or six looked like retired bikers who'd cut their hair and cleaned up their act. Then a few skinhead types and several thirtyish women, all in dresses or skirts. Not anyone you'd notice if you passed them on the street.

One of the men in a tie, maybe thirty-five, attempted to step up onto the low wall surrounding the Rock, but the students on the wall moved together, blocking his way. An uneasy murmur rippled through the crowd, which was getting larger by the minute.

"No room up here," one of the sentries growled. He was built like a football player, big in the shoulders, coffee-bean skin, wearing shades and dreadlocks.

Bully, I thought. *Since when did they let football players have that much hair?*

The man in the tie didn't protest; he simply took his stand on the steps leading into one of the flanking buildings and picked up a bullhorn, as if that had been his intent all along. "Is that the guy who's going to speak?" I whispered to Mark. The man looked like a clean-cut seminary student—except for the aging biker and skinhead types who flanked him like bodyguards.

"My guess. But see that younger guy in the red tie? And the girl?" Mark nodded toward a neatly dressed young couple clinging to the edges of the group around the man with the bullhorn. She looked to be in her late teens; he was maybe a few years older.

"I recognize those two," Mark muttered. "They're the ones who came to my house a couple of weeks ago and left that racist pamphlet."

22

$\mathcal{I}$ didn't expect a young girl. Not sure what I had expected—but not suits and ties, not a teenager in a yellow sundress.

She had a washed-out complexion, pale eyes, orangey-blonde hair hanging shapeless to her shoulders—nothing that a trip to Adele's Hair and Nails couldn't brighten up. But mostly she looked . . . scared. Like me. For a moment, I felt confused, then angry. How *dare* this hate group suck youth and innocence into their toxic clutches?

Cover the rally in prayer, Jodi. Pray for the people you see.

I decided to pray for that girl. *Jesus, I don't know anything about that girl, don't even know her name, but You do—*

The bullhorn swung up. "Glad to see *some* people on this campus believe in free speech!" The metallic bellow of the bullhorn had everyone's immediate attention. "Today's university campus is a far cry from the free exchange of ideas our European forefathers intended. Today the liberal elite talk about tolerance, but only certain ideas are tolerated—"

The sound of the bullhorn must've carried a good distance, because the edges of the crowd grew amoebalike and filled up the feeder sidewalks. A good two or three hundred by now. An undercurrent bubbled through the crowd. A few heads nodded. Whites and minorities made up the crowd in about equal numbers. I glanced uneasily around me. I had steeled myself for the kind of venom Josh had found on the White Pride Web site, the hate-filled rhetoric in the books riding on his back. Not something that actually made sense.

The man on the "soapbox" held up a purple and gold handbook. "You all recognize this. The university catalog. Padded with African-American Studies, Asian and Middle East Studies, even *Jewish* Studies! And student services galore—African-American Student Affairs, Latino Student Services . . ." He nailed the crowd with dark, serious eyes. "But where are the *White* American Studies? The *White Only* fraternities? The *White Pride* festival? Oh, no. Everybody would cry racist!"

A voice somewhere in the crowd shouted, "Tell it like it is!" A couple of the sentries ringing the Rock yelled, "Bigot!" and "Whaddya think all those Greek frat houses are, anyway?"

A hand touched my arm. I jerked it away and whirled, coming face to face with a familiar mug under a brown hat. "Ben Garfield! Don't scare me like that!" I gave the older man a big hug, nearly knocking off the hat. "Do you really want to be here?"

He settled the hat back over his yarmulke. Strange. Ben didn't usually wear a yarmulke. "Good question, missy," he grunted. "Bad for my blood pressure, but what else could I do? My brother called for the troops." He stuck out his hand to Denny. "Are we having fun yet?"

Denny chuckled. "Just getting started."

The man with the bullhorn drowned out the yelled comments. "What do they teach you at university these days? Only what the government wants you to know! A government perverted by Judeo-Christian propaganda and held captive by Jewish money!"

"Here we go," muttered Ben.

"The glorious accomplishments of the White Race in pushing back inferior races and building a great nation are now being taught to our children as mistakes and blunders! Think about it, people! Haven't you learned anything in your science classes about the survival of the fittest? Do you think this university would be standing here if we'd left this country in the hands of the so-called natives?"

Catcalls and angry comments flew fast and furious now. The same big voice on the wall yelled, "Bigot!" which soon became a chant picked up by others: "Big-ot! Big-ot! Big-ot!" The girl in the yellow dress looked frightened. She took a step closer to the slim young man in the red tie, but he seemed oblivious to her presence.

I focused on her face. If I looked around at the crowd, my heart would fail me like Simon Peter when he tried to walk on the water but let the waves sink him. *Jesus*, I prayed silently, *she's caught in a trap. Set her free, Lord.*

"You white men and white women!" yelled the man on the soapbox. "Wake up! While you party and fraternize and whine, 'Can't we all just get along?' the Jews and the mud races are taking over our country! What do you think is going to happen to your rights when the glorious white race is no longer a majority in this nation? Do you think your rights will be—"

"Big-ot! Big-ot! Big-ot!" The chanting drowned out whatever the man said next. A few of the sentries surrounding the Rock, including the big guy with dreadlocks, stepped off the wall and started pushing their way through the crowd. I caught sight of Peter Douglass and Carl Hickman standing off to the side of the crowd, as if they'd arrived late. Smart. Wished *we* were standing off to the side instead of smack-dab in the middle with Mark—

I clutched Denny's arm. "Denny! Where's Mark?"

Mark had disappeared, but a moment later he reappeared next to the White Pride guy, waving his arms for attention. "Let the man speak!" he yelled over the crowd. "People have died for the right of a person to speak freely in this country, no matter how much we disagree. Let him speak!"

The crowd, startled into submission by seeing one of NU's African-American professors defending the speaker, quieted to a restless mutter.

The young man glared at Mark. His voice still carried through the bullhorn. "I don't need your permission to speak. This is a free country."

"That's right," Mark tossed back. "I was only offering you the courtesy of my attention. If you're done, I have a few things to say in reply."

Someone yelled, "Dr. Smith! We want Dr. Smith!" Now the crowd took up the new chant, and it became obvious that Mr. Guy-in-the-Tie had lost his platform. He glanced around in frustration and then lowered his bullhorn.

A student still standing on the wall yelled, "Over here, Dr. Smith!" A path opened through the crowd like the parting of the Red Sea, and Mark stepped up onto the wall. Spontaneous clapping erupted.

But not everyone was clapping. I noticed several people clustered around the White Pride speaker as if asking him questions, even shaking hands with him. Were they White Pride supporters who'd been planted in the crowd? Or listeners who suddenly found someone who dared to speak their private prejudices and fears?

Oh God, I groaned. *Don't let the seeds of hatred settle into new hearts today—white or black.*

"Fellow professors and students! Friends and neighbors!" Mark raised an arm for attention. "Some of what you heard today has a kernel of truth. Tolerance as a virtue *has* been co-opted in today's society to mean, 'You have to agree with me.' But frankly, tolerance is particularly necessary when we *don't* agree. The real virtue is the freedom to disagree while respecting each other's humanity." Mark grinned. "Admittedly, a good deal of tolerance is needed today to listen to this man speak—"

Laugher erupted in the crowd.

"But the man has a point. *Every* ethnic and racial group should be able to celebrate its heritage and its contributions to our society, including our white brothers and sisters. But don't be fooled by the half-truths you heard a few minutes ago. The group this man repre-sents, the Coalition for White Pride and Preservation, is not inter-ested in whites celebrating their heritage along with blacks and other minorities. They believe in white *superiority*; they want to return to white *domination*. Their creed goes even further! They want to *eliminate* other races and ethnic groups—and they are prepared to go to any lengths to achieve it!"

I squirmed, keenly aware at that moment of my own whiteness. I knew Mark wasn't speaking about whites in general, but did everyone know that?

"Do your homework, men and women! Don't let this group fly under the radar until they launch their own version of a racial war.

Visit their Web site! Read their books! Learn what this group *really*—"

The crowd seemed to be pressing forward, separating me from Denny. A large figure loomed behind Josh, who was standing a few feet in front of me. "So, skinhead," a deep voice taunted. "You white folks think you gonna *eliminate* us, do you?"

I stared in astonishment at the big black guy in dreadlocks, leering behind his shades at Josh's shaved head. *No, no . . .*

Josh turned; his eyes traveled up to the student's face. "I'm not a skinhead." The muscles beside his mouth twitched. "Just shaved my head, like Michael Jordan."

The big guy belched. "Don't 'Michael Jordan' me, white boy. You look like a skinhead—what's this?" He yanked at the backpack slung over Josh's shoulder. The jerk nearly pulled Josh off his feet. The backpack thudded to the ground and spilled its contents out of the broken zipper.

The White Pride books.

It happened so fast, the moment seemed frozen in time. Fear flickered in Josh's eyes. My own stomach lurched into my throat. *Oh God! Not those books!* A sour frown creased the face beneath the shades, even as Mark Smith's voice rose and fell from the wall near the Rock.

"What's this?" The bully snatched up one of the books with its blood-red title. A string of profanity scorched the air around us. "Got your own racist library, huh, white boy?" He pushed Josh, who stumbled into me, and we both went down. I landed hard; Josh landed on top of me. Grit bit into my palms and knees. The weight of Josh's body held me down.

The big voice somewhere over my head yelled, "Get a load of

this crap!" I twisted my head and caught a glimpse of books being held aloft.

"Hey!" I heard Ben Garfield shouting. "Stop it! . . . Denny! Denny! Help me here!"

Josh was struggling to get up. I felt hands under my shoulders and saw Denny's grease-stained pant leg bending down near my head. "Jodi! Josh! What happened? Are you OK?" With Denny's help, I somehow got my feet beneath me, and the three of us struggled upward.

Voices shouted and bodies jostled all around us, making it hard to keep our footing. Denny held onto my arm like a vise. Suddenly the bullhorn's metallic voice rose over the din. "You! *Nigger!* Get your polluted hands off our sacred books!"

The atmosphere seemed to suck in its breath. Then a roar of rage swept through the crowd, as if someone had opened a dam. Josh got shoved again—but another hand grabbed him, held him upright, and Peter Douglass's voice hissed, "You guys gotta get out—*now!*"

23

eter Douglass and Denny practically dragged us through the mayhem, which was undulating like a mess of fish caught in a net. Somehow we broke out of the mass of bodies and kept going, trampling through bushes lining the walks until we'd put a hundred feet between us and the plaza and felt grass beneath our feet.

We turned back. A small riot was going on. People yelling, shoving, fists flying. The White Pride contingent was holding its own, mostly stiff-arming any students who came near their "leader," though a couple of the skinhead-types got into it with some Latino students. A campus police car drove straight up one of the walks, siren wailing; another arrived from a different direction. Cops spilled out of the cars; police bullhorns ordered everyone to break it up. People began to run in all directions, like water finding its way out the holes of a sieve.

"Ben!" I cried. "Where's Ben Garfield? He was with me! He tried to help me!" Suddenly I panicked, more scared than when Josh and I had fallen in the middle of the crowd. "Oh Jesus! Don't let anything happen to—"

"Look. There's Dr. Smith." Josh pointed. As the plaza emptied, Mark could be seen talking to one of the campus police, gesturing, looking around, while the other cops snapped handcuffs on the two skinhead guys and four or five students.

The big bully in dreads was nowhere to be seen.

"Denny! We've got to find Ben! And what happened to Carl? . . . Oh!" From the far side of the Rock, we could see Carl Hickman and Ben Garfield skirting a row of bridalwreath bushes and heading our way. Ben's hat was askew, and Carl had him firmly by the arm as if to steady him, but otherwise he looked unharmed.

"Ben!" As the two men joined our little knot on the grass, I threw my arms around Ruth's husband and started to cry.

Embarrassed, Ben patted me awkwardly; then he looked Josh up and down. "You two all right?"

I didn't know how to answer. As realization sank in that all of us were safe, so did awareness of my hands and knees, which were starting to sting like fiery nettles. And my shoulder . . . *that* was going to be sore. I nodded and squeaked, "You?"

"Who, me?" he guffawed. "Not a scratch. Except for the heart attack when Mr. Tough Guy pushed you down. Would've tackled the big jerk myself, except Superhero Hickman here whisked me away so fast I have windburn on my schnoz."

We couldn't help but laugh. Ben's nose was indeed a mottled red, though I doubted it was windburn.

The plaza around the Rock had almost emptied. The campus police who remained after the arrests were having heated words with the White Pride people. The spokesman in the black tie held his chin up, lips tight, as if refusing to answer or get drawn into a debate, while the young guy in the red tie packed up the bullhorn in its case. Mark stooped and picked up something from the ground, then trotted our way.

His face was a road map of consternation. "What happened? Are you guys OK? I thought I had everybody's attention, and then—*balloey!*" Mark held out Josh's limp backpack. "What happened to this? Where are the books?"

Josh shoved his hands in his jeans pockets and hunched his shoulders. "Uh, some brawny dude, one of the NU students, I think, jerked it off my shoulder, the books fell out, and . . ." His shoulders sagged. "Guess the rest is history. I'm really sorry, Dr. Smith."

Mark rolled his eyes and shook his head. "Should've known. Black kid? Dreads? That's Matt Jackson. Weightlifter, Wildcats linebacker, third-year student. A fight looking for a place to happen. Should've talked with him beforehand, might've—"

He stopped midsentence. A group of White Pride people were coming our way, their mission accomplished. We all fell silent. They passed by silently, as if we were invisible. The young man in the red tie and his girlfriend, I assumed, brought up the rear. I didn't know where to look; I didn't want to provoke anything by staring. But as the girl came near, she caught my eye. My heart softened. I wanted to cry out, *"What is your name? I want to pray for you!"* Our glance held for only a second, and then she looked away.

The young man in the red tie let go of her hand, deliberately stepped close to Mark, muttered something under his breath, and then hustled after his group.

We all stared at Mark. "What did he say?" Denny demanded.

"Nothing."

"Mark!"

Mark's mouth twisted slightly. "He said, 'We know where you live.'"

BY THE TIME WE PULLED INTO THE GARAGE, I was a wreck. All the things that happened at the Rock, that *could've* happened, slid into my imagination like a mudslide loosened by the respite of the ride home. Even Denny was tight-lipped. I could see it in his eyes, mentally kicking himself that he didn't protect his wife and son. Josh brushed off any concerns, even though he had a bump above one eye where he hit the plaza bricks. "Hey, I fell on top of mom. Soft landing," he joked. But he went into his room and shut the door, and we didn't see him again for a couple of hours.

Amanda was talking on the phone—surprise, surprise—but actually hung up when we came in the house. "Hey. How'd it go?" she chirped.

I left Amanda to Denny and went into our bedroom, crawled under our wedding-ring quilt, and had a good bawl. Not sure what I was crying about. Delayed reaction to being scared out of my wits. Anger. Confusion. All of the above.

I heard the door open. "Jodi?" Denny's voice. "You OK?"

I poked my head out from under the quilt. "Yeah." I grabbed a tissue from the nightstand and blew my nose. "Just a little shaken."

"Um, it's almost seven. Mind if I order a pizza?"

"Whatever. Sure, fine."

The door closed.

He obviously didn't want to talk about it right now. Maybe I could talk to Avis. Or Florida. Both their husbands had been there.

They'd surely heard all about the rally by now. They'd understand. I found the bedroom extension on the floor under Denny's dirty sweats, punched the On button, and actually got a dial tone instead of Amanda. "The age of miracles has not passed," I muttered and punched in Avis's number.

No answer. I dialed Florida.

"Jodi? Girl, Carl and Peter just been tellin' Avis and me what happened at that rally—"

"Avis?"

"Yeah. She's here. Avis! It's Jodi. Get on the other phone."

Avis picked up. For some reason I started to blubber and found myself replaying the whole no-good, terrible, rotten day. Thinking God wanted me to go to the rally. Sloshing coffee all over Denny's pants. Being late to school. Denny's flat tire and the grease stain on his *other* pants. The rally, the bullhorn, the bully, the spilled books . . .

"I am *so mad* at Josh for buying those stupid books in the first place. And I'm mad at Mark for giving them back to him *at the rally*, for heaven's sake!" I rushed on, spilling out my anger at the NU student who mistook Josh for a skinhead white supremacist and pushed him around. "We ended up being in danger, not from the hate group, but from the students we came to support! Didn't even give Josh a chance to—"

"Girl!" Florida interrupted my volcanic flow. "That's what them hate groups *do*. Get folks all riled up, try to divide people, then sit back and watch the fireworks. I mean, you can pretty much guarantee a race riot if some white guy starts calling blacks and Latinos 'inferior' and 'mud races'—even the N-word, you said. On their own college campus!"

"Jodi?" Avis's voice sounded tinny on the extension. "What did you mean, God wanted you to go to the rally?"

"Not so sure now," I sniffled. "In the middle of the night, I thought He was telling me to go, you know, to pray. But—"

"Did you pray at the rally?"

"Well, yeah, sorta. There was this girl with the White Pride group, couldn't have been more than eighteen or nineteen. She looked scared, as if she didn't really want to be there. So I started praying for her. But, well, next thing I knew I was on the ground about to get stepped on."

"Jodi." Avis's voice got stronger. "Don't you see? God did send you to the rally to pray for that girl! But of course Satan didn't like it. Everything that happened today—from spilling your coffee to the flat tire to the football player mistaking Josh for a skinhead— was part of the spiritual battle going on. Even the books last night— and I'm not blaming Josh; he had good intentions—got us distracted from the business of prayer."

"You sayin' it now, Avis," Florida chimed in. "That devil, he one tricky dude. He got all sorts of distractions to keep us from doin' business in the spirit realm."

"I just want to encourage you, Jodi." Avis's words reached out to me like a warm hug. "You were obedient, and God is going to bless your prayer for that girl. I'm glad you and Josh weren't seriously hurt, though I know it had to be frightening. I think—when is our next Yada Yada meeting? We need to do some serious study about preparing ourselves for spiritual warfare. This is just the beginning."

I lay on the bed after we hung up, thinking about what Avis said. If I was obedient and had done what God wanted me to do, then maybe I was focusing too much on the negative stuff. After all, there were many things we could praise God for. Neither Josh nor I had actually gotten hurt. Just a scrape or two. Ben Garfield was OK. Mark had stood up to the White Pride guy in a classy way. He'd showed their rhetoric for what it was: lies and more lies. Peter Douglass and Carl Hickman had looked out for us, and Ben Garfield had come to our rescue . . .

I sat up. *Wow.* In the middle of a hate rally that nearly turned into a race riot, God had knit together the hearts of friends. Jew. Gentile. Black. White. Just like Peter Douglass had said last night at the Sisulu-Smiths: *"This isn't about race or color—not in God's eyes."* It made me feel—

Hungry.

Ravenous.

I jumped off the bed and flung open the door. "Hey, Denny! Has that pizza arrived yet?"

JOSH CAME OUT OF HIS ROOM long enough to help himself to his share of the large Gino's pizza—half spicy sausage, half pepperoni, mushrooms, extra cheese. "Uh, can I use the car tonight?" He jangled his keys in one hand, and held a slice of pizza in the other.

"Where are you going?" I frowned at the bruise over his eye.

He shrugged. "I dunno. Just feel jumpy. Want to get out for a while."

I knew Denny didn't like "destination unknown" any more than I did. But he growled, "OK." Tonight wasn't the night to get tight about the rules. Except—

"Wait a minute, Josh." I ran to get the alarm clock I'd bought after Avis told me about setting an alarm for curfew. "Shut this off when you get in tonight," I told him. "You don't have to knock on our door."

His eyes narrowed suspiciously. "And if it rings before I get in?"

"Grounded!" Amanda crowed. She was enjoying this.

Josh started to roll his eyes, but I jumped in. "It's mostly for me, Josh, so I don't lie awake worrying till you're home safe. I'll set it for fifteen minutes after your curfew to give you some leeway—and you can always call if you need more time. Just so we know."

"Whatever." The back screen door banged behind him as he went out.

The phone rang as Denny and Amanda divided the last of the pizza. "I'll get it!" Amanda jumped up, sucking pizza sauce off her fingers as she dashed for the phone. A moment later she was back, her face wrinkled in a frown. "For Dad." She handed the phone to Denny and whispered to me, "Sounds like Nony Sisulu-Smith, but she asked for Dad."

My ears perked up.

Denny listened a moment. "No, not since we left the rally . . . He said he was going back to his office for a while . . . Don't worry about us, Nony; we're fine . . . Yeah, it got a little rowdy, but . . . No, they didn't stick around either . . . By the way, Mark handled the situation very well. You would've been proud of him." He laughed. "Hey. Tell those two young rascals Mr. Denny says, 'Get in that bed!' . . . Don't worry, Nony. He probably turned off his cell and forgot to turn it on again . . . OK, then."

Denny came back to the table and reached for the last piece of pizza. "Nony. She's worried. Mark's not home yet and it's past the boys' bedtime, and he's not answering his cell."

JOSH'S "CURFEW ALARM" didn't awaken me, but the phone did.

Riiing . . . riiing . . . riiing . . . riiing—

I fumbled in the dark, practically lying across Denny to reach the phone on his side of the bed. He grunted in his sleep. The glowing red digits on the bedside clock said 12:35.

Grr. If this was Josh asking to stay out later—

"Hello?"

"Jodi . . ." The voice on the other end broke and began to cry. Female. Accent.

"Nony? Nony! What's the matter? Are you OK?"

Denny rose up on one elbow and leaned an ear close to the phone.

"Jodi." Nony's voice was barely a whisper. "Can you and Denny come? Right away! The police . . . the police just left. One of our neighbors found Mark . . . badly beaten . . . behind our garage. They took him to Evanston Hospital. He's unconscious . . . maybe lying there for hours. Oh, *please.* Come quickly!"

24

*D*enny snatched the phone. "Nony, wait. Come where? To your house? The hospital? . . . OK. We'll be there in twenty minutes." He practically slammed the phone down. "Hospital. She's waking the boys, taking them with her. We'll meet her there."

Heart pounding, I was already pulling on my jeans. Then I stopped, one leg in, one leg out. "Denny! We don't have a car! Josh might be out another thirty minutes!" *Or forty-five.* I cursed myself for giving him an extra fifteen minutes.

But to my surprise, a sliver of light peeked from beneath Josh's bedroom door. I flung it open without knocking. "Thank God you're home! Dad and I have to go to the hospital. It's Mark. Stay with Amanda—"

Josh vaulted from his bed, jerking off his earphones. "Hospital? What happened? What's wrong with Dr. Smith?"

Amanda came out of her room, rumpled with sleep, confused by the commotion. When Denny repeated Nony's phone call, she burst into tears. "I want to come too!"

Fear and disbelief propelled us out of the house in an amazingly short amount of time. By the time we backed the Dodge Caravan out of the garage, Denny had called Peter Douglass and Ben Garfield. As the minivan crossed Howard Avenue and sped through the near-empty streets of Evanston, I used the cell phone to call Stu and the Hickmans. I got Chris, who didn't want to wake up his mom, but I told him I'd personally wring his neck if he didn't.

Between phone calls my thoughts tumbled, hardly distinguishable from my thudding heart. *Oh God! Oh God! Not beaten up, not Mark!* Was he hurt badly? Nony must be out of her mind with panic. Should I call the rest of Yada Yada? Maybe I should wait, see what the situation was, and make more calls later.

The parking garage of Evanston Hospital, a six-story monolith usually packed with cars like a family-size can of sardines, swallowed us whole as we hurtled past the upright arm of the empty cashier's booth. Artificial lights and shadows danced as Denny squealed around corners, passed rows of empty spaces, and pulled into the area marked Emergency Room Parking Only.

Jogging through the automatic sliding doors, we saw Marcus and Michael Smith, sweatshirts pulled over matching Spider-Man pajamas and wearing gym shoes with no socks, huddled in waiting room chairs on either side of their mother. Nony lifted her face to us, streaked with fresh tears, her braided hair hidden beneath a snug black and gold scarf tied in the back. She stood up, and we all hugged. "Thank you," she whispered. "Thank you for coming. I didn't want to leave the boys alone, but now I can go in with Mark."

"What are they—?" Denny started.

Nony shook her head. "I don't know. They haven't told me

anything yet." She disappeared through the doors marked Do Not Enter. Hospital Personnel Only.

Amanda sat down cross-legged on the floor of the waiting room, and Michael, small for his ten years, cuddled into the curve of her arm. Marcus, at twelve the spitting image of his father, touched fists with Josh and sank back into the padded waiting room chair, shoulders hunched.

We waited. Neither Denny nor I spoke. I couldn't sit. I paced. How could this happen? *What* happened? *God!* I railed in my spirit. *This isn't supposed to happen! Didn't we pray?*

Peter and Avis hurried through the automatic doors a half-hour later, Stu on their heels, her tousled long hair caught up in a butterfly clip. Jeans, sweats—the attire of middle-of-the-night dashes to the hospital. Denny and Peter shook hands grimly. Peter muttered, "Don't need to guess who did this. Does Nony know?"

Denny shook his head slightly, nodding toward the two boys. Peter pressed his lips together.

Stu pulled me aside. "Does Nony know what? How does Peter know who did it? What happened, anyway? Is it serious?"

I wanted to throttle her. Too many questions! Didn't have answers anyway. I just shook my head. None of that was important right now. Only one thing mattered: was Mark OK?

We needed to pray!

I caught Avis's eye. As if reading my mind, she said, "Let's pray."

We pulled together in an awkward clump, holding hands. Even Michael and Marcus joined the circle, clinging to Amanda and Josh.

"Lord of heaven, Satan's having a heyday right now. But he's gone too far!" Avis made no effort to pray softly, and a frowzy-haired woman sitting nearby got up and moved to a chair on the other side of the room. "We're drawing a line in the sand, Satan. You've gone this far but no further! We're standing here in the gap, wearing the armor of God, ready to face the enemy!" She paused a moment, as if shifting her focus. "Jesus! By the authority of Your name and the power of Your shed blood, we say, 'Enough!' Mark belongs to You! By Your stripes he is healed!" Her voice choked up with emotion. "Oh Jesus, Jesus . . ."

I heard sniffles and peeked. Marcus was crying, trying to stifle the tears, wiping his nose on the sleeve of his sweatshirt. *Poor kid. He's scared to death about his father.* A lump stuck in my own throat.

"God, I don't know what happened; I only know that Mark is hurt." Stu, not much of a pray-out-loud person, gripped my hand as if holding on to a life preserver. "Please, Lord, You healed a lot of people when You walked this earth. I'm asking You to take care of our brother, Mark Smith. Whatever's wrong, make it right."

Whatever's wrong. We still didn't know how badly Mark was hurt. I glanced up, trying to peer beyond the doors. *Where's Nony?*

A small voice whimpered, "Please, God, don't let my daddy die."

That undid me. Tears spilled over, my nose started running, and I had to let go of Denny's and Stu's hands to fish in the pocket of my jeans for a tissue. None, of course. I slipped away until I found a box of hospital tissues.

When I came back to the circle, somebody had started the Lord's Prayer. "—Hallowed be Your name. Your kingdom come. Your will be done on earth as it is in heaven. Give us this day our daily bread. And forgive us our sins, as we forgive those who sin against us—"

I heard a gagging sound. Male. As if the word *forgive* had gotten stuck in the throat.

"—And lead us not into temptation, but deliver us from evil. For Yours is the kingdom, and the power, and the glory forever. Amen."

A hush followed, as the words of the prayer got a dose of reality there in that emergency waiting room. *"Your will be done"? "Deliver us from evil"?* as if the phrases themselves hung in the air, waiting to hear how bad it was, after Mark Smith had been beaten and left lying in the alley behind his house, maybe for hours.

Peter Douglass expelled a sharp breath, as though trying not to explode. "Don't know if I can pray that right now, God—that part about 'as we forgive those who sin against us.' I admit it, Lord. I'm angry! I'm furious. Some of us have a good idea who did this, and it wasn't an accident. I know vengeance belongs to You, but I'd sure like to see those thugs pay for this."

"Help us, Jesus," murmured Avis.

My own emotions felt strung too tightly to pray aloud; others probably felt the same way. Avis closed the prayer time with a verse from Psalm 50, the one about "call upon me in the day of trouble; I will deliver you, and you will honor me." "We're calling, Lord. Hear the prayers of our hearts!"

Our prayer circle broke up, but I felt grateful. Avis understood our silence.

We waited some more. The hands of the clock inched past three o'clock. Michael fell asleep, his head on Amanda's lap. Marcus and Josh went hunting for a vending machine. Avis sat with her Bible on her lap—did she go *anywhere* without her Bible?—reading the Psalms. Peter paced, patting his shirt pocket from time to time as if looking for a cigarette. I smiled slightly. He must've been a smoker in another life. At that moment, I understood the urge. I wanted something to do with my hands. Something to calm me down.

I slumped against Denny, grateful for his arm tight around my shoulder, even though his grip hurt my shoulder, still aching from the fall that afternoon . . .

The fall. The rally at the Rock. Mark treating the White Pride spokesman respectfully, in spite of the man's abusive words. Josh accused of being a skinhead, of being "one of them." Mark standing on the wall. The kid in the red tie threatening, "We know where you live."

Nony appeared. I didn't see her coming; she was just there. We all jumped.

Mark! Is he—? The unspoken, unfinished question from every heart hung in the air.

Exhaustion lined Nony's exquisite face. She spoke almost as if in a trance. "They're still doing tests. A CAT scan, an MRI, a PET scan, and . . . something else. An EEG, I think. Not sure what it stands for . . ."

"Nony, sit down." Avis put an arm around her and guided her to a chair.

Amanda started to shake Michael's sleeping form, but Nony held up her hand. "No," she whispered. "Don't wake him. In a moment." She looked at each of us in turn, as if orienting herself to where she was. "He's still unconscious. They say he's badly hurt— head trauma mostly. Eye injuries, hemorrhaging . . . but they don't know how much. The police said it looks like he was struck"—her voice wavered—"with a brick. Several times. Also some broken ribs and bruising on his side, as though he were kicked—"

"Mama!" Marcus reappeared with a can of pop, Josh on his heels. Michael woke up at the sound of his brother's cry, and Nony gathered her two young sons into her arms, trying to answer their barrage of questions simply. "Daddy's head is hurt. They're doing a lot of tests. We'll know more when they finish the tests . . . Yes, somebody hurt Daddy, but we don't know who—oh!"

Nony stood up as two men in rumpled sport coats and open shirt collars came out of the Hospital Personnel Only doors and headed our way. "Detective Maxwell. Detective Rollo," she acknowledged.

A sense of déjà vu made me feel weak in the knees. *Police asking us to leave the hospital room at Cook County so they could talk to Delores's son José after he'd been caught in gang crossfire a year ago. Police looming beside my hospital bed a couple of months later while I was crazy with pain and fear, to ask me about the car accident at the corner of Howard and Chicago that left a boy dead—*

I groped for an empty chair and sat down.

The older of the two detectives, a flabby-faced man with heavy-lidded eyes, picked at his teeth with his little fingernail. "These the friends you said may have seen your husband this afternoon?"

"Yes." Nony looked at us apologetically. "I'm not sure which of you were at that rally this afternoon, but, please, tell the detectives whatever you can about what happened." Her large eyes said, *And me.*

The detectives interviewed each of us in turn, and asked where they could reach Ben Garfield and Carl Hickman.

"We know who did this," Peter Douglass insisted. "One of those White Pride guys threatened Mark after the rally. He said, 'We know where you live.'"

Nony's eyes widened; fear tightened the muscles in her face. She drew Marcus and Michael closer.

"That so?" Detective Maxwell eyed the rest of us. We all nodded.

Except Josh. He hesitated. "Well, not exactly." We all looked at him. He shifted uncomfortably. "What I mean is, the guy muttered something to Dr. Smith, and my dad asked what he said. Dr. Smith didn't want to tell us, but my dad and Mr. Douglass insisted. That's when he told us what the guy said: 'I know where you live.' Like a threat."

25

The two detectives looked at each other. "What? You don't believe us?" Peter snapped. "Mark wanted to brush it off; he didn't take it seriously. But look what happened! They knew where he lived!"

Detective Maxwell spoke with irritating patience. "I didn't say I didn't believe you. We'll check it out. But if none of you actually heard this guy make a threat, we can't arrest him on hearsay." His notebook snapped shut. "We'll need to ask Dr. Smith himself. If . . . uh, when he regains consciousness."

Nony sank weakly into a chair.

"We're sorry about what happened, Mrs. Smith." Detective Rollo tried to smooth over his partner's blunt persona. "For both you and your boys. We'll be in touch. We *will* catch whoever did this to your husband. And we wish your husband the best."

The detectives had barely disappeared when Josh blurted, "You mean they can't go after that guy? I mean, if somebody tells you ahead of time he's been threatened, isn't that enough to at least check it out?" My son backed into a chair and put his head in his hands. "*Why* did I say anything? We *know* he said it."

Denny started to say something, but it was Nony who reached over and touched Josh on his knee. "Josh, you did the right thing. Better to have the truth come out up-front than later. It will all be for the best." But she looked up at the rest of us, standing around. "That's really what Mark told you? That one of the White Pride people said—"

"Mrs. Smith?" A white-coated doctor appeared. "I'm Dr. King. Do you mind stepping this way? We have some preliminary test results and need to—"

"Is my husband going to be all right?"

The doctor, who looked all of thirty and badly in need of sleep, cleared his throat. "He's stable. But his injuries are serious and we need your permission . . ." He beckoned. "Can you come this way?"

Nony took a hesitant step. "Could I . . . could someone come with me? If decisions need to be made?"

Stu offered to stay with the young people, and Peter, Avis, Denny, and I ended up with Nony in a curtained partition in the emergency room. The situation, the doctor explained gravely, was that Mark had a skull fracture, with possible bleeding in the brain— an "epidural hematoma," he called it. Mark's other injuries—broken ribs, damage to his eyes, many lacerations—would be treated as soon as possible, but they needed Nony's permission to perform immediate surgery before the bleeding did damage to his brain.

"How . . . ?" Nony looked bewildered.

The doctor looked uncomfortable. "We need to drill a small hole in the skull to drain the blood and relieve the pressure."

"Oh God," Nony moaned. I turned away. *Drill a hole?*

"Mrs. Smith, please." The doctor's voice was kind but urgent. "Time is critical."

Nony signed the necessary papers. A nurse told us we could move to the family waiting room on the surgical floor and directed us to the appropriate elevator. On the fifth floor, the small family waiting room was empty, but we pretty much filled it.

No one needed to tell us to pray.

THE HANDS OF THE CLOCK in the waiting room moved with agonizing slowness; at other times, the time seemed to leap forward. Where did the last hour go?

As daylight filled the sky beyond the rose and green hospital décor, Dr. King returned, saying the surgery had gone well, and they were now dealing with Mark's other injuries. As soon as he arrived in the ICU, Nony could see him. He ushered her to a private room with a phone so that she could make some phone calls.

Phone calls. I should call the rest of Yada Yada. I glanced at the sign that said No Cell Phones and headed for the elevator. "Mom?" Amanda came running after me. "I'm hungry. Can we get something to eat? Something for the boys too?"

Duh. Of course. We'd been up all night. I suddenly realized how tired I was. How tired everyone must be. "We'll get something for everyone, OK?"

I sent Amanda to the cafeteria with my one and only credit card—huh! That was a first!—and told her to pick up bagels or sweet rolls, juice, and coffee; I'd come back to help her carry it upstairs after I made my calls from the parking lot.

I called Florida first to give an update. "Girl, 'bout time ya called!" She was practically yelling. "Carl and I be wearin' a path in the floor, goin' nuts. How's Mark? What's happenin'? How's Nony?" I filled her in as best I could, heard her croak something under her breath when I said they had to drill a hole in his head.

"All right now," she said, "don't ya worry 'bout calling the rest of Yada Yada. It'll give me somethin' to do till Carla's foster—till those people pick up Carla at nine. This their Saturday, s'posed to have her all day, an' for once I'm glad of it. Means me an' Carl can come up there and let the rest of you get some rest. Though I don't know how much good he'll be. Girl! Never seen him so mad." She sucked in her breath. "He told me what that kid said to Mark after the rally. Jesus! Have mercy."

Relieved at not having to call the rest of Yada Yada and go over what happened to Mark a half-dozen more times, I met up with Amanda in the hospital cafeteria and helped her carry the two trays of packaged sweet rolls, a bunch of bananas, bottles of juice, and cups of steaming coffee. I didn't even ask how much it cost; I just hit the elevator button with my elbow and scuttled inside when the doors opened.

The doors slid shut and the elevator began to rise. "Mom?" Amanda's voice squeaked a little. I looked at my daughter. Her face sagged with lack of sleep; her forehead wrinkled with worry. "The sophomore dance is tonight." Her eyes filled with tears. "What am I going to do?

THE SOPHOMORE DANCE? *How can we think about that now?* I managed a wobbly smile. "Let's get this food up to the waiting room."

Hoshi Takahashi had arrived while we were getting breakfast, her dark eyes brimming with disbelief. We hugged but said nothing. I could only imagine what was going on in her emotions. First, the trauma her own mother, visiting from Japan, had suffered when Becky Wallace robbed Yada Yada at knifepoint last fall. And now this violence against her "adopted family" in the States. But her concern seemed to focus on Marcus and Michael. "The boys are exhausted," she said to Nony in her careful English. "I will take them home and stay with them if—Stu? Could you please give us a ride?"

Even after Hoshi, Stu, and the boys left, the waiting room was getting crowded. The pastor of the Sisulu-Smiths' new church arrived, along with his wife—an African-American couple in their late fifties or early sixties. He had touches of gray in his close-cropped hair, as if it had been airbrushed; she was pleasantly plump, with a sweet, sad smile, as though she'd seen a good deal of sorrow in her life. Nony briefly introduced them as "Pastor Joseph Cobbs and First Lady Rose Cobbs," then she huddled with them, talking and praying.

I tugged on Denny's shirt. "That's the pastor from New Morning Church," I murmured. "Aren't they supposed to start using Uptown's space tomorrow afternoon for services?"

Denny frowned like one of my third graders trying to decode test instructions. "Man! That reminds me; I should call Pastor Clark. He'd want to know about Mark—if he hasn't heard it on the news already." He disappeared with the cell phone.

A nurse summoned Nony to the ICU, accompanied by the Cobbses. I felt a twinge of jealousy. *We've been replaced.* Then a spiritual slap upside my head. *Jodi, let it go. Nony needs all the support she can get.* I looked at Amanda, curled in a lump in a chair. I really should get her home and let her get some sleep. And Willie Wonka! I hit my forehead. *Good grief.* No one was home to let the dog out!

I beckoned to Josh. "Would you . . . ?" He looked at me, his eyes rimmed with red. "Never mind." Better take Amanda myself. This was no time to send my kids off to deal with this alone.

I DREADED WHAT I WOULD FIND AT HOME. Either a miserable Willie Wonka, in pain because he couldn't empty his bladder, or a puddle by the back door. Or worse. But the chocolate Lab was panting happily in the backyard, hind legs splayed out frog-fashion, keeping Becky Wallace company as she watered the flowerbeds. I half-expected Amanda to go into her daily Wonka routine, making a big fuss over the dog while getting her face and ears licked. But Amanda walked silently up the walk and into the house.

The back door was standing open.

Becky screwed the nozzle of the water hose to shut off the spray of water. "Hey, Jodi. How's Dr. Smith?" When I didn't answer, she glanced at our back door, then back at me. "Hope ya don't mind I let the dog out. I knew you guys were up at the hospital all night. Stu woke me when she got the call."

My wound-up emotions were playing on two-track stereo—but different songs. Relief that someone had taken care of Willie Wonka. Irritation that Becky Wallace had access to our house key. I had to choose.

"Thanks a lot, Becky. I was worried about the dog. You . . . did the right thing." I started for the house and then turned back. "Mark was beaten up pretty bad. He's still unconscious. They had to do surgery on his head. Other stuff too." Tears welled up in my eyes, and suddenly, standing there in the middle of our postage-stamp backyard, my shoulders shook, and I started to cry. All the unshed tears, the fear, the questions, the unknown future that I'd held in for Nony's sake, came sputtering out as if the nozzle of my emotional hose had been turned to On.

Embarrassed, I turned away, wanting to disappear inside the house. But I heard, "Hey." And felt arms around me. Becky's arms. "Go ahead, Jodi. Cry. If ya don't, it'll make ya crazy." She pulled me into her embrace. "I know."

I bawled on Becky Wallace's shoulder for a few minutes, aware that even five minutes ago I could not have imagined such a thing. I finally fished out a used tissue. "I better go inside. Amanda's supposed to go to a big dance tonight. Don't know what's going to happen about that." I gave her a wet smile. "But thanks again. Wonka likes you." *He trusts you. More than I let myself. But dogs know.*

AMANDA SLEPT TILL THREE in the afternoon. I tried to. But I no sooner dozed off than the phone rang. "Sista Jodee!" Chanda's voice squealed in my ear. "Me find a 'ouse today! Believe it! An', *heh heh heh,* you should see dem faces when I say me goin' to pay cash!" Chanda's giggles felt like salt on raw nerves. On any other day I'd whoop and holler to celebrate with Chanda. Instead, I had to throw bad news on her rejoicing. My brief, terse comments met with a stunned silence. Then a wail. "No! Don't be tellin' me dat Nony's mon got beat! No no no! God! Don' be doin' dis to me!"

As soon as I hung up with Chanda, the phone promptly rang again. "Senõra Baxter?" It was José. "We heard about Dr. Smith. Is it true? Mama's working today but wants you to let her know what she can do."

As I considered taking the phone off the hook, it rang again. It was Ruth. "Jodi. How's Nony? Would Ben take me up to the hospital? No. Tells me the car brakes are 'acting funny.' Excuses, excuses. Then Yo-Yo wants a ride to the hospital; suddenly the car brakes get healed. Off they go. So I'm having some stomach trouble. It's nothing, nothing . . ."

I finally gave up on sleep and made myself some strong coffee. Denny called when I was on my second cup, said Avis and Peter finally took Nony home to get some sleep. Florida and Carl Hickman were holding the fort at the hospital until Nony came back. Ben and Yo-Yo had come; also Adele, but she only stayed ten minutes. A number of Mark's colleagues from Northwestern came by; other visitors he didn't know. Last report from the doctor before Nony went home: Mark was stable, still sedated from the surgery, but there was concern about possible coma.

Coma? I sucked in my breath. "What does that mean?"

"I don't know, Jodi. But it's serious. I think Josh and I will—"

"Mom?" Amanda's sleepy voice behind me made me jump. I held up a "one moment" finger to her.

"—come home, maybe we can come back to the hospital this evening."

I looked at Amanda. She was holding the dress from her *quinceañera* birthday party, with its pale blue, shimmering layers. The one she planned to wear tonight to the dance.

26

wo worry lines pinched together between Amanda's eyes. "Mom? I don't know if I should go tonight. It feels dumb going to a stupid dance when Dr. Smith just got hurt so bad, and we don't . . . we don't know . . ." Her lip started to tremble.

"Amanda. We're not going to go there! A lot of prayer is going up for Dr. Smith, and we've got to believe that God is going to bring him through this!"

Suddenly I very much wanted Amanda to go to the sophomore dance. I wanted to worry about her. Wanted to get her some new underwear so she could feel special. Wanted to fuss about extending her curfew, about whether she was dressed warm enough for a cool spring evening, about . . . whatever moms fuss about. I wanted a semblance of normal life. Wanted to be reassured that the world hadn't suddenly spun out of control. "You should go. Dr. Smith would want you to go. We'll . . ."

I felt torn between loyalty to Nony and loyalty to my daughter. Where was I needed most? "We'll work out something about getting you there and back." I gave Amanda a hug. "I've got the car. Want to go shopping for new underwear? Come on."

Funny how important that new underwear had become.

Amanda shrugged. "Not really. It doesn't matter. What I've got is OK." She still hesitated. "Maybe I should call José."

"Sure. Call José. Then take a nice, long bath. Want me to paint your toenails?" *Supper. I really need to think about an early supper too.* None of us had eaten anything since our cafeteria breakfast.

Denny and Josh got home while Amanda was still in the tub, which gave me a chance to talk with Denny about getting her to the dance. Denny, usually so firmly in Amanda's corner, sank into a dining room chair and heaved a couple of deep sighs. "Gotta tell ya, Jodi, I wish we didn't have to deal with this right now."

I touched his shoulder. "I know." Weariness threatened to undo my resolve. "But no telling how long Mark's going to be in the hospital. Life needs to go on."

Denny's head sank into his hands. I went back into the kitchen to finish chopping vegetables for the pot of hamburger vegetable soup I had simmering on the stove. Out of the corner of my eye, I saw him get up from the chair and disappear into the hallway. A few minutes later, he was back in the kitchen doorway.

"I asked Josh to take Amanda to the dance and bring her home." Denny's jaw was set. "He's not happy about it, but he agreed. I did not ask him to chaperone at the dance—we have to let that one go, Jodi." He leaned a hand against the doorjamb, as if needing a support to hold him up. "I'm going to get a couple of hours of sleep, then I'd like to go back up to the hospital. I'd like you to go with me, but . . . that's up to you."

JOSH DROPPED US OFF at the Morse Street Station to catch the northbound el. Denny and I watched the red taillights of the Dodge Caravan head toward Sheridan Road, which would take them to the Lakeshore Drive and into the city. Amanda—looking pretty and sweet, if not bouncy—waved at us gravely from the middle seat of the minivan.

We didn't talk much on the Red Line train, transferring at Howard Street to the Purple Line, which took us right to Evanston Hospital. We got our visitors' badges at the front desk and took the elevator to the ICU. The only person in the waiting room was Peter Douglass, who'd changed out of his rumpled sweats into a pair of slacks and a sport shirt.

Avis's new husband shook Denny's hand and gave me a tired smile. Peter Douglass wasn't exactly the hugging type. "Nony's in the ICU. I thought she needed some time alone with Mark. But I think she'd like to know you're here, would want you to come in."

"Is Mark . . . ?"

Peter shook his head. "Still sedated 'just in case.' Tomorrow they'll wean him off the anesthesia and"—he moistened his lips— "see if he wakes up." Peter turned away, as if not wanting to speculate any further.

"You go, Jodi." Denny gave me a little push. "See if Nony wants any more company. They don't usually want more than one or two visitors in the ICU."

Peter gave me the room number, so I sidled right past the nurses' station and peeked into the room. Even though I knew Mark had been badly beaten, even though I knew he'd had surgery on his head just hours ago, even though I knew he'd been unconscious since they found him in the alley behind his home . . . I wasn't prepared for the sight of Nony's husband laid out on that hospital bed like a corpse, his head swathed in stark white bandages, his body hooked up to every kind of machine imaginable. I wasn't even sure it was Mark. The face cradled by the bandages didn't look familiar—it was swollen, darker, misshapen.

"Oh God," I groaned. I couldn't move from the doorway; I just stood there trying to take it in. A tube in his nose was dwarfed by a much larger tube down his throat, hooked up to a ventilator pumping air into his lungs. Various tubes and wires ran from his body like a ball of string that had come undone, connecting to an IV pole, a catheter, an EKG monitor above his head, and a few other machines I didn't recognize. His legs were wrapped in compression stockings, rising and falling with artificial "exercise" to keep his blood moving.

I steadied my nerves with a slow, silent breath and stepped into the room. The room seemed empty of anyone other than Mark and his machines. Where was Nony? As I came closer to the bed, I saw a dark shape bent over the chair in the corner and heard Nony's voice. I took a step or two closer. She was praying. In agony.

"Oh God, *my God!* Why have You forsaken me? Oh my God, I cry out all day and all night, but You do not answer!"

I held my breath. Those were Jesus's words on the cross; they also came from one of the psalms, but I wasn't sure which one. I waited for her to go on, but she seemed to just back up and repeat the same prayer. "Oh God! Why have You forsaken me? What have I done? Are You punishing me? Punishing us for our sins? I would confess them if I knew what they were! Show me, God! Show me! I'll do anything! Just don't—please don't take Mark away from me." Her shoulders shook in not-so-silent weeping.

I started to tiptoe out of the room, but before I got to the door, I heard my name. "Jodi? Is that you?" Nony got off her knees, shaking out the big, loose caftan tangled around her body and blowing her nose into a tissue. "Don't go. I am glad you've come."

We hugged for a long minute. Then, surprising myself at my boldness, I asked, "What psalm were you praying?"

She drew a shuddering breath, her eyes resting on Mark's still form on the bed. "Psalm 22—the first part anyway. Couldn't get past the first few verses."

I wasn't in the habit of taking my Bible everywhere like Avis and Nony, so I reached for Nony's big Bible that was still open on the chair. "Let's read the whole thing together. I'll read, OK?"

I pulled up a second chair, glad for something to do, something to say. I didn't remember Psalm 22 in particular, but I knew the psalmist often cried out in despair and then reaffirmed his faith in God. We began at the beginning: "My God, my God, why have you forsaken me?" But I kept going: "In you our fathers put their trust; they trusted and you delivered them. . . . From birth I was cast upon you; from my mother's womb you have been my God . . . Roaring lions tearing their prey open their mouths wide against me. I am poured out like water; and all my bones are out of joint"—*Uh-oh.* Should I continue?—"But you, O LORD, be not far off. O my Strength, come quickly to help me. . . . I will declare your name to my brothers; in the congregation I will praise you . . ."

When we'd read the entire psalm, we just sat quietly, holding hands, my pale one, hers a rich nut-brown, listening to the *beep, beep* of the monitors, the *whoosh* of the ventilator. Suddenly I realized that the very next psalm was Psalm 23. The Shepherd Psalm. I didn't need the Bible. I just began to pray the familiar verses: "The LORD is my shepherd; I shall not be in want . . ."

After a moment, Nony's voice joined mine. "Yea, though I walk through the valley of the shadow of death"—*beep, beep . . . whoosh*—"I will fear no evil, for You are with me . . ."

I RETURNED TO THE WAITING ROOM, and Denny went in. He and Nony both came out a few minutes later; Denny's face had paled. I glanced at the clock. Almost ten. I desperately needed to get some sleep. But I hated to leave Nony alone. *Should we . . . ?*

"Nonyameko, go home." Peter laid a hand on Nony's shoulder. "The boys need you. I will spend the night with Mark. You can come back in the morning."

I wanted to throw my arms around Peter and kiss him. Knowing Nony could go home was a gift to me too. She might even listen to Peter.

"I can sleep in the morning," he continued. "After all, New Morning Church is meeting in the afternoon at Uptown Community tomorrow, correct? I can attend their service." He smiled. "See? It all works out. Ah. Look who's here!"

Josh and Edesa Reyes walked in the door. I blinked. *Josh and Edesa?* Wasn't Josh supposed to be . . .

Edesa, looking very American—and very young—in her slim jeans and sky blue sweater, headed straight for Nony and gave her a warm hug. Josh stuck his hands in his pockets and shrugged. "Edesa really wanted a chance to see Mrs. Smith, so I gave her a ride."

"But what about Amanda and José?" I hissed, hopefully out of Nony and Edesa's hearing, who were heading out the door to see Mark. "Isn't the dance supposed to be over at ten?"

"Yes, son." Denny frowned. "You were supposed to pick them up."

Josh held up a hand. "Mom. Dad. Relax. Amanda's home already. She didn't want to stay at the dance. She called me at Edesa's and asked me to pick them up. And Edesa wanted to come to the hospital, so I thought I could give you guys a ride home. See? It all works out."

A ride home. Well, *that* part was good. I wasn't really looking forward to the el at this time of night. I started gathering my purse and jacket. "Denny? We should go. Oh." I glanced down the hall. "Guess we should wait for Edesa." I looked at Josh, frustrated. "If Amanda's so upset about Dr. Smith that she left the dance early, I'm not sure you should've left her home alone."

"Mom! Chill." There was no humor in Josh's face. "I didn't leave her home alone. José's with her. I dropped them off at the house and then came up here. I can take him home when I take Edesa. Give me a minute anyway; I want to see Dr. Smith."

Oh, great. Just great. I watched Josh disappear down the hall. *Amanda and José were home alone . . . together.*

IT WAS ALMOST ELEVEN when we finally got home. Josh was going to wait out front since he still had to take José and Edesa home, but cars were parked bumper to bumper under the dim streetlights, and the street was too narrow to double-park. He pulled into the garage and said he'd wait until we sent José out.

Denny and I walked silently to the back door. OK, this was weird. Our daughter and the love of her life were alone in the house.

Our son and the love of his life—though she probably didn't know it—were alone in the garage. Denny and I were treading the sidewalk between them, as if trying to make it across a high wire. For some reason I felt an incredible urge to laugh hysterically. Or cry.

I did neither. *Just nerves*, I told myself, as we unlocked the door and called out, "Amanda? We're home!" We needed to be careful. The trauma of Mark's beating, the all-night vigil, his surgery, the waiting, the fear, the not-knowing had all of us wound up too tight, like my grandparents' windup school clock that sprung its spring one day.

"Amanda?" Denny called again. No answer. But there was a light on in the living room and some kind of music. We headed toward the archway—and stopped.

Amanda and José were sprawled in a corner of the couch, sound asleep, in each other's arms.

27

I didn't trust myself. "Amanda! José!" Denny shook them both, his voice sharp. Startled awake, José untangled himself from Amanda's weight on his chest and jumped up, his dress shirt rumpled, his hair mussed. Amanda sat up, still wearing her pale blue *quinceañera* dress, and looked blearily at both of us in turn. Her mascara was smeared; she'd been crying. "Oh. You're home."

A touch of panic shone in José's eyes. "Señor Baxter! Señora! I'm sorry! We . . . we fell asleep! Amanda was so sad. I was, you know, just trying to comfort her."

"José. Go home. Josh is waiting for you out in the garage. Amanda?" Denny pulled Amanda off the couch. "Go to bed. We'll talk in the morning." He propelled Amanda down the hall without saying good-bye to José. I stared after them as José split one way, Denny and Amanda the other.

Well. Kick the kid out? This was a different Denny.

I locked the back door behind José and watched until the lights of the minivan disappeared down the alley, my emotions tumbling all over themselves. Had anything happened while Amanda and José were here alone? They'd still had their clothes on. Huh! As if that cinched anything. A lot of petting could go on in, on, around, and under clothes. *I should know. Denny and I strayed close to the line numerous times while we were courting.*

A whine near my knees told me Willie Wonka wanted out, so I unlocked the door again and stepped out onto the back porch while the dog scrambled down the few steps to the yard. The night was balmy and clear, allowing a few bright stars to shine through the haze of city lights. I leaned against a porch post and took a deep breath. And another. *God, I don't need this right now! Mark Smith is hooked up to a zillion machines in the ICU and maybe in a coma. Nony is a wreck, and who can blame her? She's going to need all the help she can get—care for her kids, people to stay with Mark so she can get some rest, meals, probably even stuff like grocery shopping or taking the kids to school! Somewhere out there are the evil people who did this thing. The last thing I need is a runaway romance under my own roof.*

Willie Wonka stood at the bottom of the steps as if hoping for a hand up. "Forget it," I muttered. "You're on your own." He finally labored stiffly to the porch proper, throwing in a few grunts for good measure and giving me a reproachful look as he passed. I let the dog into the house but hesitated before going in myself. Denny was uptight. Amanda was sad—and using it as an excuse to bend the rules. Josh had ended up at Edesa's apartment tonight—why? He probably needed someone to talk to. He was definitely shaken by the attack on Mark after the rally yesterday.

And me? I was beyond tired. Almost too tired to sleep. I felt like a zombie. I'd been awake for the last forty hours. Too tired to help the rest of my family weather this trauma. But how could we rest? Somewhere out there were the people who did this to Mark. An evil lurking in the shadows . . .

That did it. I bolted through the back door and snapped the lock. Then I pressed my back against the door in the dark kitchen, heart pounding. *God, I want to pray! But I don't really know how to pray against "principalities and powers." Feels like I'm still in prayer kindergarten! I need You, Lord! My family needs You! Mark and Nony need You! Yada Yada needs You! This is too big for any of us!*

A face darted across my consciousness, interrupting my silent cries to God. A pale, frightened face, young, rather plain. The kind of face that could use a good session at Adele's Hair and Nails. But our eyes had locked on the plaza around the Rock.

And that girl with the White Pride people. She needs You, too God. I don't know her name, but . . .

But God did. Wow. That was a thought.

HOW WE BAXTERS ALL GOT UP THE NEXT MORNING, got ourselves dressed, fed on cold cereal, and to church on time is beyond me. I didn't hear Josh come in. Slept right through it. Didn't set the curfew alarm either. The laundry hampers overflowed, and the refrigerator shelves yawned emptily. Life seemed to be on hold. I needed an extra Saturday just to catch up on chores.

We checked in with Nony by phone before leaving for church and found out that Hoshi was spending the day with the boys so Nony could be up at the hospital—if she could get past the media people camped out on her block. As for Mark, so far no change. They were going to wean him off the sedation this morning.

"Pray, Jodi." Nony's voice seemed to ache with weariness. "And ask Uptown Community to pray. Mark needs an outpouring of prayers."

The communion table sat in front of Uptown's meeting room with its embroidered cloth covering the "wine" and the bread. June first—the first Sunday of the month. I thought Avis might be leading worship this morning, but she came in, conservatively dressed in a black pantsuit and black-and-white print silk blouse, and sat down next to Stu and Becky. Alone. Peter must be sleeping off his night in the hospital. He'd said he was going to attend New Morning's service this afternoon.

Pastor Clark announced the call to worship from Isaiah 55: "Come, all you who are thirsty, come to the waters; and you who have no money, come, buy, and eat! . . . Give ear and come to Me; hear Me, that your soul may live." The praise team launched into the first song, but my thoughts were still on Avis's husband. Would Peter find New Morning Christian Church more comfortable than Uptown Community? Here, as a black male, he was definitely a minority. Even when he was courting Avis, he'd been visiting other churches. Maybe he'd start attending New Morning regularly and want to go there when they moved into their new building. What would Avis do then?

I felt a tiny tug of resentment. New Morning using our building was almost like having two services. One mostly white, one mostly black. Would people like the Hickmans and Douglasses end up being drawn away?

Don't go there, Jodi. Open your heart to Nony's and Mark's church— they're hurting today. This assault on Mark must feel like an assault on all of them . . .

When it was time to celebrate the Lord's Supper, Pastor Clark mentioned the assault on Mark Smith and said he had not yet regained consciousness. "Dr. Smith spoke recently at our men's breakfast about the troubling events on Northwestern University's campus," Pastor Clark added. "Many of us also met the Sisulu-Smiths at Avis and Peter Douglass's wedding. Denny Baxter? Can you tell us more than the sound bites we're hearing on the news?"

I felt sorry for Denny. He hadn't been expecting this, and I knew he was still struggling to keep his own tumultuous feelings under control. He went to the front and somehow found words to give a brief account of the rally on Friday and Mark's efforts to speak the truth about White Pride's racist and violent views. Denny had to stop and clear his throat. "The situation was tense and things got a bit out of control—"

I sucked in my breath and glanced at Josh, half-hidden behind the soundboard at the back of the room, but Denny skipped the details.

"—but thankfully, no one got hurt. Until . . ." Denny tried to clear his throat again. "Until late Friday night, on his way home, when Mark Smith was attacked in the alley behind his home. The police haven't made any arrests, but there is reason to believe this may be related to the racist rally earlier in the day." Denny shook his head. He was done. He couldn't say anymore.

Pastor Clark came alongside Denny and put an arm around his shoulder. "Dr. Smith is not only a respected member of the faculty at Northwestern and a good friend of several in our congregation—"

"Jesus! Help us!" Florida cried out. I could see Stu dabbing at her eyes with a handkerchief. I could hardly bear to look at Denny's face at the front; he looked miserable.

"—but also a member of New Morning Christian Church," Pastor Clark went on, still with a firm grip on Denny's shoulder, "the congregation that will be leasing space from us here at Uptown until they locate a suitable facility in the Howard Street area. As host to this congregation that has suffered a deeply personal tragedy, we need to keep them lifted up in our prayers."

Around the room, people began reaching out until we were all holding hands up and down the rows as various ones spoke out in prayer—praying for Dr. Mark Smith, praying for his family, praying for his congregation. And I was sure New Morning, coming together in this very room that afternoon, would be doing the same thing. I squirmed. Something didn't seem right. One building, two congregations. One body, two separate services. I stared at the communion table, waiting for us to "eat and drink together." All I could see was broken bread and spilled wine.

AS PEOPLE MILLED ABOUT AFTER THE SERVICE, Avis caught my eye and beckoned me into a corner, snagging Florida, Stu, and Becky on the way. "When is the next Yada Yada meeting . . . next week at Stu's house?" She shook her head. "We need to get together to pray before then. Today, if possible. I know everyone is praying, but God is pressing on my heart the importance of 'Where two or three come together in My name . . .' There's spiritual power in praying together with the authority of the name of Jesus."

"Girl, I'm there. Can't fight no spiritual war with little skir-mishes. We gotta call in the troops." Florida raised her voice. "Carla! Cut out that runnin'!"

Avis frowned. "There's likely to be a lot of visitors up at the hospital on Sunday afternoon, but it doesn't matter. We need to do this. We especially need to pray *with* Nony. Jodi? Can you help me call the sisters, see who can make it this evening?"

I hesitated. My weekend had already been chopped into pieces. When was I going to get my laundry done? Pick up some groceries? Denny would surely want to go see Mark. Shouldn't we see if Nony needed some practical help? The kids had youth group at five. And we hadn't talked to Amanda yet about last night . . .

Listen to yourself, Jodi Baxter! Didn't you tell God last night you wanted to get out of prayer kindergarten? That you needed help knowing how to pray against "principalities and powers"? Warfare doesn't wait for laundry and groceries! Don't worry about the details. It'll all get done. Somehow.

"Well, you know I can't come." Becky wagged her ankle with the electronic monitor attached under her jeans. Then she shrugged. "But guess it don't matter—I don't know that much about prayin' . . . or holy war or whatever ya called it, Flo."

"What? Ain't we got permission from that parole agent yet for this girl to attend Yada Yada on Sunday nights?" Florida was indignant. "Stu, you can move mountains—"

When she wants to, I thought.

"—so do your thang, girl! An' hurry up about it."

Avis gave Becky a sympathetic hug. "Your prayers are important, too, Becky. And even if you can't come up to the hospital with us tonight . . ." Avis paged through her Bible. "Pray Psalm 27. The Word of God is one of our spiritual weapons. We need to fill our prayers with the promises of God."

"Uh, I don't have a Bible."

I cringed. Wasn't I the one who'd offered to get Becky a Bible?

"Here. Take mine." Avis thrust her big Bible with the well-worn pages into Becky's hand. "Keep it until we get you one of your own." She looked at the rest of us. "Five o'clock at Evanston Hospital sound good? Jodi? Can you help make the calls?"

I nodded, feeling like a recruit who'd enlisted in the army but hadn't figured on giving up civilian life.

28

By the time Stu and I pulled into the parking garage at the hospital at five o'clock, I felt chagrined at my petty excuses. Everything got done. Somehow. We'd scratched our usual "sit-down Sunday dinner" and made sandwiches. Amanda agreed to run laundry loads while doing her homework. *Probably trying to earn a few brownie points after breaking the rules last night, but so what?* While I made phone calls to Yada Yada, Josh and Denny went to the hospital to see Mark and then took the grocery list to the store, along with a list from Hoshi for the Sisulu-Smith household. Of course, we ended up with Ben & Jerry's Super Fudge Chunk ice cream instead of the store brand, a whole salmon *sans* its head, and two enormous bags of tortilla chips—but again, so what?

Everybody was trying.

Stu pointed out a WGN-TV news van parked outside the hospital, but we didn't see any activity. *Waiting for news—the vultures.* Made me mad that the media dared to invade Nony's personal crisis and reduce it to sound bites.

When we walked into the ICU waiting room, Delores and Edesa were already there; so were Yo-Yo, Ruth, and Ben. Ruth looked her usual frumpy self and kept fussing at Nony. "You look terrible. Vitamins you need. E and B-12. I'll bring them tomorrow. You want Marcus and Michael to see their mother in the hospital too?"

Ruth must be feeling better.

The rest of us hung back until other visitors had a chance to offer condolences to Nony. Many were college age, probably some of Mark's students. I wanted to grab Delores and ask how she was doing—we still hadn't connected by phone since the last Yada Yada meeting—but I got waylaid by Ben Garfield. "Is Denny home? Do you think he'd mind if I hung out at your house till these two"—he jerked a thumb at Ruth and Yo-Yo—"need a ride home?"

"Oh. Sure. No problem." I hoped. "I'll bring Ruth and Yo-Yo to the house so you don't have to come back up here." Knowing Ben, he probably had a six-pack in the trunk of his Buick he'd be all too happy to share with Denny, but I wasn't going to go there. *Probably good for Denny to have company tonight, maybe watch a game on TV,* I thought, as the silver-haired man headed for the elevator. Denny had been unusually subdued all weekend, and we hadn't had much time to talk. Probably because both of us felt as though we were swimming through dark, murky water and were doing good just to keep from drowning in our turbulent emotions.

To my surprise, all the Yadas made it except Hoshi, who was taking care of Nony's boys like a doting aunt. Even Chanda huffed up to the ICU floor, though she announced she'd have to leave early to meet with a real-estate agent. "To go tru' me new 'ouse, you know," she said by way of announcement.

"That's nice, Chanda," I said. But any interest Chanda hoped to spark in her new house got brushed aside as a nurse showed us into a "family consultation room" where we could have privacy for our prayer time. The room was a bit tight, and several sisters ended up sitting on the floor. I already knew from Denny and Josh that Mark was not yet conscious, even though the doctors had weaned him off the sedation. I desperately wanted to ask Nony what the doctors were saying about his prognosis, but I hesitated. I didn't want to hear it if it was bad news. Didn't want Nony to have to say it.

As if sensing my questions—and everyone else's, no doubt—Nony's eyes sought out Delores. "Delores? Please, could you explain what the doctor said this afternoon?" Her voice was strained, hoarse with fear and too many tears.

Delores nodded soberly. "*Si*, of course. The good news is that they weaned Mark off the ventilator today, and he *is* breathing on his own—"

"Jesus! Thank ya!" Florida breathed.

"Also, they gradually reduced the artificial sedation, but . . ." Delores cleared her throat. "As yet, he is still unconscious. It is too soon to call it a true coma, but there is concern. They are monitoring the head injury for signs of pressure or swelling, but so far, everything is stable since the surgery."

"Yeah." Yo-Yo stuffed her hands inside the bib of her overalls, face glum. "But if he does wake up, he ain't gonna be able to see nothin' with those bandages on both eyes. That'd sure freak me out."

"Eyes? What's wrong wit 'is eyes?" Chanda broke in. "Why no one tell me not'ing?"

"Because we don't know anything, Chanda." Nony's voice had

an edge. "They were hoping he would wake up so he could tell them, you know, in an eye exam, what he can and cannot see. But he didn't wake up, did he!" She buried her face in her hands.

Chanda's lip trembled. A few eyes got wet.

Avis leaned forward. "Sisters. We don't need to know all the particulars to pray. In fact, sometimes we 'know' too much. We let the facts, the circumstances, or what people are saying dictate our prayers. Like the disciples in the middle of the storm at sea, we give in to fear. But when the storm was at its worst, Jesus appeared to them, and He said, 'It is I. Don't be afraid.'"

"That's right. That's right," Florida murmured, waving her hand in the air.

"In Matthew 18, Jesus promised that when two or three followers come together in His name, He is among them. We have come together *in the name of Jesus* to stand in the gap for Mark and for Nony and their children. Jesus is *here*. So we——"

Several voices chimed in. "——don't need to be afraid!"

"That's right. That's right," Florida said again.

"Oh God. Oh God!" Nony began to weep. "You are my refuge and strength, my ever-present help in trouble! Your Word says I don't need to be afraid, though the earth gives way and the mountains fall into the heart of the sea! But . . ." Fresh tears flowed. "Help me, Lord. Help me! Because I am afraid."

Delores and Edesa, on either side of Nony, wrapped their arms around her. My vision blurred. I was afraid too. Afraid that Mark would die. Afraid that Nony and her boys would be left alone. Afraid of the spark fanned by the hate group. Afraid of what could so easily happen when emotions exploded. And afraid of . . . afraid of what could happen if Dr. Mark Smith, professor of history, died at the hands of——

"God, we're all afraid." Florida began to pray. "But we know the Evil One wants us to be afraid, 'cause then we take our eyes off You, and we gonna be sinkin' just like ol' Peter. But instead we gonna put on the armor of God and *stand*! Stand against that ol' devil, who only comes to steal, kill, and destroy. But You! You're the Good Shepherd, who gave His life for us sheep. We're already under the blood. You already fought ol' Satan and won. We're gonna stand on that, Jesus. Stand together. You came to give us life. Life! Hallelujah! Oh Jesus! . . ."

WE PRAYED UP A GOOD STORM FOR THE NEXT HOUR. I felt my fear melting under the passion of the prayers of my sisters. *God is who the Word says He is: Elohim—All-Powerful! Jehovah-Jireh—Provider! Jehovah-Rapha—Healer! El-Shaddai—the All-Sufficient One!* Nony, too, prayed several times, her voice growing stronger each time. Don't know what the nurses or other folks thought who walked past our closed door—we got kind of loud at times—but nobody came in to tell us to be quiet.

Chanda slipped out to meet her realtor, but as I scooted my knees over so she could get by, she leaned her mouth close to my ear. "Mind if I call you soon, Sista Jodee? De new 'ouse—it's so beautiful. I want you to see." She beamed at me and closed the door behind her.

Hmph. Maybe if the sun stands still to create more hours in the day. I hadn't even had time to think about Josh's graduation coming up in two weeks!

Before we left, Avis handed out a list of what she called "healing Scriptures," and encouraged us to pray these verses every day on Mark's behalf. Then Adele closed us out by starting the gospel song based on Proverbs 18:10: "The name of the Lord is a strong tower; the righteous run to it and are safe."

I knew the song—the Brooklyn Tabernacle Choir sang it on one of the CDs we kept in the car. Later, as I headed the minivan toward my house where Ben was waiting for Ruth and Yo-Yo, I handed the CD to Yo-Yo and asked her to stick it into the player and turn up the volume.

The name of the Lord is . . . a strong tower!
The righteous run into it . . . and they are saved!

Ruth sat in the middle seat with Stu, fanning herself like a queen in exile, though she looked a little green around the gills. Yo-Yo and I were jammin' in the front seat as we came to the chorus:

Jesus is the name of the Lord! . . .

I was still humming the song after the Garfields' big Buick disappeared down Lunt Street, with Ruth fussing at Ben about something or other and Yo-Yo rolling her eyes. Still humming when Denny took the minivan to pick up the kids from youth group, which for some reason had ended up at the Reillys' house. Still humming as I picked up the trail of dishes that had migrated from stem to stern of the Baxter domicile. Including two empty bottles of Michelob Light, which I dumped into the recycle bin. I didn't care. I stuck the dishes in the dishwasher and just kept singing.

The prayer time at the hospital had not only been good for Nony but good for me. There'd been so much prayer, so much Word in that minuscule "family consultation room" that there'd been no room for fear.

> *The name of the Lord is . . . a strong tower!*
> *The righteous run into—*

The back door banged, and Amanda sailed through the kitchen without her usual kissy-face love fest with Willie Wonka. Or me. A moment later, I heard the bathroom door slam. Denny came in shortly after, pecked me on the cheek, and pulled open the refrigerator door.

I peered out the door. The backyard was empty. "Where's Josh?"

Denny shrugged. "He wasn't at the Reillys' when I got there to pick up Amanda. Rick said he stayed at Uptown." He pulled out a carton of orange juice, screwed off the cap, and chugged it down straight from the carton. I bit my tongue. Denny wiped his mouth. "From what Rick said, New Morning was still having a prayer meeting at Uptown when the kids got there for youth group. Miscommunication, I guess. Rick smoothed it over and got the kids over to his house—except Josh. Josh said he wanted to stay for a little while, listen to the service, and he'd be over shortly." Denny shrugged. "But he never made it."

"Denny! Aren't you worried? What if something hap—"

"No! I'm not worried." Denny's reply came back so quickly, it almost snapped. "He's eighteen. He's been through a lot this weekend. He needs to work it out himself." He headed for the living room, and I thought I heard him mutter, "Me too."

I followed. "Did you and Ben have a good time? Hope it was OK he came over. He kinda invited himself."

Denny sank down into the recliner. "Yeah. It was OK. We watched the Cubs pick up a few good hits. Not enough to win, but hey." He tipped the recliner back with a *thump* and closed his eyes.

I wavered between taking the hint and pretending I was clueless. I went with clueless. "So. What do you think? Should we talk to Amanda about last night? With José, I mean."

"Already did." Denny's eyes stayed closed.

"What do you mean? When?" I felt relieved. Then irritated. I didn't really want to talk to Amanda tonight, but . . . where did Denny get off doing it without including me? Or at least telling me first. "What did you say?"

Denny's eyes slowly opened, exuding forced patience. "In the car. Perfect opportunity. Had her to myself. I told her being in the house alone with José was *verboten* and she knew it. Told her falling asleep together was *over the top* and would never, ever happen again if she wanted José to step foot in this house again."

"Did you bring up her 'vow of purity' at her *quinceañera*?"

"She said she didn't mean to—you know, the Amanda 'innocence wail.' Then she said maybe it was 'spiritual warfare.'"

My jaw dropped. *Oh brother.* "What did you say to—"

Footsteps on the front porch distracted me. My ears perked. A key turned in the front door lock. Josh was home. *Thank You, Jesus!* I quickly motioned to Denny that I still wanted an answer.

A grin slipped out on his face. "I told her temptation comes from the world, the flesh, and the devil. But in this case, she could forget the world and the devil."

29

I half-expected Josh to mumble "Hi" and head for his room. But he stood in the archway of the living room, hands loose at his side. Just stood there. Like the time he was five and we got separated in the grocery store. He'd just stood still, lost, waiting for me to find him, trying not to cry.

"Josh? Are you OK?"

"Yeah." Josh slumped onto the couch. "No." His head sank into his hands. "I don't know."

The recliner unreclined with a *thump*. I sat down on the hassock. "I was worried when Dad went to pick you up at youth group and you weren't there. What happened?"

Josh glanced up, wary. "You guys mad?"

"No." Denny leaned forward, elbows on his knees. "Rick Reilly told me that New Morning was still having a prayer meeting or something when the teens showed up at Uptown, and you wanted to stay. We figured you had your reasons."

Josh heaved a sigh. "Yeah. Thanks." Then he snorted. "To tell you the truth, I was mad. Some of the kids in the youth group got real upset that somebody else was using *our* space, that we had to find another place to meet. Mr. Reilly could hardly make them shut up! You should have heard 'em! They were grumblin' and dissin' downstairs, and upstairs New Morning was praying for Mark Smith, lying up there in ICU, unconscious. Begging God to spare his life! Man!" Josh wagged his head. "Good thing Mr. Reilly got the rest of the kids out of there, 'cause I was afraid I was going to haul off and punch somebody."

"Mo-om!" Amanda's voice floated loudly from the back of the house. "Wonka's got really bad gas and needs to go out! Pee-eew."

"Then put him out yourself!" Denny and I yelled in perfect unison.

Josh barely seemed to notice the interruption. "So, yeah, I stayed for a while. Sat in the back. Nobody paid me much attention, 'cept Mr. Douglass. He saw me come in, nodded at me." He was silent for several moments, lost in his thoughts. Denny and I just waited. "New Morning is mostly black. Guess I knew that, but I started having a lot of funny feelings. Remembered us praying for Dr. Smith this morning. Then here's his own church, in the very same building, praying for him this evening. It felt . . . felt like the cafeteria at school. Latino kids at one table, blacks at another. Whites all hanging together. Just a few strays here and there crossing the color line. Made me feel weird. I mean, we were *all* praying for Dr. Smith. It seemed like we should be praying *together*."

I stared at my son. I'd sensed it, too, when we took communion that morning. Something skewed. Something not right.

Denny pursed his lips. "I can understand your feelings, son. But don't make too much out of it. I'm sure they're grateful to have a place to meet until they can move into a new space. It might be a nice thing to do something together; but given the size of Uptown's space, it isn't really practical."

Denny's words hung in the air like unabsorbed air freshener. Didn't really touch the heart of what Josh was trying to say, just made it smell nice.

Josh blew out a breath of pure frustration. "Yeah, but . . . I dunno. I started feeling confused. I got all geeked up when I heard what the White Pride group was doing at Northwestern. Told my debate adviser I wanted to do something on hate groups, ordered those books—oh yeah, Josh Baxter was really going to take it on. Now?" He threw up his hands. "I don't have the books anymore. Couldn't make my case even if I wanted to. But you know what? I don't even want to anymore. I'm glad the books are gone. Good excuse to chuck the whole thing."

Denny and I just gaped at Josh, who found his legs and started pacing back and forth in front of the couch, running one hand over his nonexistent hair.

He stopped and pointed a finger at us. "And you wanna know why I don't want to get up there and make some big argument for racial harmony? To stand there and say people like us can make a difference? Because . . ." Josh's voice broke. "Because when push came to shove at that rally, it didn't matter what I believed! It didn't matter that I was there to support Dr. Smith and *not* the White Pride guys! It didn't matter that Dr. Smith had asked us to come. It didn't matter that our families are friends. No! To that big linebacker with his loud dreadlocks, I was just a white boy. It was 'us' versus 'them'! He thought he had a right to get in my face and push me around. He pushed my *mother* down, for God's sake! And it's never going to be any different! And then . . ." Josh's shoulders heaved. "Then some white thug beats up one of the coolest men I've ever met—*just because he's black!* And we don't know if Dr. Smith's going to live or die or be a vegetable!"

Josh fell back onto the couch, his eyes tortured. "And here we are, the Christians. It isn't any different for us either. Black and white. Us and them." He put his head in his hands and began to weep. Loud, gasping sobs. "It's . . . never . . . going . . . to be . . . different!"

DON'T KNOW HOW I MADE IT THROUGH SCHOOL the next day. The kids were always squirrelly on Mondays anyway. On top of that, it was the first week of June and felt like summer already. Eighty-six degrees and humidity to match. Too many energetic third graders confined in a too-small space. Add one teacher with nerves like frayed electric wires after the events of the past weekend, and I spent most of the day shouting down squabbles, repeating class-work instructions two or three times, and marching miscreants to the principal's office. *Let Avis deal with the little criminals*, I thought, parking Ramón, Cornell, and Terrell in the chairs just inside the main office, glad to have them off my hands for even ten minutes.

When the last bell rang and my classroom emptied like runners at the starting gun of the Chicago Marathon, I collapsed at my desk, head in my hands, trying to find a solid place on which to get some emotional footing. I'd felt so helpless last night, watching my nearly grown son cry. It had unnerved me to no end. Josh had a good heart, even if he didn't know the difference between the laundry hamper and the floor. But his idealistic expectations, his hopes that good intentions could make a difference, had been body slammed into a brick wall of reality.

I couldn't help him. Denny couldn't help him. We didn't have any answers either.

"God," I moaned. "Help Josh. Help Denny and me. Help Mark. And Nony . . ." My prayer sounded hollow in my ears. *Help Josh. Help Denny and me. Help Mark and Nony.* Good grief. What kind of prayer was that? "I don't even know how to pray, Jesus. Not when it really counts."

Yes, you do, Jodi. The Voice in my spirit was so strong, I looked up, half expecting to see that Avis had walked into my classroom and overheard me. But I was alone in a sea of desks. *You know a lot about prayer. First things first. You need to praise Me.*

Well, yes. Why was that so easy to remember when I was praying with Yada Yada but so easy to forget when I was praying on my own? I squeezed my eyes shut. *Lord, You are worthy of all my—*

No. Silent praise—any silent prayer longer than thirty seconds— usually ended up getting bombarded by random Jodi thoughts and mental lists of stuff I had to do. I stood up and began to walk up and down the rows of desks—straightening a few along the way— speaking aloud my praise to God. I prayed the names of God that we'd lifted up at the hospital last night: God our Provider, God our Healer, the All-Sufficient One. "Thank You, Lord, for who You are!"

Now pray the Word, Jodi. Claim the promises God has given you for your son, for your family, for Mark teetering between life and death, for Nony in her suffering.

What promises? My mind went blank. The only verse I could pull out of the air was John 3:16. Making a beeline for my desk, I grabbed the Bible I kept in the second drawer, glad for the underlining I'd done. Neon yellow words leapt off the pages at me. "I will never leave you nor forsake you" . . . "If any of you lacks wisdom, let him ask God, who gives generously to all" . . . "If two of you agree on anything you ask for, it will be done for you by My Father in heaven."

Oh wow. I took the Bible with me as I resumed walking my classroom and prayed the verses aloud. "Thank You, Jesus, that You promised You would never leave us nor forsake us. We need You now. Mark and Nony need You! Josh needs You! And I confess my lack of wisdom. I don't know how to help Josh with the questions he's struggling with. He feels caught in the middle. But You said we can ask You for wisdom! So I'm asking, God—asking for Josh, asking for myself, asking for Denny. Asking for all of us who are confused and bewildered by what happened this weekend."

I stopped by the fingerprint-smudged window and looked out at the deserted playground, then glanced down at the verse I'd underlined in Matthew's Gospel, chapter 19: "If two of you on earth agree on anything you ask for, it will be done for you by my Father in heaven." Did I dare . . . ?

"Jesus," I breathed, "I'm here alone, praying by myself, but I stand in agreement with all my sisters in Yada Yada, with the prayers of Uptown Community, with the prayers of New Morning Church yesterday afternoon. We're asking, God, for Your healing touch on Mark Smith's body. Please, God. *Please.* In the name of Jesus . . ."

I stopped myself before saying amen. The name of Jesus wasn't just some way to sign off on my prayer, a spiritual "Over and out." If I'd learned anything from Yada Yada, it was that the name of Jesus was the *authority* I had stamped on my life, enabling me to come boldly to God, even though He was holy and I wasn't. The *authority* I had to rebuke Satan and all his evil plans and—

The door to my classroom swung open. Clara Hutchens, a first-grade teacher, poked her head in. "Coming to staff meeting? Mrs. Douglass sent me to get you." She peered disapprovingly over the top of her reading glasses.

"Uh, be right there." But I smiled to myself as I gathered up my books and papers and stuffed them into my tote bag. Avis would understand.

STAFF MEETING WAS MERCIFULLY SHORT. I realized why when Avis pulled me aside afterward. "I'm going up to the hospital now to avoid the evening crowd of visitors. Do you want to come with me?"

I did a mental check of supper possibilities—no leftovers, unfortunately, since I hadn't cooked on Sunday—and phoned, leaving a message on the machine for Amanda to pull out some bacon to thaw. *Scrambled eggs and bacon for supper. Why not?*

We rode up to Evanston Hospital in Avis's black Toyota Camry, threading through late afternoon traffic, neither one of us saying much. I almost told her about the struggle Josh was having, then decided it wasn't mine to tell. Not yet. Unless that was an excuse to avoid the awkwardness of discussing racial barriers and his feeling that "it's never going to be any different."

I turned my face to the window. *Oh God, it has to be different! We're Your body—the body of Christ here on earth! All of us!*

To my delight, Hoshi Takahashi and Nony's boys were in the ICU waiting room, drawing pictures and making signs. Michael popped up, showing off the picture he'd drawn with bright-colored markers. "We're making pictures to hang in Daddy's room," he bragged. "Ms. Enriques said we should make lots!"

I cocked an eyebrow at Hoshi. "Delores is here?"

Hoshi smiled, her silky, black hair falling over one shoulder. "Delores is with Nonyameko in Dr. Smith's room." Hoshi simply couldn't call her college professor by his first name. She peeked out the waiting room door. "I do not see any nurses at the desk. Why don't you go on in? I know Nony would want to see you."

Before following Avis down the hall, I pulled Hoshi aside. "How are you doing, Hoshi? I mean, you still have school, you're taking care of the boys . . ."

She smiled from the inside out. "Today, I go to my classes while they are at school. It is no problem. It is . . . how do you say it? It is joy." Her gaze fell fondly on the tops of the boys' heads as they busily worked on their pictures and signs. "Like little brothers."

I hustled to catch up with Avis, and together we peered into Mark's room. Even though I'd seen it all before, I still felt overwhelmed seeing Mark lying so still on the bed, his head and eyes bandaged, wires and tubes still connected to various body parts. The dark mahogany of his bare arms lay in stark contrast outside the pale hospital blankets. Delores and Nony, standing on the far side of Mark's bed, both looked up.

Delores smiled big and leaned close to Mark's head. "*Señor* Mark! You have visitors! Avis and Jodi are here." She made a sucking sound with her teeth. "So popular you are." And she laughed.

I stared. "Is he . . . can he . . . ?"

Nony shook her head, trying her best to smile. "Still no response. The doctor said he is in a coma. They do not know for how long. But Delores—and the nurses too—say we should talk to Mark as though he can hear." Her voice wobbled. "Maybe he can. Maybe he can't. They don't know."

30

aybe he can ... maybe he can't ... Nony's words haunted me all week. It felt bizarre talking to Mark, who lay wrapped and rigid on the bed in ICU like an Egyptian mummy. Chatting with him about the boys' pictures taped all over the walls, describing the colors and designs, reading their "I love you, Daddy" messages to him, over and over. Reading aloud the "Thinking of You" and "Get Well Soon" cards that piled up in a basket on the windowsill. Making jokes about the hospital having to enlarge the ICU waiting room to accommodate all his visitors. Joking that we really had to stop meeting like this!

Delores insisted, "Don't talk *about* him. Don't talk as if he's not here. The doctors are not sure why he's in a coma or how long it might last. It is, how do you say? *No saben.* They do not know. But if he can hear us, or even if he can't, we need to touch him. Let him know we're here. Speak to his spirit."

I swallowed the thought that pushed at the edges of her words. *For how long, Delores? Will he ever wake up?*

At Peter Douglass's suggestion, he and Denny, Carl Hickman, and Ben Garfield agreed to take turns staying all night at the hospital so that Nony could put Marcus and Michael to bed and get a decent night's rest. The nurses shrugged and said it wasn't necessary for anyone to stay; they would call Mrs. Smith if there was any change at all.

There wasn't. Monday . . . Tuesday . . . Wednesday . . . Thursday . . . came and went in a mechanical blur. I knew Nony was grateful that someone was with Mark during the long night hours. Grateful that someone was there to get a report when the doctors and interns came by on their early morning rounds.

Each day, I prayed several of the "healing Scriptures" Avis had given to us. "Praise the Lord, O my soul, and forget not all His benefits—who forgives all our sins and heals all our diseases. . . ." "He was wounded for our transgressions . . . by His stripes we are healed." "I will not die but live, and will proclaim what the Lord has done." *(Oh God! Mark will not die but live! And we will all proclaim what the Lord has done!)*

But they stuck in my throat on Thursday morning when Denny called me from the hospital at seven thirty to say he was going straight to work, and to tell the kids to take the city bus to school. The guys were already starting on their second rotation of hospital nights.

"Any change in Mark? Any response?" I tried to sound hopeful.

Denny's silence lasted only a heartbeat. But his hesitation spoke even louder than his words. "No. The same."

For some reason those words—*"The same"*—got my dander up. "OK, God, I want a word with You," I muttered darkly as I headed for Bethune Elementary half an hour later, eating up the sidewalk as if my walking shoes were motorized. "I don't understand this suffering You're putting Mark and Nony through. They're the good guys! They've got kids who need their daddy! Mark was finally going to take Nony to South Africa! Mark stood up to those White Pride people at the rally! The police haven't even arrested anybody yet! Are the bad guys supposed to win? *What's the point?*"

A senior-citizen crossing guard holding his bright red stop sign glared at me suspiciously, as if I might be some not-quite-all-there street person, mumbling to herself. I pasted on a cheerful smile. "Good morning, Mr. Krakowski!"

"Oh. It's you, Mrs. Baxter. Nice day—hey!" A kid on a bicycle diverted his attention. "You get off that bike and walk it across!" the old man bellowed. "You know the rules!"

Nice pair of lungs for a fellow his age. In my head, I added his bellowing tone to the prayers I was sending heavenward.

I had words with God all day. Forgot all about praising and did mostly ranting—mentally, anyway. If I'd said aloud the things I was thinking in front of a classroom of thirty impressionable young minds, the powers-that-be definitely would have had me hauled away in a little white jacket.

Huh. The kids, of course, got away with yelling stuff a whole lot worse all the time.

When I got home at four o'clock, I let Willie Wonka out the back door and poured myself a glass of iced tea from the fridge. "Sweet tea, Flo," I mumbled, holding the glass aloft in a salute to Florida *in absentia*, who'd made sure I was reeducated in the fine art of making *real* southern iced tea. "You'd be proud of me." I took my glass out onto the back porch, hoping to enjoy a moment of solitude, maybe get my prayers in working order.

"Hey, Jodi." The voice startled me. I looked up. Becky Wallace was sitting halfway up the outside stairs going to Stu's second-floor apartment, smoking a cigarette.

"Oh. Hi, Becky. Nice day to be sitting out." *Oh, that was lame, Jodi. She's probably dying for conversation, home alone all day every day, and all you can think of is "Nice day"?* "Whatcha doing?" I groaned inwardly. That was even dumber. What did it *look* like she was doing! But what was I supposed to say? *"Nice smoke rings you're blowing there"?*

I tried again. "Would you like some iced tea? Already sweet."

"Yeah. That'd be nice." She craned her neck as a car came down the alley, then she settled back against the railing as it slowly passed.

Was she waiting for somebody? I slipped back into the house, poured a glass of iced tea, and took it back outside. Wonka had lugged his stiff, arthritic legs up the steps to our back porch and was enjoying a behind-the-ear scratch from Becky, who'd slid down a few steps to our level. She took the glass. "Thanks."

"You're good with dogs. Dogs know."

She dragged on the cigarette. "I like dogs. Never had one as a kid, though." She looked away. "If I get little Andy back, I'm gonna get us a dog. A gentle one, like Willie Wonka here."

Becky wasn't looking at me. Maybe not looking anywhere. Seemed to be looking at something within, a place out of my reach. But suddenly she swung her gaze back toward me. "Uh, feel kinda dumb askin', but . . . if you got that Bible you said you was goin' ta get for me, I should probably give Ms. Avis her big 'un back. I know she's missin' it."

I slapped my forehead. "Becky! I am so sorry. I really meant to! Tell you what. I'm going to get you one tonight. That's a promise."

It isn't that far to the Mustard Seed bookstore on Sheridan Road. They'll be open tonight. Could even walk if I have to. I suddenly felt rash. "And if you'd like, maybe we could read the same book, one of the Gospels or something, and talk about it a couple of times a week—when I get home after school."

She nodded, pulled once more on her cigarette, then tossed the butt into an empty flowerpot that sat on the porch, waiting to be filled with flowers . . . someday. *Huh. Another one of my good intentions paving the road to—*

"Cool," she said.

DENNY HAD BAGS UNDER HIS EYES when he got home late from West Rogers High that evening. No wonder. The previous night was the second time he'd kept vigil in the reclining chair in Mark's hospital room. He just grunted when I said I needed the car to go to the bookstore, took his supper plate into the living room, and flicked on the TV. Didn't seem to notice I'd made his favorite pasta salad—the one with bow-tie pasta and shredded roasted chicken, spiced up with pecans, red grapes, spinach, and lemon dressing.

I had good success at the Mustard Seed bookstore. Found a hardcover *Women's Devotional Bible* in a modern language translation. Not too pricey. The whole process took about forty-five minutes. Felt pretty dumb that I'd promised to get Becky a Bible a good three weeks ago.

Better late than never. Stu's car was in the garage when I got home. I climbed the outside stairs to her apartment and peeked into the kitchen through the glass window in the back door. Stu was standing in the middle of the kitchen, purse still slung over her shoulder, car keys in her hand, glaring at the sink. I gave a timid rap on the window. She glanced my direction, rolled her eyes, and opened the door.

"How hard would it be for Becky to wash her dishes?" she hissed at me in a whisper, jerking her head to the overflowing sink. "She's here all day, for cryin' out loud!"

I put on a sympathetic face. "I thought you guys made an agreement about stuff like that?"

"Yeah, well. You want something? I just got home."

I held out the Bible. "Just picked this up for Becky. She here?" I stifled a laugh. "Guess she better be."

Except she wasn't. I knocked on her bedroom door; no answer. Not in the bathroom, not in the living room . . .

Suddenly worried, Stu tried the front door of her apartment. Unlocked. Without a word we both hustled down the stairs to the door at the bottom. It stood open . . .

Becky was sitting on the front steps, her back to us, hunched forward, blowing smoke from a skinny cigarette. A sweet, pungent smell hung in the air.

Stu was at her side in two angry strides. "Becky Wallace! Are you smoking weed?" She grabbed the cigarette out of Becky's hand. "Where'd you get this?" She sniffed the pitiful stub then threw it out to the sidewalk. "Has someone been here giving you stuff? We agreed: no drugs! Remember! *Remember?*"

Becky wiped her nose on her sleeve and looked up, her eyes bleary in the thin light from the streetlights. She shrugged and shook her head. "I know, Stu. I know. Jus' . . . I miss my baby, Stu. Ain't doin' nothin' but treadin' water here. Can't hardly stand it anymore. Feel like I *gotta* get Andy back or . . . I'm gonna drown."

Her hand snaked out, and she clutched the pant leg of Stu's pantsuit. "Please, Stu. You my only hope. Talk to that new case-worker. His grandmama don't pick up the phone when I call. *Please.*"

"Why should I?" Stu was practically yelling. "DCFS won't bring your kid back into your life until you're *clean* for more than two minutes! We had a deal! I stuck my neck out for you, Becky Wallace! What part of 'no drugs' don't you understand? Huh? N-O. None! Zip! *Nada!*"

Becky's head sank into her hands. Her shoulders began to shake. I hugged the Bible I'd just bought for her against my chest, feeling helpless, kicking myself. This sad, hurting mother practically lived under my roof, but it'd been too much bother to get her the Bible I'd promised, much less spend time with her. I took a step forward, but Stu waved me back impatiently.

Miserable, I crept back up the front stairs to Stu's apartment, laid the new Bible on Becky's bed, and went down the back stairs to our own apartment.

THE TV WAS BLARING in the front room—some stupid police drama. Probably why Denny didn't hear Stu yelling on the front porch. For once, I didn't fan the flicker of irritation I felt. *God, I know Denny's hurting—but he's not talking to me about it. He has his own way of coping.*

I hadn't been in such good shape all that day either. I leaned my forehead against the doorjamb between our kitchen and dining room. *Oh God, we're all hurting—Becky and Stu, Josh and Denny, Nony and—*

I pushed myself upright. *I really should call Nony to see how she's doing.* The kitchen phone, however, was missing—as usual. Impatient, I knocked on Amanda's door and opened it without waiting for her to answer. "Don't hog the phone, Amanda," was out of my mouth before I realized she wasn't in her bedroom.

No Amanda. No phone.

I knocked on Josh's door and waited this time. "Yeah?" On this side of the door, Josh sounded a lot like his dad. *When did that happen?* I opened the door. Amanda was sitting cross-legged on the floor, her face pulled into a big pout. Josh was sprawled on the bed, earphones clamped on his ears, obviously trying to ignore her. Seeing me, she hopped up and dragged me over to the side of the bed. "Mo-om! Lane Tech's prom is next week, and Josh says he's not going! You told *me* I should go to the dance last weekend, that Dr. Smith would want us to, you know, go on with normal life stuff." She folded her arms, huffing self-righteously. "It's his senior prom! He's gotta stop being so *weird*."

Josh rolled his eyes. "What's it to you, shrimp? I *told* you already, I don't want to go, and even if I did, it's too late to get tickets. Besides . . ." He pulled off his earphones, giving us all an earful of the thumping music he'd been listening to. Probably that Jesus People band, Head Noise or something. "I told Mr. Douglass I'd spend the night at the hospital that night. He's putting me on the rotation, starting tomorrow night. So lay off." *Both of you* hung unspoken in the air.

I hooked a finger at Amanda and backed out the door. She followed me into the hall. "The phone?" I held out my hand.

"Oh. Yeah. Uh, I left it somewhere." She disappeared into the bathroom and came out with the phone. *Oh brother.* I didn't even want to ask.

I called the Sisulu-Smith household first, but Hoshi said Nony was still up at the hospital, waiting until Ben Garfield arrived for that night's rotation. I called the hospital, got the nurse's desk in ICU, and asked for Nonyameko Sisulu-Smith. I waited. Finally an extension picked up. "Nonyameko speaking."

Her distinct South African accent gave me a pang. South Africa . . . it must seem so far away to her now. "Hi, Nony. It's Jodi. Just wanted to check in on you and Mark. Any news today?"

Silence.

"Nony?"

"Yes, Jodi. I am here." Another long silence. Then, "Mark is the same. Every day the same. No response. Just lying there. Like he's"— the soft crying began—"like he's dead. And it's my fault. It must be my fault."

"Nony!" I spoke sharply and immediately regretted it. "Don't talk that way! None of this is your fault!"

"But it must be so. Why else does God not answer my prayers? I . . . I did not want to face it. But I was reading some Scripture to Mark, some of the 'healing Scriptures' Avis gave to us, and . . ." Her weeping increased; tears gathered in my own throat. I could do nothing except clutch the phone receiver, sweaty in my hand, and wait until she was able to continue. "And the verse in James cut my soul."

"What verse, Nony?"

"Chapter five, verse sixteen." Her voice dropped, and I had to strain to hear. "It says to confess our sins to each other so that we may be healed. And it cut my heart, Jodi. Because . . . maybe Mark won't be healed until I confess my sin."

"Confess? What are you talking about? What sin do you need to confess, Nony?" This was ridiculous! Nony sin? She was one of the most Scripture-filled, God-fearing women I'd ever met in my life.

"I pushed Mark. 'Take me to South Africa,' I said! 'Let me go to South Africa! I'll die if I don't go home to South Africa!' Finally he says, 'All right, we will go.' But we didn't ask God together. I pushed; he gave in. God had to do something to stop us. So God—"

"No!" I shouted into the phone. "Nonyameko! Stop it right now!" I didn't know about pushing and giving in. I didn't know if the Sisulu-Smiths were supposed to go to South Africa or not. Maybe their decision making needed some work. But I did know one thing: *God* didn't do this to Mark Smith.

That was a lie straight from hell.

31

illie Wonka stuck his wet nose in my face at six a.m. I rolled over and groaned. It couldn't possibly be morning already! All night my dreams had been bumper to bumper with beeping heart monitors, nurses wearing prom dresses, and police raiding my house looking for drugs. I forced my eyes open, hoping consciousness would calm my psyche—but reality wasn't much better.

Denny lay on his side, facing away from me. I wanted to reach out, caress his skin, pull him close to my heart, but his back seemed like a wall. Counting all the hours he'd spent working late at the high school, keeping all-night vigils—twice now—in Mark's hospital room, or numbing himself in front of the TV, I'd barely seen him the entire week. I'd tried to tell him last night about Nony feeling guilty for what happened to Mark, about Becky smoking a joint on our front porch (which she got from *some* no-good buddy) and sending Stu into conniptions. But he'd just grunted *"Uh-huh,"* as if our connection had static on the line.

I squeezed my eyes shut once more. *God, I'm tired. Mark has only been in a coma for one week. But what if it's months? Or years? I don't know how to support Nony through something like this! And she's not the only one. Denny is hurting; Josh is struggling—and I don't know how to kiss it to make it all better. Don't know what to do about Becky and Stu either . . .*

Wonka whined. I sighed and swung my feet off the bed. Not smart to put a geriatric doggy bladder on hold. I grabbed my Bible off the nightstand, let Wonka out the back door, and followed him as far as the porch swing, working the morning kinks out of my left leg as I went. Might as well get in a few licks of Bible reading while the dog did his business by the back fence.

I let the Bible fall open, intending to look for the spot I'd been reading in the New Testament a few days ago. But a couple of underlined verses on the open page caught my eye—Proverbs 3:5 and 6. *Hm.* I was alone, so I read aloud. "'Trust in the LORD with all your heart, and lean not on your own understanding.'" *Sheesh.* It was like God talking back at me after my prayer a few minutes ago. I kept reading. "'In all your ways acknowledge him, and he will make your paths straight.'"

"Yo, Jodi." A voice seemed to come out of nowhere, but it was followed by Becky's square face peering over the railing halfway up the back stairs. "You read that thing every day? Wait a minute."

I opened my mouth to say something, but her head disappeared. She was back in thirty seconds, scooting down the outside stairs in her bare feet, the ankle monitor making a small bulge under a sloppy pair of gray sweatpants. She had the Bible I'd bought last night sitting atop Avis's giant Bible, lugging them in both hands. "What's that ya readin'? Can ya show me?" She grinned. "Thanks for the Bible. Here. You can give Avis hers back now that I got my own."

I wanted to ask Ms. Sunshine what happened between last night—when she was high on grass, weepy, and yelled at by Leslie Stuart—and *now* . . . but I decided, *Uh-uh. Not going to go there.* "Sure." I scooted over on the porch swing. "I've only got a minute till rush hour starts at our house, but I'll show you where to find it."

I showed her how to look up Proverbs in the table of contents at the front, then I pointed out the verses I'd been reading in the third chapter. "Go ahead, read them."

She squinted at the tiny type. "Uh. 'Trust in the LORD with all your heart, and lean not on your own understanding." She read slowly, with a hairsbreadth between each word. "'In all your ways acknowledge Him, and He will make your paths straight.'" She leaned against the back of the swing. "Huh. Lotta stuff 'bout life I don't understand. Sure could use some of that 'He will make your paths straight' rap."

I don't know what possessed me. I just started to pray aloud, like God was hanging out on the porch with us. Didn't even close my eyes. "Jesus, Becky and I don't understand a lot of things that have happened, things still going on. We don't understand what all You're doing in our lives. But we need direction for the paths we're on. I need Your help knowing how to be there for my kids. For Denny too. Becky needs Your help knowing how to be a mom to Andy when he's living with someone else. So we want to own up that *You're* the one in the driver's seat. We want to go where You're going. We want to walk on the paths where You've cleared the way. We . . ." I ran out of words. So I just said, "God, I want to thank You for Becky. Thank You for her Bible. Forgive me for being so slow getting her one. Show her Your paths in the Word. And give her the courage to stay on the path with You."

"Amen." Becky said it reverently, rolling the word around in her mouth like a sweet peppermint. She gave me a lopsided grin, matching the disarray of her mousy hair. "Guess I blew it last night with Stu. Don't think she's talkin' to me." She held up her new Bible. "Maybe this gonna have some help for me."

Yeah. Me too.

Willie Wonka stood with his nose to the back door, ready for his breakfast. Somewhere inside I heard an alarm clock shrilling. Yet the early morning sunlight sifting through the branches of our neighbor's tree felt warm and soft. Gentle. Like a tender nudge from God to get on with my day.

I PLOPPED Avis's oversized Bible on her desk in the school office. "Becky says thanks." I grimaced. "I finally got her that Bible I promised weeks ago. We're, um, going to do some study together."

Avis's eyebrows went up in approval. Then she looked at me closely. "Are you all right, Jodi? You look . . . stressed."

Ha. If she could have heard the way I ranted at God yesterday! I found myself blurting out the troubled waters at home since the attack on Mark. Amanda upset, using the situation to excuse her behavior. Josh struggling to make sense out of what happened to him at the rally, devastated by the assault on a man he admired, confused about all the racial boxes we end up in, tangled up in his feelings like a hog-tied calf. Denny stuffing his fears and feelings of helplessness someplace deep and not letting me anywhere near.

I sighed. "I'm guessing here. I don't know exactly *what* Denny's feeling."

Avis nodded. "I know. Peter too." She sighed. "Not what I imagined our first weeks of married life would be like. He's been calling the police every day, asking what they're doing about the investigation." She made a face. "The air in our house is turning blue. You'd think he was back in the navy."

I giggled. Even Avis had a hard time keeping a straight face. But she cleared her throat and resumed her "professional" voice. "Oh, before I forget. Peter is updating his office computers, has a couple of old ones to give away. Still in good shape for most things. You think Chanda and her kids would want one? What about Yo-Yo and her brothers? They don't have a computer yet, do they?"

"That's awesome! It's high time Chanda and Yo-Yo got their own e-mail. I'm sure they'd be tickled. You could ask them at Yada Yada. Supposed to be at Stu's Sunday evening . . . unless you think we ought to meet up at the hospital again."

Avis shook her head. "No. Let's try to get Nony *out* of the hospital instead. That girl's got to pace herself if she's going to get through this."

ON THE WAY HOME FROM SCHOOL, I marveled at the sense of peace smoothing my day, ever since my spontaneous two-minute rendezvous on the back porch with Becky and the Bible. "God," I murmured, lifting my face and drinking in the no-humidity, perfect June sunny day, "You sure do work in mysterious ways. Yesterday, I'm fussing at You big-time because *nothing good* is happening with Mark and Nony. Last night, Becky and Stu are on the verge of a major meltdown . . ."

A couple of teenage boys in baggy denim pants, crotches around their knees, slouched past me on the sidewalk and gave me a funny look. I didn't care. I kept right on talking out loud to God. "Then those verses in Proverbs practically fall out of my Bible into my lap this morning, and Becky eats 'em up like Willie Wonka scarfing up his kibbles—and it's like You telling me it's OK that I don't understand what's going on, because *You've* got it covered . . ."

I turned up Greenwood Avenue, glad I only had to walk three more blocks, since the rod in my left thigh was beginning to protest. Funny, I hadn't thought about my car accident—not since Mark got hurt. Hadn't thought about Hakim or his mother. Not even Jamal, Hakim's brother, who was buried in a Chicago cemetery on my account. Yet in a few more weeks, it would be exactly one year—

"Smile! Smile!" someone yelled. Distracted, my head swiveled to make sure no one was talking to me. A vision of chiffon and silk and sparkling rhinestones caught my eye on the porch of one of the older frame houses crunched between apartment buildings in this neighborhood. Two lovely young ladies with creamy skin and long, dark hair sat on the porch railing, posing regally. Their incredibly baby-faced dates stood behind them, dressed in tuxedos and funky open-collared shirts, sporting earrings and maximum-hold spiky hair. A long, black limo sat at the curb, hazards blinking.

My heart lurched. Tonight was prom for some of the high schools. Next week, it would be prom for Lane Tech.

But not for Josh. He was going to spend the night keeping vigil in a hospital room.

32

was hoping Denny and I would get a chance to talk over the weekend, but it didn't happen. Friday night would have been perfect; Josh took off for the hospital about seven, and Amanda had a baby-sitting job. But Denny wanted to see a movie. "Let's go out," he said, instead of just vegging in front of the TV with a video. He actually looked through the Friday section of the *Chicago Tribune* himself and found a romantic comedy at the Village North on Sheridan Road. Even splurged on a bucket of popcorn with extra butter and a twenty-eight-ounce root beer with two straws. We laughed and held hands, greasy from the buttery popcorn, and let ourselves feel like two youngsters on a date.

Make that two lovers on a date. As the movie plot became a comedy of tangled errors, Denny put his arm around me in the dark theater and absently caressed my shoulder. Or maybe not so absently. His fingers wound themselves in my hair, traced the outside of my ear, gently massaged the tension from my neck.

If he was leading up to something, it was working.

He'd felt so distant all week that I was putty under his touch, glad for anything that allowed me into his heart, even if it was through our skin. The house was still kid-empty when we got home at ten thirty, and we wasted no time shedding our clothes and tumbling into bed. Denny was tender, gentle, patient, and I was so thirsty for his touch that I didn't want our lovemaking to end . . . but later, as I lay in Denny's arms, his soft, slow breathing in my ear, a sorrowful thought crept into my contentment and pushed it aside.

Will Nonyameko ever again lay within Mark's arms, spent and happy after making love?

"GIRL, HOW YA FEEL?" Florida didn't wait for a reply after ringing me up at noon the next day. "Where's that beanpole son of yours? I gotta ask him a question about this Cornerstone jive the Uptown youth cookin' up for this summer."

I cradled the phone in my ear and stuffed dirty clothes into the washing machine. "Sleeping. Spent the night up at the hospital last night. But he said something about a bunch of Uptown youth going down to Jesus People later this afternoon—to talk about volunteering at the Cornerstone Festival this summer, I guess. Is Chris going?"

"That's what I'm sayin'. I want Josh to ask him personal, talk it up a little. So have him call me, OK? Hey, whatchu makin' for Second Sunday Potluck tomorrow?"

I stifled a groan. Potluck Sunday again so soon? "I don't know. Haven't thought about it. Haven't even done my food shopping yet. I'm waiting for Denny to get back with the car. He had to coach a game this morning. Then Ben Garfield's picking him up—they're

going up to Mark and Nony's house to mow the lawn, stuff like that
. . . Flo, wait a minute." I put the phone down long enough to pour
detergent into the washer, set the dials, and park myself on the basement stairs. "Flo? Still there?"

"I'm still here. But what's eatin' at you, girl? You sound heavy in
your mind."

Was I that obvious? Florida had radar that would pick up a low-
flying cruise missile. "Just wondering . . . how's Carl handling what
happened to Mark? I mean, is he talking to you?"

Florida's laugh was hollow. "Carl? Talk to me? Girl, we doin'
good if he's not yellin' at me or the kids. We was doin' OK in that
department past couple of weeks; the job with Peter Douglass been
real good for him. But since Mark got beat up, he's yellin' again. He's
real angry, but he don't know what to do 'bout it, so he just walkin'
around mad. But talk? Nah. Why you askin'?"

I shrugged, forgetting Florida couldn't see me. "Uh, just kinda
worried about Denny. I know he's upset about Mark, but he's
holding it all in, almost like he's scared of what he's feeling. We're
like ships passing in the night around here—not really talking."
Except for body talking last night. For that I was grateful.

"Mm-mm. Don't push it, girl. Be glad he's not goin' off half-
cocked, acting out 'fore he think about it. That'd be Carl, 'cept his
job keepin' him civilized. Your Denny, now, takes him a while to sort
things out—like what happened with him and MaDear. But he
came through. I wouldn't worry about Denny. Uh-uh. Now my boy,
Chris—he's a different story. Lord! Have mercy."

"What's wrong? He seemed to loosen up, be having a good time
when he came with us and the other kids to Great America on
Memorial Day. Even seemed interested in coming back to youth

group again. Josh wanted him to do the Cornerstone thing this summer."

"Jesus, Jesus." Florida's voice dropped. "I hoped so. But when he heard about that White Pride rally and then what happened to Mark? Jesus! That boy swore up and down nothin' was ever goin' to be different with white and black folk, an' he was done with it."

NOTHING WAS EVER GOING TO BE DIFFERENT . . .

I sat out on the back steps between laundry loads, thinking about Florida's phone call. Chris and Josh. Two very different teenagers— but coming to the same conclusion about race. *Oh God, that can't be the way it ends for our kids! Discouraged that nothing they do will make a difference in the end. Defeated before they even begin. Oh God, please, please.*

A cardinal twittered from atop our side fence. I sucked in my breath. The male's scarlet feathers riveted my eyes, pushing my despondency to the background. Such beauty in the midst of all the ordinary wrens and sparrows that normally populated our alley! I really should put up a bird feeder to attract more birds. That'd be fun; see how many different birds actually lived in the city. The cardinal was Illinois' state bird after all. There had to be a ton of them around somewhere. Why not here?

Suddenly my thoughts collided. The cardinal on the fence seemed like God's answer to my desperate prayer. *Hope is there if you know where to look, Jodi. It's that spot of beauty when everything seems dull, hopeless, colorless. It may come when you least expect it; sometimes it's already there in your own backyard. And if you want hope to stay around, you have to feed it. Invite it. Protect it from the alley cats of*

discouragement. Fight for it. Don't let it be taken over by the obnoxious
starlings and bully crows . . .

OK, maybe I was stretching the analogy a little. Or was I? Florida and I were as different as any two people could be—and not just chocolate and vanilla. Yet God had made us friends. Maybe God was the only thing we had in common—but when it came right down to it, that was enough. Our faith. Believing that God was bigger than our differences. Believing that God *created* our differences, something to enrich us and teach us, not drive us apart.

And not just Florida and me. Yada Yada itself was a cardinal of hope. And that hope had spilled over to our men, to our kids. Look at Peter Douglass and Denny, Ben Garfield and Carl Hickman. Mark had invited all of them to support his efforts at the rally. And all four of them—five, if you counted Josh—had banded together to keep vigil beside Mark's bedside at nights and give Nony a rest. Even Delores's husband, Ricardo—the inexplicable, unemployed truck driver with the mesmerizing guitar—had brought his mariachi band to Amanda's *quinceañera*, had showed up at Denny's Guys' Day Out, and had even played a Mexican love song at Avis and Peter's wedding. Our guys were as different from each other as that box of miscellaneous nails Denny kept on his cluttered workbench in the basement. Squat roofing nails; long, fine-finish nails; screws of all sizes—each with its own purpose. And you couldn't do with just one kind. You needed them all.

Suddenly anger rose up from my gut. That White Pride group had come along and nearly destroyed our hope. They'd fanned smoldering embers of fear with their bully talk. If they wanted to plant seeds of hate, bigotry, suspicion, fear, and helplessness—well, they'd nearly succeeded. Look at Ben and Ruth, who thought they'd buried painful family memories from the Holocaust. Look at Josh, giving up his youthful expectation that he could make a difference. Look at Chris Hickman, who only needed an excuse to be an angry street kid. And look at Nony's family, broken and hurting, all because—

I hit the porch railing with my fist. "Well, God, they're *not* going to succeed! We're going to fight back! Even if it means just taking a stand and not giving up any ground we've won already!"

I was so busy telling God I was ready to get tough that I didn't hear anybody coming down the steps from Stu's apartment until I heard an awkward cough. I jumped up. Stu stood on the landing twelve steps above my head, wearing a broomstick skirt, clogs, and an oversize top, all in different shades of tan and brown. Her long hair was pulled back haphazardly in a knot at the nape of her neck.

"Oh," she said. "I heard voices, thought you were talking to somebody." I almost said, *"I was talking to Somebody,"* but she obviously had something on her mind. "I was just going to ask—say, if you've got a minute, could you come upstairs? Becky and I need to talk and, well, we both agreed it'd be good if a third person could be there. She . . . suggested you." Stu hesitated on Becky's suggestion just long enough to sound surprised.

SOMEHOW, I MANAGED TO SPEND AN HOUR that afternoon with Stu and Becky, acting as facilitator while they each drew up lists of "What I Want/Need," and "How I Can Help Make This Work," and still got in a blitzkrieg shopping run to the fruit market and grocery store. Even had the bright idea to double the ingredients for taco salad so I'd have enough for supper *and* Second Sunday Potluck the next day.

I felt energized for the first time since . . . well, since Yada Yada's anniversary weekend a month ago when Avis got married and Yo-Yo and Becky got baptized. As for getting the laundry folded . . . well, something had to give.

Didn't quite know how to explain to Denny about the "cardinal of hope" God had sent to our backyard, and he raised his eyebrows when I said I wanted to go to Home Depot and get a bird feeder and some birdseed. "Right now. Like tonight." I wanted to hang the "bird feeding station" I bought somewhere near the kitchen door, but I had to compromise for a corner of the garage when Denny made a big fuss about "bird poop and sunflower seed hulls" all over the back porch.

At least he hung the thing before church the next morning.

I saved a couple of seats at my table during the potluck after service, wanting a chance to tell Avis and Florida about the "cardinal of hope" that had appeared in my backyard the previous afternoon. But as I craned my neck looking for them, comments at the table behind me distracted my attention.

"Really too bad we have to rush our Second Sunday Potluck, just so we can clear out in time for that other church to use our building. Did we agree on this as a congregation?"

"Felt like a rushed decision to me. We didn't get a chance to talk about all the inconvenience it would create. Why didn't they just rent a room from the Y or one of the high schools?"

"That's right. Two churches in one building doesn't make sense. And *we* own the building. Should we be the ones that have to hurry up and clear out? Why can't they just start later?"

"Well, I heard that last week they ran over their time and were still having a prayer service when the youth group got here. The kids were real upset."

"Hm. They don't sound very considerate to me. What do we know about these people anyway?"

I was afraid to turn around, afraid I'd spew my mouthful of half-chewed shepherd's pie all over the gripers behind me. I recognized a couple of the voices; wasn't sure about the others. A half-dozen cutting remarks almost made it to the tip of my tongue, none of which would have won me any friends or built any bridges.

I was mad. Too mad to sit there and pretend to eat. Mad at the pettiness. Mad at how little it took to keep "those people" at arm's length. Mad at how easy it was to weigh everything by what was convenient or best for "us." Mad because New Morning was Mark and Nony's church, and it felt like kicking my friends when they were down.

I took the coward's way out, found Amanda, and told her to tell her dad I was going to walk home.

33

I mentally kicked myself all the way home. Why didn't I say something? Something thoughtful and penetrating, like, *"Jesus told us to lay down our lives for each other, to be a living sacrifice. Sacrificing some of our church space and a little of our time doesn't seem like too much to ask, does it?"* Or . . . *"You might feel differently if you took the time to meet the people who are using our building, maybe even worshiped with them one of these afternoons."*

In my gut, I knew why I didn't. Because, deep down, I knew how easily the Jodi Marie Baxter who lived in my skin—self-righteous, self-centered *moi*—could've made those remarks just a few months ago. Today those thoughtless remarks felt personal—after all, Mark and Nony were my friends, and New Morning was their church. But who was I to get all self-righteous? *I* hadn't taken the time to meet others from New Morning Church or attend one of their services, not like Peter Douglass and Josh did. And I didn't want to either—not today. Not with our own worship this morning *and* potluck afterward *and* a Yada Yada prayer meeting tonight.

If I put my body where my mouth was, I'd be in church all day.

DENNY WAS PEEVED AT ME for walking home without telling him why; he said he got all worried. But we took Willie Wonka for a leisurely walk to the lake, in spite of a big thundercloud building up in the southwest, and I told him what happened. "I felt so mad, I was afraid I'd say something I'd regret or bust out crying. I kept thinking, what if Nony overheard Uptown people saying those things! Especially when New Morning ran late last week because they were praying for Mark! But"—I eyed my husband sheepishly—"I'm kinda glad I didn't mouth off. Probably would've stuck my foot in it."

The sky was getting darker. Lightning flashed off to the west. The air hung warm and heavy. Denny took my hand, and we started back home. "Thing is," he said, "if people at Uptown are not only thinking but actually *saying* stuff like that, we've got a problem. Negative attitudes feed on themselves. It's *not* convenient having New Morning share our space, but . . ." He seemed lost in his own thoughts for the next half block. I accepted the silence, aware of his fingers laced with mine, hoping the rain would hold off long enough so we didn't have to dash. "If we don't do anything about it," he resumed, "ill feelings might only get worse. The status quo obviously isn't working. Seems like we either have to back off—or dive in."

Whatever *that* meant. But I didn't have time to unravel his meaning, because fat raindrops began plopping all around us, like so many staccato beats of a percussive band. We ran, dragging poor Willie Wonka behind us as fast as his arthritic legs would pump. Made it to our front porch just as the skies dumped whole sheets of water like dancing curtains blowing in on a warm wind.

Wonka shook himself off, looking offended at the mad dash he'd been forced to make. "Hey, Wonka," Denny teased, knuckling the dog's noggin, "by the time you walk to the back of the house, this little storm will have rolled right over us and be headed toward Michigan." He disappeared inside with the dog. But I lingered on the front porch. I loved Midwestern summer storms, rolling in and then rolling right back out again with a bang and a bit of fireworks, cleansing the air and leaving everything squeaky clean.

Denny poked his head out the door again. "Think I'll run up to the hospital to see Mark. Want to come?"

I shook my head. "Can't. Yada Yada is meeting at Stu's in"—I squinted at my watch—"about an hour. Nony's coming." I was glad he was going; glad I had an excuse not to. It was painful seeing Nony's husband just lying in that stark hospital room attached to machines like a human experiment in a sci-fi movie.

An earsplitting thunderclap overhead made me jump, followed almost immediately by a bright flash of lightning. *Mm—that was close.* I peered up and down the street to see if any trees had been struck. That's when I noticed a familiar car parked in front of the house getting a nature bath.

Adele Skuggs's little Ford Escort. What was *she* doing here? Was it time for Yada Yada already? I shook my watch. Still ticking. Still only four o'clock. So why . . . ?

I tried Stu's front door. Not locked. I hollered up the stairs, "Anybody home? It's Jodi!"

"Come on up," Stu hollered back.

I found them in the kitchen. Becky was sitting in a straight-backed chair facing away from me, a plastic cape tied around her neck, her hair wet and sectioned, each strand held with a giant clip.

Adele was busy, scissors in hand, snipping away at Becky's mousy brown hair, section by section. Becky's right hand rested in a bowl of sudsy water on the tiny kitchen table; Stu bent over her left hand, carefully painting Becky's stubby nails a lovely magenta.

I blinked. The talk yesterday between Stu and Becky had been firm, fair, no nonsense. Stu had drawn a "no tolerance" line in the sand: Any drugs on this property, even marijuana, and she'd call Becky's parole officer. And she wanted household chores as "rent." On Becky's part, she said she needed a job, something— anything!—she could do at home to keep her from going crazy. She wanted regular visits with Andy. And she wanted to get her own place as soon as possible, to make a home for her little boy. Stu had agreed to look into resources for work-at-home jobs, she'd push Andy's caseworker for regular visits, and she'd be *delighted* if Becky could get her own place.

All told, they'd made good progress, but the meeting wasn't exactly what I'd call chummy. Now . . . I wished I had a camera. I could use it to blackmail Stu next time she got cranky about wet towels on the bathroom floor.

"Jodi? That you?" Becky tried to twist around to see me. "Adele won't lemme see what she's doin'! Please tell me it's gonna be all right."

"You hold still, Becky Wallace," Adele scolded, "or—"

"—I'll cut something you'll wish I hadn't!" I mimicked Adele's favorite mantra. Adele snorted. "Hush now, Jodi Baxter. A sista's gotta do what a sista's gotta do." She kept right on snipping.

Uh-huh. And you've been dying to get your scissors into B. W.'s hair ever since she showed up at Stu's front door with her toothbrush. I squeezed past Stu and stood in front of Becky, eyeing her critically—and remembering last summer when Denny had conspired with my Yada Yada sisters to get me to Adele's Hair and Nails for a makeover a couple of months after the car accident. Florida's words came popping out of my mouth: "Gotta trust your hairdresser, Becky. Relax, girl. You are going to look *good*."

SHE DID TOO. By the time the rest of the Yada Yada sisters came huffing up the stairs to Stu's second-floor apartment, Becky's hair had undergone a transformation—a richer brunette color with auburn highlights; short and feathered in the back, a bit longer in the front, creating a playful swing every time she turned her head. Her nails—fingers and toes—had color, and I noticed a smidgeon of rosy blush, lipstick, and mascara.

"Girl, where ya been hidin' your beautiful self?" Florida turned her around. "Mm-hm. You lookin' *fine*."

"*Si!*" Delores beamed. "You can throw away that bandana now."

Edesa gave Becky a hug and one of her big smiles. "I hope you will be coming to all our Yada Yada meetings now. *Si?*"

I caught Stu's eye. If Stu followed through on calling the parole agent, she would. Could.

Chanda looked Becky up and down. "Now you be needing somet'ing new to wear. A woman wit' nice, skinny legs as you got should be showing dem off. Baggy ol' sweatpants, uh-uh. Dey gotta go." I hid a smile. Chanda's own plump legs had gotten a good deal of exposure lately in the tight, short skirts she'd been buying.

Becky's eyes glistened at all the attention.

Yo-Yo showed up—without Ruth. "De lady sick again?" Chanda asked, helping herself to two of Stu's lemon bars.

Yo-Yo shrugged. "Dunno. She just said she was tired."

"Humph." Chanda wagged her head, her mouth full. "Time we sistahs got to worrying. Dat lady either got cancer or got 'erself pregnant."

Ruth's recent absences weren't funny, but it was hard not to laugh. "I'm sure there are other possibilities," Stu said dryly, handing a pitcher of iced tea to Chanda. "Here. Make yourself useful."

I counted noses. "Are Nony and Hoshi coming?" I asked Avis, who looked strangely undignified in one of Stu's wicker chairs. Stu's wicker furniture required a good slouch, and I was sure Avis hadn't slouched in all her fifty-plus years.

Avis shifted, trying to get comfortable. "She said she would try. Might have to bring the boys. She doesn't want to leave them with a sitter."

"No problem," I said. "Amanda and Josh are both home tonight. Youth group got cancelled since they went to Jesus People yesterday to sign up for Cornerstone as volunteers. The boys can hang out with them."

As the lemon bars and iced tea got passed around, Avis said, "Almost forgot! Chanda and Yo-Yo? Would either or both of you like a computer? Peter's getting some new ones for his office and—"

"For real?" Yo-Yo's eyes widened. "Ya mean, like, he's giving them away?"

"Sure. Passing on the blessing." Avis smiled.

"All right by me." Yo-Yo's grin practically hit both ears. "Pete an' Jerry gonna fall right outta their skin."

Chanda waved a finger back and forth. "T'anks, but not for me. Dis girl don' want no more hand-me-downs, secondhand, gently used, or whatever name it go by. Tired of being a charity case—an' no need now." She sniffed. "Me be getting a computer soon, but I tell you true, it going to be spankin' new from top to bottom." She sat back and folded her arms across her chest.

Avis shrugged. "It's up to you. Just wanted to ask my sisters first, before Peter—"

"Uh . . ." Becky Wallace, sitting on a kitchen chair just off to the side, cleared her throat. "If nobody else wantin' that computer, I'll take it. Might help me get some work I could do while I'm stuck on house arrest." She aimed a meaningful eye at Chanda. "When a body don't got nothin', secondhand sparkle like gold an' diamonds."

"Good. It's yours," Avis said hastily, cutting off Chanda, who looked like she was ready to come out sparring. "Let's begin with a prayer, shall we? Edesa, would you?" And with Edesa's simple, sweet opening prayer, Avis had deftly steered us into our prayer time.

After Edesa closed the prayer, Avis asked, "Delores, can you tell us what the doctors are saying about Mark?"

Delores seemed to search for an answer but ended up shaking her head. "The doctors are . . . how do you say it? *No decir cualquier cosa*—not saying much. He is still critical."

Storm clouds gathered on Adele's face. "An' the police aren't saying nothin' about who did this either. If you ask me, they're afraid to call it a hate crime. Don't want to set off any racial mess." She folded her arms across her generous chest, as if holding in what she *really* thought.

I jumped in with my two cents. "At least they ought to haul in that jerk in the red tie for questioning—the one who left hate litera-ture at the Sisulu-Smiths and then threatened Mark at the rally. I'd like to see *him* in jail." The moment the words were out of my mouth, I saw Becky wince and regretted my big mouth. *She probably thinks we talked about her like that after the robbery last fall.* I winced myself. We probably did. *Oh Jesus.*

Avis cleared her throat. "Sisters, while we're waiting for Nony and Hoshi, I'd like to read a few verses from Ephesians, chapter six—the passage that talks about putting on the whole armor of God." She paged to the last section of her big Bible. Several others with Bibles hunted it up too. "Here it is. 'Be strong in the Lord and in his mighty power. Put on the full armor of God so that you can take your stand against the devil's schemes' . . ."

Becky, sitting a bit apart from the rest of us, leaned forward, elbows on the knees of her skinny jeans and chin in her hands, as if to catch every word.

"'For our struggle is not against flesh and blood,'" Avis continued, "'but against the rulers, against the authorities, against the powers of this dark world and against the spiritual forces of evil in the heavenly realms.'"

Yo-Yo blew out a breath. "Sounds creepy—all that stuff about 'dark powers' and 'forces of evil.' Like a slasher movie."

"That's why we need to understand what Scripture says about fighting spiritual battles. Our struggle *isn't* against 'flesh and blood.' *People* are not the real enemy. Not the White Pride Coalition, not even the guy in the red tie." Avis gave me a teasing smile.

"Wait a minute." Stu had her hackles up. "You don't mean we should just let these creeps get away with what they did!"

"Of course not. We should pray that the person or persons who attacked Mark will be brought to justice. But even if they are, the battle is not over. Because the attitudes of hate and violence behind this attack are *spiritual* in nature, so we need to use spiritual weapons to fight back."

"I don't get it." We all looked at Becky Wallace. This was only her second time meeting with Yada Yada, and the first time she'd opened her mouth during a discussion. "*Spiritual* weapons? Ain't that a contradiction? I mean, I thought being a Christian was all about love an' stuff."

"Not a contradiction. Love *is* a spiritual weapon! That's the weapon God used to overcome sin and death." Avis flipped in her Bible again. "John 3:16 says, 'For God so loved the world that he gave his one and only Son'—meaning that He let Jesus take the punishment for all our sins. And the very next verse says, 'For God did not send his Son into the world to condemn the world, but to save the world.'"

"Thank ya, Jesus! Or my butt would be fried for sure!" Florida wagged her head, making us laugh.

Becky shifted in her chair. "Yeah, guess I understand that. 'Cause I'd still be in prison if you guys hadn't, well, been nice to me."

Adele snorted. "*Nice* didn't have much to do with it. Some of us didn't feel so 'nice' after what you did." She shrugged. "But like Florida said, all of us are in the same boat. You, me, Yo-Yo, Avis . . . Love covered over our sins. God expects those who 'get' to 'give.'"

"So love . . . that's it?" Yo-Yo sounded skeptical.

"I don't feel much like loving those White Pride people," I admitted. "Not after what they did."

"But our sister is right," Delores said. "About love being a spiritual weapon." She hunted for something in her Bible. "In the Sermon on the Mount, Jesus said, 'You have heard people say, "Love your neighbors and hate your enemies." But I tell you to love your enemies and pray for anyone who mistreats you.'"

"Or mistreats your brother," Edesa murmured.

We sat silently in Stu's melon and lime living room. Finally Yo-Yo blurted, "Can't say as I got much love for the dudes who messed with Mark, but guess we're supposed to pray for 'em, huh?"

Stu's doorbell rang. While she let Nony and Hoshi in, Yo-Yo's words pricked my conscience. *Pray for them.* God had told me clearly to go to the rally, to pray for the people there. God had seemed to point out the White Pride girl, the one with orangey-blonde hair. Had I been praying for her since the attack on Mark?

No.

If I'd thought about her at all, it was wishing I could slap her upside the head.

34

"S orry we are late," Nony said apologetically. "The boys were visiting their father." A plain black head wrap hid her usually sculpted hair; the bright African prints were missing, replaced by an ordinary pair of beige slacks and black top. Her eyes seemed large; strain lined her face. Even so, she was beautiful. "Can the boys do their homework somewhere?"

I crooked a finger at Marcus and Michael. "Come with me. Amanda and Josh are studying too. You can hang out with them."

Amanda, doing homework at the dining room table, gave both boys a big grin and made room for them at the table. Knowing Amanda, she'd probably haul out the makings for caramel popcorn balls given half an excuse. When I ducked out to go back upstairs, Josh, who was supposed to be studying for his last two finals, came out of his room and started shadowboxing with the boys, creating unrestrained youthful glee.

Wasn't sure how much homework was going to get done, but maybe Josh and Amanda needed Marcus and Michael as much as the other way around.

When I got back upstairs, Yada Yada was singing. I squeezed onto Stu's futon between Edesa and Delores, closed my eyes, and just listened.

> *If the sun says I won't rise*
> *If dark clouds fill my skies*
> *Lord, just know that I*
> *Will always give You praise . . .*

Oh my. Could I sing this song if I were in Nony's shoes? I peeked at Nonyameko. She wasn't singing either. Her eyes were closed, and tears slid down her face. My own throat tightened. The words sank in deep.

> *No matter come what may*
> *I'll always give You praise . . .*

The room was quiet when the final phrase died away, except for a few sniffles and blowing of noses. Then Hoshi spoke up quietly. "That seems—how do you say it?—a lot to ask. To praise God when evil things happen. It was hard when—" She stopped, suddenly flustered. She seemed about to say, *"When Bandana Woman cut my mother's hand"*—and then realized Becky Wallace was sitting right there in the room. Hoshi blinked fast, swallowed, and recovered her composure. "It is very hard to feel like praising God when Dr. Smith is in a coma, day after day with no change, no response."

Yo-Yo, at home on one of Stu's floor cushions, nodded vigorously. "Yeah. Me too. I don't feel much like praising. Feel more like throwing things."

Murmurs of assent traveled around the room. Nony, curled up in another one of Stu's wicker chairs, just shook her head, as though she couldn't find a way to put her feelings into words.

"Nony?" Avis's voice was gentle. "It's all right. Say what you need to say."

Nony rolled her eyes and gave a bitter laugh. "It's not pretty, what I am feeling today. Today I am angry. So angry I—yes, Yo-Yo. I want to throw things." She looked around the circle. "You are not surprised. You are angry too. Ah, but you are angry at the people who hurt Mark. Or maybe you are angry at God for letting this happen. Yes, I have been angry that way too. But today . . ." She laughed again, a strange, hollow sound. "Today I am angry at Mark. *I am so angry with him!* Angry that he had to wade right into the middle of that hate group, when he knew—*he knew!*—they were out for trouble. He—he risked our family, he risked our future to protest one stupid rally." Her hands clenched; her voice trembled. "I am angry that he has left me alone, left my bed empty, abandoned our boys, who need their father . . ." She covered her face with her hands. "Oh Jesus. I don't know how to praise You. I can't. I don't even know how to pray anymore."

I stared at Nony. Was this the same woman, who just a few days ago had struggled with feeling guilty, saying what happened to Mark was all her fault? But now it was *Mark's* fault? I thought I knew her, this woman whose heart and mouth were always full of Scripture, who fed on God's promises like bread and butter, whose compassion for hurting people so far outweighed my own . . . but *this* Nony seemed like a stranger to me.

God's Voice in my spirit put brakes on my tumbling thoughts. *Pray for her, Jodi. Grief has to cycle through its seasons—heartache, fear, anger, helplessness . . . Just be there for her until the season of strength and courage.*

I squeezed my eyes shut. *I want to, God. Help me. I don't know how.*

No one said anything for a few moments. Then Adele started to sing in her rich contralto voice. *"Say the Name . . . of Je-sus . . ."* Recognizing the song from one of Clint Brown's CDs, I joined in with the rest:

> *When you don't know what else to pray*
> *When you can't find the words to say*
> *Say the Name . . .*

As the tender song trailed off, Delores cleared her throat. "Nony, my sister, *es bueno* you can say you are angry. No use pretending; God knows anyway. And He understands. But as the first song said, we must keep praising! It doesn't have anything to do with *feeling* like praising." Her eyes lowered to her lap, and her voice softened. "Believe me, I know. My Ricardo—something is not right. He is gone many nights. He will not say. He takes the dog. I tremble with fear. Darkness threatens to shadow our home. But I praise anyway. I fill my heart with praise. When I praise, there is no room for fear. It is the only way."

I reached for Delores's hand beside me and squeezed. *Oh Jesus. What's going on with Ricardo? No wonder Delores has seemed troubled lately.* It sounded like even Delores didn't know.

"Thank ya, Jesus!" Florida blurted. "You're a good God, and don't let us forget it. Ol' devil wants to make us blind to Your love and goodness, wants to make us think all the misery he sendin' our way—not to mention all the mess we cook up for our own selves—

somehow is *Your* fault. But we know *You* are the Light of the world, King of kings, and Lord of lords! An' he ain't nothin' but the prince of darkness. Light stronger than darkness anytime. Don't even have to wrestle. Light just gotta show up and darkness gotta go. Thank ya! *Thank* ya!"

Florida's prayer opened up a regular flood of praise and prayers, several speaking at once. Even Nony's head nodded now, her lips whispering, "Yes, yes. Help me, Jesus." We ended up gathering around Nony and laying our hands on her, as Avis got out her little bottle of oil and anointed her forehead. Someone pushed Delores into the center of the circle, and Avis anointed her, too, as we prayed for God's light to shine through the darkness.

After the prayers, Nony blew her nose and mopped her wet face. "Thank you, my sisters. Thank you so much for helping me touch the hem of His garment, when I couldn't get through the crowd of pain and anger on my own. My heart feels"—she smiled sheepishly—"maybe not healed, but more at peace."

A puzzled look crossed Yo-Yo's face. Becky's too. I wanted to giggle. I could almost hear their minds trying to plug "hem of His garment" into their own frame of reference. Well, maybe that was a story Becky and I could read together from the Bible at our back porch rendezvous next week.

We moved on to other prayer requests. But I was only half-listening. Snippets from our conversations that evening kept running into each other. *Love is a spiritual weapon. Praise chases away fear. Light is stronger than darkness. Pray for our enemies.* An idea began percolating in my head. It became so strong I had a hard time waiting till Yo-Yo finished what she was saying.

"—or maybe it's Ben we should be prayin' for. He got Ruth lined up with the doc next week." Yo-Yo grinned. "Whether he can wrestle her into the car and make her go, that's a diff'rent story."

We had to laugh. Dear, opinionated Ruth was one stubborn lady.

I jumped in. "Um, this isn't exactly a prayer request, but it's about praying. What about doing a prayer walk?"

Half the group looked interested. The other half had *Prayer what?* plastered on their faces. "Go on," Avis said.

"Well, I've been thinking about what we said tonight, about light and darkness. Jesus is the Light of the world, right? By lifting up the name of Jesus where there's darkness, the things that need darkness to survive get chased out, right? And the Bible says that we aren't supposed to hide that light in a corner; we're supposed to let it shine where darkness is hiding evil—or something like that."

Delores, Adele, and Avis began flipping pages in their Bibles. "Mm-hm." Adele thumbed her well-worn King James Version. "Matthew five and fifteen says, 'Neither do men light a candle, and put it under a bushel, but on a candlestick; and it giveth light unto all that are in the house.'"

Delores had her finger in the Gospel of John. "'Light has come into the world, but men loved darkness because their deeds were evil.'"

Avis read from Ephesians. "'Live as children of the light . . . Have nothing to do with fruitless deeds of darkness but rather expose them.'"

Wow. All that support for what I wanted to say, straight from the Bible. "That's it. But I was thinking, just praying here at Yada Yada is a little like hiding the light. We need to take the light to where the darkness is. Like the campus of Northwestern. All those incidents that have been happening up there? The hate literature, the swastika somebody painted, White Pride holding that rally? What if we did a prayer walk around the campus, praying for God's protection from those deeds of darkness?"

I WAS SURPRISED how excited Yada Yada got about my idea for a prayer walk. In fact, before we went home, people were suggesting we split up and some of us do our prayer walking on campus, and some of us pray God's protection over the Sisulu-Smiths' home and neighborhood. On one hand, doing it next weekend made sense, but Saturday seemed too far away. We finally decided on this Thursday at six o'clock, whoever could make it after work.

Even Nony said she'd come if she could.

Denny was home from the hospital by the time I got downstairs, digging into some nacho chips and salsa at the dining room table. He looked wrung out. "It's hard keeping up a one-sided conversation with a guy in a coma," he admitted. Ben Garfield had showed up after dropping off Yo-Yo at Yada Yada, so that helped.

He listened while I told him about our discussion at Yada Yada, about love being a weapon of spiritual warfare, about taking light into the darkness, about our idea for a prayer walk. I even got out my Bible and read some of the verses.

I didn't notice Josh leaning against the archway between the hallway and dining room until he said, "Mom? Read that one again about exposing deeds of darkness."

How long had he been there? "Um, sure. It's Ephesians five, starting at verse eight. 'Live as children of light (for the fruit of the light consists in all goodness, righteousness and truth) and find out what pleases the Lord. Have nothing to do with the fruitless deeds of darkness, but rather expose them.'"

He nodded thoughtfully, propped against the archway, hands in the pockets of his jeans. "That's what Dr. Smith was doing at the rally, wasn't it? Exposing deeds of darkness."

Denny and I glanced at each other. Denny cleared his throat. "That's right. He was."

Josh walked over and held out his hand. "Can I see that?" He took my open Bible and walked away toward his bedroom.

"What are you going to do?" I called after him, thinking there was something different about Josh. Couldn't put my finger on it.

"I dunno. Maybe nothing. Maybe something." His bedroom door clicked shut.

I suddenly realized what was different about Josh. A shadow of sandy hair covered his head—longer than his hair had been since he first shaved it off last fall.

Was Josh growing out his hair?

35

ecided to keep my mouth shut about Josh's hair, sure that the moment I expressed anything remotely complimentary about this new growth, off it would come. Not that I saw much of him the next few days. It was finals week, and on Monday he stayed at the high school library till suppertime, then holed up in his room studying. As I let Willie Wonka out for one last pee at ten o'clock, Josh emerged from his room holding a couple of pieces of paper covered in scrawl. "Computer free? Gotta type something up."

"Thought all your final papers were due last week! Is it late?"

"Chill, Mom. I wrote something for the student newspaper. *The Warrior's* last issue. An opinion piece."

"Oh." My curiosity was piqued. "Can I read it?"

He snorted, waving the marked-up and crossed-out paper out of reach as he booted up the computer in the dining room. "Even I can't read it in this state. Maybe later."

Uh-huh. I knew when I'd been given the brush-off.

It might have been the last full week of school for Josh, but Amanda still had two weeks to go, and so did Denny and I. I managed to squeak in a half-hour of Bible reading with Becky Wallace on Tuesday, but a staff meeting after school got me home late on Thursday. *What's with Avis, anyway?* I grumbled to myself, trying to look alert and interested in the most recent statistics of the "No Child Left Behind" legislation. *Doesn't she remember Yada Yada agreed to do the prayer walk tonight?* But even Avis Johnson Douglass couldn't change district school schedules around just for our ragtag prayer group.

Once home at four thirty, I racked my brain for something I could eat on the run, while leaving some decent pickings for Denny and the kids. I finally pulled out the leftover chicken from last night, tore the meat off the bones, chopped it, and tossed it together with a head of romaine lettuce, a can of mandarin orange slices, green onions, sliced almonds that had been hiding in the freezer since Christmas, and a can of dry Chinese noodles for a passable oriental chicken salad. I stepped back to admire my handiwork. *Hey, girl. Someone might think you actually planned this thing!*

Denny wasn't back with the minivan, so I called Stu at five thirty and begged a ride with her up to Northwestern. Josh loomed over my shoulder as I hung up the phone. "Think Stu would mind if I rode along? Something I gotta do at Northwestern."

"Do? Like what?"

He shrugged me off. "Someone I gotta see, OK?"

WE WERE SUPPOSED TO MEET the other Yada Yadas at the Rock at six. Stu parked her Celica on a side street, and Josh trotted off, promising to meet us back at the car in one hour.

"What's he doing?" Stu jerked a thumb in the direction Josh had disappeared.

I rolled my eyes. "I'm just his mother. I'll be the last to know."

We were the first to arrive at the Rock. It felt strange standing in the same spot where the White Pride rally had taken place less than two weeks earlier. So serene and quiet now, the Rock painted yet another color, the bridalwreath bushes bursting with dainty flowers and shades of green. A few students sat on the low stone wall surrounding the Rock, noses in their books, drinking coffee or soft drinks from disposable cups. No one paid any attention to us, even when Florida, Avis, and Adele showed up, followed in short order by Edesa, Delores—and Ruth Garfield.

"Ruth!" we screeched. She seemed embarrassed by all the hugs.

"Down, girls. Save the excitement till the Cubs win the pennant." She shrugged. "So I missed one little meeting."

"Two!" Stu waved two fingers under Ruth's nose. "Out of the last three. Did you see your doctor yet?"

"Oh that." Ruth waved a hand dismissively.

Nony and Hoshi joined us just then. Yo-Yo, Ruth said, had to work at the Bagel Bakery that evening, and no one had heard from Chanda, so we decided to go ahead. We divided into two groups: Florida, Adele, Delores, and Stu agreed to walk over to the Sisulu-Smith neighborhood and walk around the surrounding blocks, praying. "Four is enough," Nony agreed with a slight smile. "The neighbors might get nervous." The rest of us would pray at different points on the campus, and we'd meet back at the Rock in an hour.

We held hands in a circle and prayed before the neighborhood group set off, generating a few odd looks from passersby. *Which you wouldn't even know about if you'd keep your eyes shut, Jodi Baxter,* I scolded myself. I concentrated on Florida's prayer.

"—standing on the same bricks where that rally took place a couple of weeks ago. Jesus! We ask Your blood of forgiveness to pour over all the hateful things said an' done that day. We prayin' for all the students, all the young people here that day, whatever stripe or color. Sift what was spoken, so that every evil thing will be blocked from their hearts an' minds, an' every good and God-fearin' thing settle right into their spirits."

I pictured that Friday afternoon in my mind, the restless crowd, the White Pride group—some in suits and ties, others just tough guys who needed to build themselves up by putting others down. And the girl in the sundress, clinging to some false identity offered by this group of white supremacists. Yet I remembered her eyes. Uncertain. Insecure.

I added a P.S. to Florida's prayer. "Lord God, I especially want to pray for the young woman I saw that day with the White Pride group. I don't know her name, but You do. Call her out, Jesus! Call her to Yourself. Find her, Lord! Show her a better way."

We split up then. As the other group disappeared across Sheridan Road to the Smith's neighborhood, Hoshi spoke up. "Why don't we start praying right there? It is Dr. Smith's office." She pointed to a plain building looming along the south side of the plaza. Sure enough, the sign said Harris Hall, History Department.

To my surprise, Edesa spoke the first prayer as we gathered at the entrance. "*Jesú Cristo*, we thank You for Your great love, even as we stand here with hurting hearts. There is an empty office in this building, a professor who is not here for his students, a husband who is not here for his wife, a father who is not here for his children . . ."

It was too much for Nony; she began to weep. Edesa and Hoshi each put an arm around her waist and let her lean on them, but Edesa continued to pray. "But one thing we know, loving Savior! *You* will never leave us nor forsake us. And that includes our *hermano*, our brother, Mark Smith. You have not forsaken him or his family. No matter what the circumstances look like, we claim what is true."

Ruth cleared her throat. "God, it's me, Ruth. What a prayer walk is, I don't know. But I figure, it can't hurt. Evil raised its ugly head on this campus in recent weeks—the same pride and hatred that has caused havoc around the world for centuries. Gentiles hating Jews, whites against blacks. Ugly stuff. The stuff that causes wars and riots, leaving misery in its wake. But we're asking You to turn it around, God. Right here, at the history department of this great university."

Ruth jumped when her prayer was met with several "amens" and "That's it, Jesus!"

Hoshi prayed simply, "Father in heaven, may Your kingdom come and Your will be done on this campus, even as it is in heaven. And, please, inspire others to continue the work Dr. Smith began on this campus, bringing students of all nationalities together to learn from one another, and even—as he did for me—to learn about You."

The prayers were so powerful that we just strolled in silence for a while along the paths curving between weeping willows and beautifully landscaped lawns. It was tempting to just gawk at the enchanting mix of old and new architecture, but we stopped beside several of the university buildings to pray briefly, naming the department housed there and praying for the administrators, professors, and students.

Pausing under a willow tree near the imposing university library,

Nony, her tears subsided, voiced a heartfelt prayer from the Psalms. "I love You, O Lord, my strength! You are my rock, my fortress, and my deliverer; You, my God, are my rock, in whom I take refuge. You are my shield and the horn of my salvation, my stronghold! I call to You, O Lord, who is worthy of praise, and I am saved from my enemies. But I pray not only for myself, God, but for all the young men and women of this campus, those who know You and those who don't, that You will be their defender from the Evil One."

Avis, picking up on Nony's prayer, prayed for the spiritual battle raging for the hearts and minds of students on this campus and on campuses all over the world. "Break down the strongholds of unbelief," she prayed. "Raise up a Moses, a David, an Esther, a Paul on this campus who are willing to step forward as God's messengers in this day and in this hour!"

As the minute hand of my watch nudged closer to seven, we found ourselves walking up the path to the Norris University Center, NU's student center, overlooking a sleepy lagoon. "We can use the restrooms here," Hoshi suggested. Then she smiled slyly. "Willie's Too has fruit smoothies."

Ruth perked up. "Prayer and smoothies—that's a marriage made in heaven, if you ask me."

We laughed as we headed down the stairs to the ground level of Norris, feeling energized and almost lighthearted by the prayer walk. But as we started to walk into the student café, I put out an arm to stop our charge. "Wait. Shh. Don't go in."

The other Yada sisters stopped, confused. "What is it, Jodi?" Avis asked.

My heart thumped like the bass drum in a Sousa march. I peeked into the large lower room with its wooden tables and padded booths, hanging TVs, the enticing smell of coffee and pizza, and wall of windows overlooking the lagoon, just to be sure my eyes had not been playing tricks on me.

They weren't. Josh was standing beside one of the tables nearest the door, his back toward us, talking to an African-American student wearing a Northwestern T-shirt, shorts, and sandals. Big guy. Legs solid as tree trunks. Looked like a football player. Wearing dreadlocks. Next to him, Josh looked like a skinny middle-school student.

"So?" The big guy's voice suddenly carried our way, a mixture of scorn and frustration. "You're still white! Maybe you're not part of that White Pride group, but you're still walkin' around with all that white privilege in your pocket you people take for granted. Deal with it, man!"

Impulsively, I took a step forward, my thoughts spinning. *What on earth is my son doing here? Is that guy threatening him? Josh is going to get the stuffing beat out of him!* At almost the same moment, Florida grabbed my arm and pulled me away, practically pushing me back up the stairs and out the nearest exit. "Not a word, Jodi Baxter," she hissed in my ear. "That boy's doing a man's work in there. Facin' his own moment of truth."

STU AND I WERE ALREADY WAITING IN THE CAR when Josh ran up out of breath, ten minutes late. I managed to keep my mouth shut until Stu parked the Celica in the garage and disappeared up the back stairs to her apartment. Then I grabbed Josh's arm before we went into the house.

"Josh! *That* was the 'somebody' you were going to meet? The same guy who pushed us down at the rally? What were you *thinking*?"

Josh flopped onto the porch swing, resting his arms along the back and sticking out his lanky legs. "What? You were spying on me?"

"No such thing!" I explained that we were heading for the student café when I saw him talking in the eatery. "Didn't mean to eavesdrop, but the guy's voice carried like he was using a megaphone." I sank down on the back steps. "He didn't sound too friendly."

Josh shrugged. "I wasn't expecting friendly. Just wanted to clear up his presumption that I was part of the White Pride Coalition. Dr. Smith said his name was Matt Jackson, so I located his dorm. Somebody—roommate, I think—told me he was hanging out at Norris. Kinda surprised me that I actually found him. But I wanted to give it a shot. I prayed that I'd find him. And I did."

I gaped at my son in amazement. Would I have gone to talk to a big bully like that after he'd pushed me around? Not likely. And not when I was only eighteen, for sure.

"From what I heard, he didn't sound very open to what you had to say. You're white, that's it, end of subject."

Josh shrugged again. "Yeah. But he let me have my say; then he had his say. That's a start. Besides, I got in the last punch."

I raised my eyebrows. "What'd you say?"

"Wasn't what I said. I told him he had a point, and I *was* trying to deal with it. Then"—Josh grinned—"I shook his hand."

36

I had to look twice to see who was pulling weeds in the flower garden when I got home from school Friday afternoon. Still wasn't used to Becky's new look. Her face seemed . . . younger. Fresher. Could definitely use some new clothes, though. Her new Bible was sitting on the back steps. She obviously was going to hold me to my promise to study the Bible "a couple of times a week."

Becky brushed the dirt off her jeans, took the glass of iced tea I handed her, and plunked down on the steps to Stu's apartment, facing me on the swing. "Been doin' some readin' in the Gospel of Matthew, like you said. Guess what I found?" She grinned, wiping her mouth with the back of her hand, leaving a dirty streak on her face. "That story 'bout the woman touching the hem of Jesus' robe, or whatever they called it. Man! *Zap*, she was healed. After bleedin' all those years." She wagged her head. "Never knew the Bible talked about female problems like that."

I laughed. "Well, yeah. The Bible isn't for the fainthearted. Gets pretty graphic sometimes."

"Blows my mind, Jesus healing all those sick people. Right and left! Deaf guys. Blind guys. Even a dead girl!" She shook her head. "But what I'm wonderin' is . . . all you Yada Yadas been prayin' for Jesus to heal Nony's husband, an' He ain't answerin'. Why is that? I mean, if He's *God* . . ."

I pushed the swing with the toe of my shoe. *Huh. Good question, Becky. Wish I knew the answer.* The swing swayed gently, giving me time to collect my thoughts. *Lord, help me here!* I took a deep breath. "I ask that question all the time, Becky. Jesus did promise that if we ask anything in His name, He will do it. But there's a story in the Gospels about two sisters—Mary and Martha—whose brother was sick. They sent for Jesus to heal him. Jesus got the message, but He didn't come right away. And Lazarus died. The sisters were devastated, and they scolded Jesus when He finally came. Told Him that if He'd come when they'd asked Him to, Lazarus wouldn't have died. But Jesus had a reason for waiting; He had another plan in mind. He raised Lazarus from the dead—after four days in the grave! But the whole purpose was to bring glory to God, to do an even greater thing."

Becky leaned forward, and I realized she was listening intently.

I pressed on, reaching for the faith that had been building in me the last year. "I guess what God has been teaching me lately is that it's my job to ask, and it's God's job to answer, according to *His* plan. Sometimes His answer is yes, sometimes it's no, and sometimes it's 'wait.'" I shrugged. "I admit, it's kinda hard to swallow the 'no' and 'wait' answers. But we gotta keep praying. Gotta keep asking."

Inside the house, the phone rang. "If you want to read that story about Lazarus and his sisters, it's in the Gospel of John, chapter eleven—" The phone was insistent. "Excuse me a minute, Becky. Be right back." I hustled into the house and snatched up the phone. "Hello? Baxters."

"Sistah Jodee?" Chanda's voice squealed into my ear. "De 'ouse is mine! Closed today, bless Jesus!"

"You closed on the house already, Chanda? That's fast!" I glanced out to the back porch. Becky was hunting in her new Bible for the Gospel of John with the help of Willie Wonka's nose pushing into her lap.

Chanda chuckled with glee. "Yes! Yes! Mountains, dey move when you pay cash!" And she laughed again.

Cash. I could hardly imagine paying *cash* for a house. And knowing the price of houses in the Evanston-Skokie area, she must have paid a pretty penny.

"Oh, Sistah Jodee. It's one big 'ouse! Four bedrooms! One for Dia and Cheree, one for Thomas, one for me, and one for guests! Maybe me mother will come visit from Jamaica!"

"That's wonderful, Chanda. I'm very happy for you." I was too. Not the least bit jealous.

Liar. Even in Downers Grove we didn't have a guestroom.

"I want you to see, Jodee. I got de keys to de house now. If you give me a ride, we could go together."

I pressed the fingers of my free hand to my temple. Surely I didn't have time for this. What was happening on Saturday? Lane Tech's prom, but Josh wasn't going. Amanda had final exams next week; she should be studying. State playoffs were over, West Rogers High didn't place, so Denny didn't have to coach this weekend—but wasn't he training a new batch of suburban volunteers for Uptown's outreach to the homeless this Saturday?

"Jodee? You still dere?"

"Yes, Chanda. I was just trying to think." Oh well. Why not? Chanda needed somebody to share her joy. I stifled a sigh. "Sure. I could probably drive you up to your new house tomorrow. Could we make it in the morning? Ten o'clock?"

I WAS HUNTING FOR MY CAR KEYS the next morning when I heard thumping on the front porch. I peeked out. Peter Douglass was wrestling a box with computer logos all over it into Stu's front door. Becky's "new" computer! *Well, hallelujah.* Peter would probably get it set up and running, too, since computers were his specialty. Was he going to do the same thing for Yo-Yo?

Avis sure did get herself one heckuva good man. I found the keys in my jacket pocket and headed for the back door.

I dropped Denny off at Uptown for the outreach, then headed for Chanda's apartment building on Juneway Terrace—better known as Juneway Jungle, a street straddling the north edge of Rogers Park whose name was synonymous with drugs, gangs, and absentee landlords. There was a big push to "gentrify" the neighborhood and bring in new business to the Howard Street area, but I was sure Chanda was glad to get out of there.

I was surprised, though, when she came out of her building alone. "Don't the kids want to see the new house too?" I asked as she climbed into the front seat of the minivan. I'd assumed half the reason I'd been invited was to help ride herd on her three kids.

"I am sure dey do." Chanda smirked. "Me jus want a chance to soak up de pleasure of me new 'ouse wit'out having to chase t'ree kids upstairs an' down. Left Thomas in charge for a few hours. Saturday cartoons save de day."

I smiled. OK, this was nice. Just Chanda and me. I began to look forward to seeing Chanda's new "blessing."

Fifteen minutes later, we pulled into the driveway of a white two-story house in a quiet neighborhood in north Skokie, just west of Evanston. Skokie had everything from little brick bungalows and new yuppie condos to upper-middle-class homes on quiet, tree-shaded streets. A tad more modest than the ritzy mansions along the lakeshore that could probably house two or three families, each living separate lives. But this house was just . . . nice. Really nice. Two-car-garage nice.

I smiled at Chanda with new respect. "I love it already! Show me around!"

Proudly, Chanda walked up the short walk to the front door—no porch or veranda—and used her key to open the door. The house smelled of fresh paint. The wooden floors in the foyer and dining room gleamed. Four wooden stools lined up along a breakfast bar that divided the kitchen from the family room. A fireplace hugged one corner of the family room.

I fell in love when I pulled open the sliding doors along the backside of the family room and stepped out into a screened-in, four-seasons porch. "Oh, Chanda. I *love* screened-in porches! I am going to go home, pack my suitcase, and move in here today!"

Chanda beamed. "Me hopes you will come visit anytime, Jodee. Your man too. De whole family! Anytime!"

The doorbell rang. Chanda's eyes widened. "Who can dat be? Me not expecting nobody no how."

"Go on," I giggled, giving her a shove toward the front door. "It's probably just one of your new neighbors or the UPS man."

Chanda cautiously opened the front door and peered out. I held back but peeked over her shoulder. A fortyish man, medium tall, wearing slacks and a sport coat, stood on the front stoop. "Yes?" Chanda said. "What you be wanting?"

"Oh!" The man smiled cheerfully. "I'm Paul Schoenberg, co-owner of Schoenberg Realty"—he jerked a thumb at the real estate sign still on the lawn—"and I just came by to pick up the sign. One of our other agents handled the sale. When I saw the car in the driveway, I thought it might be the new owners, and I just wanted to—"

Chanda opened the door wider and crossed her arms across her chest. "Take de sign down? Dat's good, good. You do dat."

Just then Mr. Schoenberg caught sight of me standing next to the banister of the carpeted stairs going to the second floor. "Oh! You must be Mrs. George." He stuck his hand out in my direction, a big smile on his face. "Let me be the first to welcome you to the neighborhood."

His hand hung there, suspended in the middle of a ghastly silence. Chanda's mouth popped open. I was so startled, two fat seconds went by before I found my voice. Then I started to babble. "Oh, no! No, you've got it all wrong—"

Chanda cut me off. "Mistah, *I* am Ms. George, de new owner of dis 'ouse." Both fists settled on her wide hips. "An' dis is me friend, Mrs. *Baxter*. An' *you* can take your sign and get out." She shut the door in his face.

Chanda leaned against the door and stared at me. I stared back. And then we started to laugh. We laughed until our stomachs ached. We laughed until I realized Chanda's laughter had turned to sobs.

"Oh, Chanda." I put my arms around her. "He's just ignorant. Don't mind him. It's going to be OK."

She shook her head, and now the tears were coming freely. "He . . .

he tink me jus de maid." She sank onto the carpeted stairs, pulling a tissue out of her pocket. "Oh, Sistah Jodee. What if dey don' accept me in dis neighborhood? Keep all dey kids away from my t'ree kids?"

I hardly knew what to say. It hadn't occurred to me to ask if the neighborhood was diverse. Had it occurred to Chanda? Would *she* feel comfortable here?

Chanda suddenly raised her head, mopping her face with the soggy tissue. "No more tears. Dat's jus' Satan, trying to steal my joy!" She stood up, found another tissue, and blew her nose. "Don' have time to be offended, or I'd be a sorry mess one day to de next. Come on. Me show you de bedrooms." She practically ran upstairs. "Come see! I got me own bathroom! Believe it, girl!"

CHANDA'S NEW HOUSE was just five minutes west of Evanston Hospital, so Chanda and I decided to visit Mark Smith on our way home. Nony rose from the chair when we walked into his room in the ICU, a light on her face. "He moved!" she blurted.

"He what?" Chanda and I sounded like a Greek chorus.

"Mark's leg moved! I saw it! I was sitting right here when his leg moved. I got so excited. I called the nurse . . . but she told me it was involuntary. That people in a coma sometimes make involuntary movements. But . . ." There was no denying the hope in her voice and the smile on her face. "I saw him move. Oh, sisters. It is a sign. A sign of hope!"

I stared at Mark's body, lying motionless on the bed, still hooked to bags that fed and watered him, still hooked to machines that monitored his vitals, his eyes bandaged. He didn't look hopeful.

"Let's pray," I said, grabbing Nony's and Chanda's hands. But all

I could think of in that moment of time was the Lord's Prayer. So I prayed it anyway. We sounded like a trio without music, speaking different parts, as my Midwestern flat accent bubbled along the words with Nony's South African lilt and Chanda's Jamaican *patois*. ". . . Thy kingdom come, *Thy* will be done, on earth as it is in heaven!"

"Oh, yes, Jesus," Nony moaned. "Yes, yes."

Pastor Cobbs and his wife from New Morning Christian Church arrived just as we were saying good-bye to Nony. "Pastor Joe and Mama Rose, have you met my friends? Chanda George and Jodi Baxter. Jodi's family attends Uptown Community, where New Morning is meeting."

"Yes, yes," said Pastor Cobbs. Both he and his wife shook our hands warmly. "Pastor Clark has been very gracious, gracious indeed."

Rose Cobbs held my hand in both of hers. Her eyes were dark and deep. "I hope you will visit our service sometime. Anytime. We would love to see you."

"I would like that," I blurted. And then I realized that what I said was true. I *would* like to visit their service. And I'd just been personally invited. "Tomorrow," I said. "I would like to visit your service tomorrow."

37

The third Sunday of June promised to be a scorcher. My T-shirt and shorts were already sticking to me when I let Willie Wonka outside and headed down the back sidewalk to fill my new bird feeder. Now that summer was here—well, not "officially" till the twenty-first, but tell *that* to the heat index— I'd been enjoying having my quiet time on the back porch and watching the birds squabbling over their breakfast.

I no sooner got the garage door open where we kept the birdseed than I heard our phone ringing inside the house. *What?* It was only seven o'clock! That's like six on a weekday. I hustled back to the house in my bare feet and barely snatched up the kitchen receiver before the answering machine kicked in.

"Jodi?" It was Nony. "Did I wake you?"

"No, no. I was outside. Are you OK? Is Mark—"

"Mark is the same. I am sorry to call early. I did not mean to worry you. But I have a favor to ask, if you—"

"Sure. What's up?" Footsteps coming down the outside stairs

distracted me; I glanced out the window in time to see Stu hustling out to the garage, shutting the yard-side garage door behind her. Where in the world was she going this early on a Sunday? Some DCFS emergency situation probably. Guess we could take Becky to church if Stu didn't get back—

"—Mark's birthday is this week," Nony was saying in my ear. "I know it might seem pointless, but I'd like to have a birthday party for Mark at the hospital Tuesday evening. For the boys' sake, more than anything. And I was wondering, could you e-mail Yada Yada and let everybody know they're invited?"

A birthday party? For Mark? I felt like crying. But I sucked it up and said, "Sure. Be glad to. Anything else you want me to do?" *Now you're getting reckless, Jodi—don't forget Josh graduates this week!*

Nony let me off the hook. "No, no. It will be very simple. The boys want to bring balloons and have a cake and ice cream. It is . . . important. To keep the hope alive."

Yes. That was it. Keeping the hope alive.

I BRIEFLY ENTERTAINED THE IDEA OF SKIPPING CHURCH at Uptown if I was going to visit the New Morning service in the afternoon, but Denny said he'd been thinking of visiting their service that afternoon too—and *he* got ready for church at Uptown as usual. *Ah well.* Playing hooky had always been more of a fantasy in my lifetime than something I actually *did*. Good ol' responsible Jodi Baxter.

I was glad I didn't skip.

Stu called on her cell about nine o'clock and said she wasn't going to make it back in time; could we give Becky a ride to church?

Ten minutes into the praise and worship part of the service while everyone was standing and singing (and sweating), I saw Stu out of the corner of my eye scooting into the row behind us. She leaned forward and tapped Becky on the shoulder. "Psst. Becky. You've got a visitor."

Becky turned; I turned. Half our row turned. Three-year-old Andy, his soft, rusty brown curls bouncing, beamed up at his mother, giggling. "Surprise!" he shouted, his voice carrying right over the words of the Tommy Dorsey hymn we were singing.

Precious Lord, take my hand, lead me on, help me stand . . .

Becky, speechless, reached for her son, hauled Andy right over the back of her metal folding chair, and wrapped him in a bear hug. The child snuggled into her neck as she rocked back and forth.

. . . Thru' the storm, thru' the night, lead me on to the li–ight . . .

I shook my head at Stu, even though I was smiling. Why didn't she just tell Becky she was going to bring Andy instead of making it a surprise? Sometimes I just couldn't figure out Leslie Stuart.

But as we sang, Stu leaned over the pew and whispered in my ear, "His caseworker arranged an all-day visit for Andy and Becky for today, but I had no guarantee the grandmother would have Andy ready in time to get him here for church. Didn't want Becky to be disappointed."

Becky definitely was not disappointed. She was so excited to have Andy with her in church that she didn't want to let him go for children's ministry, so she tagged along with him when the young children went downstairs to the classrooms. I smiled to myself. Becky knew so little about the Bible, maybe she'd learn something right along with the kids.

When the children returned at the end of the service, lots of people crowded around Becky and Andy. Several children—including Carla Hickman—seemed to have fallen in love with the beautiful little boy and kept trying to pick him up or tease him into playing tag around the rows of chairs. I thought Andy might feel clingy and want to stay with his mom, but he seemed delighted with all the attention and let Carla pull him away to go get some punch at the kitchen pass-through window.

"Wish Stu had told us Andy was coming," I grumbled on the way home. "We aren't going to see much of him if we go to the New Morning service this afternoon."

Denny gave me a look. "Andy didn't come to see us. He came to see his mom. Probably just as well we aren't going to be around every minute."

I stuck out my tongue at him. "Well, we could've planned lunch together or something."

Josh looked at me in the rearview mirror from the driver's seat. "Mom. Andy's three. If you want to do lunch, just offer to make some peanut butter sandwiches!"

I stuck out my tongue at him too. My menfolk were ganging up on me. What did they know about forty-something women who needed a little-kid fix every now and then? I didn't actually *want* to be parenting a preschooler in my forties, but an afternoon with Becky's little sweetie sure would go a long way to scratching the itch.

As it turned out, our two households—upstairs and down—pooled sandwiches, chips, fruit, veggies, and cookies and ate together on the back porch, while Josh and Amanda rigged up the hose and sprinkler on one side of the yard, much to Andy's delight. He was much more interested in running in and out of the water than he was in eating carrot sticks. I saw Stu watching him as he squealed with laughter when the water "caught" him, her paper plate of food barely touched . . . and remembered what it must cost her to bring Andy to her home. Andy and Stu's baby, David, who shared the same birth date—or due date in David's case. If Stu hadn't . . .

My own eyes blurred with sudden tears that I blinked hastily away. Becky didn't know about Stu's aborted baby. But maybe she should. Maybe that's what stood between these two women even more than the dirty dishes in the sink and wet towels on the floor.

New Morning's service started at three o'clock, so Denny and I left the backyard party at two thirty and headed back to Uptown Community. It felt odd to see total strangers piling out of cars and pulling open the doors of Uptown's two-story storefront; even weirder to be greeted at the top of the stairs by a pleasant couple as if *we* were the visitors. Which I guess we were, though I had to admit I felt a tad possessive as we sat down in the familiar, awful metal folding chairs. Uncomfortable as they were, they were *our* chairs and this was, after all, *our* church.

Good grief, Jodi, listen to yourself! You sound just like those women complaining about New Morning last Sunday at the potluck. True, true. *Help me, God.*

The still, small Voice that seemed to enjoy dissecting my Old Jodi thoughts jumped in. *Your church, Jodi Baxter? Correction. My church. This building is just four walls, some windows, and a door with a mortgage. It's just a temporary house for part of My church. My church is all these people who have come here to worship, and the ones who were worshiping here this morning, and the ones who are worshiping Me in different buildings all over Chicago today. That's My church.*

Chastened, I glanced around as the chairs filled up. To my

surprise, New Morning wasn't all black. Pastor Cobbs was confer-
ring with a Latino man, who might be a deacon or worship leader
or something. A couple other Latino families filed in, and several
college-age singles—mostly black, several Asian, and a few who
might be Middle Eastern.

Peter Douglass acknowledged us with a wave as he filed into a
row on the other side of the room. That didn't surprise me; he hadn't
been at Uptown the last three Sundays. Then I saw Avis right
behind him. When I caught her eye, she looked as surprised as I
felt. I hadn't mentioned Denny and I were going to visit New
Morning's service today; obviously she'd had the same idea. I
grinned at her, telepathing my thoughts: *We really should talk more!*

The Latino guy, who turned out to be the worship leader, gave
the worship band a nod, and they lit into the first praise song. Denny
grinned at me. He really liked the addition of a saxophone to the
usual drums, electric bass, and a keyboard. Everyone stood and I saw
Peter really getting into the music—clapping and raising his arms.

For one brief moment, jealousy reared its ugly little head again.
Maybe Avis would leave Uptown and start attending New Morning
with Peter. I fought down my resentment of this little church that
had invaded our lives. *OK, Satan, I know your tricks. You're trying to
cause division here. Didn't God just remind me that we are all His
church? You've got me figured out. You know I get protective of what's
"mine." You know I can get distracted when what I should be doing is
focusing on why I'm here—to worship God. So beat it!*

I was so busy back-talking the devil that I didn't see Nony and
the boys come in until she gave me a wave from the end of our row.
And Pastor Clark! When did he get here? Nony was mouthing
something at me. *"Thank you."*

Thank you? For what? For just being here? I closed my eyes as the haunting notes of the saxophone moved the congregation into the popular worship chorus: "Here I am to worship, Here I am to bow down . . ." *I want to thank You, God, for nudging me to come today.* This was Nony's church family. Nony's and Mark's. This was probably her first time back since Mark got hurt more than two weeks ago. It was good and right that we should be here this particular Sunday to worship together, to pray together, to celebrate God's big church, of which we were all a part.

THE SERVICE WOUND DOWN around five o'clock—usually the time the Uptown youth met at the church for youth group, but Rick Reilly had wisely moved the group to his house for the duration. I thought we'd get a chance to hear Pastor Cobbs preach; he was wearing a black robe and looked very dignified in spite of the muggy heat. But it didn't turn out that way.

"Before the message," he said, "we want to pray for our brother, Dr. Mark Smith, and his precious family, who are facing the most grievous trial of their lives. Sister Nonyameko?" He motioned her to come forward, then asked his wife, Rose, and Pastor Clark to join him at the front. Spontaneously, several other church members also went forward, surrounding Nony in a circle, laying hands on her. Peter and Avis joined the circle. Was this an open invitation? I wanted to go up, too, but felt too timid, not knowing the protocol of New Morning Church.

But the prayers! No murmurs to be heard by the circle around Nony. Voices boomed out, praising God for His great goodness even in the middle of dire circumstances. Several prayed for miraculous healing. "Even today, Father God! Give our sister a good report! Bring this man back to his wife, to his family, to his students, whole and healthy and on fire for the gospel, Lord God! For which we will give You all the honor and praise and glory!"

The next forty-five minutes turned into a rousing prayer meeting. More and more people joined the prayers at the front. But that didn't stop the people still sitting or standing in the rows of chairs. Prayers went up all over the room, not only for Mark's healing and strength for Nony and her children, but for justice and truth, an end to racism and bigotry.

The most moving prayer to me was Pastor Cobbs's. "Lord God, we would be remiss if we did not also pray for the perpetrators of this serious crime." He had a surprisingly strong voice without shouting, even though he was probably in his early sixties. "We don't hate them, Father God, for what they did. There is too much hatred in this world already. We pity them, because they are lost, sick with sin. But we know You died for their sins, too, same as for us. While we were *all* still sinners, Christ died for us. And Christ said on the cross, 'Father, forgive them. They don't know what they're doing.'"

Yes, Lord, my heart whispered. *The girl in the sundress. She doesn't know what she's doing. Forgive her, Jesus.*

"So help us, precious Savior," New Morning's pastor went on, "to follow Your example and be willing to forgive, just as You have forgiven us. We don't want to compound this great sin against our brother by letting Satan get a foothold in our hearts with thoughts of vengeance, or even using this situation to excuse our own hatred for those who misuse or abuse us. Your last prayer on earth, dear Jesus, was for those who believe in You to be one, just as You and the Father are one. For this spirit of unity we pray. We need a breakthrough, God! For a 'new morning' in this nation when God's people would break down the barriers of prejudice and mistrust, and be living witnesses of God's kingdom! And let it begin with us . . ."

Shouts of "Amen!" and "Hallelujah!" went up all over the room. The praise band began to play, the saxophone echoed, and all around us people began to sing a song new to me.

> *I need you; you need me*
> *We're all a part of God's body . . .*

All around the room, men and women and children took the hands of the people beside them, reaching across the aisles and over the backs of their chairs. The prayer circle in the front broke up and joined the larger mazelike circle as the song continued . . .

> *I won't harm you with words from my mouth*
> *I love you; I need you to survive.*

Beside me, Denny suddenly began to weep. He dropped my hand and fished in his pocket for his handkerchief. Big, gut-wrenching sobs shook his body, and he sank down into his chair. Startled, I touched his arm; I just kept my hand there. Several others around us moved close to him and just touched him lightly on his back, on his head. I was touched by their concern, but for a few moments, I felt confused. Why was Denny crying so hard? Granted, the worship service and prayer time had been spiritually moving, but this—this was something deeper.

Then suddenly I understood. It was grief, finally coming out. Denny had been grieving for Mark, hardly knowing what to do with his feelings. But somehow, here at New Morning Church, something had pulled that grief to the surface.

Pastor Clark was one of the people who came over to Denny. As Denny's sobs subsided, he stood up and whispered something in Pastor Clark's ear. Uptown's pastor nodded and went forward to speak to Pastor Cobbs, then motioned to Denny. Denny moved to the front. The music died away.

Denny cleared his throat a couple of times. "God wants to do something. I feel it deep within my spirit. I don't know what, for sure, but . . . I don't believe it's an accident that God brought our two churches together in this place. Mark Smith was . . . is . . . my friend. But I sense that even what happened to Mark is only part of the puzzle God is putting together." Denny made a face. "I know, I'm probably not making any sense . . ."

"That's all right, brother!" Peter Douglass's voice. "You say it."

"That's right. That's right," several other voices added.

"I want to make an invitation to the brothers here. Sorry, sisters." He grinned sheepishly. "Uptown Community has a monthly men's breakfast on the third Saturday of each month, and I want to invite any of you brothers to join us this coming Saturday, right here at eight o'clock. Can't promise you a low-carb, low-calorie, low-anything breakfast—we cook it ourselves, you know. Or sneak in Dunkin' Donuts."

Laughter sprinkled around the room.

"That's all. Please come." Denny struggled with his emotions for a moment. Then he said, "We need each other to survive."

38

First, the alarm rudely assaulted my sleep. Then, my conscience hit me with a double whammy. *Good grief! I forgot to send out that e-mail about Mark's birthday party at the hospital tomorrow night!* I crawled out of bed with a groan. Not even six thirty on Monday morning yet, and already I was behind schedule.

As I booted up the computer to send out Nony's announcement, still bleary-eyed without my first cup of coffee, the last full week of school stretched out before me like a trek across the Sahara—hot and endless. The birthday party for Mark was a great idea, but when would I find time to fill out all the end-of-year reports for my students? Not to mention the main event of the week: Josh's high school graduation on Thursday evening. The graduation announcements said it would be held in the Lane Tech Sports Stadium at 7:00 p.m. Outdoors. No air conditioning. *Hot . . . endless . . .*

I sent up a hasty prayer for an overcast sky, cooling temperatures, and no rain.

The Baxter hurry-scurry kicked in as two more alarm clocks went off. I ducked into the bathroom before the who-gets-the-shower-next dance began, then set out bagels, cream cheese, and OJ for breakfast.

"Kinda wish Grandma and Grandpa Jennings could come for my graduation," Josh said wistfully as he grabbed a bagel on his way out the door that Monday morning.

"I know. They would if they could, honey." I hid a grin. My dad would *love* to see Josh's head once again covered with hair, though still army-boot-camp short. But my parents had called last week, saying my mom had been called back to have a retake on a colonoscopy and would not feel up to the long drive. No, no, nothing to worry about, they'd assured me. Another time.

The Baxter GPs had also sent regrets, saying they'd be on a cruise to the Bahamas for eighteen days. They'd enclosed three one-hundred-dollar bills for Josh. "Knowing Josh," Denny had muttered, "he'll probably hand it to the first homeless guy who hits him up for a quarter."

I'd made a face. "Would buy a lot of college textbooks, but, oh yeah, Josh isn't going to college next year."

We'd stopped bugging Josh about college—for now—but it was hard to let it go. Josh was such good college material. He'd probably love it! But he seemed determined to wait a year and do some kind of service work or volunteering after graduation.

Graduation . . . I'd hardly had time to think about—much less plan—any celebration for my firstborn's high school graduation. I mulled over that one all the way to school . . . but didn't have time to think about it anymore until I was on my way home again. What did parents do for their high school graduates? A BMW was out. So

314

was a trip to Cancun. *My* parents gave me a set of indestructible luggage to take me off to college. Still had a few pieces of the ugly things. But for Josh? I didn't have a clue. Or much money.

So pray about it, Jodi. I dumped my school tote bag, stuffed full of reports I needed to complete, on the dining room table. Pray. OK. Seemed kind of a trivial thing to bother God about when we were sending up urgent prayers about healing for Mark Smith, but . . .

"OK, Jesus," I said aloud as I let out the dog, poured myself a glass of iced tea, and booted up the computer to check e-mail. "I need some help knowing how to honor Josh at this milestone in his life. He's a good kid. Thank You for the privilege of being his mom . . ." I stopped what I was doing. *Have I ever told Josh that? That I'm proud to be his mom? That he is God's gift to us? What I appreciate about him?* I should. I really should tell him how I feel. Not just a schmaltzy graduation card, but a personal letter. It'd be a start at least.

The e-mail Inbox was jammed with the typical "Fw: Fw: Fw:" junk mail Amanda and her friends passed around. I scrolled through the new messages quickly. Several Yada Yadas had responded to the birthday invitation. "Wonderful!" Stu wrote. "I'm so sorry! I have to work P.M. shift Tuesday" (Delores). "Can I bring anything?" (Edesa). "Can I bring the kids?" (Florida). "Cool!" (Yo-Yo).

I did a double-take. *Yo-Yo?* I grinned as I called up her message.

To:	Yada Yada Prayer Group
From:	YoSista@wahoo.com
Re:	Mark Smith's Birthday

Cool! Will come if I can hang a ride with Mister B.

How do u guyz like my new computer? PD set it up for

me. He's the Man! Also worked some kinda magic and presto, e-mail. Ruth sent me Jodi's mssg about the B-day party. Add me on the regglar YY list, OK?

Yo, Jodi. U gonna do a name thing for Mark like u did for my B-day?

Yo-Yo

I stared at her message. What a great idea! Hadn't even occurred to me. I quickly minimized the e-mail program and called up the Internet, clicked Favorites on my toolbar, then clicked one of the baby name Web sites I'd found. Marc . . . Marcus . . . Mark . . . There it was.

Mark. Latin: Warrior. Warlike.

I sat numbly in front of the computer screen. *Warrior. Warlike.* How terribly appropriate. The warrior, cut down in the heat of battle. Cut down, but not . . .

I had to get my Bible. I jumped up so fast, the chair tipped over, scaring Willie Wonka, who was, of course, stretched out on the dining room floor as close as he could get without sitting in the chair with me. I found my Bible on the back porch swing, then hunted in the concordance until I found what I was looking for: Isaiah 42:3 and 4.

"'A bruised reed he will not break, and a smoldering wick he will not snuff out,'" I read. That was it. *Cut down, but not broken. Burning dimly, but not snuffed out.* That's what I wanted to use for Mark's birthday.

I started to close my Bible, but the verses that followed caught my eye. "In faithfulness he will bring forth justice; he will not falter or be discouraged till he establishes justice on earth." *Oh God. Mark is cut down, but You are still fighting on his behalf to bring about justice.* I read on. "This is what God the LORD says . . . 'I, the LORD, have called you in righteousness; I will take hold of your hand. I will keep you and will make you to be a covenant for the people and a light for the Gentiles, to open eyes that are blind, to free captives from prison and to release from the dungeon those who sit in darkness."

I had to quit reading then. Tears blurred my vision, and a lump stuck in my throat. But strong words from my spirit rose to the surface of my thoughts.

Fight on, my brother. The Lord is with you!

I WORKED ON MY END-OF-YEAR REPORTS late that evening and for a couple of hours after school on Tuesday to make time for Mark's birthday party up at the hospital. Had to beg off our Bible-reading time with Becky; said I'd try for Wednesday and Friday instead.

My emotions fought with each other as we drove up to Evanston Hospital. Part of me dreaded trying to "celebrate" with Mark lying in a coma. Part of me felt excited. I knew, I just *knew*, somewhere deep in my spirit, that God was at work doing—what? something!—in spite of what the circumstances looked like.

The entire Baxter tribe (*sans* dog) took the elevator to the ICU floor and made our way to the family waiting room. Inside the room, a bevy of helium balloons hugged the ceiling, announcing a party in progress. A good smattering of Yada Yada sisters and families were there, plus Pastor and Mrs. Cobbs and other New Morning people. Everyone was doing their best to talk in hushed tones. Two elderly brown women I'd never seen before sat quietly in a corner of the room. *Friends? Family?* They laughed behind their hands as Nony's boys and Carla Hickman gleefully batted around two errant balloons that wouldn't stay afloat.

Flo wiggled through the standing bodies and handed me a plastic glass of punch. "Girl! How Nony got permission to throw this party on the ICU beats me. Lines up right behind the Israelites crossing the Red Sea!"

I grinned. "I know. Isn't it great? Marcus and Michael are obviously delighted to be having a birthday party for their daddy."

Yo-Yo arrived with Ben and Ruth Garfield, bearing a gaily decorated chocolate cake from the Bagel Bakery, with MARK and *38* written in sunny yellow icing in the center. Ruth pulled a box of birthday candles from her big leather purse and stuck three on one side of Mark's name, then lined up eight candles on the other side.

"Three . . . eight . . . thirty-eight. Cute," I said.

"Didn't do it to be cute," Ruth huffed. "Had forty candles on my cake for the big Four-O. Ben insisted on lighting them. Set off the fire alarm. Not taking any chances."

I was still laughing when Pastor Cobbs asked for quiet and opened with a short prayer of thanksgiving that we could come together to celebrate the life of Mark Smith. Then he swept a hand in Nony's direction. "Sister Nonyameko? It's your party!"

Nony welcomed everyone with a gracious smile. She was dressed in a brilliant blue caftan with gold embroidery around the neck and sleeves, her hair braided into a zillion tiny braids and swept up into a coil. "Thank you, dear friends. Thank you for coming tonight. I especially want everyone to meet two special guests . . ." Nony swept over to the two older women and gently pulled them to their feet. "I want to introduce Mark's grandmother, Mrs. Bessie Smith, and her sister, Auntie Bell, all the way from Peachtree City, Georgia."

The room erupted in spontaneous clapping. Hoshi Takahashi beamed, but tears glistened in her eyes. I suddenly had an awful thought: *Would Hoshi's family come from Japan if she ended up in the hospital? They didn't even write since—* Just then a nurse opened the door and gestured frantically for us to be quiet. The noise settled down.

"We're not going to make this long," Nony went on. "But Mark is the only patient on this side of the ICU tonight, praise God. So we have permission for several of us—not all, I'm afraid—to take a few balloons into Mark's room and sing 'Happy Birthday.'" Her smile took on a sly look. "I told them it was therapy. Even got a doctor to agree with me. Medicine doesn't know for sure what comatose patients can hear or understand, and they need a certain amount of stimulation. But first we're going to share 'verbal gifts' to Mark." She motioned to her son Marcus, who held up a small boom box with a small microphone. "Marcus is going to record the verbal gifts so that his daddy can hear what we each have to say . . . later, when . . ." Nony blinked rapidly and her lip quivered. She quickly went on. "Who would like to be first?"

Nony's younger son, Michael, waved his hand. He bent close to the mic Marcus held in his hand. "I love you, Daddy. Happy birthday. P.S. Get well quick."

Taking Michael's cue, several others gave "verbal gifts," speaking directly to Mark rather than about him. Peter Douglass praised his courage. Pastor Cobbs thanked him for all his support of New Morning Church. Stu said God had given him the gift of encouragement. By now, tissues and handkerchiefs were coming out in droves, but the verbal gifts continued. Denny thanked Mark for his friendship. Josh thanked him for being a role model. "I can't even begin to tell you how you have influenced my life, Dr. Smith," he said. "As I walk into manhood, I want to be like you."

I was weepy-eyed now. But decided I might as well give my verbal gift now since my family was up to bat. I pulled out the paper with the meaning of Mark's name and the Scripture from Isaiah 42, which I'd printed out on vellum, rolled up, and tied with a purple ribbon. As I read, murmurs of "Beautiful, beautiful" and "So true" rippled around the room. After I finished, I managed to say into Marcus's microphone, "You *are* a warrior, Mark. God's kind of warrior. One who speaks truth and makes peace. But the battle is not over, Mark. We need you."

Finally, Marcus clicked off his boom box. The room was quiet. Nony, her eyes wet but still smiling, said, "Thank you, Yo-Yo, for making the beautiful cake. Will you light the candles? Then we'll sing 'Happy Birthday,' and Marcus and Michael can make a wish."

"Got it," Yo-Yo said, whipping out her cigarette lighter. I glanced in panic at the closed waiting room door. I was sure lighted candles would break at least a hundred hospital rules, but . . . oh well. They'd get blown out in a minute. We sang a don't-wake-the-baby version of "Happy Birthday"; then Marcus and Michael blew.

No one doubted what they'd wished.

To my surprise, Nony asked Denny and me if we'd go into Mark's room with her and the boys, Hoshi, the Cobbs, Mark's grandmother and aunt, and Peter and Avis Douglass. We tiptoed down the hall, each carrying a balloon, and slipped quietly into the room. The nurses had propped up the patient by raising the hospital bed and plumping an array of pillows under his arms and legs—

probably to change his position. The compression stockings wheezed gently. The heart monitor and blood pressure machine still beeped; a bag of fluid dripped into his arm. A nasogastric feeding tube disappeared into his nose, and a small wire ran from the top of his head to another machine, which I'd been told monitored the pressure inside his brain.

A lot of the bruising had disappeared from Mark's face, and I was surprised that only one eye was still bandaged. I didn't have time to ask Nony about it, because she moved the boys close to their father on one side and encouraged Grandmother Bessie to hold his hand on the other. Denny closed the door, and once again we softly sang "Happy Birthday."

When the last note died away, Michael said, "Happy birthday, Daddy. We had chocolate cake—your favorite."

Mark's grandmother, tears sliding down her cheeks, leaned close and kissed Mark on the cheek. "You be a good boy, Marky," she scolded. "Don't do anything your Grammy Bessie wouldn't do."

For a moment, I thought I heard a murmur, a mumbled reply.

Bessie Smith's head jerked up, her eyes wide. "He—he said, 'I won't, Grammy'!"

We all froze. Then Nony said gently, "No, Bessie. He can't—"

The little woman drew herself up to her full five feet. "Don't tell me he can't. I heard him say, 'I won't, Grammy.'" She leaned over her grandson on the bed once more. "Mark. You listen to your grandmother. If you can hear my voice, squeeze my hand."

We saw it then. Ever so slowly, Mark Smith squeezed his grandmother's hand.

Auntie Bell fainted dead away.

39

*P*eter Douglass caught Auntie Bell before she hit the floor and maneuvered her into a chair. Nony and the two boys crowded close to the bed. "Mark! Mark, can you hear me? It's Nony! Marcus and Michael are here too."

"Daddy! Daddy, wake up!" Michael pleaded.

We all held our breath. For a long moment there was no response, and I was afraid we'd imagined the whole thing. And then—Mark's lips moved. "Nony," he said in the barest of whispers. His unbandaged eyelid fluttered.

Nony burst into tears. "Oh, praise Jesus!" She practically lay across Mark's body, cradling him in her arms. "Thank You, Jesus, thank You, thank You . . ."

Most of us were too stunned to say anything. Peter was fanning Auntie Bell. Marcus and Michael clung to Hoshi. Avis lifted one hand in the air, her eyes closed, and kept saying, "Hallelujah! Thank You, Jesus. Oh God! You are good, so good. *Jesus!*"

Pastor Cobbs stepped out of the room, and I heard him calling,

"Nurse? Nurse! Come quickly." Avis followed him out. I knew she wanted to shout, to praise God with her whole self, and she would look for the first place she could do that without upsetting hospital protocol.

A nurse came running into the room. Assessing the situation, she ordered everyone out except Nony. I gave Nony a quick hug and scooted out behind Denny and the others. Michael ran ahead of us and darted into the waiting room, shouting, "Daddy woke up! My daddy woke up!"

I DON'T KNOW WHEN WE FINALLY GOT TO SLEEP that night. Once we got home, I called everyone I could think of who wasn't there to tell them the good news; even called Delores at work at the county hospital. We cried and laughed together for several minutes, then she peppered me with questions about exactly what happened. "Mm-hm. *Bueno*. But we must not expect everything to change overnight. Recovery from a head injury happens in stages; it will take time. Nony will need to be patient. I will talk to her." Delores's voice drifted off as if she was thinking aloud. "*Sí, sí*, I will go to the hospital as soon as I get off work."

Stu and Becky both came downstairs to our apartment, and the six of us rehashed every detail at least ten times, drank iced tea, stuck a frozen pizza into the oven (Gino's pizza it wasn't), and inhaled two bags of chips, a jar of salsa, and the last of the Oreos in the cookie jar. When I finally glanced at the clock, it was almost midnight. "Ack! Tomorrow's a school day!" I yelped. But even after Denny and I had crawled under the sheet and turned on the window fan, I didn't go to sleep for ages.

Mark Smith woke up from his coma. Thank You, thank You, Jesus . . .

I was exhausted when I got home from school the next day, and I still had a few end-of-year reports to finish. But Becky was waiting for me on the back porch with her Bible, so I woke myself up with a can of Pepsi, and we read a little further in the Gospel of Matthew. In chapter 9, just after Jesus got criticized for eating with "sinners," Becky read Jesus' reply: "It is not the healthy who need a doctor, but the sick. But go and learn what this means: 'I desire mercy, not sacrifice.' For I have not come to call the righteous, but sinners."

"Man! How cool is that?" Becky shook her head. "An' all this time I been thinkin' that, ya know, goin' ta church and all this religious stuff was just for the good folks."

I told Denny what she'd said as we drove up to the hospital that evening after throwing together a couple of sandwiches for a paper bag supper. He digested her words. "Yeah. Guess we need people like Becky and Yo-Yo to help us read the Bible like it's supposed to be read—as good news."

We found Nony alone in Mark's room in the ICU when we got there. She was stroking his hand and reading from the Bible on her lap. " . . . 'When the Lord restored his exiles to Jerusalem, it was like a dream! We were filled with laughter and we sang for joy' . . ."

Mark's unbandaged eye was closed; all the machines were still attached. For a moment, it looked as if nothing had changed—and then I saw it: the nasogastric feeding tube was gone. Had he been able to eat or drink today?

" . . . 'the other nations said, "What amazing things the Lord has done for them." Yes, the Lord has done amazing things for us! What joy'!" Nony looked up at us and smiled all over her face.

I looked over her shoulder to see if those last words were from the Bible or if she'd added them herself. But there they were in Psalm 126: "The Lord has done amazing things for us! What joy!"

"Read . . . more." Denny and I jumped. It didn't sound like Mark's voice, but it definitely came from the bed.

Nony stood up and touched her lips to his. "Later. Someone's come to see you." She nodded at us and stepped away from the bed.

Denny clasped one of Mark's hands. "Hey, man. It's Denny. You look like Rip Van Winkle—without the beard."

Again, for a long moment there was no response. Then Mark's unbandaged eye blinked open. He seemed to be trying to focus. Denny leaned close to his line of vision. Mark grunted. "You don't . . . look so hot . . . yourself. Got . . . four eyes." He tried to smile and winced. Then his eye closed, and he seemed to fall asleep.

Nony walked with us out of the room. "They still don't know how much damage he's sustained to his eyes. The left one is still full of blood. But he can see out of his right eye, though probably double vision, as you heard."

"And his head?" I asked.

Nony hesitated. Then she said, "The doctors seem hopeful. They won't know for sure if there is any permanent brain damage until he continues to recover and regains his faculties. So keep praying—and please, keep coming to visit. He needs the stimulation." She hugged us both. "See you tomorrow?"

I shook my head. "I'm so sorry, Nony. We can't. Josh graduates from Lane Tech tomorrow night, and they expect the parents to show up." I gave her a wry grin.

"Of course. Give him my love. Josh . . . He . . ." Her eyes got a distant look, as if she wanted to say something else. After a moment, she took one of Denny's hands and one of mine and brought all our hands together. "God has plans for that young man. Not your plans. Don't stand in His way. I believe . . ." Again Nony hesitated. "I believe God will use your Joshua like the Joshua of old, to fight a battle that the older generation did not fight."

THE SCHOOL PARKING LOT was already crammed when we pulled in the next evening. Graduates had to arrive no later than six for the seven o'clock graduation. Josh shot out of the car with his shiny green robe and mortarboard under his arm, still folded in the plastic package it came in. Before he disappeared between the rows of cars, he turned and yelled, "Sit on the west bleachers! Then I'll know where to look for you!"

I smirked at Denny, who was cracking the minivan windows an inch and locking the doors. "That's nice. I thought maybe he wouldn't want to acknowledge that he had parents. You've got the tickets, don't you?"

Denny's eyes rounded. "Tickets? What tickets?"

My mouth fell open. "The tickets! They were on your dresser! We can't get in without—"

Denny pulled something out of the inside pocket of his sport coat. "Oh. You mean these bookmark thingies?" His dimples gave him away.

"Denny!" I punched him on the shoulder. Hard. "Don't do that to me! I'm already so nervous I'm sweating right through my antiperspirant."

He laughed and gave me a teasing hug. "Why so nervous? You don't have to do anything. After listening to half a dozen boring speeches, Josh will walk up there and get his diploma, we will completely embarrass him by yelling 'Yea Josh!' at ten decibels, and then we can duck out! After all, he'll go up with the *Bs*."

Amanda rolled her eyes and lagged a few steps behind us. "You guys are nuts, you know that? I'm hungry. Wish we'd eaten supper before sitting through Torture 101."

"Suck it up, kid," Denny said. "You'll need lots of room for Ron's of Japan later."

Sitting on stadium bleachers was not my idea of a good time, but at least the graduation ceremonies started at seven o'clock sharp. The Lane Tech concert band launched into the processional as a parade of teachers, administrators, and dignitaries filed into the stadium, followed by the senior class—all one thousand of them, give or take fifty or so—to resounding cheers all around the stadium.

"There's Josh! I see him!" Amanda pointed excitedly as the students, shiny green robes flying in the stiff June breeze, crossed the cinder track and filed into the rows of chairs on the grassy playing field.

As the ROTC color guard presented the flags, a lump of gratefulness caught in my throat. We'd been so fortunate that both Josh and Amanda had been accepted at Lane Tech College Prep when we'd moved into Chicago two years ago. The school drew students from all over the city and applications had to meet a wide range of "college prep" standards. Denny had been impressed by the diversity of the student population: Hispanics and Caucasian made up about 70 percent of the population in roughly equal proportions, and Asian and African-American students equally shared the remaining 30 percent. One of Josh's teachers once told me that at least 90 percent of graduates went on to college.

Not that Josh is going to college, a nasty little voice whispered in my ear. And then I heard Nony's voice in my other ear: *"God has plans for that young man. Not your plans. Don't stand in His way."*

I put my hand over my heart and heartily sang "The Star-Spangled Banner" with the Lane choir, all in matching blazers, trying to drown out both voices in my head.

We politely listened to the valedictory speech, the citizenship awards, and presentation of the class gift in spite of aching spines. Amanda sighed loudly. I bumped her affectionately with my shoulder. "Two more years, and it'll be your turn," I whispered. "And we'll be just as proud."

"Shh," Amanda said. "What's that guy saying? I thought he said Josh's name!"

My head whipped up. One of the vice principals was at the microphone on the stage set up on the stadium playing field. "—a student opinion piece in the last issue of *The Warrior*, our student newspaper. This is a bit unusual, but we have asked the author, Joshua Baxter, to read what he wrote as a graduation challenge to all of our students—and not only our students, but to us as parents, teachers, and administrators."

Denny and I stiffened in complete shock as the tall figure of our son rose like a leaping trout from the sea of square green "lily pads" and made his way to the platform. The vice principal shook his hand and sat down. Josh leaned toward the microphone and said, "Good evening." That was all. He fished under his robe, pulled a folded piece of paper from a pocket in his dress slacks, and unfolded it. A quiet born of curiosity settled over the stadium.

Josh cleared his throat. "Three weeks ago, I learned something I didn't really want to know. And that is: words have power. So does silence. Words can be used for good or evil. So can silence. And we are responsible for how we use both." My eyes riveted on my son. The paper shook slightly in his hand—or was it a breeze? "In this great country of ours," he read on, "we have been given many rights, including the right of free speech. To say what we think and believe. But we don't often talk about the fact that exercising that right has consequences. And how we respond—or don't respond—to those exercising that right also has consequences."

I saw Denny lean forward, elbows on his knees, chin on his fists, listening to Josh describe the events of three weeks ago: a "free speech" rally organized by a local hate group, a university professor who knew the power of words to affect attitudes, an angry crowd—and then a cowardly act in the middle of the night that left that same university professor in a coma.

"I went to that rally full of idealism; I went home thinking nobody is going to listen. Nothing is ever going to change. What I think or say or do won't make any difference. I wanted to chuck it all. Just look out for myself. That's what everyone else is doing." Josh looked up from his paper. "But I was wrong."

I could hardly breathe. My heart pounded in my ears. I strained to listen.

"A courageous man lying in the hospital taught me that to remain silent is to allow evil words and evil attitudes to fill the empty spaces. An angry student at that rally, who assumed I was a racist skinhead—" Josh ran a hand over the fuzz on his head, looked up from his paper, and grinned. "Well, not so bald now," he quipped. Laughter rippled over the stadium. "That student taught me that if I don't correct wrong assumptions, they become bigger than life and actually become true. Because silence speaks."

Josh looked down at his paper. "There's an old saying from my parents' generation"—I poked Denny and mouthed, *"Old?"*—"'If you aren't part of the solution, you're part of the problem.' I didn't want to believe that. Because it demands that I stand up and be counted for what I believe, just like Dr. Mark Smith. Just like many other brave men and women who have shown us the path to brotherhood against the forces of prejudice and fear. And many paid for their courage with their lives. I don't know if I'm that brave. But there is no middle ground. Silence is not an option, because the voices of hate and division and violence are growing stronger."

The mortarboard on Josh's head tipped up, and he looked toward the west bleachers, as if he were talking directly to us. "I want to be part of the solution. I want to follow in the steps of that courageous man, Dr. Mark Smith, who believed one person can make a difference. *My* attitudes. What *I* say or don't say. What *I* do or don't do. It has to begin with *me*."

Josh folded his paper. He started for the steps of the stage. Before he reached the ground, a swell of clapping brought the students of his class to their feet. The dignitaries on the stage followed. Parents and families in the stands rose all around us. The senior class began to chant, "Bax-ter! Bax-ter! Bax-ter!"

Tears dripped off my chin. Somewhere deep in my spirit I heard Nony saying, *"God will use your Joshua like the Joshua of old, to fight a battle that the older generation did not fight."*

40

*B*ecky Wallace was waiting for me on the back porch when I got home from school the next day. "How was graduation?" she asked, stubbing out her cigarette and flicking it into the unused flowerpot. "You guys got home kinda late last night."

"No kidding." I resisted the urge to wave away the last vestige of stinky smoke and flopped down on the porch swing while Willie Wonka wobbled down the back steps. What I really wanted to do was beg off from our Bible reading date and take a nap. By the time we'd pried Josh away from clusters of giddy classmates last night, snapped pictures, and inched our way out of the parking lot, it was already after ten. And we still had to eat.

I yawned. "We took him out to celebrate, kind of a fancy place. Ron's of Japan." I saw Becky's face wrinkle up in that *never-heard-of-it* expression of hers. "It's a Japanese restaurant where they cook your food right at the table. Good thing we'd made reservations, because the place was really packed last night. Gotta admit, it was fun. I think Josh had a good time. Oh!" I pushed out of the swing. "A really neat thing happened at graduation."

I popped into the house and came back out thirty seconds later holding a copy of *The Warrior* folded open to Josh's opinion piece. I tapped my finger on the newsprint. "Josh read that during graduation. Big surprise to us."

Becky frowned as she read, tucking a tuft of stray hair behind her ear. She finally looked up. "Your kid wrote this?"

I nodded.

"Man! He sure used a lot of big words. But I like what he said. 'Specially that bit about if you ain't part of the solution, you're part of the problem." She heaved a sigh. "Guess that's my trouble. Been part of the problem too long."

She wouldn't get any argument from *me*, though I didn't think Josh was talking about Becky-type problems. I let it pass, thumbing the pages of my Bible until I got to the Gospel of Matthew. The sooner we got started, the sooner we'd get done; and maybe I could still sneak in a nap before supper.

Becky was fishing in the flowerpot for her cigarette stub. She pulled it out, relit it with her cigarette lighter, and blew out a satisfied puff of smoke. "Say, ain't this a Yada Yada weekend? Where we crazies meetin' up, anyway?"

"Oh, uh . . ." I stared at her. "Did you say 'we'? Becky! Did you—"

She grinned and blew another puff of smoke at me. "Yep. Parole officer called, got it all squared. Jus' hafta give him a couple of days' notice where I'm gonna be—address, phone number, time in and out, stuff like that."

Now the cigarette really had disappeared down to the nub. She flicked it back into the flowerpot, still grinning. "That ain't all.

Andy's caseworker called me, tol' me she set it up so I can have Andy every Sunday till five. All worked out, 'long as somebody willin' to go pick him up for me." She rolled her eyes. "'Cause his grandmama sure ain't gonna lift a finger to get my baby here."

"All right, Becky!" Laughing, I gave her a high-five. "Got plenty of drivers under this roof. Four, counting Josh. I think we can make this happen."

DENNY WAS IN A BIG HURRY to get out the door the next morning to Uptown's monthly men's breakfast. He seemed disappointed that Josh didn't want to go with him, but Josh had made his priorities clear for this particular Saturday: sleep in till noon and then hang out at the beach the rest of the day. "Might be my last chance to do either, once my internship at Jesus People kicks in," he groused.

As Denny went out the door, I saw him grab a copy of *The Warrior*, the one with Josh's opinion piece. *Uh-huh.* Josh wasn't dumb. He knew his dad would be bragging on him to all the guys, and he definitely wanted to be someplace else.

Both kids were still asleep when I left the house to grocery shop and run errands. *Well, let 'em.* Amanda was done with final exams and just had to show up Monday and Tuesday to officially end her sophomore year. Me, I still had a third of my end-of-year reports to write. "No fair," I grumbled to Wonka, as I scribbled notes to the kids and taped them where they'd be sure to see them—on the bathroom mirror. "I'm the last one with homework."

I glanced at the kitchen calendar on my way out. Today was the first day of summer. Why the school year ran so late this year was beyond me! But the day was too gorgeous to be down in the mouth. The weather guy on channel 7 had promised midseventy temperatures with low humidity. Couldn't get any better than that!

Well, yeah, it can. I grinned in the rearview mirror as I backed out of the garage. Denny and I had gone up to the hospital last night to see Mark. Nony said the nurses had had him up out of bed earlier that day, but he was so weak and disoriented that he only lasted five minutes. *"That ought to steadily improve,"* Nony had added, as if giving herself a pep talk.

"You bet!" Denny had said. *"I'll come back on Saturday and walk him around a bit. Maybe play a little touch football in the hall."* Even Nony had burst out laughing.

"Thank You, Jesus!" I laughed aloud with renewed hope as I headed the minivan toward the Rogers Park Fruit Market. Second stop, the big Dominick's grocery store on Howard Street. It was my turn to restock paper goods in the kitchen at Uptown—paper plates, napkins, plasticware. I felt a twinge of anxiety as I waited in the long checkout line. *Hope the guys didn't run out of supplies for their breakfast this morning, especially if some of the men from New Morning came.* Too late now if they did. But if I hurried, I could at least drop off the stuff at the church while the door was still unlocked.

As I pulled out of the parking lot with my groceries, I noticed a large, butcher-paper sign in the windows of one of the large, unoccupied storefronts in the big new shopping center. Bold, black letters declared FUTURE HOME OF NEW MORNING CHRISTIAN CHURCH. I stomped on the brake. I knew that New Morning was looking for space to lease somewhere in the Howard Street area, but I had no idea they'd found space in the shopping center. It would need a lot of work. But the space was huge! Twice as big as Uptown's meeting space. *Wow*, I thought. *Pastor Cobbs must plan on doubling in size.* But what a great location for outreach. I felt a little envious. Uptown was already feeling scrunched in our space.

Five minutes later, I found a parking space on Morse Avenue near Uptown's front door, hauled out the plastic bags with church paper goods, and quietly slipped up the stairs, hoping I could sneak in and out of the kitchen without disturbing anyone. A quick glance into the main room showed a larger group of men than usual, chairs drawn into a circle, a number of them African-American. They were praying, and I thought I heard Mark Smith's name mentioned, along with a lot of "amens" and "hallelujahs."

I smiled as I ducked into the kitchen. So some of the New Morning men had actually taken up Denny's invitation last Sunday! I was glad. Denny would be so pleased. And it was a good thing. If our two churches were going to share building space for a while, it was important to develop some personal relationships.

As I stored the last of the paper plates, I thought I heard Denny's voice. I opened the kitchen door a couple of inches but remained a few steps inside. "—feel like God is saying something to me this morning, if . . . Could I have a few minutes, pastors?"

"Go on. Go on, brother." Pastor Cobbs's voice. I strained to listen.

"No one is happier that Mark Smith has turned a major corner than I am. Well, maybe his wife would argue with that." General laughter. "But a certainty has been growing in my spirit—I have to admit, this is new language for me—that this whole business isn't just about Mark Smith. A certainty that God wants to use this terrible event to do something new—with me, with my church, maybe with all us guys here. In fact, it was my son who put his finger on it and helped put it into words for me. Do you mind if I read something he wrote for his school newspaper?"

I leaned against a counter in the kitchen, listening as Denny read the now-familiar words from *The Warrior*. The novelty had worn off, and the words twisted deeper into my spirit, like a corkscrew slowly embedding itself into a cork. "*—who believed one person can make a difference. My attitudes. What I say or don't say. What I do or don't do. It has to begin with me.*'"

I held my breath. What would the reaction be? To my surprise, a long silence yawned after Denny quit reading. Didn't the guys like it? Did they think Denny was just showing off? And then I heard Peter Douglass's voice puncture the stillness. "Well, I'll be! Kicked in the butt by a teenager."

His comment seemed to pull a plug. Immediately there was a babble of men's voices. "Got that right!" "Can you read that again?" "What I'm thinkin' is—"

I slipped out the kitchen door and down the stairs . . . but later that day, when Denny and I had a chance to meander down to the lake towing Willie Wonka, Denny told me that Josh's essay had kicked off a heated discussion among both Uptown and New Morning men.

"Like what?" We stopped to get a couple of snow cones from a vendor in Loyola Park and found a bench so encrusted with layers of paint it would probably stand up by itself if the wood ever rotted out underneath. Wonka flopped, panting, under the bench, giving up hope that one of the snow cones might be for him.

"A lot of feelings about what happened, for one thing. Anger that the police haven't made an arrest. Some of the African-American guys admitted that they've felt more defensive around white folks since Mark was attacked." Denny crunched thoughtfully on his flavored ice. "A lot of us admitted we've felt helpless, not knowing what to do with our fear and frustration. And hopeless, like Josh said. That nothing has really changed."

I set my paper cone on the ground and let the dog lick it. "What about Pastor Clark or Pastor Cobbs? Did they have anything to say?"

"Yeah, well, Peter Douglass kind of put both of them on the spot." Denny laughed. "For one thing, his reaction to Josh's essay was—"

"'Kicked in the butt by a teenager.' Yeah. I know."

Denny squinted at me suspiciously. "How do you know that?"

I confessed. Told him I'd snuck in to put away the paper goods. "But that's all I heard. Honest! Don't stop now. What did Peter say?"

"Well, it was really something, Jodi. I don't know what's going to come of it, but it's sure something to pray about. Gave us all a lot to think—"

"Denny!" I punched him on the shoulder, making him drop his paper cone. "What did Peter *say*?" Willie Wonka crawled out from under the bench and finished off the snow cone in two gulps.

"All right. All right!" Denny threw up his hands in mock defense. "Two against one. No fair." But he leaned forward, scratching behind Wonka's ears affectionately. His early-summer tan glowed in the late afternoon sun. "Peter reminded us about Joseph in the Bible. How what his brothers meant for evil, selling him off as a slave to Egypt, God turned into a greater good. He said maybe we should look at this whole hate group thing that way. If those White Pride people are responsible for what happened to

Mark, they certainly meant it for evil. But maybe God wants us to look for ways to turn it into a greater good."

"Like . . . what? Returning good for evil? We've been praying for those people."

"Well, that too. But Peter said he didn't believe it was coincidence that put our two churches together these past few weeks, right in the middle of this tragedy. The hate group wants to create division and suspicion between the races. But what if we merged our two churches? What better way to bring good out of Mark's tragedy? Uniting instead of dividing? Healing instead of bitterness? A mostly white church and a mostly black church becoming . . . well . . . a church. Together."

I was speechless. A dozen conflicting thoughts fought for prime-time attention. *Uptown would never agree! Would New Morning even want us? We'd have to do it in their space. Who would be the pastor? I don't want to lose Pastor Clark! But what an amazing idea. Peter and Avis could stay in the same church. Carl Hickman would be more at home with more blacks. Maybe Chris too. And we'd be in the same church with Nony and Mark.* Bubbles of excitement swirled around all the questions and obstacles. *Only God could make it work. We'd have to really get down on our knees.*

I finally breathed. "Oh, Denny. Do you think . . . ?"

He shrugged. "I don't know. Feels daunting. Probably like the Israelites facing the Red Sea. But we all know what God did there." He grinned, exposing his dimples. "At the very least, Pastor Cobbs is inviting Uptown to a joint celebration in the new space they found. A week from Sunday."

41

*D*enny and I batted about the pros and cons of merging two churches from different cultural backgrounds all the way home. Had other churches done this? Could they help us avoid the pitfalls? "The pastors would have to be sold on this one hundred percent," Denny said as we came into the house through the front door, "or it'll never happen." He unsnapped Willie Wonka's leash. "Even if they are, we'd probably lose some people from both churches."

"That's why we really have to pray about it, be sure that's what God wants us to do. Otherwise . . ." The house seemed awfully quiet. "Amanda? You home?"

"Out here." Amanda's voice squeaked from the direction of the back porch. She sounded funny. Denny and I looked at each other and hustled in that direction.

Amanda and José were sitting on the steps, their backs to us. José was hunched over, his head in his hands. Amanda had her arm around him, her head on his shoulder. But she looked up as we came out the screen door. She'd been crying.

"Amanda! What's wrong?" I couldn't keep the alarm out of my voice. She hadn't said anything about José coming over. But at least they were outside.

Denny stepped around them down the stairs and put his hand on the boy's shoulder. "José? What is it, son?"

José looked up at my husband. His shoulders seemed to shake. "*Me padre*. He says I have to drop out of school next year, get a job."

"What?"

"Dad! You gotta talk to Mr. Enriques! José wants to go to college. But he can't, not if he drops out of school! It's so unfair!" Amanda started to cry again.

Wonka whined at the screen door. When I let him out, the dog headed straight for Amanda and licked her face. I sank down on my knees beside her.

Denny's voice gentled. "But why, son? Why would your father do that?"

Even from the side, I could see José's handsome young features glower. "Because Mama found out he's fighting that dog. Alley dog fights. For money."

"Dog fighting! That's illegal," Denny said.

"Tell me something I don't know!" José spit his words. "Mama says he has to stop it, or she'll call the cops." José's shoulders sagged. "That's when Papa said it was either the dog fights to bring in some money—or I had to get a job to help support the family."

GOOD GRIEF. What was Delores's husband *thinking*? I wanted to call her, but I had to get over being mad first. Delores had suspected something wasn't right for some time. *Wonder when she found out?* I felt disappointed too. Ricardo Enriques had seemed like a real person when he played that fancy guitar of his in the mariachi band. Underneath his brooding exterior, the man had a *soul*. Delores said he even cut down on his drinking and seemed less depressed after he got those restaurant gigs, even though it'd been really tough going after the trucking company downsized him last summer.

Denny was still kicking himself the next day as we got ready for church. "I've made friends with the other Yada Yada husbands, but haven't really connected with Ricardo."

"He came to your Guys' Day Out a couple months ago," I reminded him. "He and José."

"Yeah. I know. Haven't followed through though. And his son is courting my daughter. You'd think . . ." Denny stopped buttoning his shirt and scowled. "Guess I've been leaving all the communicating to you and Delores. Stupid reason too. My Spanish isn't so hot, and Ricardo doesn't really *converse* in English. Where do I start now? Can't just call up the man and say, 'I think you're being a real jerk. Both of your so-called options are *stupid*.'"

I couldn't help but laugh. Might not be a bad idea, if you asked me. But Denny was probably right. He didn't have enough deposit in the relationship bank with Ricardo to make a big withdrawal right now.

We arrived at church wondering what would happen after the big idea had landed like a water balloon in the middle of the men's breakfast yesterday. Peter Douglass showed up with Avis; Pastor Cobbs and his wife, Rose too. *Interesting.* Stu came in with Becky and Andy, big grins on their faces. But nothing was said during worship about merging our churches, though I'd be willing to bet half the congregation had heard about the idea already.

However, at the end of the worship service, Pastor Cobbs stood up and invited all the Uptown members to share a thanksgiving celebration with New Morning Christian Church next Sunday morning at their new facility. Spontaneous clapping broke out at the news that New Morning had found a space to meet. "Don't get too happy," Pastor Cobbs joked. "The space needs a lot of development before we can actually move in, but we want to thank God up front for His provision, and we also want to thank our brothers and sisters here at Uptown Community for your hospitality."

"Did he say Sunday *morning*?" I whispered to Denny.

Beaming, Pastor Clark accepted the invitation on Uptown's behalf, reiterating that next week there would be no service here on Morse Avenue. Rather, Sunday's service would be a joint celebration at New Morning's new location.

"Hm. That was smooth," I murmured to Denny as the praise team launched into the closing song. "Are they trying it on for size?"

We come rejoicing . . . into His presence . . . !

Denny put his arm around me and pulled my ear close to his mouth as the familiar words of the Brooklyn Tabernacle praise song pulsed around us. "Maybe," he hissed. "But don't go running ahead on this, Jodi. We just have to take it at face value: a thanksgiving celebration together. That's *all*." But the quirky little smile on his face told me Denny Baxter wasn't doing so good following his own advice.

LITTLE ANDY TUMBLED AROUND THE BACKYARD with Willie Wonka that afternoon, hanging over the dog's back, trying to feed him grass, blowing dandelion fuzz in his face. Wonka just panted in the sunshine, looking for all the world like an indulgent canine parent with a two-legged puppy. "I think Andy comes to see the dog, not me," Becky groused as she watched from the back steps. "Glad Wonka's so gentle."

"Mm-hm." There'd been times I wished Willie Wonka *wasn't* so gentle—like when Becky Wallace made her first unwelcome appearance at this very house. *But You're so good, God, so good. You kept us all safe that day. Even Wonka.*

"Becky!" Stu's voice from above. "We gotta go!" Stu's face appeared over the upper porch railing. "Oh. Hi, Jodi. We have to take Andy back, then we'll meet you at Ruth's house. Don't do anything radical till we get there, OK?"

Andy set up a wail when his mother plucked him up on her way to the garage with Stu, but he settled for leaving one last kiss on Wonka's forehead. At the last minute, Becky stuck her head out of the garage door and yelled, "Hey, Jodi! Can ya save me the job want ads from your Sunday *Trib*?"

Easier said than done. Josh and Denny had pretty much trashed the Sunday paper all over the living room. But I finally found the employment ads section, stuck it in Stu's mailbox, and headed out the back door, where my impatient family was waiting for me in the minivan. Plans were heating up for Uptown youth's volunteer assignment at the upcoming Cornerstone Festival over July Fourth, and Josh and Amanda wanted to get to youth group on time. Denny decided to go with me to the Garfields' and rescue Ben from a houseful of Yada Yadas. So he said.

"Uh-huh. You wouldn't just happen to be hankering for some lox and cream cheese at the Bagel Bakery, would you?" Knowing Ben, I wouldn't be surprised if he'd throw in a couple of beers to wash it down.

Denny just waggled his eyebrows.

I was glad we were meeting at Ruth's. Last time we'd met here, I'd sneezed all over Stu's birthday cake. Or was it Ruth's birthday cake? We'd had two that time. That was the start of a lot of sickness for me last spring. Without a spleen to bolster my immune system, I had to be careful. Just hoped whatever bug Ruth had been struggling with wasn't catching. When I'd asked if she was up to hosting Yada Yada at her house, she said she felt fine, not to worry, she wasn't dead yet.

For the first time in a couple of months, all Yada Yadas were present and accounted for. Even Nony and Hoshi came! And with Becky, we now numbered thirteen. A tight squeeze in the tiny living room of the Garfields' brick bungalow. I noticed that this time Becky joined Yo-Yo on the floor instead of hiding back in a corner. I managed to catch Delores before we settled down and whispered, "José told us a little bit what's going on with his dad." I gave her a hug. "Are you all right? I love you."

She nodded. "*Sí*. We will talk. Later." *OK*. I knew it wouldn't come up tonight.

Our praise time, however, was charged with joy. Mark Smith's comeback, slow as it was, was nothing short of a miracle, and we let the world (well, the Garfields' neighbors) know it. We sang song after song: "Our God Is a Great Big God," "Give Thanks with a Grateful Heart," and my personal favorite, the one with the line, "Never will a rock cry out in my place! He is worthy of all my praise!"—which generated a "Wait a minute! What in the heck does *that* mean?" from Yo-Yo.

So Avis shared the story from the Gospel of Luke, where the religious leaders wanted the crowd to stop singing "Hosanna! Son of David!" as Jesus was riding a donkey into Jerusalem. And He told them that if the people kept silent from singing praises, the stones would cry out in their place.

Becky gave me a sideways look that said, *"You better show me that story when we do our next Bible reading."*

"Me got someting to t'ank Jesus about," Chanda cut in. "Me and de t'ree kids will be moving in a couple of weeks. Into our very own 'ouse, praise God!" Tears glistened in her dark eyes. This time others in the group seemed genuinely interested, asking questions about how many rooms and what school district. Chanda painted a glowing description of the house, but deflected when Adele asked about the neighbors. "Hmph. Enough to say de welcome wagon not come yet."

Florida said, "Girl, you jus' tell us when you packin' up, and we all be there." She eyed us like a Mafia boss "volunteering" the Family. *"Won't* we, sistahs?"

Adele grunted. "You sure we want to scare her new neighbors by all showing up?" Right away, everyone volunteered, laughing.

Maybe it wasn't a joke. If I were Chanda, a Jamaican cleaning-woman-turned-millionaire, would I be brave enough to buy a house in an all-white neighborhood on the North Shore? Despite how progressive the Chicago bedroom communities thought they were, people could be pretty snobby about who moved in next-door. And from what I'd read, some of the White Pride people even came from those privileged families! Maybe they had professional parents who gave them everything money could buy but were too busy to realize their kids were growing up loners, needing to belong—somewhere. Like that girl in the sundress at the rally . . .

Pray for the girl, Jodi. Fight for her.

I was so startled by how strong I heard that Voice that I looked around the room to see if one of my sisters was talking to me—and realized Nony had started to share. I shook away my thoughts and tried to concentrate on what she was saying.

"First," Nony said, "I want to thank all of you sisters for standing with me during this difficult, difficult time. We . . . have a long way to go. But Delores, bless her, helps me to understand it may be a long process of recovery and to not get discouraged when Mark seems, well . . ." Nony hesitated. "Not like himself. It will take time."

"So what about goin' to South Africa and all that?" Yo-Yo blurted. "I thought maybe since he was wakin' up and startin' to walk around, you guys might still go."

I winced. As always, Yo-Yo said what many of us had probably been thinking. That had to be a hard one for Nony.

To my surprise, she smiled, sad and serene. "I wouldn't be honest if I said it's been easy to give up that dream. It seemed so close to coming true! Mark had agreed; he was taking a sabbatical; he'd even applied to teach at the KwaZulu-Natal University for the winter term. But God is showing me I need to let go, that we weren't ready to go to South Africa." She looked down at her hands.

Adele frowned. "Not ready. Huh! Say some more, honey. 'Cause from where I sit, the only reason you ain't goin' to South Africa is because some hatemonger got a little too handy with a brick."

Nony nodded. "I know. Believe me, I've wrestled with God many nights about that, wondering how God could allow something like this to happen to a good man like Mark. And, I confess"—she held up a hand, palm out—"I don't pretend to know *how* this fits into God's big picture. But, what I'm trying to say is, God did show me one small reason He allowed this to happen at this time. We weren't ready. Mark and me." Nony took a big breath.

"Unity has not been one of the strong points in our marriage. Mark and I are both strong, stubborn people. We both have our 'good' reasons. During the long hours I sat by his bedside in the hospital, God whispered to me that we had to back up and start over with the whole decision to go to South Africa. Because, you see, we never *prayed* about it together. Oh, yes, I prayed!" She rolled her eyes. "I prayed that Mark would change his mind! And I can only guess what *he* prayed while I nagged him for years!"

Laughter tucked into all the unoccupied places in Ruth's living room.

"But we never," Nony continued, "we *never* held hands and prayed about it *together*. 'Lord, is this what *You* want us to do? Am I willing to stay? Is he willing to go? This is my heart's desire, Lord, but stay or go, what I really want is what *You* want for *us*, for the Sisulu-Smith family.'" Nony shook her head. "No, I was too headstrong. Too sure I was right. But now I know—and you sisters will need to remind me!—that any future decisions Mark and Nonyameko Sisulu-Smith make, we must both pray until God gives us the same direction."

The effect on the group was electric. Delores's face was wet with tears; I knew her heart was breaking for the disunity in her own marriage. Avis just kept waving a hand and saying, "Glory! Oh Jesus! Teach us!" Others nodded or murmured understanding, knowing that the struggle for unity in *any* relationship is great.

"Well, then." Ruth cleared her throat as if asking for our attention. She'd been unusually quiet so far that evening, especially given that we were meeting in her house. "Grandmother Zelda would turn over in her grave on the day Ben and I agreed about anything. He disagrees with me on principle!" She shrugged. "Can't say I'm so quick to agree with anything *he* says either. A miracle it would take. But . . ." Ruth chewed on her lip. "A miracle we're going to need."

We all stared at her, waiting. Finally I blurted, "Ruth! What are you talking about? What kind of miracle do you need?"

Delores was hot on my heels. "Did you go to the doctor? Is that what this is about? What did he say?"

Ruth fluttered her hands. "Yes, yes. Ben made me go. But I didn't need a doctor to know what's going on. Ben . . . he'll never stand for it."

We waited two seconds, then half the Yada Yadas yelled, "Stand for *what?*"

A teary smile wet Ruth's face. "I'm pregnant. Me. Pregnant. And I'm so *happy!*"

42

*R*uth was pregnant. That was the first shock wave. Ben didn't know it yet. That was the second. "Ruth? Pregnant?" Denny sputtered when I told him half a block away from the Garfields' house. "Ben didn't say a word about it tonight!"

"I know. Because she hasn't told him yet. She has to tonight, because now *we* all know."

Denny gaped at me, almost missing a stop sign in the process. "But why wouldn't she tell him? And how did she get pregnant in the first place? Isn't she, you know, the change and all that?" The tips of his ears turned red.

"*How* did she get pregnant?" I giggled. "Need a little refresher course, do you?"

"You know what I mean. Isn't she too old?" He turned and looked at me again. "How old is she, anyway? I mean, Ben's at least sixty."

"Get this. She's forty-nine. And yeah, she thought she had

started menopause. But, well, I guess things happen." My eyes misted as we picked up Touhy Avenue and headed toward our end of Chicago. "The thing is, Denny, she's thrilled. She's always wanted a child, had a couple of miscarriages, then was going to adopt that little girl she and husband number two fostered—till the birth mother wanted her back. Ruth was devastated. Got real upset when Florida wanted *her* kids back from the foster-care system. I think they've pretty much worked that through. But it's still a bit of a touchy subject."

Denny tapped his fingers on the steering wheel at a long red light. "Why not tell Ben? It's his kid too."

"Because. Like you said, Denny. Ben's at least sixty. When they got married ten years ago, he made it clear he didn't want kids. And recently, when he was bugging her about going to the doctor to see why she was throwing up, so fatigued, all that stuff, she made a wisecrack about maybe being pregnant, and he went ballistic. Said that wasn't funny, and it was a good thing abortion was still legal."

Denny made a strangled sound. "He didn't."

"He did. Ruth's really scared to tell him. But she's just so *happy*! Her dream of having a family has finally come true! You should have heard Yada Yada screech when she told us. Surprised you didn't hear it over at the Bagel Bakery." I shook my head. "Makes me mad that Ben threatened abortion if she ever got pregnant."

We rode silently for the next couple of miles. Then Denny said, "Maybe he's scared, Jodi. We're talking a high-risk pregnancy here. Ben . . . you know how he is. Hides his real feelings under that gruff exterior." He glanced at me from the driver's seat. "If we were in their shoes, I'd be scared too."

RUTH HADN'T SAID ANYTHING ABOUT POSSIBLE RISKS. But she'd be fifty by the time the baby was born. Not exactly prime time for childbearing. I meant to call her the next day and ask about what the doctor said. At least e-mail her to ask how Ben was taking the news. But with Tuesday being the last report card pickup day at Bethune Elementary, I was still plowing through end-of-year reports until midnight Monday evening. Ruth slipped my mind entirely.

I walked into school Tuesday morning feeling smug. Done. *Fini.* I'd survived another year as a third-grade teacher at Mary McLeod Bethune Elementary School. And all my kids were passing on to fourth grade. Even Kaya, who could barely read at the beginning of the year. She still wasn't reading at grade level, but she'd come so far!

I'd even written a report for Hakim Porter, though he'd left my classroom six weeks ago. I'd mail it and include my phone number. Maybe his mother would call and tell me how he was doing.

Fat chance, Jodi.

OK, I needed to be realistic. But I was still going to mail it. At least Hakim would know I thought about him. Still cared. Still had positive things to say about his time in my classroom.

As it turned out, I didn't have to mail it.

I almost missed him in the flurry of parents and students who stopped into my classroom to pick up report cards. Some of my kids showed up with little gift bags—a refrigerator magnet boasting "#1 Teacher," crackers and cheese, even a colorful neck scarf. There wasn't really time to talk—just handshaking, some hugs from the kids, hunting for the report that wasn't in alphabetical order.

As the crowd thinned, I saw him. Sitting at his desk I'd left in its place, the one with the jagged lightning scar he'd scratched in frustration. When my mouth dropped open in delight, he grinned, pleased with his little surprise.

"Hakim!" I squatted down to his level. "I'm so glad to see you! I was going to mail your report card, but"—I gave him a hug; to heck with school policy!—"here you are!"

He just nodded, still grinning.

"Um, did you come with someone?" I glanced around the room, where a few parents and kids still lingered. "Is your mom here?"

His smile dimmed slightly. "She's waitin' for me out in the car. I'm s'posed to come right back out."

"Of course. I'll get your report card." I returned to my desk, found the manila envelope, and then realized he'd followed me. The room was almost empty now. On a sudden impulse, I sat down in my desk chair and took his hand. "Hakim. I want to tell you something. I know you know it was my car that hit your brother, Jamal. I'm so sorry about what happened." Tears welled up in my eyes. "I've talked to your mom. But I've never told *you* how sorry I am."

He nodded, the smile gone, his expression sober. "I know. It was an accident, Ms. B. You didn't mean to."

"No. I didn't mean to." My voice caught. "But I was still wrong. I wish I could make it right, but I can't. I learned a hard lesson. But there's one good thing I thank God for." I beamed at him in spite of my running nose and eyes. "I met you. You are a special boy, Hakim. I'm proud of you. And I'm glad you're my friend."

Hakim just looked at me a moment. Suddenly, he threw himself into my arms and gave me a stranglehold hug. Then, clutching his report card, he was gone.

I COULD HAVE SLEPT IN THE NEXT MORNING. No school! No school! But even without the alarm clock, my eyes popped open at six o'clock. The house was quiet. The morning was still cool. The wind chimes my parents had given me danced and sang in a little breeze. The birds were chirping and trilling—

The birds! I sat up. When was the last time I'd filled my new bird feeder?

I practically bounced out of bed, feeling like a kid who didn't want to waste a minute of summer vacation. Putting the coffee on, I scurried outside to fill the bird feeder, turned on the sprinkler, unloaded the dishwasher while the coffee took its own sweet time, and finally settled on the back porch swing with my Bible and the biggest mug I could find for my caffeine fix.

Wow, Lord. My heart was so full, I couldn't think of anything else to say. For several minutes I just soaked up the new morning, watching the birds squabble over the birdseed. Hakim showing up yesterday was such a gift. *Wise healer.* As far as I was concerned, he was already living into his name. He was getting academic help. He offered me forgiveness in that hug. And yet . . . his family still grieved the loss of their older son.

Joy and sorrow.

I'd called Ruth after report card pickup yesterday. Ben answered. "B-Ben!" I stammered. "How are you?"

He'd muttered something unintelligible, then yelled, "Ruth! It's for you."

Ruth picked up an extension. "I'm fine, Jodi. Who wouldn't be, with ten doctors suddenly interested in the pregnant old woman? Next thing I know, I'll be giving interviews to the *National*

Enquirer." Ben, she said, told her all the perils of late-in-life preg-
nancies at least ten times a day. "Suddenly he's concerned about my
health?" She snorted into my ear. "*Mishegaas.*"

Joy and sorrow.

And last night, all four of us Baxters went up to the hospital to
see Mark Smith. I was still amazed to see his one eye open, to see
his head turn at the sound of our voices. Yet it seemed to take him
several minutes to register who we were. Nony repeated each of our
names slowly. Finally he nodded, a smile twitching on his face.

"I'm hoping we can bring him home soon," Nony had said to us
out in the hallway. "But he'll need a lot of therapy. Even has to
relearn simple things, like tying his shoe. He gets easily frustrated
now. And"—her chin trembled—"the doctors think he's suffered
irreparable retinal detachment in his left eye."

Joy and sorrow.

I'd never realized before how often joy and sorrow walked hand
in hand.

A familiar trill interrupted my ping-pong musings. I squinted
into the trees along the alley but couldn't see anything at first.
Then—a flash of scarlet landed on top of the garage . . . then down
to the gutter . . . fluttering to the bird feeder. I smiled. My "cardinal
of hope."

Hope. I was looking forward to Sunday. The joint thanksgiving
celebration was a hopeful sign of something good coming out of
Mark's attack. Yet the police still had no suspects in the case. *That*
stuck in my craw. Those White Pride people were basically getting
away with attempted murder—

Pray for the girl, Jodi. Pray hard. Fight for her soul.

Suddenly I knew why God got me up early this morning. I was

supposed to pray. Supposed to fight a battle I didn't understand for someone I didn't even know. God was up to something. But as Florida always said, "God is God all by Himself!"

I didn't have to know.

But I did have to pray.

THE FIRST FEW DAYS OF SUMMER BREAK always felt like riding the tilt-a-whirl at a carnival. *All* our schedules were different now that school was out. And we had one car, three drivers, and four schedules to juggle. Only Willie Wonka maintained a steady course: eat, sleep, go outside, pee, poop, eat, sleep . . .

Within a few days, things got sorted out. Denny got his usual jobs coaching at park district programs. Josh applied for a job at a summer day camp in one of the parks since Jesus People said they couldn't talk about a more extended internship until after the Cornerstone Festival was over. The phone rang relentlessly for Amanda as Uptown moms called to book their favorite baby-sitter for afternoons at the beach or backyard entertaining while they ran errands. One working mom asked her to be a full-time nanny all summer, but Amanda turned it down. "Sheesh, Mom. I'm just a kid myself."

Right. I'd remind her of that the next time she wailed, "Mo-om! I'm not a kid!"

Since both Denny and I worked during the school year, we'd decided that one parent should be home in the summer when the kids were out of school, so I'd always had summers "off." I felt vaguely guilty about it, now that the kids were practically grown and had summer jobs themselves. But right this moment, this week, I was glad. Because I felt like I was on assignment.

God wanted me to pray. Pray hard. For that anonymous girl in the White Pride group. And for Mark and Nony. Ruth and Ben. Delores and Ricardo. Florida and Carl and Chris—well, the whole Hickman family . . .

I had what Avis called an "unction." I had to pray. Had to. Once I started, I hardly knew where to stop. Even with Mark slowly getting better each day, I felt a burden I couldn't explain. And so I prayed. Called Avis and told her God wanted us to pray for "that girl." Called Delores and prayed with her on the phone. Ditto Ruth. Prayed for Becky to find a work-at-home job—and not just because she was borrowing the want ads from our paper every day.

I was praying in the back porch swing early Sunday morning, feeling excited about the joint worship service with New Morning Christian Church that day, when Becky Wallace peeked over the second-floor stair railing. "Hey, Jodi. Know it's early, but can I borrow the Sunday want ads? Wanna check 'em out before little Andy gets here."

"Sure. Check the front porch. The paper should be here by now." She disappeared back inside the second-floor apartment, and I tried once again to focus on my prayers. *God, I don't know what You're doing in some of these situations, but I want to trust You. To give You praise in the middle of difficulties, not just when the answers come. Your ways are not my ways, Your thoughts are not my thoughts . . . but I want to line up with the Word of God. I want to be so full of the Word, like Nony, that it comes pouring out when I—*

A human screech from the direction of the front of the house cut off my prayer like a carving knife. Outside, not inside. "Jodi! Stu! Somebody!" I launched myself off the swing and tore through our house to the front. Becky's voice. From the front porch.

As I unlocked the front door and tore it open, I heard Denny's bare feet thudding down the hall right behind me. Stu spilled out from her front door in lounging pajamas, long hair askew. Becky Wallace was standing on the front porch, holding the newspaper, eyes popping. She looked up at us and then held out the paper. "Look!"

Denny snatched it. We all crowded around. There on the front page, the headline blared BREAKTHROUGH IN UNIVERSITY ASSAULT. And a subhead: "Hate group member fingers those responsible for attack on NU professor."

"Let me see that!" I snatched the newspaper from Denny and began reading the story aloud. "'Evanston police say that a female member of the group calling itself White Pride came forward and—'"

The printed words sucked the breath right out of me. "The girl! The girl in the sundress! It's gotta be!"

43

We turned on the TV and radio. It was all over the Chicago area news. Two men, identified only as members of the Coalition for White Pride and Preservation, had been arrested during the night. Names had not yet been released. The informant was in police protective custody.

Our phone started ringing. Had we heard the news? Yes, yes, praise God for His justice! Everyone had questions. *Who was the informant? Why did she decide to turn them in? Who got arrested? Was it any of the White Pride people we'd seen at the rally? Or had they just sent a couple of thugs to do their dirty work?* Nobody had answers.

Pray for the girl, Jodi. Keep praying! Put a hedge of protection around her!

Somehow, in the midst of all the excitement, we got ourselves into the minivan and drove to the mall on Howard Street. The large, unfinished storefront with its butcher-paper sign declaring FUTURE HOME OF NEW MORNING CHRISTIAN CHURCH was filling with people. We parked in the mall parking lot and joined the stream of people moving slowly through the double-glass doors. I saw what the hangup was: Pastor Clark, Pastor Cobbs, and Mrs. Cobbs all stood just inside, greeting people with handshakes and hugs. Pastor Clark was introducing Uptown folks to the Cobbs, and vice versa. I couldn't help but smile. Pastor Clark, tall and gangly, and Pastor Cobbs, shorter, dignified, looked a bit like a fudge ripple version of the old comic-strip characters Mutt and Jeff. *Bless them, Father. Bless them!*

"Yes, yes, we have met the Baxters." Pastor Cobbs smiled warmly and shook our hands. Rose Cobbs enveloped me in a warm hug. She smelled like lavender. "Bless you, my sister," she whispered in my ear. For some reason, her greeting brought tears to my eyes.

Denny nudged me playfully as we moved further inside. "We ought to feel right at home. Look. Uptown's sorry chairs."

Sure enough, Uptown's poor excuse for folding chairs were all mixed in with newer-looking chairs that had Ric's Party Rentals stamped on the back. I rolled my eyes. Stu better get her chair fund kicking—soon.

As people found seats, my heart swelled to see the Hickman family come in—even Chris, though he certainly was playing up the "gangsta" fashion to the max: baggy jeans ten sizes too big barely hanging on his butt, oversize shirt, gold chains, sullen expression. *Oh God, protect that boy. Let something be said today that touches his heart.* Carl had Carla by the hand, dressed in a summery knit shift and sandals and looking older than her nine years.

Avis waved at us from the coffee table, but Peter was busy greeting everyone who came within hailing distance. *Oh God, is Peter's dream possible? Could these two churches merge and become one?* I shook my head. That definitely fell in the category King David must have been talking about in Psalm 131: "I do not concern myself with great matters or things too wonderful for me. But I have stilled and quieted my soul . . ."

Yes. I needed to leave that one in God's lap. Today, I was just going to enjoy this extraordinary joint thanksgiving service with New Morning.

The praise band and worship team took their places against the unpainted wall facing the chairs, a fruit salad of Uptown and New Morning musicians. Microphone wires snaked to a soundboard off to the side. I wondered if Nony and the boys would come this morning, but I hadn't seen her yet. Stu, Becky, and Andy came in and found seats just as Pastor Cobbs tapped on the central microphone. "Are we on? . . . Good."

A black metal music stand substituted for a pulpit. Pastor Cobbs took the mic out of its stand and cried out, "This is the day the Lord has made! Let us rejoice and be glad in it!" The New Morning keyboardist punched a couple of loud chords to accompany the chorus of "amens" and "hallelujahs" around the room.

"Praise God! Praise God!" Pastor Cobbs walked back and forth at the front of the room. "We are delighted today to welcome Pastor Clark and our brothers and sisters from Uptown Community Church, who have been our gracious hosts this past month. And as you can see . . ." He grinned, waving his free hand at all the unfinished walls and heating ducts overhead. "You'll probably have to put up with us for a while longer until we get some more work done here." People laughed appreciatively. No mention of merging, I noticed.

Leave it in My lap, Jodi.

Right. *Sorry, God, I forgot.*

Pastor Cobbs picked up his Bible from the music stand. "Most of you have probably heard the news this morning—"

Spontaneous clapping and shouting went up all over the room, drowning out whatever he had planned to say next. When it finally died down, Pastor Cobbs said, "But we're not here to talk about what the newspapers are saying or the sound bites on TV." He held his Bible aloft. "We're here to talk about what the Word of God says about all this!"

Drums and electric keyboard joined the clapping and shouting this time. But Pastor Cobbs held up his hand to quiet things down. "Let me read our text for today, second book of Kings, chapter six, talking here about the king of Aram who wanted the head of the prophet Elisha."

New Morning's pastor had a surprisingly dramatic voice as he read: "Therefore . . . they came by night and surrounded the city. And when the servant of the man of God arose early and went out, there was an army, surrounding the city with horses and chariots. And his servant said to Elisha, 'Alas, my master! What shall we do?' So he answered, 'Do not fear, for those who are with us are more than those who are with them.' And Elisha prayed, and said, 'LORD, I pray, open his eyes that he may see.' Then the LORD opened the eyes of the young man, and he saw. And behold, the mountain was full of horses and chariots of fire all around Elisha."

Pastor Cobbs's eyes sparked with triumph. "Open your eyes, brothers and sisters! Do not fear! For those who are with us are more than those who are with them! I'm not talking about the police. I'm not talking about the U.S. Army. I'm talking about *God's army* that is fighting for us! That has been fighting for our brother Mark Smith even as he lay comatose on that hospital bed! That has been battling this hate group! That is fighting for our families! Fighting for our young people! Fighting Satan's schemes to keep people of faith separated and suspicious of one another!"

Pastor Cobbs once more held his Bible aloft. "And what are the weapons we possess to fight alongside heaven's armies?"

By this time, most of us were on our feet. "The Word of God!" several shouted. "Prayer and praise!" "The name of Jesus!"

Pastor Cobbs lifted his hand as if to signal the praise team to begin—and stopped with his hand in the air. His lips parted; his eyes widened. He was looking out the windows that ran along the front of the spacious room. Heads began to turn. What was he looking at? I craned my neck, trying to see past Denny's big shoulders.

A Medicar had pulled up right in front of the doors of New Morning's new space. Its side doors were open. A technician lowered a wheelchair on an electric ramp. A woman stood with her back to us, wearing a flowing caftan with gold braid around the neck and sleeves. Two boys in suits and ties ran up to her as she took the handles of the wheelchair and pushed it toward the door.

My heart nearly stopped. Nony! And Mark!

People scrambled to open the doors. Nonyameko pushed the wheelchair into the room. Mark sat in the chair, dressed in slacks and an open-necked shirt. Bandages still wrapped his head and covered one eye. Scars still raked one side of his face. But there was no disguising the broad smile on his face.

People all around the room broke into applause. "Thank You, Jesus!" "Glory!" rang out from all corners. I could barely see for the tears in my eyes. Pastor Cobbs must have recovered and signaled the praise band and worship team, because the room filled suddenly with a Sion Alford song:

My God is a great big God!
My Lord is a mighty Lord! . . .
He's my help in the time of need!

I let the words roll over me and fill me up. I caught Nony's eye where she stood beside Mark's wheelchair in the midst of our two churches, worshiping together. She winked at me and mouthed, *"Watch out, devil!"* And we both started to laugh as the musicians led into the bridge of the song:

I don't care what the devil may do
I'm gonna praise the Lord!

Book Club Questions

1. As Book 4 opens, the Yada Yadas have lots of reason to celebrate! But God's Spirit prompts Jodi, *Don't let down your guard. Satan likes nothing better than to lull us to sleep spiritually when things are going well.* How can we keep spiritually alert?

2. Leslie "Stu" Stuart invited ex-con Becky Wallace to share her home—a well-meaning gesture that turns Stu's orderly life upside down. Do you think it was worth the risk? Why or why not? How does Stu's rash decision compare to the Sermon on the Mount (Matthew 5–7), where the things Jesus advocates seem to go against common sense?

3. The Yada Yada Prayer Group has to "get tough" to battle the events that threaten to crush them. What are the weapons they use for this spiritual warfare? What weapons would you add to this list?

4. Psalm 8:2 in Today's New International Version says: "Through the praise of children and infants you have established a strongold against your enemies . . ." How does praise build a stronghold against the enemy? What is the significance of the psalmist mentioning children and infants?

5. What does it mean to you to pray "in the name of Jesus"?

6. Like Jodi praying for "the girl in the sundress," have you had a burden to pray for someone but you didn't know why? If so, what was the result?

7. Jodi's son and Florida's son concluded that "nothing will ever be different" when it comes to racial relations. How did they each get to that point? Do you sometimes feel this way? In what other areas of life or relationships do you feel discouraged that nothing will ever change? Why?

8. "One person *can* make a difference. *My* attitudes. What *I* say or don't say. What *I* do or don't do. It has to begin with *me*" (chapter 39). Why did Josh Baxter find hope in this perspective, even when the circumstances were so huge? Apply this to yourself: what needs to begin with you?

9. After weeks of struggling with the attack on Mark, Nony reflects, "God is showing me I need to let go, that we weren't ready to go to South Africa" (chapter 41). Why weren't they ready? What needed to be different about future decisions? What role does prayer play in your own family decision making? What needs to change to bring about more unity when making decisions? (Be honest!)

10. The biblical story of Joseph reminds us that what Satan meant for evil, God can turn into a greater good. Why does Peter Douglass think merging Uptown Community and New Morning fits into that concept? Is it realistic? What would be the challenges? The blessings?

11. Read 1 Corinthians 12:12–26. How can we learn to appreciate the different parts of the body of Christ (i.e., other churches in your area that may be culturally or denominationally different)? Do you *need* these other parts of the body? (Reread vv. 21–26).

Starting a Yada Yada Prayer Group

*I*s God tugging at your heart to start a prayer group but you feel totally inadequate? God will give you wisdom! (Read James 1:5 and *ask*.) There is no one-size-fits-all formula for putting together a prayer group, but here are a few things to consider:

First, prepare yourself . . .
- **Bring your desire to God** and pray about it! (Funny how often we skip this step.)
- **Ask another sister to pray with you.** "If two of you agree . . . about anything, it will be done for them" (Matthew 18:19).

Then . . .
- **Share with your pastor** what you want to do. Choose a meeting time for your prayer group that does not conflict with other church meetings or activities.
- **Determine who needs a prayer group.** A prayer group for women in your church is perfectly legitimate. (Many "church" women are lonely or alone.) Or maybe God is calling you to reach beyond your circle of friends—to neighbors, co-workers, other parents at your child's school, or across cultural or racial boundaries.
- **Invite other sisters to join you.** If two of you are in agreement about starting a prayer group, each of you could invite one

more. That's four. Then those four each invite one. That's eight. A good beginning!

- **Meet in your home**—or ask another sister to host. Or share hosting among all the members of the prayer group. Meeting in homes helps create a circle of intimacy. Also, women who are not members of your church may feel more comfortable coming to a home meeting. (But if God directs you to meet at the office, at the park, at Starbucks, at the jail, or at the church—do it!)
- **Don't let the group get too big.** Twelve is usually maximum for a small group. Eight to ten is a good number. (If lots of women want to participate, you may need to divide into two groups! What a wonderful "problem" to have.)
- **Find other leaders to help.** Be sure one or two of the sisters who are well grounded in the Word of God are willing to function as leaders/facilitators.

The meeting . . .

- **Fellowship.** Allow at least fifteen minutes for women to arrive, get snacks or drinks, and unwind.
- **Worship.** Begin with a scripture, a song, or prayers of praise to get your focus where it needs to be—on God alone.
- **Word/Prayer.** Your group may be a Bible study with prayer or a share-and-prayer time. Either way, you will need someone to facilitate so you *do* leave time to pray.
- **Respect!** Agree together that personal things shared in the group are to remain in the group—not fodder for gossip. (However, if things come up that are too big to handle in the group, the leaders may need to seek outside counsel.)

Last, but not least . . .

- **Pray during the week** for the women who attend the group. Call to check on anyone who is missing; pray for them over the phone if need be.
- **Expect God to do great things** in you and through you as you pray!

Find out how the Yada Yada Story begins . . .

I almost didn't go to the Chicago Women's Conference—after all, being thrown together with 500 strangers wasn't exactly my "comfort zone." But I would be rooming with my boss, Avis, and I hoped that I might make a friend or two.

When Avis and I were assigned to a prayer group of 12 women, I wasn't sure what to think. There was Flo, an outspoken ex-drug addict; Ruth, a Messianic Jew who could smother-mother you to death; and Yo-Yo, who wasn't even a Christian! Not to mention women from Jamaica, Honduras, South Africa—practically a mini-United Nations. We certainly didn't have much in common.

But something happened that weekend to make us realize we had to hang together. So "the Yada Yada Prayer Group" decided to keep praying for each other via e-mail. Our personal struggles and requests soon got too intense for cyberspace, so we decided to meet together every other Sunday night.

Talk about a rock tumbler!—knocking off each other's rough edges, learning to laugh and cry along the way. But when I faced the biggest crisis of my life, God used my newfound girlfriends to help teach me—Jodi Baxter, longtime Christian "good girl"— what it means to be just a sinner saved by grace.

ISBN 1-59145-074-8

BOOK 2

When they get shaken up, The Yada Yada Prayer Group Gets Down

I had never felt so violated! The Yada Yada Prayer Group was "gettin' down" with God in prayer and praise one night when a heroin-crazed woman barged into my house, demanded our valuables and threatened us with a 10-inch knife—a knife that drew blood.

We wondered if we'd ever get back to normal after this terrifying experience. I assumed we would (although "normal" doesn't usually describe the 12 of us mismatched women anyway). After all, we'd been through a lot already as spiritual sisters. This was just one more hurdle to conquer, right?

But then a well-meaning gesture suddenly incited a backlash of anger in the group, forcing us to confront generations of racial division, pain and distrust—and stretching our friendships to the limit. Initially I thought, Surely I, Jodi "Good Girl" Baxter, am not responsible for other people's sins—am I? But a shocking confrontation in my third-grade classroom forced me to face my own accountability, and God used the Yada Yada Prayer Group (and my own husband, of all people) to show me what true forgiveness really is.

THE YADA YADA PRAYER GROUP GETS DOWN
ISBN 1-59145-151-5

BOOK 3

God gives the Yada Yadas a crash-course in forgiveness

After all that we Yadas have been through in the past eight months, I told God I could sure use a little "dull and boring" in the new year! That was before Ms. Perfect herself—Leslie "Stu" Stewart—moved upstairs in the same two-flat as us Baxters. And before Delores Enriques' son wanted to throw my Amanda a party for her 15th birthday, Mexican style. And before Avis—*our* Avis—started being courted by a man we don't even know!

I guess I should have realized that with 11 Yada sisters as diverse as a bag of Jelly Bellies, life would always be unpredictable. At least Bandana Woman, who held up our Yada Yada Prayer Group at knifepoint last fall, was safely locked up in prison . . . or so I thought. We visited her, like the Bible says; even sent her something for Christmas. But then she ends up back in our face. I mean, how far is forgiveness supposed to go?

All I know is that the longer we Yadas pray together, the more real things are getting, not only with each other but with God. Dull and boring? Not a chance.

THE YADA YADA PRAYER GROUP GETS REAL

ISBN 1-59145-152-3

AVAILABLE WHEREVER BOOKS ARE SOLD

Your chance to "yada yada" with God

A prayer journal to go with a series of fiction novels? Whoever heard of such a thing! Yet the Yada Yada Prayer Group novels have impacted thousands of lives as these rollicking prayer sisters have inspired a heart-hunger in readers to "yada" (know and be known intimately by) God and each other, and to "yadah" (give praise to) our Lord.

Now you can join author Neta Jackson on a journey that will take you even further into the three books' themes of grace, forgiveness and redemption. Each of these 60 daily devotions include an excerpt from one of the novels, Neta's personal reflections from her heart to yours, thought-provoking questions with relevant scripture and prayer guides . . . and space to respond with your own thoughts, prayers and praise.

Using this journal will not only change you, but may even ready you for the next step: your own prayer group of "Yada Yada" sisters. For Jesus said: "Where two or three are gathered together in My name, there I am in the midst of them" . . . and where Jesus is, something glorious happens!

THE YADA YADA PRAYER JOURNAL
ISBN 1-59145-285-6

AVAILABLE WHEREVER BOOKS ARE SOLD